MADRIGAL

'The most tortuous, tantalising plot of
any spy yarn to date races to the
requisite blood-and-guts climax.
Mr. Gardner has succeeded in fashioning
this million-piece jigsaw of a story into a
slick, intelligible thriller which beats
even his first B.O. saga, *The Liquidator*,
for excitement, hilarity, and wit.'

SHE MAGAZINE

'This must be another hit book for
John Gardner, who whips his tale along
with ferocity of language and action.'

YORKSHIRE EVENING POST

Also by JOHN GARDNER

THE LIQUIDATOR
UNDERSTRIKE
AMBER NINE

and published by CORGI BOOKS

JOHN GARDNER

MADRIGAL

CORGIBOOKS
A DIVISION OF TRANSWORLD PUBLISHERS

MADRIGAL

A CORGI BOOK   552 08004 7

Originally published in Great Britain
by Frederick Muller, Ltd.
This edition revised by the author

PRINTING HISTORY

Frederick Muller Edition published 1967
Corgi Edition published 1968

The quotation from 'Room Five Hundred and Four'
on page 110 is reprinted by permission of
Chappell & Co., Ltd.

This book is set in
Baskerville 10/12 pt.

Corgi Books are published by Transworld Publishers, Ltd.,
Bashley Road, London, N.W.10

Made and printed in Great Britain by
Richard Clay (The Chaucer Press), Ltd., Bungay, Suffolk

FOR SUSAN

Tell me where is fancy bred,
Or in the heart or in the head?
How begot, how nourished?
　　Reply, reply.
It is engender'd in the eyes,
With gazing fed; and fancy dies
In the cradle where it lies.
　　Let us all ring fancy's knell:
I'll begin it,—Ding, dong, bell.

All: Ding, dong, bell.

Shakespeare,
a madrigal from
The Merchant of Venice

ACKNOWLEDGMENT

I should like to acknowledge the invaluable help and data given to me by Captain E. Mercer, DFC, Mr. Hugh Miller, Miss Miranda Riley, and Mr. Jon Tremaine, the mind-reader, part of whose act is described in Chapter VII.

Especially I am deeply indebted to Mr. Simon Wood, without whom this entertainment would never have been written.

CONTENTS

PART ONE

THE LAST LIQUIDATION

If you like it ... Straight?

I. WARBLER

Made poetry a mere mechanic art;
And ev'ry warbler has his tune by heart.
                    Cowper, *Table Talk*

'*Ach*, Herr Oldcorn, it is good to see you again.'

Boysie Oakes, yet to get used to his cover name, looked about him to see if the small man was addressing somebody else. Then, remembering that *he* was Oldcorn: 'I don't think'—Boysie stopped himself from finishing the sentence—'we've met before.'

'Nice to see you, Herr Warbler,' he said instead.

'Come. I have transport outside.' Warbler, his face a picture of benignity, hustled Boysie to the Berlin hotel's car-park exit like a smiling sheep dog.

Warbler was a small man in whose conception Groucho Marx and Norman Wisdom could both have had a part. Like most of the foreign boys whom Boysie met in the field, Warbler was conspicuous. It seemed to have become a trademark. Gone were the days when operatives merged into the crowd, skulked black in the shadows, clad traditionally in belted raincoats. The secret sixties was a time for individuality. Perhaps it was the influence of the CIA. Warbler wore a long, checked gabardine and a cap to match. His age was indefinable, due mainly to the drooping and decidedly thin moustache that fell from his upper lip in an oval of wispy hair. His eyes, though shielded by gold-rimmed and thick glasses, flickering brown and merry, reminding Boysie of childhood winter evenings spent reading *The Wind in the Willows*.

Warbler's transport was a decrepit VW which looked as though it had been used as a practice vehicle for either stock-car racing or inexperienced panel beaters. Boysie's nose turned up. 'Got mine over there,' he said cheerfully, pointing to the bullet-proof Jensen standing proud, aloof, and snobbish twenty yards away.

Warbler's eyes glistened. 'We go in mine. I could not possibly handle a beast like that. Not in Berlin traffic.' He chuckled.

Warbler, thought Boysie, is a joker. The interior of the VW was as beat-up as the exterior. Bits of wire protruded from the rear off-side seat.

'There are many birds in the spring in England,' said Warbler from behind the wheel.

'Yes,' said Boysie, lost. There was a pause.

'I said, "There are many birds in the spring in England."'

'And I said "yes." Oh Lord.' Boysie's shuffled memory caught on the code-pass sequence. 'Yes. And the cuckoo sings loudly. Who the hell thinks up those things?'

'It is rumoured,' said Warbler, putting the car in gear and starting off with a series of short kangaroo hops, 'that it is the same person who writes slogans for film advertising. I'm sorry to rush you out like this but it is better that you should know the plan straight away. And it is safer to talk in the open.'

He was negotiating the traffic with accomplished dash, causing Boysie's stomach to whir like an egg whisk. They flushed out a covey of pedestrians bent on crossing the Kurfürstendamm and narrowly missed shunting a Merc 220. Boysie closed his eyes and rendered himself up to St. Christopher, whose medal hung from the dashboard.

Warbler grinned and flicked the silver disc with his left forefinger. 'I got that by accident.' He chuckled.

Boysie finally opened his eyes to see a sign that read Des Juni Strasse. 'Where are we going?' A plea more than a question.

Another grin from Warbler. 'The Reichstag, a suitable place for conference. Well, not exactly the Reichstag but near enough. The Platz der Republik in front of the Reichstag. It is good open ground and we will not be overheard. After, we can see the sights and enjoy ourselves.' An all-embracing smile and a quick flick of the wheel to avoid a weaving cyclist.

Boysie did not like to say that the last thing he wanted—at least until Griffin arrived—was to enjoy himself. Already the alternating hot and cold sweats were invading his nervous system. It had taken all Mostyn's and the Chief's charm, heavily impregnated with threats, to get Boysie as far as Berlin. Mostyn had promised it would be the very last 'pressure.' Boysie was the only person who could do it, the Chief had said. There would be an outstandingly large bonus—ten thousand pounds, Mostyn had said. (At this point they had handed out more drink.) Elizabeth's jeer about growing up was still lingering in Boysie's ears. Eventually he had come to the conclusion that, in his midforties, it was time to face the inevitable. This state, and the heavy alcoholic intake, had combined to suppress any marks of neurotic fear. Again, he had shown considerable resistance when they had outlined the circumstances of the forthcoming kill and the identity of the target. Boysie had never been one-up in the bravery stakes, and the thought of crossing the Berlin Wall, going right into the core of the Deutsche Demokratische Republik, and disposing of his former mistress-enemy, Irish MacIntosh, had not appealed strongly. (Another round of drinks.) However, Mostyn had pointed out that even though Boysie held only a technical rank they could courtmartial him *in camera* on a number of charges ranging from direct disobedience to cowardice in the face of the enemy. On reflection, Boysie had realised that this was all a load of old horse feathers. But the heat was on and the protesting Boysie had been driven by force of circumstances into the pipeline.

It had been just after ten o'clock on that damp evening when Boysie Oakes had brought his new silver-grey Jensen FF to a spectacular standstill outside the building which housed his flat off Chesham Place. He slid from behind the wheel and slammed the door viciously. Big, muscular, on the wrong side of forty, Boysie's usually placid good looks showed signs of irritation. Getting out of the lift cage, he nearly trapped his hand, an incident that caused a spurt of foul language.

Once inside, Boysie made straight for the bar, trickled a good quarter of a pint of Courvoisier into a balloon glass, and tripped the stereo switch on the Dynatron. Sinatra swooned 'Memories of You' across the palatial living room. Boysie pursed his lips and gazed at himself in the mirror. He looked frightened, angry, and sweaty. He was frightened, angry, and sweaty—hair deranged and a mild pallor showing through the even sunlamp-inflicted tan. The reflection blurred. Boysie screwed up his eyes and the vision cleared. Too much booze. The eyes stared back from the mirror, watery, red-rimmed, not recognising what they saw. He stepped back to take an objective look. The set of the dark maroon tie was not right, flying one wing low. A stain slewed down one of the watered-silk lapels of his dinner jacket. Boysie lifted his chin, viewing the left profile—the Mona Lisa side. The corner of his mouth twitched in a spasmodic nervous tremor. Frank had swung into 'I'll Be Around.' Boysie took a throat pull at the brandy and walked, as though through a mine field, to his favourite leather armchair and picked up the telephone. He misdialled, then got it right, rocking the chair to and fro as the signal brut-brutted at the far end of the line. The rocking motion fell into step with the signal. It went on and on, then the hollow clunk as the receiver was lifted. Heavy breathing. Someone had used a lot of energy getting to the telephone.

'Hello?' Elizabeth's voice, whispering as though half MI5 was at her elbow.

'It's me. It's Boysie.' Taking up the whisper and trying to sound cheerful.

'Boysie.' Exclamation. Irritation. 'What's the matter? It's nearly half-past ten and you know the situation. Sandy's ill.'

'Wanted to talk to you, Liz. Miserable, Liz. Please come home. Need help. Personal column. Come home all is forgiven love Boysie.'

'Well, phone Suicides Anonymous or whatever they call themselves. You *are* drunk.'

'Don't be like that. I need you. Come over. Please.' A staccato urgency, prerecorded in the brain while the telephone signal had been ringing.

'Boysie, I can't. You know I can't. Sandy's really poorly. She mustn't be left. Doctor says I've got to stay with her.'

'She's only got flu.'

'*Only* got.' Internal combustion. 'Yes. *You* only had flu last month. You were bloody dying, weren't you? The last rites. Talk about Mimi.'

'Liz, for Christ's sake, I'm in trouble. In a jam. And who the hell's Mimi?'

'*Bohème* Mimi, you selfish oaf.' Pause, followed by a slight change in tone. 'Your jam, is it work?'

Boysie's reply did not come too quickly. He could never lie easily to Elizabeth. 'You're rotten. It's Sandy, she's been getting at you again.'

'Is it work?' Insistent.

'Partly work. A jam.'

A long silence this time. Elizabeth knew what Boysie meant by a jam; she had been on the fringes of so many that she was fully case-hardened. Elizabeth held the record as Boysie's 'London steady.' At twenty-five she was his junior by almost a score, but three years previously a wet night, a film première, and a shortage of taxis had paired them off.

Boysie, she was convinced, often thought lasciviously about that night, for he was never done confiding in her that despite a full life she had been his first virgin. She never had the heart to tell him that he had not seduced her. If anything, it was the other way round, and from the beginning she suspected that Boysie was no born seducer. His girl friends were usually available ladies. Yet since that first night, whenever Boysie was stationed in London, Elizabeth could usually be found at the scene of her undoing: the flat off Chesham Place. Otherwise she returned, for companionship, to the digs in Hammersmith shared with a fellow secretary at the Board of Trade—Sandy, a straight-laced Presbyterian minister's daughter, who borrowed her underwear and stockings, read her long lectures about the inadvisability of being at the beck and call of a man like Boysie, and subscribed to both the *Spectator* and *New Statesman*.

Elizabeth let the moralising slide swiftly in through one internal auditory meatus and out of the other. She knew exactly what Boysie meant to her. As a man he was an open book with which she was wholly familiar. Boysie's foibles, fears, insecurities, fads, pomposities, and nightmares she had explored in depth. What remained unknown to her was the manner in which he kept himself in comparative luxury. He had something to do with Defence: he held a military rank and spent a great deal of time in Whitehall. She knew his immediate boss was a man called Mostyn—a figure able to put the hex

15

on Boysie quicker than anything or anybody. Time and again he returned to Chesham Place angry and frustrated, hurling abuse and obscenities against the man. Once, at a West End first night, Boysie had pointed him out, a smooth-looking Mephistopheles with tight curls and the infuriating manner of one in high authority.

From time to time Mostyn would call Boysie away on business. Always Boysie left like a man in some fearsome trance returning often to terrifying dreams. But Elizabeth never pried. She got her cut of the loot, in kind if not in cash, with a great deal of care, tenderness, and consideration thrown in. In return she tried to steer Boysie into those moments of peace and tranquillity which she knew lay at the vortex of his whirling life. Sometimes, lying awake in the restless early hours, she worried at the recurrent thought that he had somehow got into a quicksand not of his own making, a swirling clutching morass from which he could never be extracted and which would eventually suck him into oblivion.

When Boysie was out of London, or even out of touch with her, Elizabeth sensed that he was often lost even to himself. There was also a stockpile of evidence which told her that she was far from being the only woman in his life. It was a great wonder to her that again and again he was pulled back, from luscious, sensual and sophisticated creatures, to her own dumpy, snub-nosed, ordinary workaday mind and body. Yet, in a befuddled world, Elizabeth felt that her relationship with this big, secretive, handsome, nervous, middle-aged clown was something to be envied. Whatever he did, she had the best of him; something she shared with nobody else.

At the moment Elizabeth was absent from the Chesham Place flat only to nurse Sandy through a particularly vile bout of influenza. Boysie's 'jam' could be one of three things—an urgent summons abroad on business, a clash with the infamous Mostyn, or the age-old problem. Elizabeth's eyes were fully open to the fact that, once they were separated, it was a safe bet on Boysie's being off with the first girl who showed interest.

'Well,' she said at last, a modest impression of an angry rattlesnake, 'who is she? And how is it going to help if I come back?'

Boysie swallowed, switching on his sincere voice. 'Honestly, Liz, I'm sorry. I try. You know. I don't mean to——' He could not keep things like this from Elizabeth. 'Oh hell, yes, I'm a bit pissed. You were away. I was lonely and fed up. I had the afternoon off.'

'What else did you have off?'

'Eh?'

'Do I know her or is she a public woman?' Witch voice.

'No. Nobody knows her. Except—oh hell, that's the trouble.'

'What's her name?' Patience screwed to the top of her head.

'Susan Scrivinas.'

'What happened?'

'Everything.'

'Oh.'

'I met her in Hatchetts.' As though that excused the whole thing. 'Quite accidentally.'

'How accidentally? She dropped something and you picked it up, I suppose?'

'It wasn't like that, Liz. Truly she's not that sort of——'

'Girl. I know. None of them are.'

'I knocked over her pink gin.'

'Her pink gin—how absolutely devastating for you, and in Hatchetts.'

'An accident. Truly.'

'Yeah.'

'And we had lunch together, then came back here.'

17

'Original.'

'Then I took her to the Whimsey.' Shamefaced.

'I never get taken to the Whimsey.' Bristle.

'You don't like it. You hate the Whimsey. You told me.'

'I hate *you*.' It was the best repartee Elizabeth could manage.

'Liz.' Wheedling.

'Where's the trouble? All this is infantile. You've laid somebody else and now you've got drunk and maudlin and guilty.'

'No. You haven't heard the worst. We were having dinner and she suddenly started on the marriage line.'

'You're joking.'

'Truth. The love-at-first-sight bit.'

'Serve you right. So?'

'So, when was I going to meet Mummy and Daddy and they would adore me just as much as she did and how furious Mummy would be if she knew what had happened and her uncle would be especially livid——'

'Her uncle?'

'Her uncle. A colonel. Something very hush-hush. Name of Mostyn. Uncle Jimmy.'

Elizabeth began to gurgle. 'Where is she?'

'Left her at the Whimsey. Paid the bill and pretended to go to the loo.'

'You walked out on her? You've done it proper, darling. She'll have your——'

'Liz.'

'No, Boysie. Screw off. Isn't it time you bloody grew up? You're a rabbit, love. A dirty, great, middle-aged buck rabbit.'

The line clicked dead. For a moment Boysie sat staring at the receiver clutched in his large paw. It was all Mostyn's fault. Everything. When you traced trouble to its logical source the first cause always turned out to be

Colonel James George Mostyn. Had not Mostyn conned him into the job? Offered him the golden carrot? The eternal Pools winner. In exchange for what? Death? A hundred deaths? It was Mostyn who had suggested a life of glamour, riches, and gloss. Ten years ago. Ten years of living it up. But the ball had become interspersed with horror, and with the horror Boysie was slowly declining into intense hatred. As far as British Special Security was concerned, for the best part of ten years Boysie Oakes had been their unofficial killer. The man with the code letter L—L for Liquidator.

Boysie set the telephone back into its cradle. Almost immediately it started to ring.

'Hello,' said Boysie gingerly.

'Major Oakes?' The voice of authority.

'Yes.' Boysie swung back out of his black period with a pinch of pride. They had just upped his technical military rank, and for the past week he had been trying it on for size.

'Duty Officer. Number Two just called down. He wants to see you in Number One's office as soon as possible.'

A brace of jellyfish squeezed themselves into Boysie's main arteries. 'What's it all about?' Constricted. Concern zigzagging between the words.

'Dunno, mate.' The Duty Officer unflurried. 'But they're both up there with foul tempers. I think Number One's gone spare. Keeps muttering something about rabbits.' Boysie closed his eyes and wished he had paid more attention to Scripture lessons.

'Damn Bolshy swine've got Rabbit.' The Chief blurted out this somewhat dramatic statement before Mostyn was half-way into the familiar plush office at the top of British Special Security Headquarters near Whitehall. Mostyn quietly closed the door behind him. Being a man of some ambition and ruthlessness, he thought about chains of command quite literally in terms of chains. The most highly polished, super-brilliant link was, of course, himself, while those around him had a tendency to dullness. Tarnish even. The boozy old ex-admiral who was Chief of Special Security had become in Mostyn's mind both a figurehead and a rusty uncertain hook on which the chain hung. When Mostyn was most able to delude himself, he sought comfort in the fact that if anything gave way it could be blamed on that rusty hook. Yet in dark-bright moments of truth Mostyn knew intuitively that the Chief was banking on his Second-in-Command being the weak link. The Chief had even taken opportunities to make little file marks in Mostyn's mettle.

At this moment Mostyn was feeling far from his best, having been called from the warmth of a fallen Bunny girl, with strange fetishes, earlier that drizzling evening. 'Rabbit?' he queried, doing his best to keep the snap from his voice; then, making alarming contact, 'Good grief, Chief!'

'Ye-es,' snarled the Chief, intent on broaching a new bottle of Chivas Regal. 'Good old Rabbit Warren. They've got 'im.'

'Chopped?' Mostyn's irritation turned to uncertainty.

'Don't talk like a bloody cabin boy, man. Got 'im in the bag. Wouldn't chop a bloke like Warren in Moscow.'

'We've chopped their blokes here.'

'Different matter entirely.' The Chivas Regal was open.

'How'd it happen, Chief?' Mostyn careful, greasy as the little curls on his head.

''Otel Ukraine. Meetin' with Chateaubriand—bloody silly code name for that little shit. Ought to change that one, lad. Understand it was something quite important. Supposed to be bringin' the stuff back in the Diplomatic

Bag tomorrow.'

Mostyn sat down, mouth open with rage and eyes narrowed to nasty little slits. 'Why wasn't I told, sir? My area. My operative.'

The Chief turned, bottle in one hand and glass in the other. 'Got news for you, little Mostyn. We could both be up the fornicatin' creek. Information concernin' Warren's detention came through odd bloody channels.' He passed the brimming glass of whisky across the desk.

Mostyn took it with some gratitude. 'Odd?'

The Chief nodded sagely. 'Information came direct to me in confidence from the Foreign Secretary.' The Chief grinned nastily.

If he crossed arms under his chin he would look like the Jolly Roger, thought Mostyn. The whole atmosphere was edgy with conflict. Warren, one of the most experienced field operatives, often doubled with the diplomatic couriers behind the Curtain. That the news should come direct from the Foreign Secretary verged on catastrophe. The Foreign Office, Home Office, and Paymaster General, not to mention the Treasury, had long sought to combine Special Security with one of the other existing Intelligence branches. The slightest chink in the Department's armour could lead to drastic reorganisation—plus the loss of jobs for the Chief and his Second-in-Command. For years the whole of Special Security had been balanced precariously on the dodo line.

'Thinkin' of your nasty neck, Mostyn?'

'To be frank, Chief, yes.'

The old boy nodded. 'So am I, lad.' There was sincerity in every word. 'Happily,' he continued, 'there are certain things on our side.' He took a gulp of whisky, which would have done for most experienced drinkers, got up, and crossed to the tape-recorder table, which stood, like an altar, beneath a mediocre reproduction of Annigoni's portrait of Her Majesty. 'FS was in a bit of a panic when he got in touch. Y'see, he had the news straight from his opposite number in Moscow. Scrambled line of course. Had the monitor tape sent up here. Interestin' listenin', Mostyn. FS wants our help and I've promised to destroy the tapes.'

The Chief took another major swallow and touched the side of his nose with a bony forefinger. 'We play this on tipitoes, little Mostyn. Listen, mark, and inwardly digest right through your watery bowels.' The gnarled finger swooped on to the playback key and a wave of static filled the room. 'We must think ourselves bloody lucky. Listenin' to history, Number Two, history.'

Voice began to permeate the static, then a series of clicks and a whir.

'Foreign Secretary, sir?' The stewed-prunes voice of a ministerial switchboard operator. 'Personal call from Moscow on the red phone, sir.'

'Ah'm on th' bloody red phone.' The unmistakable North Country accent which endeared that eminent politician to so many of his disciples.

'Switching you now, sir.'

'Hello.' Another voice now. A dark accent beamed into the Foreign Secretary's bedroom from way below the iron shutters which ring East from West. 'Hello. Is that you, Basil, my friend?'

'Aye. Who th' 'ell's that?'

'Illyich.' Expansive. 'From Moscow. You remember our last meeting—in New York for the UN?'

'Oh, aye. Aye. Illyich. Nice to hear from yer. 'Ow are ye, lad? What canna do for thee?'

'You remember New York, Basil? Vhat a night! Vhat vere their names? Two cute cookies, eh, comrade?'

Mostyn looked at the ceiling with grave devotion. The Chief wore a satisfied smirk.

'What canna do for thee, Illyich?' The bluffness gone in defence of dignity.

'Well, little brother, it may be that I can do something for you. One of your Embassy couriers has got himself into trouble. Always happening, isn't it?'

'Now luke 'ere, Illyich, If you've been pullin' them damn camera tricks again, by Gow, I'll——'

'Basil.' Soothing. Keep it friendly. 'Nobody knows about this. Not even the Ambassador. Certainly not the press. Not yet anyway. He is a boy called Warren. Timothy Warren. He works in your Department of Special Security under the amusing code name "Rabbit." Quite good that, Basil, no? Rabbit Warren?'

'Never 'eard of 'im. Don't know what yer on about.'

'No, of course not. It's sordid—only your underlings deal with things like this. But old Boris Khavichev has had an eye on Warren for some time—a fatherly eye, you understand.'

'Aye. Coom on, out wi' it.'

'Tonight Boris pulled him in, and truly, Basil, we can go the whole bundle on this. Make it look very bad for you.'

'What d'ye want?'

'That's better, Basil. No publicity. A straight swap within a week. You have the choice of place, though I would suggest the Wall now that the heat is off there. We release no information about Warren or the switch—either before or at any time after the event. You get him back in exchange for a young woman called Iris Mac-Intosh who is at present languishing in the Intelligence Detention Area of Holloway Prison under the severity of a life sentence.'

Mostyn shot forward as if scorpion-stung in the rectum. He was making motions like a landed fish. 'Iris bloody MacIntosh,' he seemed to be saying.

'Ah'll luke into it.' The politician's voice was still coming flat from the tape. 'Ah promise nothin', Illyich, but ah'll 'ave an answer in twelve hours.'

'I can expect no more than that, Basil. No more, no less. It has been good talking with you. Be well. Be happy. And, by the way, Miss MacIntosh's prison number is 26589300. She occupies the cell next to Helen Kroger.'

The Chief stopped the recorder, and Mostyn began to splutter. 'Iris bloody MacIntosh. Of all the—— It's not on, Chief. It's not on.'

'On the contrary, little Mostyn.' The Chief wound the tape off the machine, removed the spool, dropped it in a container, and tapped it with his right hand. 'Life insurance, old boy. Bloody man from the Prudential couldn't have called at a better time.'

'I presume you're not going to destroy that tape.'

'You're jokin', Number Two. Just a couple of sentences on it, but while the present lot are in power we have the Foreign Office buttoned up. Now let's get down to cases. Sinister plottin' and all that cock.' The Chief refilled his glass and seated himself behind the desk.

'We can't let Iris MacIntosh out of the country, Chief.' Mostyn telling him as opposed to warning. 'Quite out of the question.'

'Stow it, you lubber.' The skinny hand moved towards the IN tray and fastened on a bulky red file. Mostyn could read the tags. 'Took the liberty of gettin' the MacIntosh file sent up.' The Chief's voice held a hint of hidden treasure. 'I see those psychologists at Sheep Dip have had no luck in de-indoctrinatin' her. One of your big bloomers, eh, Mostyn? Real purler. Secretary to the Second-in-Command of Special Security working for Redland. Girl must have a gold mine of information still tucked away, and she's highly resistant if even Sheep Dip can't wash it away.'

'We cannot let her go.' Finality.

'Seem to remember that she was highly involved with your boy L.'

'Yes, Chief.' Mostyn's voice had the cutting edge of a Wilkinson's sword blade. 'Boysie was involved. Heavily, sexually, and insecurely.'

'Together you chose a purler. Nearly went arse over elbow. Nearly did for your scheme.'

'What scheme?'

'Mostyn.' Reproach. 'Your wheeze for liquidatin' security risks.'

'Look, Chief——' Mostyn gave up before starting. The involved, undemocratic and highly unofficial method by which Special Security cleared its books of suspects had first sprung from a germ deep in the Chief's ocean-washed mind. Mostyn had put his scheme into operation, chosen Boysie as the executioner, trained him, and pressed the button when necessary. Since then, the Chief had just not wanted to know. The ball was always left firmly embedded in Mostyn's court. If there were any questions, investigations, or raps to be taken, Mostyn, as the Chief's Number Two, would be at the blunt end.

'Been thinkin',' said the Chief. 'Time to clear the decks for action. Get the skeletons out of our cupboards. We want Warren, can't let MacIntosh go.' He looked hard into Mostyn's face, eyes playing at being gimlets. 'Also get the feelin' these days you're not too happy with your boy L.'

Mostyn was silent, trying to work it out. This was a change of tune from the Chief. Mostyn always approached changes of key, pitch, or tune with the greatest delicacy and a certain amount of mistrust. He began slowly. 'To be honest, Chief, I use him as little as possible. Boysie tends to be accident prone.'

'Thought as much. The Coronet business, Understrike, then the goddam lot in Switzerland, Amber Nine. Nearly buggered the lot of us.' He put his hands together in an attitude of prayer. 'How would it be, Number Two, if I arranged the deal? Wednesday today, say on Monday evenin'? We swap at Checkpoint Charlie. All above-board except that we've sent L, Boysie, into—how do those curious novelists put it—into the cold?'

Mostyn's face showed no reaction for five seconds. Then a smile began to trade up his cheeks. 'Bloody marvellous, Chief. Marvellous. We get Warren. They get Iris MacIntosh. But Boysie's waiting there with his little pop-gun. He chops Iris, and they'll never let him out alive.'

'Pre-bleedin'-cisely, gets rid of all our garbage. Start with a clean slate.'

'Well, I have been using somebody else for quite a time.'

'Oh, I know all about that. 'Nother problem alto-gether. Get rid of this one first. And if by any chance he does come back, then the bleeder deserves to stay with the Department. Desk job, of course, where he can't get into any trouble.'

Mostyn gestured towards the telephone.

'Be my guest,' said the Chief, unusually jaunty.

Mostyn picked up the instrument. 'Duty Officer? Number Two. Get Major Oakes up to Number One's office as soon as you can, will you? There's a good chap....'

Boysie almost kicked his way through the anonymous swing-doors which were the entrance to Special Security's Headquarters. For once in his life Boysie was boiling for a fight. He had always known the end would come, but never had he envisaged its precipitation through a stray bit of consorting with one of Mostyn's slag relatives. Elizabeth's words still burned in his ears. 'Isn't it time you bloody grew up?' All right, he was thinking, they can stuff it. He had lived the schizophrenic life pretend-ing to be their hired hatchet for long enough.

'Come in, Boysie, nice to see you.' Mostyn, all glowing

and obese with charm, opened the door and withdrew the wind from Boysie's frantic sails.

'Come in, Major Oakes.' The Chief hearty from behind his desk. 'Good of you to turn out.'

The door shut quietly behind him. 'Now look here——' Boysie began loudly.

'A chair,' said Mostyn.

'Most interestin' assignment for you.' The Chief beamed.

'Oh no.' Boysie, firm but seated and by this time with a glass in his hand.

'Big bonus,' smeared Mostyn. 'Very big.'

'And a chance to see the world,' said the Chief.

'I am not doing another operation.' Boysie felt his voice did not carry conviction. 'I resign.'

By mid-morning he was being processed through a cover story. A new name: Bertram Ian Oldcorn. A new occupation: sales manager for Bone Demolition (Hatch End) Limited, combining business with pleasure on a sales-sightseeing tour. Background and normal pre-operational screening followed fast, and between each of the usual twenty phases Boysie worked out his reserves of nervous energy desperately trying to contact Griffin. Charlie Griffin was Boysie's escape chute. While Boysie was willing to fight for his life (even to kill *in extremis*), he had never managed to summon up the required stomach to execute in cold blood. Boysie was the hangman incapable of pulling the bolt, the O/C firing party unable to deliver the *coup de grâce*. Hence Griffin, quiet, laconic, an ex-undertaker, an expert in the death-game; the man whom Boysie had, over the years with the Department, subcontracted whenever called upon to dispense cold-blooded murder. But as Wednesday night approached, Boysie became more frantic and Griffin still remained unavailable. No answer from his telephone, no reply to the three telegrams. At this point Boysie, true to form began to build up a mental block. It would be all right on the night, he thought with a nervous laugh. The mind stopped at the point where he would be called upon to squint down the telescopic sight and put Iris MacIntosh's head slap between the cross-wires.

On Thursday morning he sent a last telegram:

CONTACT ME BERTIE OLDCORN SOONEST HOTEL BRISTOL KEMPINSKI BERLIN IN PERSON

He signed it with his humiliation initials B.O. and rang Elizabeth, who could not talk because there were a dozen people in the office. Frustrated and with the preliminary twinges of despair leading him to resignation, Boysie picked up his carefully packed, battered tan Revelation and headed for the door. The telephone rang while his hand was still on the knob. Despair changed to active abhorrence as Mostyn's voice slid, oily, through the earpiece.

'Just calling to wish you luck, Oaksie.'

'Get stuffed.'

'Oakes.' The grease wiped away. 'This is important. Now you listen. Your contact in Berlin will be Warbler. Got it? Warbler.'

'Warbler,' repeated Boysie without enthusiasm.

'He's good, so watch it. He'll contact as we arranged.' Then loudly, as though to an animal, 'Now move, boy. Kill.'

Warbler turned off the Strasse des 17 Juni and took the VW up a straight, broad road flanked by flat grass rectangles. Ahead stood the crumbling grey pile of partly restored masonry, once the imposing, powerful Reichstag, Germany's House of Commons. The sky was darkening, but Boysie could just make out the inscription *Dem Deutschen Volke* above the tired colonnade.

There was a sad loneliness, a feeling of lost greatness in the air. Warbler pulled over to the right and stopped the car.

'Are we near the Wall?' Boysie ventured.

'Your first time here?' Warbler switching to serious mood, eyes now dull, dead behind the thick glasses. Inscrutable.

Boysie nodded.

'It is the first thing you all ask,' said Warbler, relaxing again. 'Yes, we are quite near the Wall. Part of it is over there, behind the trees. There, you can just see the top of the Brandenburg Tor. That's in the East. In Commie country.' His English precise, worked out over schoolbooks and polished on the international market. Even the slang was meticulously accurate.

Over the trees Boysie could see the ironic Goddess of Peace sitting, through all weathers, on top of the Brandenburg Gate. Above her the Red Flag whipped out against a sky that had become menacing. Boysie shivered.

'It is going to rain,' said Warbler. 'Tomorrow you will see the Wall. And on Monday evening you will cross it.' He burrowed in his gabardine pockets and brought out a large envelope from which all crispness had been erased. 'You like Brecht?' he asked, looking straight at Boysie.

There was no point in playing for time. 'Never tried any,' said Boysie with his open, homely grin.

Warbler guffawed. 'Good. Good. Bertolt Brecht, the playwright.'

'Still haven't tried any.'

'You are going to see one of his masterworks on Monday.'

'That'll be jolly.'

'*Dreigroschenoper.*'

'Yes.' Boysie a long way behind.

'That is the name of the piece. *Dreigroschenoper.* In your language *The Threepenny Opera.*'

'Oh.' Boysie's voice full of recognition. 'I know the theme song, 'Mack the Knife.' Hey, I know about that.' Happily surprised.

'Yes.' Warbler rocked backwards and forwards, gurgling with laughter. 'Yes. "Mackie Messer." We thought it appropriate.' He began to sing quietly to the tune of 'Mack the Knife':

> *'Irish MacIntosh was discovered*
> *With a bullet in her breast.*
> *Boysie strolls on down the dockside*
> *Knows no more than all the rest.*
>
> *Oh, the shark has pretty teeth, dear,*
> *and he keeps them pearly white.*
> *But Boysie has a knife and*
> *He keeps it out of sight.'*

'I'm not using a knife,' Boysie bridled.

'Poetic licence.' Warbler tapped his knee. 'Parody. You will enjoy this *Dreigroschenoper*, even though I am told the new production toes the party line. Now to work. All work and no play, you know. And do I want to play tonight! On your expenses, of course.' He pulled a pile of papers, a map, and some photographs from the envelope. 'Tomorrow, as I have said, you will be shown the Wall. On Monday night you cross normally, here.' He laid a small section of map between them. It was barely visible in the gloom. 'Checkpoint Charlie.'

'What do you mean, normally?'

'Just like any other tourist. They do it all the time, you know.'

Boysie swallowed, and Warbler continued. 'You go straight on down the Friedrichstrasse on which Checkpoint Charlie is situated, on over the Unter den Linden, and across the river. The Bertolt-Brecht-Platz is on your left. In the Platz stands the Berliner Ensemble Theatre. There is plenty of room to park your car.' He passed over a photograph, but it was already too dark to scrutinise. 'That is marked "Photo One." Shows the Berliner Ensemble from the Friedrichstrasse. You should begin to cross at about six on Monday night in case there is any holdup.'

'What sort of holdup?' Windy.

'Oh, they sometimes like to spin it out. You know what they're like. Formalities, formalities. They're not too bad with foreigners. With West Germans they can be tedious.'

Boysie nodded. 'So I get to the theatre and park my car.'

'The performance is scheduled for seven o'clock. It usually starts promptly at eight minutes past seven. Your ticket.' He passed over a small envelope. 'Take care of that. If the checkpoint officials want to know where you are going, you can show them. Good. You sit through the first half of the play. If they start on time, the interval comes at eight-thirty. And here you must move.' Another photograph over to Boysie. This time Warbler illuminated it with a pencil torch. 'Photo Two, you must study this with care. It is taken from the steps of the Berliner Ensemble.'

Boysie could see a tree in the foreground, then a road and fence. Beyond, and to the left, a bridge. Behind that a long five-story building of grey stone, flat roofed. Warbler talked on. 'As soon as the interval begins you move out of the main doors, across the road, and over the bridge. You are making for the right end of the building, only about seventy metres from the theatre. A block of apartments.'

Boysie nodded.

'Good. The door is obscured in the picture, but I have marked it.' His index finger pointed. 'Here.' The torch went out. 'You must know that picture by heart. It is essential. If you have time to spare before the performance, locate the door and do the walk from the theatre. You have a stop watch?'

'Yes.' Boysie flashed the Navitimer he had 'won' from the last operation.

'Good. You will need it. When you get to the flats, go straight in through the door I have marked, then up to the second floor. Two flights, remember. Two flights of stairs. Flat Number 12.'

'Number 12,' said Boysie as though confident.

'The door will be open and nobody will be there. Empty. Lock the door and go through to the bedroom window.' Another piece of paper. 'Plan of the flat. The window looks straight down on to the Friedrichstrasse. Ideal view. You are about fourteen metres from the ground. Oh, how do you work it out in your damn foots and inches? Anyway, from my notes I know your first possible shot will be from around a hundred yards.'

'A hundred yards.' Boysie had long learned to say the right thing at the right time when being briefed for something he knew Griffin would be doing. Suddenly he found himself again considering the possibility that he might, on this occasion, have at least to get as far as the window.

Warbler was still talking. 'On the floor by the window you will find a Mauser rifle. The 98K. You are familiar with the 98K?'

'A Mauser 98K?' Mild shock showing in the tone of the larynx.

'Yes.'

'Bit ancient, isn't it? You haven't got an old Winchester or something from the US Fifth Cavalry days lying around by any chance?'

Warbler grinned in the gloom. 'The 98K is a very accurate weapon still, friend, and with the kind of bullet we are providing I don't think you will have much trouble.'

'Well, I suppose it is designated as a sniper's rifle.' Boysie grudgingly. Whatever his weaknesses, he knew guns. 'Telescopic sight?'

'No. It will be dark, but the area is quite well lit—those awful yellow lamps. Your weapon will have been adapted for the Hythe night-sight system.'

'The radium cylinder on the foresight.' Very knowledgeable.

'That's it.' Warbler suitably impressed. 'The rifle takes a clip of five rounds, as you know. There will be one spare clip in case you run into difficulty.'

Boysie made a disgusted face. Once more he had the feeling that he was really going to do this operation.

'The switch between Warren and MacIntosh,' continued Warbler, 'is timed to the minute. It takes place on Checkpoint Charlie at exactly 8.35. She should pass your position at 8.38. There will be no slip-ups at that end, and you will have no real difficulty—we have arranged for a truck to break down. Your target will be travelling in the back of a black Zil III.'

'Like a Buick.' Boysie knew it *all* this evening.

'As you say, like a Buick. It will be going quite fast but shall have to slow down for the truck. They should have the lights full on.'

'And she'll be in the back?'

Warbler's body jerked in affirmation. 'Probably with someone else. Too bad about him.'

'No chance of them changing cars? Switching her again?'

'Not likely. There wouldn't be much point, and they won't be expecting our kind of trouble.'

'And what about the ammunition? You said something about that. What am I using? Explodable bullets or something?'

'Plenty of time to worry about that. Tomorrow night we will go out to the field firing range at Ruhleben. They have fixed up a tower for you at approximately the height you will be shooting from. We also have a radio-controlled car for you to practice on. It will be fun.' Gleefully.

'I'll bet.' No enthusiasm from Boysie. 'And what if things really go wrong? If the performance starts on time—at seven?'

'Then you will have eight minutes in hand. When it is all over, use your own discretion about getting away. I suggest you go back to the theatre if you can. Certainly you must stay over there until the performance is finished. And don't panic when you cross into the West again. They will have tightened up the checkpoint control, but that shouldn't worry you. Tomorrow I give you an address. If things get very bad, you can lie low there for a while.' Warbler raised both hands in a manner of finality. 'Now, my friend, put the papers away safely and work on them later tonight.' Another envelope. 'Just a few more details from Headquarters. Tomorrow we rehearse everything.' He started the VW as the first drops of rain sprayed on to the screen. 'Food,' said Warbler, his voice crammed with gluttony. 'Food at your hotel. They do you well there.'

Still no word from Griffin at Reception. Boysie surrendered himself to the dogma of making the most of it and joined Warbler in the polished extravaganza that was the foyer lounge. A couple of dry martinis while tropical fish did five turns around a massive wall tank and shallow fountains splashed peacefully, generating the feeling of comfort and luxury that was the Bristol Kempinski's great selling line. Prosperity loomed large, hanging on the vicuña shoulders of the men or flashing in diamonds from the Rubinsteined necks of their women. Warbler chatted endlessly, his inconsequentialities laced with long gusts of birdlike laughter. He came more into his own when they moved into the restaurant, to a meal and service that banished all thoughts of the danger which lay only hours from Boysie. With the last sip of brandy, Boysie realised that he was unmistakably contented. Who cared about Monday night—it might never come anyway. So this was the hub of the Cold War. Bloody good place to be. So what about NATO and the Rhine Army and those bloody great Russian divisions on the other side of the Curtain?

'Now,' said Warbler smacking his lips, 'now I show you some of the night life of Berlin.'

The streets seemed to contain nothing but clubs— Rififi, Club Sexy, Rio Grande, Rialto, The Berlin Hotpoint. They spun out on either side in a blast of crimson neon, winking in a montage, flooding fire over the death-mask faces of occasional girls haunting doorways or passing the time, with uniformed commissionaires, between clients. The rain had turned to an apathetic drizzle, cold for late spring. Warbler stopped at the Ritz Kursal, the small entrance belying the opulence of its name.

'They tell me there is a very original girl here,' he said as they passed from the relative brightness of the street into the heavy murk that pervades this kind of club from Brewer Street to Brazil. Warbler was obviously expected —a table by the small dance floor, a bottle, glasses.

Boysie's eyes gradually adjusted to the smoky lack of light. They were in the original L-shaped room, low-ceiling, the walls half panelled in a cheap stained wood. Near the door two girls, isolated and for hire, sat at the bar. On the dais in the adjacent corner a trio throbbed an unmerciful beat, making the Rolling Stones sound like the London Philharmonic. It was the clientele which made Boysie do a double-take in quadruplicate. Sedate at the tables tightly packed around the floor sat family after family of solid citizens, the men upright in Sunday suits, with their womenfolk, some of whom still sported the tough huntin' and shootin' type headgear. Only two other tables were occupied by unattached, lonely young men, eyed expectantly by the brace of tarts at the bar.

'*Ach.*' Warbler doubled up with laughter. 'You are surprised. Here it is not just for the tourists. I know what you call in England the middle-class people would not come to a club like this. We come for the family outing. Very healthy. A few glasses of beer. An eyeful of the girls. Stimulating for the marriage. A song. Nice. *Gemütlich.*' He looked around, nodding approval. 'I have known this place for a long time. *Ach——*' Falling apart at some hidden hilarity to be told.

A very funny fella, thought Boysie.

'Here,'—Warbler choked—'here, there used to be a stripper called Sexy Hexy. Too fond of the drink, Hexy.' He mimed with a trembling hand. 'One night in the winter, Sexy Hexy had too much. She went upstairs, slipped, and fell out of the window. So there she was, on the pavement outside, in the rain, twenty-one years old, dead. Sexy Hexy.' Paralysed with mirth. 'Sexy Hexy.'

Boysie gave a little polite laugh. Very funny fella, he thought again. Funny sick.

There was a roll on the drums. The lights dimmed, which was more than Boysie thought possible, and a single spot ripped through the smoke. Into the illuminated circle strode a heavily dyed blonde wrapped skilfully in gold lamé. She greeted the audience in German, wooing them with a series of leers and winks understandable in any language. Then, like a Lufthansa hostess, she switched on her English.

'Good evening, ladies and genellmen. We are glad you have come to our club and hope you will leave with some stirring memories. My name is Merry Fern. A happy name, no? First, as an apéritif to our main act of the

36

evening, I like to introduce Margot. Here she is, give her a big hand. Margot.'

Margot needed a big hand. She looked on the grubby side and was about four stones too heavy with breasts like hybrid breadfruit. The trio banged away at the bumps and grinds while Margot slowly uncovered down to the last minute G-string, doing some highly obscene things with her stockings on the way. A second apéritif followed—Heddi, as skinny as Margot had been plump. Heddi did odd things with her off-white suspender belt. Boysie had seen better performances in Soho, but the audience seemed to like it.

Heddi had barely scampered from the floor before Merry Fern was back in the spotlight. Through the murk Boysie could see the trio creeping away from their dais. An attendant pushed a low, heavily decorated sofa on to the floor. At one end was a neat pile of what appeared to be clothes. The attendant completed his scene setting by placing a pair of high-buttoned Victorian ladies' boots and a silver button hook by one leg of the sofa. The audience shifted with expectancy.

'Here it comes. The new act,' whispered Warbler with an elbow jab to Boysie's ribs. Merry finished her German introduction. The audience buzzed appreciatively.

'And now, ladies and genellmen, what you have been waiting for. The toast of the evening. Our flower from the Orient. Our China doll. Miss ... Rosy ... Puberty.' Deafening applause. From somewhere a stereo player poured liquid Eastern noises into the haze. The spotlight whipped from the floor, faltered, then settled on a door at the far end of the bar. The door opened, and out came Miss Rosy Puberty, somewhere around five feet tall, jet shining hair piled high over a strong oval face, dark eyebrows above perfect lashes and deep dark almond eyes slanting away from the elegant nose, nostrils flared for a fraction, while, below, her mouth mixed generosity in equal portions with that kind of sensual promise which is the sole copyright of young Chinese women. Miss Puberty was stark naked, the light from the spot striking off her smooth olive skin, making it glint around the wonderful curve of her neck and the upthrust circlets of young breasts, each centred with a wide brown bull's-eye of nipple. The body hair had been shaved below the tiny dark cavern of her navel, and she walked with a slow careful pleasure, an ease, in flowing movements of her thighs, as though it was complete happiness for her to bring joy to the audience, who sat silent as animals watching some unobtainable prey.

Boysie was unaware of the music, of Warbler, of anything but the graceful girl moving towards the sofa. As she reached it she turned with arms outstretched and feet slightly apart; then, rocking a little, she completed the circle so that the whole of her body passed before the eyes of everyone in the room. The music softened, and Miss Puberty bent to take, from the piles of clothes, a wisp of black, a tiny pair of sheer panties, into which she placed first one foot and then the other, slowly pulling it up tight around hips and buttocks. She turned full circle again, hands spread wide across her flat stomach. Then one hand drifted away to take from the pile a corselet, fragile and frothed with lace, small, bowed suspenders hanging from the one-piece garment, which nipped in her waist and cupped the lower halves of her breasts.

Despite the intricate fastening, Rosy Puberty made this business of clothing her body, from thighs to breasts, an infinitely more stimulating moment than most strippers can manage during the final seconds of their divesting. She now sat on the sofa to pull on her long black silk sockings, her fingers caressed the silk and flesh in a manner that conveyed the sense of touch to every man in the room, the fastening of each suspender a moment of pure delight. Garters, narrow rose lace, delicate and precisely placed. Then the buttoning of the boots, the body undulating into a different position with each subtle move of the button hook. Boysie could hardly breathe; the hairs on the back of his neck stood to attention like the Royal Marines Queen's Squad. He had not seen anything so blatantly sexy and off-beat since Albert Finney had done the eating bit in *Tom Jones*.

Rosy Puberty was now stepping into an ankle-length grey skirt, fastening the side buttons with a deft one-handed flick of finger and thumb, the ball of the thumb, kneading each button into place. Last a lacy blouse, with leg-of-mutton shoulders and a collar up to the chin. Rosy folded her hands and lowered her head. Coyness. Innocence. The complete Victorian governess from China. The lights went up, and the audience screamed their heads off while Rosy walked to the bar where Merry Fern stood with a waiting drink.

'Good.' Warbler nodding with all the seriousness of a professor vetting a pupil's essay.

'Good?' said Boysie, wiping a film of perspiration from his brow. 'She's bloody marvellous.' He looked up to see Merry Fern approaching their table, leading the handsome Miss Puberty by the hand. Warbler and Merry Fern greeted each other like old sparring partners. Boysie rose and stood grinning like a goat, not knowing what to do with his hands, embarrassed and submerged in a glut of German. Warbler was nearly on his knees, offering Miss Puberty his heart, wealth, the whole quota. Then Warbler came to his senses and turned to Boysie.

'*Ach*, my friend here is English. Please, Mr. Oldcorn, meet my old and intimate friend, Fräulein Fern.'

'Hello.' Boysie beamed, wiggling his fingers.

'And Miss Puberty.'

Boysie took her hand and tried to will charm from his fingertips into her palm. Play it cool, carefully, buster, said the nasty, whispering voice in his head. Pretend you do not want it. Rosy was even more gorgeous at arm's length than onstage. There was a gentle pressure between their hands with her eyes looking hard into his.

'Care for a drink?' Boysie making it casual.

'Ver' kin' off you.' Moving towards him as she spoke.

The foursome rearranged itself around the table, Warbler well away with Merry Fern, Boysie the envy of every lecherous eye in the place. A waiter descended like a white owl. He did not have to ask either Fern or Puberty what their liquid would be.

'Liked your act.' Boysie using all his self-discipline.

'Thank you. It is a way of making money. I do not choose it myself. But girls cannot always choose.'

'No,' said Boysie, feeling that line of conversation was at least temporarily closed.

'Please, I did not catch your name.' Her voice lifted and fell in the fascinating classical way of the Far East, though the pitch was basically lower than that of the few Chinese Boysie had previously met.

'Oak—Oldcorn.' He got it right after a stumble. 'My friends call me Boysie.'

Warbler momentarily came out of his rapt conversation to shoot a warning stiletto in Boysie's direction. Rosy laughed. For Boysie, delicate glass bells tinkled from a pagoda lit by a crescent moon. There were also a couple of willows, weeping copiously, in there somewhere. Boysie's knowledge of the Far East stemmed mainly from *chinoiserie*.

'It is a strange name, Boysie. How you come by it?'

'Don't know really. Started when I was a kid. A child. Never thought about it much. What about yours' Rose Puberty?'

Again she laughed. Boysie's mind did a quick reprint of the pagoda scene.

'That not my real name. Only name for stripper.'

'But you're not a stripper. You're a dresser.'

'All right, my real name is Mu-lan Tchen. Mu-lan is girl in ver' old Chinese poem. She went to war instead of father.'

'You don't look very warlike to me.' Boysie beginning to nudge in.

'You be surprised, Boysie. Often ver' bad temper.' She sipped the anonymous drink served by the hovering waiter, never taking her eyes from Boysie's face.

'And where were you born?' Boysie keeping the conversation in play.

'China.' The almond eyes wide.

If you ask a silly question, thought Boysie. 'Whereabouts in China?'

'North China.' She pronounced it 'Shina.' 'You know Chinese silk? That is where I come from. Shantung.'

'Where the silk comes from?'

'Yes.'

'And when were you last in Shantung?'

'Oh my.' Rosy slid her pupils to their apogee. 'Many, many years ago when I was still tiny baby.'

'You went to Hong Kong?'

'Taiwan—oh, sorry, I use Chinese name. I mean Formosa.'

'Family?'

'Yes, with family. It was ver' good in Formosa. Ver' happy there.'

'Then how did you end up like this? In a club.'

'Oh, you know how it is. I spend happy years with family in Formosa, then father die, and I want travel, want be big movie star but have no talent.'

'You've got a lot of talent. Anyway, you don't have to have talent to be a movie star, just——'

'Big breasts or talent. I have neither. Only talent to read palms and nerve to walk naked and dress in front of men.'

'You read palms?' Boysie a little afraid of himself. Like

most people with neurotic tendencies, he feared the unknown, rigidly disbelieved in palmistry and astrology, yet always felt a distinct magnetic pull towards it.

Rosy nodded, smiling.

In spite of himself Boysie extended his right hand. Rosy reached forward and took his left hand, then pulled both of them towards her. 'In Chinese palm-reading you need both hands. This hand, the right hand, tells of your life before birth. This tells me about you now.'

Her fingers soft on the back of his hand. Might be resting them in a nest of petals, thought Boysie. 'I'm going to marry a rich Chinese heiress and have fifteen children,' he said.

Rosy did not reply; she sat still, gazing into his hands. 'You are ver' soft-hearted, kind, romantic, sometimes too soft-hearted.' Her voice had gone as flat as last night's saki. She let go of his hands.

A colony of ants got to work in Boysie's intestines. Once he had seen a bit of stage business where a palmist took one look at the sucker's palm, then folded it up and returned it to him, making little negative sucking noises. 'Give,' he said throatily. Instant twitch.

'I do' know. There is something. Boysie, I see great danger for you.'

The ants developed wings. Persistent little devils.

She took his hands again, this time in her palms. 'One other thing. I am not bad girl, Boysie. I promise I am not bad girl. Not take money for making love with men like those.' She nodded towards the bar where the whores still lounged, bored with custom. There was a tremor in Rosy's voice as if she were short of breath. 'Bu' in your hand I see we are good for each other. I see that we correspond with much between us.'

Under different circumstances Boysie would have been flippant, even cynical. It was a brand-new approach, and she was a creamy dish. But the palm-reading had edged under his skin, the reality of the situation brilliant before him. Griffin had not yet turned up. He would probably never turn up. The thing which Boysie had tried to submerge came popping up through the loose layers of psychological self-bluff. He was being forced into doing this one himself—the most dangerous one of all. Yet Boysie still could not face the truth; as always when he was on the run from facts, his physical self came into play. It was back to the womb, the need and desire to be close to a woman, any woman. Preferably this woman with the midnight hair and deep, drowning, slant eyes.

'You ready?' he said.

The girl nodded solemnly.

'What do I call you, Rosy or Mu-lan?'

'I like you call me Mu-lan best.'

As they rose, Warbler and Merry Fern looked up from their conversation. 'We're just going,' said Boysie, avoiding Warbler's eyes.

'*Ach*, but my friend we have the papers to see about yet. We cannot play all night.' Warbler sounded horribly confident about his authority. 'I do not think your managing director would like that.' Firm as a threat. Checkmate to Warbler.

Boysie turned aside and muttered to the Chinese girl, 'It's no good. Tomorrow or Monday?'

She nodded briskly. 'I give you telephone number and address. I write them down. Please, tomorrow or Monday, Boysie.'

Outside, in the Volkswagen, Warbler said, 'I'm sorry, but what can I do? Definite orders from Number Two. He gave me the orders personally.'

'Shaft Number Two,' spat Boysie, pocketing the piece of paper on which Mu-lan had written her address and telephone number.

By four in the morning Boysie had not slept. A small volcano of dog ends mounted steadily in the grotesque glass ashtray by his bed. In the end he was forced to look at the papers provided by Warbler. Apart from the photographs, drawings, and tickets there was the final envelope. 'Just a few more details from Headquarters,' Warbler had said. The envelope contained two sheets of flimsy. Both were marked 'Classified. Destroy after assimilating.' The first was a terse instruction from Mostyn.

This operation is of the highest importance. You will carry it through to the end without thought of outcome or consequence to yourself. N2SS

The second sheet proved to be a stapled clip of notes, circulated to all departments by K1, the Supervising Ktentologist for the Ministry of Defence, dealing solely with the science of killing. Boysie was sickened by what he read. At one point he looked up and caught a glimpse of his face in the mirror across the room. That sickened him even more. The signs of harass were beginning to show. K1's notes were prefaced by a single line that read:

'For guidance should your Department be called upon and/or authorised to carry out a mission of this nature.

Twin snakes of anxiety wriggled even faster through Boysie's nervous system. The heading served only as a reminder that the post of Liquidator to British Special Security was entirely an unofficial appointment. There was no 'out' but one—feet first in lead, mahogany, or cement.

With disgust Boysie slowly tore both pieces of flimsy

into small pieces, carefully placed them in the ashtray, and started a miniature bonfire. Somehow, the charred ashes which remained stank of death, provoking a definite increase in Boysie's heartbeat. Picking up the remaining documents, he went over the plan a couple of times, lay back, lit another cigarette, and allowed the timing and sequence to run smoothly through his mind. He slipped out of bed and unlocked his only other piece of important luggage—the gimmicked, slim-line Samsonite briefcase—inserted the documents, locked the box, and pressed hard on the left-hand lock. Anyone attempting to open the steel-reinforced case would immediately trigger an interior flush element, so destroying all contents. It worked well, as Boysie knew to his cost, having once, on a routine pick-up in Rome, tried to unlock the case (containing a set of priceless blueprints) without unsetting the mechanism. It was difficult to erase from his memory the look on Mostyn's face when he reported back with an envelope full of embers.

He woke at ten the next morning in a hot unpleasant sweat, emerging from a nightmare of walls, windows, flashing lights, and weird noises. Like one of Pavlov's dogs, Boysie automatically reached for the telephone. There were no messages. Nothing from Griffin. Sunday morning. Tomorrow night was Iris night.

Warbler arrived at noon, and they lunched at the Big Black Buffel up the road from the hotel. The service was diffident and the food vaguely American in the sense that it had little taste. The bill, which Boysie stupidly picked up, was exorbitant.

After lunch Warbler took him on a tour of the Wall. The German pointed to a notice rivetted to it. 'I know you do not read our language, my friend. It says, "The road is blocked because of the wall of shame." '

For the rest of the tour Boysie was dejected. Concrete

blocks and bricks, the everlasting wire, the initials KZ for concentration camp—and *Denk an Eichmann* chalked large on the bricks; too often the sad little pole-and-wire memorials of death: *Unknown escaper shot here by Vopos on 9th June 1965 at about 9 p.m. To the unknown escapist 4/9/62. Rolf Urban 6/6/1914 to 17/8/1961*

Later, as they drove round the streets near Tempelhof, Boysie recited each stage of the plan while Warbler questioned and cross-questioned with the verve and dash of Perry Mason. At times he became blatantly nasty. Finally they headed out to take a peek at Checkpoint Charlie. The atmosphere was haphazard on the West side, the whole vista being less colourful than it appeared on the postcards on sale at the Bristol Kempinski, though less grey than it appeared in spy movies. Dusk was moving in quickly. A tinge of panic trickled down Boysie's spine.

'That's where you go over tomorrow,' said Warbler without any inflection of feeling. 'Now we have a light meal and then I will take you for some practice with the rifle. Yes?'

Boysie nodded, the vomit of funk rising into his throat. He clenched his teeth, made a supreme effort to quell the distress, praying hard that Griffin would turn up.

II. NIGHTINGALE

I will roar you as 'twere any nightingale.
                              Shakespeare,
                    A Midsummer Night's Dream

As Boysie and Warbler drove away from Checkpoint
Charlie, Special Flight A5—an Aeroflot TU-104B—was
lowering its landing gear about twenty miles to the south
over the Eastern Zone. At just over four miles from the
theshold of runway 25L at Schoenefeld—East Berlin's
main airport—the TU-104B began to descend. High
above, two shadow aircraft, Mig-21s (NATO code *Fish-
bed*-C), broke away and turned off, heading for their
eastern base.

The TU-104B has a maximum load of seventy-five
passengers. Special Flight A5 carried only five people,
apart from the crew and two bulky hostesses. Timothy
Warren sat well forward, flanked by a brace of silent,
heavy gentlemen in badly fitting raincoats. His formerly
good-looking face was aged by ten years, his eyes tired
and glazed as though by a film of ice. His seated pose was
rigid, as if held by an invisible clamp, giving the impression of being locked in a shell of private hell, ignoring
the pair of obvious security men who had long since
given up trying to make conversation.

Towards the end of the aircraft two other men, more
neatly tailored, talked in occasional bursts of quiet
Russian. One was exceptionally tall: over six feet, with
dangerously broad shoulders and a facial skin of rough-

47

grained texture. He smiled rarely during the scattered dialogue and seldom kept his wide eyes in the same position—the restless look of a watcher, an observer, one constantly aware. Even in the relative solitude of the aircraft's cabin those eyes stabbed from subject to subject like an animal searching for prey or ready for the unexpected.

In government circles throughout the world, the tall man's face was well known—particularly in the major security departments of the West. There could be no doubt about his identity: Boris Piotr Khavichev, Director of Soviet Counter Espionage and Subversive Activities. A big man. A wide-radius wheel in the override game.

'There it is,' said Khavichev to his companion, looking down from the starboard window as the aircraft dipped into its tight turn. 'The West pretending to be a golden carrot as usual. *Ach*, look at the Kurfürstendamm. Sucker bait, as the Americans would say. Sucker bait among a pile of rubble.'

'Whom are they trying to fool?' The other grinned—a repulsive effect, for his face was terribly marked, a bizarre wrinkling of the skin and flesh overlaid with a criss-cross of scars. Bad burns badly patched up.

Special Flight A5 touched down lightly on Runway 25L at Schoenefeld and taxied into Parking Bay 4 by the main terminal building. Two black Zils, with the slatted grey blinds down, swung across the apron and drew up close to the boarding steps pushed into position at speed.

'We're here.' One of Warren's guards spoke in English, unclipping his seat belt.

Warren nodded, sullen and apprehensive. He started to get to his feet, but the other guard clasped his arm hard and pushed him down. Khavichev passed along the aircraft to the forward door, followed by his friend. The friend was small, dreadfully crippled, and took time, moving slowly with two rubber-tipped sticks, arms

48

trembling each time they took the weight of the warped body. Neither he nor Khavichev even glanced at Timothy Warren.

Boysie and Warbler ate at a coffee shop opposite the Kaiser Wilhelm Gedachtniskirche; sandwiches, black bread, and sausage, three cups of coffee. Boysie wanted a drink, but Warbler was in his firm mood. 'No alcohol before the practice and none at all tomorrow.' He did not even smile. It was nearly seven-thirty by the time they returned to the car.

'Now we go and see how well you can use this gun,' said Warbler, starting the engine, which coughed like a bad case of bronchial pneumonia.

'Where?' asked Boysie, unhappy and resigned.

'Not far. Ruhleben. The NATO field firing range. All is ready for you. I gather they have gone to much trouble.'

'What time will we finish?'

Warbler wheezed out a chuckle. 'Too late for Miss Puberty.' A fatherly pat on Boysie's knee.

They headed northwest, branching from the Ernst-Reuter-Platz, into the Otto-Suhr-Alee. On, out towards Ruhleben, the dark world around them outside the VW became more bleak and miserable. Boysie lost track. They passed through a small village and turned off on to a third-class road that eventually transformed itself into a rutted cart-path. The Volkswagen protested violently. Warbler had his lights full on, but even they disappeared into nothing when the big searchlight hit them. Warbler swore in German—a nasty-sounding word which Boysie did not even have to guess at in translation. The car jolted to a standstill and there were four uniformed men at the windows. Boysie slid his hand automatically under his coat and undid the safety strap on the Browning. There were some L2A3 Sterlings around—ferocious little submachine guns.

Warbler cranked down his window and flashed a magic card. Through the glare Boysie saw one of the uniformed quartet raise his hand and click a torch signal towards the searchlight. The blind of light beams faded. One of the L2A3's gave a sweeping motion intended to be a friendly wave forward. Boysie kept his hand on the small Baby Browning's butt. The nervous itch continued road trials up his vertebrae.

They bounced up the track for another hundred yards or so. In the distance there were more lights. Barbed wire. A notice in German and English: NATO PROPERTY. DANGER. KEEP OUT. Gates. A wooden hut. Soldiers. A Land Rover containing a driver and three males in service greatcoats. Warbler flashed the card again at the gate. Two armed guards there, one British and one American. The gates swung open, and Warbler drove through as one of the greatcoated figures detached himself from the Land Rover and approached the Volkswagen. Epaulettes flashed in the dim light. A major, British.

'Dead on time if you'll pardon the expression, old boy.' He peered into the car, giving Boysie a look which mixed intense interest with distaste. About 60/40 in favour of distaste. 'Just follow us. It's all set up.'

They parked next to the Land Rover behind a hut—dark and vaguely unsafe. To the right a watch tower rose, rickety, a wooden scaffold topped by a low flat box. It looked like a rush construction job. A broad stretch of concrete curved to the left and right, dotted on either side with tall lamp-posts, bending forward, throwing flat yellow pools of light on to the road, giving their faces the primary symptoms of jaundice. It was cold out of the car, enough for Boysie to turn up the fur collar of his short suede driving coat. They followed the three men from the Land Rover into the hut; the Land

Rover's driver was left standing by the vehicle, stamping feet and blowing on his hands after the traditional manner of frozen soldiery. Inside it was hot, and the light had a clear brilliance. The major's companions turned out to be a young down-faced subaltern and a large American top sergeant. The sergeant carried a 98k Mauser rifle casually under his arm. The subaltern clutched a small green metal ammunition box. There were no introductions, and the top sergeant arrogantly started the action.

'Which one, suh?' he asked the major, swivelling his eyes between Warbler and Boysie. Warbler indicated Boysie with a histrionic gesture. An MC introducing the comic turn of the evening.

'Okay, bud, there she is. Catch.' The Mauser did a slow curve from the sergeant's hands, landing broadside against Boysie's chest. He fumbled but managed to retrieve without dropping the weapon. Anger replaced the twitch and tremble.

'You can cut the tom-tit, sergeant. I hold the rank of major and I don't like tricky boys.' Boysie almost regretted the violence latent in his voice as he spoke. Warbler's hand dropped to Boysie's forearm. Firm pressure. The British major looked down his nose. The sergeant looked insolent.

'Ah'm sorry . . . suh.' The poor timing of the 'Suh' was a masterpiece. 'Ah'm sorry . . . suh, but we don't understaynd that kinda talk where Ah come frowm.' Deliberately doing a Southern drawl. 'Suh? What is tom-tit, suh? Sure don't know that, like what it means . . . suh.'

The subaltern raised his precious head. 'I believe it is what is known as rhyming slang, sergeant. It has cockney and Australian origins. Er—tom-tit, it means sh——'

'We know what it means, Rothley.' The major shearing the backchat.

The sergeant's face glowed into a huge smile. 'Ah. Shit.

Geeze. That's good. Remember that, suh. Tom-tit.'

Boysie did the bayonet thrust with his eyes, making them into slim daggers aimed straight at the American's nose bridge. The left side of the mouth twitched unmercifully. Once more fear elbowed into its normal hiding place. The supreme effort. Anger was his only counter.

'Let's sit down, gentlemen.' The major, rock-strong and edgy. 'The—the major here'—indicating Boysie—'he has to be put in the picture before we do this experiment. I gather that it is only an experiment?' Looking long at Warbler.

'A mere test exercise.' A hairbreadth too smoothly from the German.

'Right.' The major with disbelief. 'I'll give you a run-down on the test then. Your job is to destroy the occupants sitting in the rear of a car moving at between twenty and thirty miles an hour through a reasonably well-lit street at night. You will be firing from a window roughly fourteen metres from the ground with a good view of the road on both sides. As you probably noticed on the way in, we have created these conditions here.'

Boysie lifted his head in acknowledgement.

The major did not pause. 'You will be using a Mauser 98K fitted with the Hythe night-sight system. Familiar?'

'I am familiar with all weapons.' Anger at the sergeant's attitude coupled with anxiety fused into a particularly unco-operative mood. Quite unlike Boysie. He began to wonder about himself. 'The 98K's okay,' he said almost inaudibly; then louder, 'a bit old but accurate enough. What am I going to use in it?'

'Lieutenant Rothley will deal with ammunition in a moment. I'm only concerned with the test. We are going to run a normal type of target fast along the road for you to get accustomed to the firing point and range. Then we'll try the real thing—a radio-controlled car, complete with dummy figures, which your friend here has laid on for us. We'll run the car through on a radio beam, at around twenty-five mph once for you to do a test sighting. The second time you can do the real thing. Okay?'

Boysie looked down at his feet, lips tight. Then, 'Okay.'

'Good. Now ammunition. Rothley's in charge of that.'

Young Rothley knew his stuff even though he had the visage of a chinless, noseless wonder.

'Well, sir.' It was the sort of drawl you could hear nightly in places like The Blue Angel. 'For the ordinary target shoot we'll use a normal 8-mm. round, but for the actual car we're giving you an armour-plated 7.92. Centre of the bullet is hard steel with a soft lead exterior. If I may suggest, after you have fired on the approach, try to get a couple in near the base of the rear window. A couple of these.' He had opened the green box, rolling out two cartridges on to the table. 'With luck you might even take the back right off. Certainly cause extensive damage.'

'Yes.' Boysie flat, trying to sound unimpressed, again praying that Griffin would make it on time, trying to blot out the thought of steel penetrating the back of the car with Iris MacIntosh sitting unsuspecting and shocked by the sudden tear of bones and the flash of pain before eternal darkness.

'Sergeant Gazpacho will be with you at the firing point.' Rothley glanced apprehensively towards the American, who was making with the dead eyes.

Boysie brightened. 'Sergeant Gazpacho?' Cheesy grimace. 'Bet all your friends call you Soupy.'

The sergeant wagged his head, the smile of a cadaver with its throat cut.

'Top Sergeant Gazpacho is a first-class shot.' The major twenty degrees below freezing point.

'Sure lookin' forward to seein' what you can do ...

53

suh.' Gazpacho unpleasant.

'Let's go and see then.' Boysie's voice coming out crisp while his guts crunched rapidly into small pieces. Cautiously he slid his hands behind his back so that no one would catch the tremble running from a point behind the neck down the arms, through the hands, and into the fingertips. A proving moment approached; he felt it; could smell it. It was essential that he should *get* the sergeant. A time for one- (even two- or three-) upmanship.

A door at the far end of the hut opened, revealing an emaciated RCS corporal. 'Target and radio control all set, sir.' To the major.

'Come along then, we'll get it over. I shall be with the radio boys and Lieutenant Rothley. We'll be in contact. R/T's checked out, corporal?'

'Sir.' Affirmative.

'Good shooting then. Mr.—er—Major——'

Boysie looked blandly at the major and tried his know-it-all smile, then turned to the American. 'After you, sergeant.'

'Oh no, suh.' Picking up the green ammunition box. 'After you-all.'

The climb up the outside of the tower was not Boysie's most hilarious experience. Three feet off the ground had always been high enough for him. Up a scaffold ladder fourteen metres to a wooden box, in a heavy suede coat, with a Mauser slung round him, the cold sloshing over his hands and the stiff breeze shaking the whole structure was not fun. Worse, the sergeant turned out to be cattishly agile, well ahead of Boysie and through the entrance to the tower a good minute before Boysie's head came level with the oblong opening. The first thing that came into view was Gazpacho's left foot. The sergeant stood three or four paces from the open hatchway and the foot was not encased in a regulation GI boot. Instead, Gazpacho wore thin, mirror-polished shoes. So the sergeant is a dandy, thought Boysie. Even in this swaying, high, cold, anxious situation, clinging to the ladder's final rung, Boysie did a mental slow smile. It was time for the old 'Ouch' trick.

'You want some help through the hole, suh?' Gazpacho not offering to move or stretch out a hand.

Long deep breath through the nose. 'I can get through any hole, Buddy.' Boysie willed himself not to look down into the blackness below and heaved himself up through the entrance. Gazpacho still did not move. Boysie un-slung the Mauser, holding the rifle gently by the stock just above the trigger guard, butt down, and walked forward. The wooden plank floor bent and creaked unsteadily. Coming abreast of the sergeant, Boysie's eyes did a quick flit downwards to align the rifle butt with the polished shoes. His right hand opened and the butt dropped with full force on the centre of Gazpacho's shining footwear. It was all a matter of timing. At the moment of impact, Boysie moved in close and let out a loud yell of pain. Gazpacho jumped back. 'Sorry . . . suh. Ahgghugh!'

Boysie's yell and the bruise of pain on the sergeant's toes were just far enough apart to fuddle Gazpacho for five-tenths of a second before reaction. It was enough.

'Sorry, chum,' said Boysie cheerfully, grasping the rifle by the muzzle.

Visibly, Gazpacho was attempting both to contain anger and control pain. Impossible. Round one, thought Boysie; now let's scare the arse off him with the gun. He looked round. The bend of the floorboards did not help. The tower was small, roughly ten feet square and seven high. Light filtered yellow and foggy through the open oblong, which was the firing point at the far end. Boysie knew he had to relax. Whatever happened tomorrow night he was committed to going through his paces here.

55

Relax. Relax. Gently.

He reached into his left breast pocket (past the shoulder holster) and removed the skin-tight black leather gloves he always used for rifle work. The sergeant watched without comment as Boysie played at being a brain surgeon preparing for a leucotomy. There was a shelf near the window. The sergeant hobbled forward, took down the small Vigilant transmitter/receiver, and, showing a certain amount of care with his left foot, squatted beside Boysie, the green box on the floor and the Vigilant nearby, now with aerial extended.

'Ready for the target?'

'Just give me a minute.' Boysie closed his eyes. It had to be right. Deep breath; relax; loosen all muscles; he had done it a hundred times before. Clay pigeons; thirty-nine out of forty one afternoon in a matter of fifteen minutes with the .303, not twelve bore or scatter shot. He could knock the centre pip out of an ace of spades with any known gun at fifteen yards and rip it apart with most rifles at five hundred. This was only a target. A target and an empty car. Close your eyes. Breathe deeply.

Boysie shifted to the left, towards the direction from which the target would come rolling up the road. He closed his eyes again. 'Let 'em send it down.'

Gazpacho pressed the mike switch. 'Nightingale to Control. Ready for target. Over.'

There was a pause. Boysie's thumb slid off the safety lock.

The major's words came out pat. 'Control to Nightingale. Target coming on a five count down. Five ... four ... three...' Boysie opened his eyes. Butt into the shoulder. Sharp glance at the rear slide, then the cheek nuzzling against the weapon. '... two ... one ... zero.'

It came faster than he expected, but the black bull was plainly visible right in line with the foresight blade and the rear V. Boysie got three shots in before the target passed below, then an easy two as it moved away out of sight.

They waited in silence for the result. It took a full three minutes before the Vigilant crackled. The major's voice portrayed minute respect.

'Control to Nightingale. Point. Please give our congratulations to the major. Group of five centre of bull radius eight inches.'

'Tell them not to bother with the dummy run. I'll do the car in one. We're wasting our time. And yours,' said Boysie. He nearly repeated it, the sentence and delivery sounded so cool.

Gazpacho passed on the message. A calmer, less cocky Gazpacho.

'If that's what he wants.' The major placid over the Vigilant receiver. 'Report when ready. Over.'

'Give me the steel-core bastards then ... sergeant.'

Gazpacho handed over a clip of the 7.92 ammunition. Boysie reloaded the rifle, rested his eyes for a few seconds, then signalled the sergeant with a grunt. The radio procedure ran identically with the target shoot.

This time Boysie saw it coming a long way off. The headlights dipped, a squat black shape. Again he managed five shots. The first, a little early and a shade low, knocked the rear near-side tyre. The car swerved violently across the road, spinning full circle. As it spun Boysie's second bullet shattered the left window. This time the car was pushed right off the road, still moving away, decelerating. Three bullets into the back. Boysie saw the great gashes opening up the window and boot, heard the pathetic roar, whine, stumble, and final silence of the engine. Smoke began to filter from the car.

'Cease fire. Cease fire.' From the major at the other end of the transmitter. Boysie ejected the last empty cartridge case.

'You heard the man,' said Gazpacho.

Boysie pressed down on the magazine in order to push the bolt home. He clicked the trigger, rolled over, and tossed the empty weapon casually towards the American.

'Catch,' said Boysie with a smile. 'I'll leave you to pick up the pieces.'

Gazpacho gave him a killer look. Boysie had thrown with some force. One bruised foot and some sore ribs. Game, set, and match to the lad. Boysie glanced out of the firing-point opening. There was a lot of activity around the car. He humped himself into the suede driving coat. Gazpacho crawled around clearing up the spent cartridge cases. Boysie looked down; the green ammunition box lay open at his feet. It was divided into three portions marked with sticky labels: *8-mm., 7.92-mm. SC.,* and *Dummy*. There were four clips in each of the first two sections and three in the *Dummy* partition. Almost on impulse, Boysie slipped out a clip of dummies and popped them into his pocket. Subconsciously a plan was germinating: another escape route in case Griffin failed to materialise. Gazpacho still had his back to Boysie, limping and picking the empty cases from the creaking wood.

'You look like a flower plucker,' chanted Boysie as he made for the exit.

Gazpacho mumbled something about the sexual habits of Boysie's forebears.

When Boysie reached the bottom of the ladder he realised that his legs were trembling. Queasy, that was the word. All confidence suddenly drained. He could all but see it flowing from him. The test was over. Unavoidable reaction had set in. A couple of yards away to the right, across the road, they had set up some sodium arc lights, there were vans. He recognised a big Stalwart support truck. The brightness of the lamps threw the scene into macabre relief. It had the feel of some shocking disaster. The major, subaltern, Warbler, and one or two others were gathered close around the wreckage. Someone was taking photographs, and there was an odd smell. As he crossed the road Boysie identified the odour. It was coming from himself, a combination of cordite and sweat—even in the cold, an unpleasant, hot, stinking sweat, which had associations with violence, fear, and death. As he got nearer the smell changed. Petrol fumes and smoke. A pair of asbestos-clad soldiers had foamed down the front of the automobile.

'*Ach*, good shooting. They damage, those bullets, eh?' Warbler cheery as an in-grouper at party time.

'Damn good.' The major really impressed, sounding as though he were talking to his jockey. 'Lesson for everyone on my staff.'

Boysie said nothing. The car looked hateful, jagged gashes into which a man could crawl. Inside, through the smoke which still drifted out from under the bonnet, the dummy figures were obscenely ripped apart. A head was entirely missing from one that had been strapped into the rear. The dashboard looked as though King Kong had gone to work on it with a sledgehammer. Embedded in one long crack—originally the main line of instruments—was a wooden arm from the man-sized doll driver.

Boysie turned away, imagination coloured and working on truth. What is truth? Ideals? Imaginary? Fact? Realised fiction? He could not see imitation bodies, only the projected horrible things, the tangled hair, flesh, bone, and blood. As slowly as possible he walked away, trying to keep down the retching fluid as his stomach punched up, pulsing mechanically, lifting and controlled.

'Jesus,' blasphemed Boysie quietly. How the hell——? Why——?

When they got back to the hotel Boysie made his now

customary enquiry at the desk. Nothing. Without asking, Warbler followed him up to the fifth floor.

'I offer you anything?' Boysie hinting that Warbler was *persona non grata*. He glanced at his watch. Still reasonably early. Still time to call Mu-lan Tchen. Warbler spotted Boysie's Freudian slip of sliding his eyes from watch to telephone.

'*Ach*, comrade, I am sorry. We have been naughty. Your telephone will not work. Not tonight anyway. And no alcohol. We wish you to rest and sleep well. Please do as I say; it will be for the best. I would like you to go to the bathroom and get ready for bed. Coffee will be ordered, and I have a little pill here.' He held what looked like a licorice torpedo between thumb and forefinger. 'You will sleep until midday. Stay in bed and rest, order lunch. I will leave books for you to look at. Then I will come personally at about four.'

'Ah, now come on.'

Warbler shook his head. 'As far as the hotel authorities are concerned, you are my patient. Dr. Warbler's patient. I will leave special instructions.'

The manipulation of circumstances had passed out of Boysie's hands. With realisation came resignation. He removed the suede coat and hung it carefully in the wardrobe, hoping Warbler would not start searching the pockets. Without a word he headed for the bathroom, picking up the mauve silk pyjamas, slinkily spread across the bed, on the way. The feel of the silk caused a reactive twitch in his loins. ('North China. You know Chinese silk? That is where I come from. Shantung.')

Coffee was waiting when Boysie returned. He tried to pretend Warbler was not even there. It was all a gigantic embarrassment. A compromising bad dream. Warbler poured the coffee, chattering all the time.

'Two books I am leaving. You might as well enjoy yourself tomorrow night. It is a great thing to see the

Berlin Ensemble. Especially in *Dreigroschenoper*.'

'Can't wait.' Boysie dead-pan.

'Now, a nice cup of coffee and this tiny pill.'

Boysie sighed and reached out for the proffered cup and sedative. Warbler talked on quietly. The coffee was cool and the capsule went down easily. Warber continued to talk. Boysie took two more sips of coffee before the cup and saucer began to slip. Warbler stretched forward and removed the coffee. Boysie's hands sank peacefully on to the bedclothes, his head lolled, and the breathing took on a peaceful, heavy rhythm. Warbler put down the cup, switched off the lights, and left quietly.

It was like being wrapped snugly in a warm, black-velvet bag. No dreams, colours, or sensations. Death, or the time before conception. Utter unknowing until first one layer of velvet was removed; then, slowly, another; and another. Boysie felt his body drifting to life. Conscious of toes, feet, shins, thighs, belly, and chest. Next the fingers, hands, wrists, arms, shoulders, neck, and head. His eyes snapped open. It was like the snapping of a hypnotist's thumb and forefinger. Fully alert, no hangover; all senses operating and a feeling of well-being. He moved voluptuously under the soft feather comforter.

'This is the life.' He sang softly, reaching out for a cigarette. The two books lay next to his packet of B&H Filters. Memory. Nausea. Tonight. Iris. Tomorrow?

Boysie's hand wavered over the cigarettes, paused, and moved on to the telephone. Nothing but a hollow buzz. Banging at the receiver rests made no difference. In the end he gave up, pressed the bell for Room Service, opened the bedside drawer and took out his Hugo's *How To Get All You Want When Travelling in Germany*. riffled the pages to the section on 'Ordering a Dinner' ('Give me the bill of fare' was the first phrase). He looked at his watch. Warbler's prediction had been pretty accurate. It was just after midday. Happily, when the waiter arrived, he spoke English and behaved with the old-world charm of the Admirable Crichton. Having been spared groping through *Geben Sie mir die Speisekarte,* Boysie decided to go through the condemned-man routine and stuff himself. The Bristol Kempinski had already proved itself a peer for gourmets. Pôtage Crême de crevettes (Boysie had a *grand passion* for shrimps); poulet sauté à la bordelais with pommes lyonnaise (Boysie was a martyr to onions but who cared) and petites pois. To round it off, some of their excellent Pflaumenkuchen, which, after all, was only a fancy German name for greengage tart. Oh, and half a bottle of Dom Perignon '55. Yes, sir, and of course the waiter would see if there was any mail or messages to be sent directly to his room.

Boysie lay back and rubbed his hands. No messages came, and when the waiter (this time accompanied by a white-coated assistant) arrived with the trolleys, there was no Dom Perignon. The waiter was sorry but Herr Oldcorn's doctor had stipulated anything but alcohol. Would a nice Perrier water be acceptable? Of course, Boysie told him with a smile, his mind performing a complete *karate uechi* thrust at Warbler.

Satiated in the aftermath of food, Boysie lay back on the pillows, lit a cigarette, and planned for the night. Within half an hour he knew exactly what he would do, and damn the consequences. He swung out of bed, opened the wardrobe, and transferred the clip of dummy ammunition from the car coat to the breast pocket of the Hawkes two-piece worsted. Back in bed, he opened the first of the two books, Willett's *The Theatre of Bertolt Brecht.*

He was still sitting propped up and reading when

Warbler arrived. The time was four-thirty, and Warbler carried a larger briefcase than before.

'All set. The big moment, eh?' Warbler said cheerfully.

Boysie retasted the greengages in the back of his throat. It was going to happen. He nodded, mouth twitching.

'Good. Go get dressed.'

'Passport and papers?' asked Warbler when Boysie returned to the bedroom. Boysie touched his pocket, nodding.

'There is nothing I can say then but good luck. Come back quick.'

'Thanks,' said Boysie. Now he could taste the chicken as well as the greengage.

'I'll be waiting at Checkpoint Charlie between ten-thirty and eleven. I hope you will be there.'

'I'll be there.' Forced confidence. They shook hands. Boysie swallowing hard every second; he shouldn't have had the Pflaumenkuchen on top of all that chicken. The shrimps had joined in.

In the car park the Jensen started in one. To the left Boysie saw Warbler climbing into the Volkswagen. He put the Jensen into drive, released the brake, and moved slowly out into Dahlmannstrasse, then into Kurfürstendamm, heading towards the Friedrichstrasse and Checkpoint Charlie, a cigarette between his lips and terror coursing every fibre. In a strange way the terror drove him on like a kind of fantastic death wish.

At the same moment Boysie was leaving the Bristol Kempinski, British European Airways Flight 569 from Zurich turned at a height of 15,000 feet, in the Epsom holding stack ready to make her approach to Heathrow. In the tourist compartment of the Trident, Charlie Griffin sat cheerfully reading Truman Capote's *In Cold*

Blood. He had been taking a fortnight's holiday near Lake Maggiore. Griffin had fallen for Maggiore the previous year when he had visited it at Boysie's request, and to some confusion. Idly Griffin glanced up from the page and wondered if there would be much mail waiting at home. He would eat out tonight; the house had been empty and Rubin was not due back until the morning. Might even put up at some hotel, thought Griffin, returning to the tragic affair at Holcomb, Kansas.

III. SHARK

When the shark has had its dinner
There is blood upon its fins.
Brecht, 'Moritat,'
From *The Threepenny Opera*

TAUT at the wheel of the Jensen, Boysie tried singing to himself. It was a nervous throaty hum, eventually emerging as 'I Wonder Who's Kissing Her Now'; as the car drew nearer to the Wall and Checkpoint Charlie, the mind backed away from the facts, hiding behind an old lyric as an alcoholic hides behind a bottle. The street lights were yellow, like those at the firing range on the previous evening. Yellow. Yellow. Boysie forced his thoughts away from the shattered car, an act more physical than mental, vomit rising from the undigested contents of his stomach. Chicken. (Yellow.) Greengages, Shrimps. Yellow Rosy Puberty. Mu-lan. Back to the womb. Elizabeth was far away, Mu-lan was here. Boysie could turn away from the Wall and be with her in a matter of minutes. With her. Having her. Escape to the comforting prenatal state by vivitombment in soft, yellow flesh.

The Jensen rolled gently into the Friedrichstrasse. Ahead were the hutments of Checkpoint Charlie; the lights more brilliant. Boysie changed the lyrics. 'I wonder who's Kiesinger now?' He laughed aloud, hysteria hovering somewhere in the background. A mental check: passport, ticket to the Berliner Ensemble, no weapon (safer, he had decided), clip of dummy ammunition in his right jacket pocket, leather shooting gloves in left breast pocket, watch synchronised before leaving the hotel. The time was exactly 5.55. An NCO in German field-grey greatcoat waved him through the western checkpoint, hardly looking at the car. Boysie need not even have reduced speed. As he drove through, he had the impression that several uniformed men stood inside the main hut looking towards the Eastern Sector. One of them, he was certain, was Gazpacho. Someone was certainly using big night glasses.

The business of getting into East Berlin took only twenty minutes and, to Boysie's surprise, was relatively easy. When the barrier raised, Boysie drove through, still on the Friedrichstrasse but now on the other side. It was psychological, he told himself, this feeling of bleakness.

There were quite a lot of people about. They looked happy enough. There were two young girls giggling. What the hell? Use your loaf, Boysie-boy, what did you expect? Ape men? Wagonloads of prisoners? Bloody great Russians with snow on their boots muttering *Da* and shooting up the joint? Berlin Capone-style? Still there *was* that feeling, the intangible something. A stark quality? A difference? A mental sour odour.

The Berliner Ensemble Theatre was just where Warbler said it would be, exactly where the map showed it—the dark classic façade with the cheap white banner hanging over the entrance, announcing that *Dreigroschenoper* was playing tonight. Boysie parked the Jensen, positioned for an easy get-away, slid from the driving seat, and locked up. The Bertolt-Brecht-Platz was definitely bleak—there was no psychological blunder over that. Mud; the black untidy shape of the theatre; a couple of unhealthy trees; a red-brick cinema wall bearing an excruciatingly bad poster for (of all films) a Western—the guy in the Stetson and Levis carrying a

Peacemaker had a vague Germanic look about him. The area was reasonably lit; a clank of trams filtering from the bridge, an occasional glint from the river across the road. Boysie slowly walked up the theatre steps, turned, and looked at his watch. Nearly 6.30. Half an hour. Time to walk through the moves as Warbler had suggested. Not that it particularly mattered now. His mind was made up. They could do what they liked about it when he got back, whether they believed him or the other thing. It just did not matter.

Even under the street-lighting conditions Boysie recognised the view, etched into his brain from Warbler's photographs: the bridge and, behind, the angular rise of the apartment building. He clicked down on the stop-watch stud of his Navitimer and began to walk quickly towards the bridge. It was easy enough locating the door in the apartment building. At a fair, unrushing speed it took three minutes and eight seconds from the theatre to the green peeling paintwork entrance. Boysie double-checked that it was the correct door. Nobody about. The timing would be all right. Hands driven hard into the suede coat pockets. Boysie walked back towards the theatre and *The Threepenny Opera*.

Dangerously, Boysie thought, Warbler had acquired one of the most conspicuous seats in the house for him—a well-placed box to the right of the stage. For some reason, which he could not quite place, the name John Wilkes Booth kept running through his head. He did not know anyone called Booth. There was Booth's Gin, of course. Something he had read somewhere? Perhaps the guy was an actor. Boysie had been to see the Royal Shakespeare Company at the Aldwych a couple of times lately. Could be one of that lot. The name worried him. Yet, as the lights dimmed and the curtain raised on the garish, strange Soho street with the 'beggars begging, thieves thieving, whores whoring,' and the ballad singer nasalising the 'Moritat,' Boysie, with only a couple of words in his vocabulary, became engrossed in Brecht's politically rejigged version of the musical.

When the first half was over, the Navitimer showed exactly 8.30. Boysie just sat there befuddled, coming out of the dream. He had broken through a language barrier and understood. Him, the twit Oakes, Mostyn's little puppet, had understood through the force of actors acting and singing their guts out in an alien tongue. He looked down stupidly at the watch, the second hand moving in its relentless circle. Time present. Time passing. Every fractional second was vital. Who the bleeding hell was Booth? He was losing valuable time. At least the deal had to have the feel of reality. Move now. Reluctantly, as ever, Boysie stood up. Stepping through the crowded corridor outside the box, he headed down the side staircase, through the foyer, and out into the open, beaming-in on his death date with Iris Mac-Intosh.

There is a rule in Eastern-bloc countries, as in many European cities, that overcoats must not be taken into the auditorium. Grim, tubby ladies enforce the regulations, and attendants even shout at you if you try to get a Dannimac into the dress circle. Nobody seemed to have taken this into consideration, and, if the timing was to be right, Boysie had no chance of picking up his coat in exchange for the brass disc used as a cloakroom ticket. The result, outside in the chill, was a feeling of complete conspicuousness and a specific touch of the brass monkeys. Frost was creeping into the night air, and Boysie moved faster than intended. He crossed the bridge and reached the apartment building like an Olympic walking champ. A good thing, he told himself, lost some time in the theatre; anyway, get the farce over, hustle back for the second act. He was looking forward to the brothel scene.

There was nobody inside the apartment entrance. A sour smell of stale vegetables, grey, rough-painted walls, broad, curving stone steps. Boysie took them two at a time. First landing. Second landing. The numbered doors. His shoes made too much noise, an echoing clunk in the emptiness. A door faced him. Number 10. Boysie moved to the right. The next door was Number 9. Wrong way. Music coming from behind the door of Number 9: martial, a military band creeping noisily through a poor amplifier. Back, past 10 ... 11. Flat Number 12. Boysie stopped, breathing heavily, anxiety catching up with him again. This time it was horrible black beetles frugging in his lower bowel. Coleoptera, that was the posh name for beetles, Boysie had read it in a book, *Children's Encyclopaedia* or something. Copulating Coleoptera. In clogs. His hands shook as he pulled on the tight black leather gloves. At least the brain still functioned and the sequence was running true.

The door opened smoothly and closed quietly. The key turned silently in the newly oiled lock. The Berlin network knew its stuff. Boysie stood still for a moment, eyes growing accustomed to the darkness, getting his bearings, mental thought-pictures shifting from Warbler's photographs to the plan of the flat. The bedroom door was straight ahead. There was more light there, coming in from the street with the faint rumble of occasional traffic. The bottom half of the window was open and the Mauser lay on the floor. Next to it a spare set of ammunition. Hell, he had forgotten about the spare clip. That would be difficult to explain. Think of something later. No time now, the watch showed 8.35. At Checkpoint Charlie they would just be doing the swap. He had about three minutes. The window was an ordinary eighteen-pane, cheap wood-and-glass effort, not sturdy. Poor workmanship, Boysie reflected somewhere at the back of his thoughts.

He worked quietly. Safety catch off, bolt pumped back to eject the steel-core bullets.

Five clicks, five live rounds spinning away and thudding dully on to the carpet: one hit the end of the bed with a clack-thwump. Boysie picked up the spare clip of live cartridges and dropped them into his inside pocket. then to the right-hand jacket pocket for the dummies. He had to tilt the rifle towards the light source from the window to get the clip in place. Down with the thumb. Bolt home. One dummy round up the spout and four in the magazine ... 8.36

On his knees, Boysie took up the aiming position, looking over the sight up the Friedrichstrasse. He had to push the bottom part of the window sash up another couple of inches. It rattled, badly worn. A game. If Mostyn could play games with life and death, so could Boysie. Christ Mostyn would never have him again, the bastard. If this job proved anything, it cleared up the fact of Boysie's independence ... 8.37.

Left eye closed, the bright sliver of foresight gleaming and accurate between the backsight V. Do everything. Adjust range. Boysie gingered the range screw with leather-coated thumb and forefinger. Butt into the shoulder once more. Cheek cold against the woodwork. Sweep the whole target area. Comfortable. Coming up to 8.38. Time for baby. It was almost real, looking down the sights for the car. Two heavy lorries went by, then a mixture of vehicles. Boysie identified a cream Skoda and a couple of rattling Zaporojets. Then something was coming fast with lights full on. Outriders as well. Motorcycles. They had not estimated that—three in a Victor formation ahead and some behind. Lights not dipped. The glare murderous. Impossible to sight. A very doubtful business if the ammunition had been the real thing. With the outriders, he would not have stood a chance. Coming in very close now. Sighting towards the rear.

Bloody dodgey. First pressure on the trigger, then a shriek of apprehension before the cold muzzle of the automatic pistol touched the back of his neck and all the lights in the flat flared on.

The voice in his ear was rough, low, and most unfriendly, apart from being deplorably accented.

'Just put it down and stand up quietly, Herr Oakes.'

Supreme effort controlled Boysie's bowels, yet the training of the Department of Special Security set off mechanical brain signals. From the front Boysie sadly saw the motorcade sweep away. He partly turned his head to the left. The hand which held the Stechkin machine pistol behind his ear was encased in a military glove, a bit of uniform sleeve showed as well, and Boysie got the impression that the Stechkin was fitted with a shoulder stock. Nasty. It made the odds most uneven. There was no question of bravery. Boysie could feel his shoulders go rigid with shock, and the left corner of the mouth twitching with all muscular control gone. The upper part of his thighs churned into a kind of meat jelly. Filletted Gelée de viande, as the French would have it. But the mechanism of self-preservation remained. Boysie bowed his head. How would those actors at the Berliner Ensemble convey defeat? He tried to think himself into it, slowly lowering the rifle from the shoulder towards the floor, crossing and changing the hands so that the butt came round to the left. Let the shoulders droop. Now the right knee up, foot flat, balanced on heel and ball, still lowering the rifle and beginning to push up, as if to stand and leave the Mauser on the ground. Very slowly. Then the flash of action. In one movement, Boysie swung to the right, away from the Stechkin's muzzle, at the same time bringing the butt end of the Mauser up and back hard, very hard in the general direction of the heist man's crotch. An audible phlump.

Boysie heard the man scream and saw the automatic pistol, complete with shoulder stock, fall forward as the assailant jack-knifed in extreme agony, clutching at his past, present, and future. The rest was easy, taking, in terms of time, the hairbreadth of a second. Boysie pivoted on his left foot and went into the third and fourth movements of a judo block and throw. The hefty character who had held the Stechkin was in uniform and at a fatal disadvantage. As Boysie began the throw, it flashed through his mind that the uniform was Russian, not East German. The attacker somersaulted over Boysie's hip, his buttocks and legs hitting the window as Boysie pressed inwards against the man's thigh, heaving downwards, hands locked on his victim's arms. There was a ripping smash of glass and woodwork as the man's heavy back struck the window.

Boysie had been right—it was either bad workmanship or the landlords just did not bother about maintenance. The whole window went out in a concave of splintering wood and glass. Boysie gave an extra pull, then let go. The Russian's original scream of pain turned into a high-frequency note of terror, fading as he fell. There was a quick glimpse of a frightened, red, bulging face slashed by broken glass as the body tumbled out to streak untidily down to the pavement.

At the same moment a burst of automatic fire roared from the direction of the bedroom door, flinging great chips of stone from the wall to the left of the incapacitated window. The burst went upwards, blasting at the angle where ceiling met wall.

A sharp peal of command. The language Russian. The meaning plain. 'Stop!' Explosively authoritative.

Boysie turned, ready to dive for the rifles. Useless. The bedroom was painted a dirty white, the end of the double bed a faded pink board, scratched and old. Somewhere there was relief, a painting over to the right by another piece of furniture, he thought. Three men stood inside the door. Two wore the sheepskin coats and red-starred fur hats of the Soviet Militia, the third was in a civilian greatcoat and black 1930s broad hat. All three held Stechkins with shoulder stocks, the pair of Militia men handling them in the offensive manner, turned sideways with the butts pushed into the elbow, so that on automatic fire the high cylic rate pulled the weapon round to the right in a raking movement. The civilian was reloading his pistol. There were other people behind the door to the living room from where the command had come. Boysie did not have to pretend any more. His knees collapsed like broken sticks, arms shooting upwards as if operated on pulleys.

The civilian finished reloading, banging the magazine into place. He held his pistol level (hence the row of chipped masonry up the wall). Boysie became conscious of pain in his right cheek. Blood. A piece of flying stone? You did not have to draw any conclusions. Even the Militia men were KGB. The three moved in close. The uniforms on one side, civilian on the other. Boysie thought his lungs were going to burst. Breathing all wrong. Three muzzle eyes directed at his head, three index fingers curved behind the trigger guard. He looked away through the door. A pair of polished shoes, well-pressed trousers, neat overcoat. His eyes travelled upwards. Jesus, this was a big bloke! Wrestler perhaps? The Red Giant from the Salt Mines. 'My Lords, ladies, and genellmen. In the left corner, 'Orrible Oakes at fourteen stone, and in the right corner, at gawd knows what weight, the Red Giant.'

Boysie's eyes reached the face. He really was going to be sick this time. It wasn't much. One retch on to the dirty carpet. At Special Security HQ the Chief had a blue dossier on the man locking eyes with him; Mostyn's file was black leather and there was one in the Classified cabinets at Operations Control. Every department must have one. On the first page of those files was a series of photographs. He had seen the physiognomy many times. Read the description and crossed swords, at a distance—a safe distance—with this man.

'You know who I am?' said Khavichev in good, modulated English. He was smiling.

Boysie had a go at saying yes. It would not come out, so he tried again. 'Yes.' A whisper. God, the back of his mouth tasted vile.

'I suppose I should say something melodramatic, like "so we meet at last"?' It amused Khavichev.

'So we meet at last,' said Boysie like a parrot. Then, 'Look I wasn't going to—I mean they wanted me to—but —well, just look at the rifle—dummy ammunition. I took out the real stuff. Honestly, Mr. Khavichev, I wasn't going to——'

A flash bulb exploded behind Khavichev's shoulder. There was a photographer in the room, dressed like a movie journalist in a belted raincoat. Khavichev looked at Boysie with distaste.

'We will talk later. A long talk. There is much to discuss.' He turned and said something to the photographer. Two more flash bulbs. It was going to look great in *Pravda*. Front-page lead with a banner headline and Boysie grovelling with his hands up, shock tearing out of every wrinkle.

'We will talk later,' Khavichev repeated, making a signal to someone else in the living room. A trim girl came in carrying a small black bag.

'Roll up your right sleeve,' she commanded. Her English had an American touch, the figure and face good-looking in a severe sort of way. Institutional. Boysie went on looking—the blue uniform was well fitted.

'Your right sleeve. Quickly.' The girl was on her knees with the bag open. It was a medical kit. Swabs. Hypodermic. Vials. Boysie did as he was told, pulling his jacket up to the elbow and unfastening the jade cuff-links. Elizabeth had bought him the jade cuff-links, oblong and smooth. Paris? Did she buy them in Paris? He could not remember. But she bought them, no doubt.

'Quickly,' repeated the girl. To help, the civilian pushed his pistol nearer. Boysie rolled back his shirt. The swab cold on his inner arm below the elbow. The tiny jab. Blackness swallowing him.

The two Militia men moved their safety catches to 'safe,' locked elbows under Boysie's armpits, and dragged the unconscious, unknowing, framed, unwanted nit past Khavichev out into the living room, where a stretcher waited.

The room was dark, and Boysie was lying on his side, the right arm cradling his face. No nausea or giddiness, consciousness returning quickly, like an express train coming from the darkness of a tunnel into a misty early evening. His brain was fully active with total recall (guts-drop at the memory of humiliation, photos, the playful attitude of the KGB men. He did not open his eyes completely, just narrow slits, trying to acclimatise. There was light coming from another room. People talking. Someone near him as well. Boysie tried to swivel his eyes. There was someone sitting there. The urge of curiosity was too much. Boysie shifted on to his back and turned his head. It was a middle-aged, plump woman in a white overall, sitting with hands crossed on her lap. Through the gloom their eyes met. Without a word the woman got up, went over to the door, and spoke a few words, low, in Russian. It was Khavichev's voice that came back, harsh, angry. She stood aside as the big man came quickly into the room, a great paw reaching for the light switch. The light made Boysie blink. Bright white walls, high-powered light reflecting like a white sun at high noon.

Mexico. Spain. A few seconds later it cleared, and his eyes began to adjust. Khavichev was standing over him, storm warnings carved into his rough wooden face.

'So. You are awake.'

'Yes. Look, I wasn't——'

'You feel all right?'

'I think so. Yes.' Boysie wanted to off-load a lot of things.

'Then we can have our talk.'

'I'd like to talk.'

Khavichev bent low over the couch on which Boysie was lying. There was a sweet smell to the Russian's breath. Sweet-sickly.

'You will talk, *tovarich*. A lot of questions.' His face relaxed almost into a smile. '*Ptcha*. I am getting melo-dramatic again. I really must give up watching your Western television spies.' He stopped short and sprang the big intimidating shout coupled with the 'Kitchener-Wants-*You*' point. 'Why were you set up for us? Why dummy ammunition?'

'I used dummies. I don't do it in cold blood. I can't——'

'So you use a remote method instead. Or your bosses do. You know, of course, that Spensky, my Militia man whom you so cleverly hoisted out of the window, is dead. So that's one more notch to you.' Khavichev's lips were pursed hard. 'You may not know you were being given to us on a plate. Sold out. You may not even know that Iris MacIntosh is dead anyway.'

'But I didn't——'

'On the other hand, you may know.'

'How? Iris? For Christ's sake——' Boysie swung his legs off the couch to face Khavichev. The room floated slightly.

'How? She had a drink sometime before they handed her over. On the way here she became drowsy in the car.

76

She was unconscious when she arrived. She died within an hour.' Khavichev slid a piece of cheap blue paper from his inside pocket. 'They have just sent over the post-mortem report. The lovely Iris was given a large brandy before coming over the Wall. She does not look so lovely now. There are pictures outside. The brandy was a large-large, missile-sized. A chloral hydrate cocktail. Three hundred grammes of chloral hydrate and about three fluid ounces of cognac.'

Boysie got the implications with a flood of emotional, sensitory, and motor excitement. Autonomic discharge. The end. Impending doom. Sold out. Death hovered, a tiny lethal helicopter in his brain. If Khavichev was telling the truth, why had the Chief and Mostyn sent him over to shoot up the car? To destroy Iris? In case the chloral hydrate did not work? Or...? Was it a trick on Khavichev's part? Bewildered. Khavichev sensed his disbelief.

'Some things can be faked, Boysie Oakes.' Khavichev gave him a hang-dog look. 'But I can provide you with photographs and samples if you like.' Those kinds of photos and specimens floated over Boysie's consciousness. Vividly. Churning. There was a short silence. Khavichev's eyes did not leave Boysie's face. Boysie had stretched back on the couch again, feeling as though he were disintegrating. Mind crowded with mixed phrases like, 'God, I'm dying.... Those buggers in Whitehall fixed me.... If it's true, they never intended me to do the kill at all.' Childhood forced its way into his memory, an automatic escape from reality. Robert Louis Stevenson. Lying in bed. Measles or chicken pox. Reading Stevenson. What? *Treasure Island*. The words as fresh as yesterday. Total recall. (*'Belay that talk, John Silver,' he said. 'This crew has tipped you the Black Spot in full council, as is dooty bound; just you turn it over, as is dooty bound, and see what's wrote here. Then you can*

77

talk.') Bleeding pirates, Mostyn and the Chief. Silver Mostyn and Cap'n Flint Chief. All right, he *would* spill it. Talk. Stool. Spew it out. Knickers to Mostyn. Suspender belts to the Chief. Doom still weighed heavily as he opened his mouth to speak.

Khavichev cut in. 'There is much to talk about.' Frosty. 'We have our interrogation pattern like your own people. In the case of you, Boysie Oakes, it is probably going to take time, and there will be much propaganda.' Then, more softly, 'Why were you there with dummy ammunition? Why did your friends make sure that we knew about it? You've been a naughty boy? Stepped out of alignment? Have you become a risk? Has Jimmy Mostyn found out about you?'

The questions hit Boysie like great blows above the heart. High-calibre pistol shots at least.

'Dummy ammunition,' he repeated, an automaton. Then, gathering strength, 'Yes, they wanted me to come over and get Iris. She still holds classified information. High resistance to wash-outs. Our brainwash boys—the Sheep Dip—couldn't erase anything.' He gulped, soreness in the back of the throat. 'All right, Khavichev, I work for the Department of Special Security. For some time I was their private liquidator, but I'm not made that way. You needn't believe it, but I can't do the thing in cold blood. I'm not the boy wonder, the cool killer. *I use people.*'

'We know all about Charlie Griffin.' Khavichev smiled, oozing self-satisfaction. The dead complacency on the face of a putrefying suicide corpse. 'You've still done quite a number of things which have troubled us. A regular crown of thorns in our flesh. And you *have* killed for the British. Only a few hours ago there was my man Spensky.'

'Self-defence. Look, I've never had the bleeding guts to do a cold one. And that's the truth, Mr. Khavichev. The colonial plucking truth. I'm a country boy at heart. Some twit decided I was a dead ringer for the secret-agent act and I fell for it. What the hell, the money was good.'

Khavichev ignored Boysie's flare of venom. 'There was a very specialised operative called Gorilka,' he continued. 'My prize man, a Doctor of Law, Philosophy, Medicine, and Languages. You had a hand in him as well. But I believe you. I find your story credible. You are basically a coward.' The final word stressed with vicious scorn. 'Also you are despicable. You hold the rank of major in the British Department of Special Security. You have made a lot of mistakes, taken money under false pretences, and, however you may have double-crossed your own Department, have been instrumental in causing many problems to me and my associates. Just take the rout of my Assault One group last year in Switzerland. Another good man went then. Several people went.'

'That was Mostyn, not me. A balls-up from start to finish.'

'If there is one thing at which you are expert, it is balls-ups, Boysie Oakes. As I have already pointed out, despicable.' Pause to the count of three. 'Still, most security men are despicable one way or another. It is part of our nauseating job.'

('Isn't it time you grew up? You're a rabbit, love...' Elizabeth's words floating into his ears through time and space.)

'What I really want to know,' said Khavichev, 'is what about the dummies? The dummy ammunition? You came over here yourself, no private substitute. No Mr. Charlie Griffin.'

'I tried to tell you, you mammoth moron——'

Khavichev did not even bother to raise his voice, but the timbre had the entire menace of The Death of a Thousand Cuts. 'No one——' Iron. Lips closing like mantraps at each word. 'No one, not even the President, speaks to me like that.' A pause, more dangerous than uncomfortable. 'You will see.'

Boysie's larynx had gone unserviceable.

Again the question. 'Why the dummies?'

Six seconds, feeling like six hours. Then Boysie let out a long, hissing sigh: a tired, clapped-out steam loco-mative reaching the final engine shed. What with Eliza-beth, the strain of the past few days, the double-cross, all his senses told him he was finished. Capitulation. Stuff the Official Secrets Act. Stick it up Mostyn's bum. He was done for anyway. The last reel in the serial.

'All right, I'll tell you.' He rested his head back on the pillow, closing his eyes against the glare. The first fingertips of a headache were beginning to feel their way upwards towards the cerebellum. 'I couldn't contact my usual man,' he said. Christ, his voice sounded tired. 'I couldn't refuse. Big money. Booming great bonus.'

'Your usual man? Charlie Griffin?'

Nod. 'So I gave in.'

'It's taken you long enough to build up your nerve.'

'You're joking. I still couldn't go through with it.'

'No.' Confirmation. 'But what about all that fair-ground stuff at the Ruhleben range last night?'

'You knew about that?'

'There's not much we don't know. We are profes-sionals. I'll show you your file sometime. That was good shooting last night and on your monthly check-up in Hampshire last week.' Khavichev allowed himself an un-familiar smile. 'You are a good shot. Pity you haven't the guts to use your talent.'

'Why don't you shut your——' Boysie had the sense to bite off the retort.

'Go on talking.' Kharvichev's smile lap-dissolved into hard leather. 'Why the farce at Ruhleben?'

'They wanted to check me out. Get me acclimatised to

80

conditions.'

'No.' Patiently. Categorical denial. 'They wanted to—how do the Americans say it?—they wanted to con you. Make you think you were really doing the kill.'

'Don't be stupid.'

Khavichev's face changed from Jekyll to Hyde.

'Look.' Boysie pleading. 'Okay, it was me. I chickened. I brought the dummy ammunition over the Wall with me. For Christ's sake, you must have found the real stuff—one clip in my pocket and one lot scattered all over the floor after I'd ejected and reloaded with dummies. I was playing it by ear. Going to concoct some story when I got home.'

Khavichev threw back his head and wheezed. It was a second or so before Boysie realised that the wheeze was a laugh.

'You poor foolish idiot. I've seen men set up before, but never like this.' He turned his head towards the door and shouted in Russian, then looked at Boysie again and chuckled. The noise of a hyena in pain.

A young Russian orderly came in, saluted Khavichev, and handed over two small white boxes, a slim red one, and a manila envelope neatly labelled in Russian script. Khavichev rested the boxes on his knee. 'You enjoyed the play? What you saw of it? The Brecht?'

'Great. Like to see the second half.' Boysie calmer.

'Your agent Warbler got you a good seat. A box.'

'You saw me?'

'One of my men.'

Silence. Boysie thinking about *The Threepenny Opera* ... Booth? Why had he kept thinking about Booth? Automatically he turned to Khavichev. 'You seem to know most things. Do you know an English actor called Booth?'

'English?' He raised his pupils in thought. 'There's a very popular young man called Anthony Booth.' Musing more than telling. 'Why? Did one of the Ensemble remind you of him?'

Boysie's face puckered into worry lines. 'No. It was before that. Sitting there in that bloody plush box. I kept thinking of the name Booth.'

A laugh hawked from Khavichev's throat. 'I learn more about you every time you open your mouth.' The big, hard man spoke with a hint of softness. 'I am lucky.' He nodded the whole of his body. Rocking in the chair. 'Not always easy to keep at the top either. The regime, quite rightly, is merciless. So am I.' He stopped talking and stared into space, away on some personal worry.

For the first time Boysie really looked at the man. Tall, shoulders like a nineteenth-century pillory, hands that could fill an omelette pan. Boysie concentrated on the face. Lines of character deeply engraved into the barklike texture. Authority and a dependability. Ruthless, he had said. Obvious. Yet there was the attribute of justice. The feared, merciless Boris Piotr Khavichev took on an avuncular appearance, from the grey hair and strong features right down to his boots, good leather and polished glass sharp.

'Your mind works in an obvious pattern.' Khavichev in a consulting-room manner. 'You were sitting in a box near the stage of a theatre. You were about to shoot an ex-girl friend—I don't have to explain the love-hate psychology, do I?'

No reply.

'You were sitting in a box about to perform an assassination. You thought of Booth. Now who was Booth?'

'I don't know, that's what's worrying me. I thought I needed a drink at first. We have a gin in England called Booth's.'

Khavichev recited, parrot-fashion, 'On April 14th, 1865, the President of the United States, Abraham

Lincoln, visited Ford's Theatre in Washington, DC, to see a performance of a mediocre piece entitled *Our American Cousin*. He sat in a box overlooking the stage——'

'Oh, Jesus, of course! How stupid can I get. Honestly, Mr. Khavichev——'

'*General* Khavichev——'

'Sorry, General Khavichev. Know how you feel, they just made me a major——'

—a man called John Wilks Booth entered the President's box——'

'Yeah, and shot him behind the left ear——'

'—with a——'

'Derringer.'

'You remember now,' snapped Khavichev with the spleen of an overwrought schoolmaster.

'Silly of me. Of course. Idiot.'

Khavichev opened one of the white boxes and set it aside. Leaning forward, concentrating on Boysie. 'We understand that when you arrived at the apartment overlooking the Friedrichstrasse the rifle was lying by the window, the firing point. Is that correct?'

Boysie reflected on Khavichev's English. It was good. The attitude was that of a policeman establishing facts. A normal interrogation. He could have been sitting in West End Central with a pipe-smoking super. Quiet, no brow-beating.

'That is correct?' asked Khavichev, calm as a BBC news reader.

'Yes. The Mauser 98K.'

'The rifle was loaded. That was prearranged?'

'Yes.'

'And you ejected the cartridges, substituting dummy ammunition?'

Boysie confirmed with a long nod.

'What kind of cartridges did you understand were in

the Mauser's magazine when you entered the room?'

'Specials—7.92 armour-piercing, with a soft lead outer casing.'

'Like those you used on the car at Ruhleben?'

'Uh-huh.'

'And where did you obtain the substitute dummies?'

'Pinched them at Ruhleben.' Conspiratorial grin. 'From a crafty American sergeant called Gazpacho.'

'So you ejected the live rounds of ammunition from the rifle and left them lying around where they fell. Where they were thrown by the ejector mechanism?'

'Yes. One hit the foot of the bed. I heard the thump. Remember being annoyed at making extra noise.'

Khavichev moved his head in a sign of comprehension. 'Then you inserted the dummies. You had no other ammunition?'

'No. I brought the dummies in from the West.' Pause. Boysie lightly bit his lip. Brow creased. 'No, there were more. They left another clip of live stuff by the rifle. I put that in my inside pocket. They said I should have some extra in case I got into trouble.'

'Mumm.' An indefinable noise from Khavichev. Now a slight change of tone. 'Boysie, *tovarich*, I must tell you that our conversation now, and before this, is recorded and can be used in evidence. I want to try and prove something to you. With your Western indoctrination you will probably think it is simply a dirty Communist trick.' He tightened his lips. 'A trap to incriminate you. We have evidence enough already.' Khavichev lifted a hand and told off the points on his fingers. 'You have admitted working for the British Department of Special Security. Whoever did the jobs, *you* were paid for being a hired assassin. You have also worked in close contact with Colonel Mostyn, Special Security's Second-in-Command. So you have much information at your disposal. What I do not understand is why you had to go through all the business of even leaving the Berliner Ensemble and sitting at the window—pretending to fire at the motorcade—when you did not even intend to exterminate Iris.'

'I had to go through the routine to cover myself. To have a story. God knows, I was probably being watched.'

Khavichev weighed the answer, making up his mind. Stretching out his hand, he lightly touched the open white box, then dropped his index finger on to the second box. 'As I have told you we have evidence— evidence through which I can prove to you that they were taking you for a ride. Disposing of you. Your own people were liquidating you.' Khavichev opened the manila envelope, withdrew a stock of photographs, and spread the first three in front of Boysie. 'You will agree that this was the kind of rifle provided for you?'

The pictures unequivocally showed a Mauser 98K.

'It is in fact the rifle we took from you.' He spread another batch of pictures on the table. Assorted close-ups of various sections of the weapon dusted with fingerprint powder. Smudges and prints showed clearly. One of the shots showed the butt with strands of fibre adhering to the wood and metal. Another turned out to be detail of the Hythe night-sight system.

'First, this is to prove to you that in the Soviet Union we do everything right. By law. With evidence. These photographs, as I have said, are of the rifle you were using. Your fingerprints are not on the weapon, you used shooting gloves and there are plenty of glove smudges. We have, however, identified the prints of two suspected reactionaries. They have already been arrested and are being interrogated by a mutual friend. A friend of yours and mine, Boysie.'

Boysie took out a cigarette.

'Their evidence is of little importance. You are a self-confessed Western agent whom we can identify with several killings. We have eyewitnesses to your murder of my man Spensky. Further evidence is here.' The long finger touched the photograph of the rifle butt. 'The fibres match Spensky's uniform where you caught him in the—where you hit him. So we have definite evidence of murder——'

'In self-defence——'

'—murder against you. But that is not the main point. My real project is to prove how your Western bosses put you on the spot.' He pushed the open white box towards Boysie. 'I will agree that the Mauser rifle was loaded with dummies when we caught you, and you had undoubtedly ejected the ammunition from the loaded rifle. One of the bullets made a nasty scratch on the foot of the bed by the way. There were five rounds in all. These are they.' He tapped the open box.

Boysie looked down. Five 7.92 cartridges nestled in cotton wool.

'We picked these up from the floor. They show none of your fingerprints. Only those of the two men we have under arrest.'

More photographs. 'I promise you, though you will think I am lying, that these are the five cartridges with which your rifle was loaded. The five you ejected. Take the tweezers and examine them.'

Boysie hesitated as Khavichev pushed the large tweezers towards him across the table. Gently Boysie picked up the tweezers and lifted the first bullet from the cotton wool. He felt his heartbeat quickening, the familiar bowel churn at what he could see. He replaced the first bullet and took up the next. The same.

'The third one,' said Khavichev quietly, 'has a mark on the actual bullet. That is where it struck the bed.'

Boysie took up the third round. 'But they're all——'

'Yes.' Confident and self-satisfied.

'This can't be the bloody ejected ammunition. They're

all'—he struggled for the correct oath—'they're all dummies.' He reached for the fifth; they were all easily identifiable. Boysie dropped the last cartridge into the box in an attitude of despair. 'I don't believe you. It's a load of old cobblers.'

Khavichev opened the second white box, revealing a full clip of cartridges. 'These were in your pocket. The ones left by the rifle. The extras in case of trouble. No fingerprints of yours. Just smudges. Have a look.'

Boysie picked up the clip with the tweezers and again put the magnifying glass into action. The result was the same, dummies. He threw the clip back into the box. By this time Khavichev had opened the slim red plastic container. Five more cartridges. 'These have your fingerprints all over them. You obviously handled them in the West. They are the dummies we found in the rifle.'

Boysie did not even bother to look at them. Any anxiety had long given way to anger. 'You tricky bastard——' he began.

'Do I have to remind you again?' The chopping voice. 'Try to remember, my dear Boysie. Make sure your brain is engaged before putting your mouth into gear. I am telling you the truth.'

'You're trying to tell me that my Department deliberately killed off Iris themselves and left me in a room with a rifle and dummy ammunition. Put the finger on me.'

'I am not trying to tell you. I *am* telling you. The evidence is here.'

Boysie's brain spun like a buzz-saw. A Khavichev trick? A Mostyn trick? Could be either. That bastard Mostyn could do it. Would do it. He had known the end was imminent anyway. A window. A rifle with dummies. Complete denial by the Consulate or Foreign Office. Boysie Oakes acting on his own. No proof. After all, the Russians had more to gain from Iris alive than dead.

Christ. Where? When? How? Why? Who? He looked down.

'What happens to me? Whatever?' He looked squarely at a blurred Khavichev.

'Whatever?' Khavichev callous. 'A big trial. A propaganda trial. You're strong meat. Better than Powers or Wynne. A real headliner. British denials do not matter. There will be a trial with all the evidence.'

'No way out?' Boysie clutching at haystacks.

Khavichev came slowly back into focus. 'Why should I give you any chances? What I have told you is true. Once sentence is passed there is no hope. Life imprisonment, and your people will not want you back. Ever.'

'Christ.' A prayer, not blasphemy.

'Of course.' Khavichev's voice trickled a pinch of hope. 'You are a coward, a reprehensible person of little moral fibre. You have worked in Mostyn's personal office for a long while. There must be certain things you know.'

'I hardly know anything.'

'You would be surprised at what could be of use to us. A few sessions and we might come to some arrangement.'

Boysie thought for a minute. His reactions were even slower than usual. 'It's a trick. It is you, not Mostyn. Information. That's all you're after.'

Khavichev spoke softly, as to a small child. 'You must use your reason. Work it out for yourself. Only you can make up your mind, come to a decision. I offer nothing. There is a chance, but at the moment the only thing I can see is a full spy trial as the Western press would call it. There is no other way.'

'There is another way. I know what I would do.' The voice came from the door. Boysie's head jerked round. The light was all wrong. The face in the doorway simply a silhouette, grotesque, leaning on two sticks, but the voice was familiar. Slowly, painfully, the heavy little body advanced, one stick and one leg dragging in front of the other. The man emerged into the light. Khavichev stood up and pulled a chair near to Boysie's couch.

Boysie stared incredulously at the man. The last time he had seen him was from a helicopter off San Diego. By rights he should be dead, engulfed in flame from the AIM-4A missiles which had flashed from a brace of Voodoo fighters finishing off a PT boat and a Redland-mounted operation in which both Boysie and the warped man had played a large part during the Understrike affair.

'You have met Gorilka?' said Khavichev with a twitch of humour.

'You're dead.' Boysie incredulously.

'Bang, bang.' Gorilka's face was changed since their last meeting. Flame from the rockets had taken their toll.

'How in the name of——?'

'No thanks to you, Boysie Oakes. I was thrown clear of the PT boat. Unconscious and badly injured, as you can see. But our motor launch picked me up and finally got me back to base. There was an enquiry but I was exonerated. Happily my brain is not impaired.'

'They talked?' Khavichev's question purposely cutting off any more of Gorilka's reminiscences.

'Like angels. We can make three more arrests if we want. It's all on tape and being transcribed now.' Gorilka's voice came horrendously happy from the Munster-mask face. 'I often wonder about those stories of heroism. Men not talking. The closed mouths. I fear that if the tight-lipped brigade ever existed at all they have now gone forever. They all talk for me.'

'Possibly your natural charm,' said Khavichev. Not a spectre of a smile.

Boysie went cold. Gorilka was deadly. As Khavichev's man in the field during the Understrike affair in America, he had nearly done for a NATO Defence Project, the British Prime Minister, and Boysie himself. A brilliant intellectual, Gorilka was also a grim psychopath.

'Gorilka'—Khavichev's voice chilly with an undercurrent of uncertainty as he spoke to Boysie—'Gorilka is my Second-in-Command of general staff.' Turning to Gorilka. 'You said you know what you would do, comrade. What you would do to Boysie Oakes? What?'

There was no feeling in the way the deformed man spoke. 'Shoot him. Slowly. The feet first. Then bullets through the legs. The bone shattered. A day later one carefully placed stomach wound. Pain for a week. Then the chest. Another week. A throat wound. A great deal of pain for three weeks or so until death. Killed while trying to escape.'

'You are a vicious man.'

'We shall see.'

Boysie got the fleeting impression that Khavichev somehow feared Gorilka.

'I have pointed out the true position,' Khavichev said. 'His own people will never want him back, but we could come to a deal. I don't think he quite believes that Mostyn framed him.'

Gorilka gave an imitation of a laugh that would have assured him a part as one of the witches in Shakespeare's Scottish play. 'Fool. We need no trials or deals. Information can be extracted painlessly. The pain can follow. Don't forget all the equipment is still intact from Stalin's era. The golden age. You should know about that, Comrade General.'

Khavichev was silent. Then, just as he was about to speak, a knock came heavy on the door.

'*Viadee te.*'

This time it was a young officer, facial inscrutability trying to hide concern. He moved with immaculate military precision, the salute to Khavichev being obeisance to the man, not the rank. Khavichev, in the eyes of most of his staff and the whole of Soviet Intelligence, was more of a myth than a legend. The officer's left hand came forward, handing a long, folded sheet of paper to the General.

Khavichev opened the document, showing no sign of concern until his eyes began to move across the page. The strong face slowly sagged. Confidence began to disappear from the usually alert eyes. Gorilka watched, his wrinkled and horribly clawed face set tight as plastic. Khavichev allowed the paper to fall between his knees. Involuntarily he spoke in English to Gorilka. 'We've failed. They've got Warren. Got him from the English.'

Gorilka spat out a phrase in Russian which obviously meant, 'Not in front of the serfs.' Tension, the unbearable concern of defeat between the two men. Then Khavichev turned his whole body towards Boysie. He spoke sharply.

'That will be all today. I will see that you are taken care of. I promise what I have said is the truth. Your English masters have failed you. Remember that. Remember also that you are a man of little principle. We might have work for you. I do not know yet. It is a germ. A germ of an idea.'

'You talk nonsense.' Gorilka had taken the paper from Khavichev and scanned it hurriedly. 'Number Four Group can deal with this.'

'And break their cover? Your experience is limited in the field, Gorilka. I make the decisions.' He turned to Boysie again. 'We will see you later. Within hours you may well have to decide your fate. *You* may well have to decide. Think logically about what has happened. Mostyn tried to get rid of you. I promise that.'

Gorilka, disregarding Boysie, was already halfway to

the door, hobbling slowly like a battery-operated toy. Khavichev made his exit with a straight back. At least he was a soldier. Depression immersed Boysie. The black ink of an octopus, the terror of drowning, the touch of suckers and tentacles.

IV. DRAGON

. . . and with weak hands though mighty heart
Dare the unpastured dragon in his den?
                                    Shelley, *Adonais*

THE hand was clamped to his shoulder, shaking violently. Boysie, fist clenched, tried to beat the arm away, but it was like banging against hard metal.

'Oakes. Waken. Waken. Up. Come on. Up ... up ... up.'

Boysie opened his eyes. The lights were on, slashing pain momentarily above the eyes. A hand on his shoulder was still tight, clasped, fingers digging and pressing into the deltoid muscle. Khavichev stood over him, pummelling consciousness into the mind. Boysie started to sit up.

'How long have I been out?' Boysie shocked at the change in Khavichev's face.

'Only the night.'

'How long? How long have I been here?'

'I told you, just the night. We picked you up at about twenty to nine last night. It is Tuesday morning.'

Boysie, now fully in focus, stared at the General. It was hard to believe that this was the same strong man, the hammer of Soviet Counter Espionage and Subversive Activities. His leather-grained face had taken on a surface sheen of grey, the sharp eyes were dulled, showing an underlying, preoccupied stare of stress, sunk into

93

black sockets. The big body gave the impression of having dwindled, shrivelled overnight. Khavichev looked hard back at Boysie—through Boysie.

'You feeling all right?' Though he was at Khavichev's mercy, the question was demanding to be asked.

'No.' Khavichev's voice dull as his eyes. He took a deep breath. 'I have dismissed the guards. The electronic equipment is turned off. Gorilka will not disturb us. He is still under medical care and does not rise until eleven. There is not much time but I must talk to you. Make you an offer.'

There was a desperate, suspended state of silence before Khavichev spoke again. The vocal note was a plea.

'What I told you last night. Have you seen reason? I must have the truth. Do you now believe that Mostyn and his superiors arranged for your capture? Or do you still not trust me?'

The toss of a coin; the spin of a wheel; the dice ('Baby needs a new pairs of shoes.... Snake eyes.... Sorry chum'); pull the handle and up come the three lemons— or more likely a peach, a pear, and an orange. It was all a gamble. Boysie made the quickest decision of his career. He plumped for Khavichev.

'I believe you,' he said softly.

'You are right. If you ever get back to London you will find out.'

'So what happens?' Some fundamental change of mood had given Boysie a new attitude. He did not really care any more.

'I have much to tell you.' Khavichev sounded dreadfully tired. A broken man. Even an old man. 'Things no one else has heard. Things very few people know of. Why should I tell you? I have held more power than you can ever hope to hold. We have been enemies. I could even have you shot now.' He stopped. Then, loudly with drama, 'The great Khavichev is finished.' Bitterness. He raised his hands and dropped them in an attitude of finality. 'Unfortunately Gorilka has many important friends. You must have seen last night that he is unfit for his job. Our legal system—whatever your Western propaganda says—is strict. Certainly we in espionage, in security, elicit confessions. Gorilka meant what he said. That is the way he would have killed you; out of spite, vindictiveness. And he would have broken our legal code.' Khavichev raised his right hand as though holding a pistol and pulled an imaginary trigger. 'I fought hard to prevent Gorilka's appointment as my Second-in-Command. He wanted my job, and now I suppose he will get it. For a while anyway. Unless I get him first. Before noon today.'

'Noon?' Boysie concentrating.

'I too have my friends. I was tipped off this morning, at four o'clock. They are flying in from Moscow today. Around noon I will be relieved of my command, placed under arrest, and taken back to Moscow.'

'You? But why? That message last night?'

'No, that is something quite different. More important. We will come to it in a minute.' A clearer light returned to the General's eyes and with it a smile circling the corners of his mouth.

'I told you that our legal system is strict. My big chance against Gorilka is the fact that one of the two men who signed confessions concerning the Iris liquidation last night died under pressure. Gorilka was in charge of the interrogation, and in our criminal code he is most vulnerable.'

'Then why are they——?' started Boysie.

'Getting rid of me?'

'Yeah.'

Another painful sigh from Khavichev. 'A long story. I've kept it quiet for many years.' The eyes glazed over as though he were speaking to someone beyond Boysie, some person from the past. 'I got my present appointment on February 20th, 1956. Five days later, if you know your history, Khrushchev made his six-hour speech denouncing Stalin.' He was back with Boysie again. 'Since that moment, since the beginning of my appointment, I have never felt safe. My tracks were covered, but I never felt safe. You see, Khavichev has not always been my name.'

Khavichev lowered his head. 'Some of the things,' he said, agony winding between the words, 'some of the things we did. I did. I have done. Stalin taught me the trade. Security, intrigue, espionage, intelligence. I served directly under him when he was appointed Commissar of Nationalities, when we had control of all the security organisations. And now'—a cynical lilt, once more the hands lifting and dropping in defeat—'and now they have found out. And you know what happens to Stalinists, even today. There is documentary evidence. Letters. Papers. My assumed names.'

'And you're willing to get me away from Gorilka?' Hope raging in Boysie's voice.

Khavichev smiled to himself. He had still not lost the knack of grinning like a predatory monster. 'Oh no, not without something in return. Gorilka cannot last long, but I am a true Communist. I believe in the way, the truth, and the life of Communism. I believe that it must spread and engulf the entire world. Inevitable.' He hesitated, his timing like an actor's, letting the words sink home. 'But, Boysie Oakes, I do not believe in the sacrifice of mankind. Russia, America, and Britain could be closer now than they have ever been at any time. The danger lies in China, in her way of spreading the gospel—the leveller through annihilation. Do you really understand the situation between China and Russia?'

Boysie looked perplexed. 'Well, I know old Criss-Cross-

Cruisechoff and Cosy Gin didn't see eye to eye with Mousy Tongue.'

Even Khavichev got the gag line. 'If it were only as simple as that,' he said. 'China is determined to be the number-one nation. The progress of their nuclear research and their power rise goes on. Their aim is a takeover bid for the entire world. China may be a little disoriented—or may seem so. The Orient has always seemed disoriented. But the power is there, being tapped, and the organisation is growing.'

'The old Yellow Peril.'

'The new Yellow Peril. They already have a security network and espionage system that at least equals our own. The Jen Chia, the police apparatus. The Am Chuan Jen Chia, that is the central apparatus for the Party, with a European HQ in Albania. Then there is the Pi Mi Jen Chia, the government-controlled apparatus, not to mention the People's Liberation Army's Jen Chia. And they intermingle, Boysie, they overlap. Just think of a simple illustration: all those Chinese restaurants in the world's major cities.' He paused again, this time to light a cigarette.

Boysie began to find the room unbearably hot.

'Take your own country,' continued Khavichev. 'There are six Chinese restaurants in the city of Oxford, fifteen in Liverpool, and twelve in Manchester—they are the licensed ones. God knows how many in London and other cities. I am not suggesting that any of these have a connection with the Chinese People's Republic Security Services, but they could. It could happen. There are Chinese everywhere. Intrigue everywhere. And don't forget that from the nuclear point of view they are still working on the level of Nunn May and Fuchs. Still after atomic secrets.'

Boysie could feel the big bang coming any minute.

Khavichev continued. 'They are shrewd, cunning,

clever. And one of their major operations is aimed at your own country.' The General leaned closer. 'That is why we gave Warren back. Your poor old Rabbit Warren.'

He clenched his right fist and thumped a knee, hard. 'My fault. The stuff Warren was taking over the Wall from us was of little consequence. Even he knew that. But he did have specialised information about the Chinese situation, information we could not get. Information about a major Chinese action aimed at England. Something already in operation. We were naturally anxious that he should get that information back to your people. It would have been easy. We should have just let him walk out.' Another snort of laughter. 'But I was too clever.' Bitter. Cynical. 'The all-seeing Khavichev. Huh. Thought I could kill two birds with one stone. If we offered to exchange Warren for Iris there was a chance that we might get her back. But it was obvious that some attempt would be made on her life. So we also considered the chance of getting you, Boysie—and my palms have been itching for you. It has been a long while.' A drawn-out hiss from between clenched teeth. 'But I have failed. Your colleague Warren has *not* got through.'

Boysie felt nothing. 'Dead?' he asked. It was a dream. Chinese restaurants and the Yellow Peril. Untrue. Unreal.

'I do not think so.' Khavichev tomblike. 'I do not think they have killed him. Not yet.' His hand extracted a slim, folded sheet of paper from his inside pocket. 'The cable I received last night was from KGB HQ in Moscow. I had it translated for you.' He passed the paper to Boysie. 'Take no notice of the Russian heading. It is only the KGB HQ address and code number.'

'All Greek to me,' said Boysie, concentrating on the translation.

Boysie read the cable aloud. 'Dragons?' he repeated.

'Obvious.' Khavichev in a Sherlock Holmes voice. 'Our code reference for the Jen Chia apparatus.'

Boysie looked down at the cable again. *Contact immediate for details and action,* he read. 'So what's happened to Rabbit?'

'Your disorganised military and intelligence services happened.' Khavichev itchily critical. 'If your wretched government were not so stingy, Rabbit would probably be in London now. They could easily have had an RAF aircraft waiting to take him straight home. That information about Chinese action against England would have been in the right hands now. But in the spring British European Airways has only one aircraft out of Tempelhof each day, a Viscount Flight 685 leaving at fifteen hours. He was scheduled to go this afternoon. In the meantime they were putting him up at the Hilton. Your man was waiting for Warren at Checkpoint Charlie —a Merc, the lot. Three more of your operatives followed the Merc in a Volkswagen, and two of our operatives tailed them. Rabbit was taken to his room at the Hilton. Your man left him for half an hour—a little less—so he could bathe and clean up.'

'He was alone? They deserted him in the Hilton?'

'For thirty minutes or so.'

'And?'

'He disappeared.'

'Did a Houdini.' Fast. Dry as a martini.

'Your men had the hotel under surveillance. Our men had your men under surveillance. No one saw a thing.'

'Disappeared into thin air?'

'Not quite. A waiter has reported seeing him leaving

the building through the servants' entrance. Three men with him. The waiter says they were Japanese or Chinese, not Caucasian.'

'So they led us up the Yangtze without paddles.'

'There has been more information since than. At midnight four Chinese diplomats and a European boarded a special flight and left for Tiranë.'

'Where the hell's Tiranë?' A mechanical Boysie incompetence. Then, with a quick lift of his hands in a shoving motion, 'Don't tell me. Let me guess. Albania?'

'The capital of Albania.'

'And the bloody Ham Chew and Jen whatsit have their European headquarters in Albania.'

'The Am Chuan Jen Chia, China's main security organisation. The European answered Warren's description, carried a British passport, Number 56718, and was supposed to be part of a cultural diplomatic mission. He was not well and had to be driven out to the aircraft on the tarmac. They said he had been drinking and wanted to avoid scandal.'

'So Rabbit's in Albania.'

'For the time being.' Khavichev's eyes, still sunken, bored into Boysie's face, a hard electric drill. 'I am going to be realistic. By noon I will have no authority. Before then it is possible that certain things can be put into operation. Things that could be of value to my beliefs. If I choose to leave you here, Gorilka will dispose of you. The shooting, the feet, legs, and upwards. A long death.'

A skeleton hand closed painfully round Boysie's bowels.

'I have already convinced you,' continued Khavichev, 'that the Department of Special Security doesn't want to know. Except to see you as a corpse.' He continued to bore his eyes into Boysie's face. 'I am offering you a job.' Spoken slowly and with force.

'Me?'

'As I see it, you have no choice.' Khavichev's hand went into his pocket once more. A passport spun across the bed, landing on Boysie's lap.

He picked it up. An American passport. He flicked through the pages. Brian Ian Oshiemer from Toledo, Ohio. The rear pages were crammed with valid visas. Iron Curtain countries predominated, all stamped with dates going back to 1963. The photograph and description were Boysie's. It looked like a masterpiece, the real thing.

'That's you, Oshiemer.' Pointing towards the open passport. 'Executive Sales Manager of Steel-Thru Bullet-Resistant Glass Incorporated. You do a lot of business in Europe. A lot behind the curtain.'

Boysie glanced up from a vanity-case viewing of the passport photograph. By now Khavichev had a stack of documents on his lap. Light began to dawn in Boysie's slow brain as another passport sailed over the bed, settling the right way up. A document he knew.

'There's your own passport.' Khavichev lifted his head. The black-circled eyes dimly reflected scorn. 'Herr Oldcorn.' More of smear than sneer. 'Colonel Mostyn's sense of humour is slightly childish. Old Corn.'

Boysie did not have time to reply. A slim, thickly stuffed envelope followed the second passport.

'Ten thousand dollars, in fives, tens, and hundreds,' said the General. 'Easily convertible currency. Happy money. Expenses.'

'Look.' There was no bite to Boysie's reaction. 'I do read you? You're asking me to go double? Do a Blake?'

Khavichev made a jeering noise, a rasp of odium from the back of the larynx. 'If you are getting technical, a double agent, or counterspy as officialdom calls them, is a person posing as a spy for one side in order to learn their secrets.' He gave the jeering noise again. 'Secrets? What secrets? A double agent—what the hell, you know this already—often works for two sides, sometimes three. Sells to the highest bidder. One week a job against some country, and in the same week he undertakes a spot of subversion on behalf of the country against which he is contracted, my dear Boysie—I may call you Boysie?' He stopped, politely waiting for an answer.

'Of course.' Stunned that Khavichev should take this turn of courtesy.

'Good. I feel I have known you long.' Smile from the heart, a true smile. 'Boysie, you realise that you cannot be a double agent. It is not possible because you do not work for anybody. The Department of British Special Security, I presume, imagines you are already dead or awaiting trial. They are probably puzzled, waiting for news of you. But they cannot do anything. They sent you out here to get caught. I lose my rank, authority, position. You cannot work for me. So you work for nobody.'

Boysie gave the matter some full-fathom-five thought. If one accepted Khavichev's original premise regarding Soviet Security having been given the squeak, Iris's death by poisoning, and the dummy ammunition laid out for him at the firing point above the Friedrichstrasse, the whole thing was logical. After an era of silence he spoke. 'It's all very well, but I'm still under the erotic bloody Official Secrets Act. In dead lumber with them if I work for you.'

A cynical twist of the lips from Khavichev. 'You have probably heard this many times before from your old masters. But you are on your own, working for the good of humanity, Boysie. You will certainly not be working for me because, as I have said, I suppose I will cease to exist within a month or so. Apart from the political machinations of the gruesome Dr. Gorilka, my removal from office does not come as a great surprise. I had a slight heart attack last year and I was bound for retirement—retirement can mean different things under our regime.'

'I heard about that. The heart attack.'

'It is all inevitable, like life and death,' said Khavichev quietly, his face set into an autumnal sadness. Then the manner changed with the speed and force of a racing driver doing a change-up on the straight. The sharpness of authority returned. The heavy thump of the executioner's axe on the block. 'I am concerned that the total facts of China's operation against Britain reach the right quarters as soon as possible. The Am Chuan Jen Chia will undoubtedly be interrogating Warren to see how much he really knows, where he got his information and how accurate it is. They know we, the Soviet Government, are deeply concerned. But the Am Chuan Jen Chia will expect a unit of our organisation to be taking action. I doubt if they will be bargaining for you.'

'So I go to Albania and get Warren out?'

'Or procure the information from him and get it back to Whitehall.' The General glanced at his watch. 'You must make up your mind quickly so that I can arrange suitable remuneration through our British and Swiss cells. You have the dollars. For undertaking the operation the sum of twenty thousand pounds sterling will be paid into a numbered account. In Switzerland, of course. If you succeed, a further fifty thousand pounds will be paid. This will automatically go through whether I am in power or not. If I arrange it now, today, nobody can trace it for at least six months. What do you say, Boysie? Slow death under Gorilka, or a chance for freedom and cracking the dragon men. Eh?'

Money, big money, was involved—always a magnet to Boysie. There was also the chance that he could welsh on everyone. At least he would get into the West again.

It was as though Khavichev could read his thoughts.

'And no pulling a fast one, friend. I still have good contacts. If you cross me on this, somebody will get you soon and quickly. I promise you that. I am taking as much of a risk as yourself. You have already proved to be notoriously unreliable.' He spoke with point. Reminiscent of a gangster in an old movie.

'It's bloody suicide,' said Boysie aloud. 'Chop suicide.' But he had no real option. He nodded a painful affirmative. 'All right. How do I get to—where is it in Albania?'

'Tiranë.'

'Tiranë.'

'Your car is waiting outside. Nice motor, that Jensen. You can be across the Wall and into the West quite quickly.' He sucked his teeth thoughtfully. Mild concern. 'Unfortunately we cannot get you out to Tiranë from here. Too much risk. You will have to go from the West. From Tempelhof.'

'Fly?' The words came out in a strangle of panic. Boysie had a natural aversion to taking airplane rides. It was a state bordering on the pathological. He was sick in aircraft and usually in a state of slight shock from take-off to touch down. 'I have to fly?' he questioned, voice quavering on the frontier of near terror.

'You cannot very well walk or drive to Albania.' An inkling of Boysie's problem showed in Khavichev's eyes and the creased lines of his forehead. 'There is another point,' he continued. 'You are going to have to be very careful in the West. The situation is like Rabbit Warren's. I must get you out of here today. Out of the East. Today is Tuesday, and you cannot start your journey to Tiranë until tomorrow. At eleven.'

Another envelope changed hands.

'Tickets. Itinerary. A difficult journey. You do not arrive in Tiranë until Thursday.'

'If I'm lucky.'

'Then on, you play it by ear. I want Warren, or the

full details of this Chinese business, passed to your Department at speed. Within hours. At least within four days.'

'Where the hell do I start?'

Khavichev shrugged. 'The Am Chuan Jen Chia head-quarters are housed in the basement of the University Research Library. I should start there.'

'I can't do it.' Boysie suddenly brimming with panic.

'All right.' Khavichev unmoved. 'Stay here and let Gorilka shoot you. A piece at a time.' He gave a thin-lipped smile.

'Strewth, he looks grey, thought Boysie.

Khavichev, slowly and with feeling, said, 'Think of all that lovely money.'

Boysie thought, and moved his head in assent.

'Good.' Khavichev withdrew a silver snake of keychain from his pocket. 'You will want to freshen up while I deal with the money in Switzerland.'

He began to cross the room and, for the first time, Boysie noticed there was a door, hardly visible, set into the gleaming white wall at the far end. Khavichev inserted a key. 'Go ahead. You will find all you need in there.'

Boysie looked terrible, gazing at himself in the long mirror. Suit crumpled, unshaven, dark-ringed eyes. A shower, followed by a session at one of the three wash-basins. Glass shelves were neatly laid out with male and female cosmetics. Mainly American. Boysie chose Wal-dorf Astoria Shaving Lotion (the best in the world), a Gillette Aristocrat Razor with Super Silver blades, and English Leather Aftershave. While he shaved, his suit hung on a British Corby electric trouser press. In twenty minutes he looked, and felt, a different man. Clean, neat and tidy, and with shoes polished on an automatic machine.

Khavichev was waiting for him, sitting on the couch.

He looked even more tired and concerned.

'It has all been arranged.' He spoke as soon as Boysie entered. For the first time that morning, Boysie noticed that the General's appearance was sloppy, creased and untidy.

'A draft for twenty thousand pounds is already on its way to Account Number 4897A at Leu and Company, AG, Zurich. It is the largest private bank in Switzerland, so there will be no trouble. Details will be posted to your London address. Whatever happens to me, the other fifty thousand pounds will be deposited once you have successfully carried out the assignment.' Khavichev spoke with complete confidence.

Boysie found it hard to believe. His mind built up a glossy picture of the money in actual notes piled high. Khavichev pulled him back to reality. 'You had better be armed,' he said, offering him a pistol, butt first. A Walther P38, heavy and horribly lethal. 'It's loaded, safety on. And I have four full magazines for you.'

'Where the hell do I carry this cannon?' Boysie said, gingerly grasping the automatic and examining it. He noticed that it had once belonged to a member of the Third Reich. There were tiny German eagles engraved on the slide and above the trigger guard. The left side of the slide bore the legend 'ac43.' Nazi Forces Armament manufactured by Walther in 1943.

'Stick it in your waistband.'

Boysie pushed the gun into place. It felt uncomfortable. He slid it farther to the left, out of sight even with his jacket open. The spare clips were easily distributed: left- and right-hand hip pockets, left inside jacket pocket.

'Another thing.' Khavichev spoke with acute earnestness. 'Your room at the Bristol Kempinski is now bugged. Group Four again. It is a standard telephone and room microphone/transmitter. While in place it will pick up all telephone conversations and tap the whole room at the same time. As soon as you get back, unscrew the phone mouthpiece and disconnect the bug. It simply lifts out, but you had better smash it to pieces. Better safe——'

'——than sorry.' Boysie looked solemn.

'Well.' Khavichev glanced at his watch again. 'We just have time for a drink. Or would you prefer tea?'

Boysie wanted a stiff Courvoisier but decided to play it safe. 'Tea, I think.'

'Russian tea is always good. It rejuvenates.' Khavichev gave a grunt, the edge of a half-laugh. Then silence. An embarrassment. Things unsaid between the two men, things which could not be said. Eventually Khavichev spoke, placing a hand gently on Boysie's knee. A single pat. 'Strange, is it not, that we should be sitting talking like this? Enemies for so long. Me, an exalted Chief of Soviet Counter Espionage; you, Britain's Security Liquidator.' He stopped talking and gazed straight ahead, trying to get the right words for the thoughts. 'At times we have nearly trapped you. Now, we meet, and I have to let you go. We talk, and I like you.'

'We might have got on quite well together.' Boysie was developing an almost sentimental feeling for the man.

'That is the real trouble with the world.' The General shifted his bulk and took a long swig at the tea. 'People do not meet and talk enough. Or, with politicians, when they meet it is all so formal. They do not know. They do not get inside each other's minds. It has become a game. All on the surface. Chess.'

Another lull.

'I hope——' started Boysie. He had difficulty finding the correct words. 'I mean—well—I hope they don't make things too bad for you.'

General Khavichev's hand closed around Boysie's

107

upper arm, squeezing a message of thanks. Boysie winced. Khavichev's squeezes were like overtight tourniquets.

'Thank you.' No emotion. 'One of two things will happen. I will be publicly denounced and humiliated, expelled from the Central Committee, like Molotov, Shepilov, and Malenkov in '57—sent to some outlandish place as a minor official. Remember, they made Molotov Ambassador to Outer Mongolia? At least you have a chance that way. Otherwise there will be arrest, Public trial. Charges of teason. Then a short time of horror. A moment of fear. After that, rest. Sleep. It is of little consequence. It has to happen one day.' He stood up, facing Boysie. 'Now it is time for you to go. You know what to do. It is for everyone's benefit. In everybody's interests. Do it well. Check to see you have everything.'

The P38 weighed a ton in his trouser waistband; spare magazines were in place. The American passport and dollars bulged next to one of the magazines in Boysie's left-hand pocket. The travel documents and his British passport were on the opposite side.

'Everything,' he reported after checking.

'Let us hope you are not searched in the West then. On this side all is arranged. I have a man waiting in your car. He will guide you to the checkpoint and leave before you reach there. He speaks good English. You will be all right. They are expecting you, but it will be necessary to go through the routine. Both sides watch each other's procedure. When you go into the passport and customs office they will simply ask you to wait for a few minutes before going back to the car. Come.'

Khavichev led Boysie out of the room and along a narrow corridor. A left turn. Then another. A short flight of steps and an entrance hall. Two armed soldiers in Russian uniform came to attention as Khavichev appeared. Ahead through the big glass doors Boysie could see the Jensen standing by the curb, a figure sitting in the passenger seat.

Khavichev put out his hand and grasped Boysie's right forearm in the Russian manner of a handshake. 'Do it well,' he repeated. 'Do it well.'

Boysie went through the doors, down the stone steps, and climbed into the car's driving seat. He did not look back.

At Schoenefeld Airport an Antonov An-12 was just touching down on Runway 25 Right. On board, held safe in their seat belts, sat five senior officers of the KGB and three civilians. By evening they would all be back at Sheremetyevo Airport, Moscow. By then they would have an extra passenger: General Boris Piotr Khavichev.

The trip back passed without undue incident. Back at the Bristol Kempinski, Boysie made straight for the desk clerk.

'Give me a cable form, and where can I use a typewriter?' No messing about with easy English or half German. The man behind the desk gave him a sphinx look and pushed a cable form towards him.

'At the far end. They will let you use a machine there,' he said without courtesy or arrogance. He just did not care.

'I'll take my key as well. Room 504.'

The clerk fumbled among the pigeonholes and banged the key on to the desk. At the far end of Reception an under-manager in black pin-stripe said it was no trouble at all. Of course he could use one of the typewriters.

'I just don't want there to be any mistakes about this cable,' said Boysie. They lifted a hinged lid and let him through to sit at one of the secretaries' desks. With great care Boysie typed his cable:

JAMES MOSTYN, QUEEN'S MANSIONS, PORCHESTER GARDENS, BAYSWATER, LONDON W2

CLIENT GONE YOUR WAY STOP ROTTEN RESIGN UNLESS HELP IMMEDIATE STOP BACK HERE THROUGH CONTRACT INVOLVING RED AND YELLOW LINES IN YOUR FAVOURITE COMMODITY STOP DO NOT KNOW DONKEY FROM FOREARM STOP STOP STOP HELP.

OLDCORN

Once finished, Boysie silently read over the message aimed towards Mostyn at the Queen's Mansions contact address. That ought to do something. The under-manager bowed and said he would have the cable sent off straight away. Boysie handed it over and headed for the lift.

As he put the key into the lock Boysie looked up at the number of his room. It had not struck him before. The years slipped back and he heard a verse from the old wartime sentimental ballad tripping melodically through his rotating mind:

> *We turned the key in the door,*
> *We didn't dare to ask the price.*
> *Just for one night our paradise.*
> *That seventh heaven on the old fifth floor,*
> *In room five hundred and four.*

'Shit,' said Boysie loudly as he banged the door open.

'Watcher, Mr. Oakes. Sorry if I'm a bit late. On 'oliday. Got 'ere soon as I could.' Charlie Griffin sat in the easy chair facing the door, a lurid detective magazine open to display a poor colour drawing of a man leaning out of a window. The man had a rifle in the aiming position, squinting down a telescopic sight. In scarlet letters the

110

caption blazed across the page: THE KILLER WHO NEVER
FIRED A SHOT.

'You're all I bloody need,' said Boysie, slamming the
door in fury.

PART TWO

GRIMOBO

If you like it ... Funny?

V. PIGEON

Though not thought to be the wisest bird;
The pigeon sends its mate away at the first
sign of bad weather.
Pien Fu Yuan-ting, *The Pigeon*
(Translated by Art Fairbank)

'Now don't be like that Mr. O. I mean I only do it for you as a favour.' Griffin looked shocked at Boysie's display of evil temper.

'Don't do me no favours.' Boysie having a go at his Marlon Brando imitation for the hell of it.

Griffin went on. 'I mean I told yer that larst year out in Switzerland. In Locarno. Just been there ag'in. Back to loverley Locarno. Little 'oliday. Well, does yer good to get away, don't it? 'Ave a break, eh? S'why I never gotcher messages till Monday night. Yer telegrams and that. Over 'ere as quick as I could, mind yer. First aircraft out. I've always played fair with you, 'aven't I?'

'Hey.' Boysie waking to the fact that Griffin had got into his room without a key. 'How'd you get in?'

'In?'

'Into my room. In 'ere—here.'

'Ah.' Griffin in mood melodramatic, finger to the side of his nose. 'Ah, well, always been 'andy with locks, Mr. Oakes. See, when I first started, that was in the undertakin' business, like what you might call the packagin' side of the trade, we 'ad a stand-in pallbearer who 'appened to be a locksmith by profession. Good old Sam.

114

Sammy Yale, 'is name was. Wonder what ever became o' Sammy? Useter see a lot of each other——'

'I bet.' Boysie brought Griffin to a halt. There was an odd feeling about the room. Something indefinable. Then he remembered Group Four, the West Berlin cell of what was once Khavichev's major network.

'Shshshsh—for Christ's sake, shshshsh!' Leaping across the room like a student fakir having his first go with the carpet of hot coals. Gently, right hand still in the shshshshing position, Boysie lifted the telephone receiver and began to sing the more obscene verses of an old Scots ballad well known to the rugby football fraternity, and more debased persons, as the 'Ball of Kirriemuir.' Griffin watched with interest as Boysie, still singing, unscrewed the mouthpiece and carefully tipped the flat, circular electronic bugging device into the palm of his hand.

'We bin——?' started Griffin.

Boysie made a shshshshing motion and carried the bug, with almost ceremonial care, into the bathroom. Griffin followed. Boysie placed the device on the imitation marble floor, bent low over it, and, with tongue between lips, took in a massive breath which he expelled as a thunderous raspberry. Quickly straightening up, Boysie lifted his right foot and brought the heel hard down on the eavesdropping instrument. Three times the heel was raised and crashed down, leaving a small pile of metal fragments and wires, which he gathered up and popped into the lavatory bowl. He dropped the lid, pulled the flush handle and stood to attention. 'So perish all electronic swine,' said Boysie.

'We was bein' bugged then?' Griffin not amused.

'Bugged and buggered,' blustered Boysie, bouncing back into the main room to replace the telephone receiver.

'You all right, Mr. Oakes?' Griffin infuriatingly bland.

'No, I'm not bloody all right.'

'Come on, Mr. Oakes, please. I never done any 'arm to you. No need to turn nasty with me.'

'Well.' Boysie petulant, still almost cross-eyed from swivelling his face around in search of more clues to Group Four's visitation. 'Well, so would you turn bloody nasty.'

'It doesn't do to upset yerself, Mr. Oakes.' Griffin smiled a faraway smile and shook his head. 'Spot of bother you've 'ad then? Girls ag'in? Not them girls ag'in, is it?' Jokingly remonstrating with a finger wag.

'A spot? Whole bloody festering rash of trouble. And no ... it's ... not ... girls.' Slowing up with a smile as Rosy Puberty, the delicious Mu-lan, rode full tilt into his thoughts. How ever could he have forgotten the little yellow lovely?

'Not—er—not Mr. Mostyn then, by any chance?' Griffin tentative.

'You guessed,' said Boysie in mock sorrow. Where had he put Mu-lan's address and telephone number? Then, fast reaction. 'What do you know about Mostyn anyway?'

'Not exactly blind, deaf, and dumb, Mr. Oakes. All part of the service. Part of the job to keep my eyes open.'

'Yes, but you're not doing a flipping job, are you? Only for me, so you say.'

Griffin hastily swung in the subject's direction. 'Talkin' about jobs. What about this one?'

'Which one?'

'The one we're on now.'

'*We!*' Boysie shouting. 'You mean the one *I've* been on.'

Griffin started, startled at Boysie, a look of respect filling his face. 'You mean you done one? By yerself yer done one? Cor, Mr. Oakes. I knew one day...'

Boysie preened. Why not play it to the limit? 'Like

diving really, isn't it?' he said smugly. 'Once you've done it off the high board and all that.'

But Griffin was cagey. 'What's upset yer then? This spot of trouble?'

Boysie waved his hand in what was meant to be a dismissive motion, oblivious to the fact that his action assumed the aspect of a landed fish. 'A mere bagatelle.' He had read the phrase once in an old novel.

'I see.' A sterner Griffin. 'So what went wrong? Something I gotter clear up?'

'Nothing that can't be handled.' Boysie had started to search the wardrobe. Group Four had easily found the special compartment in the Revelation, the Baby Browning and all the spare ammunition. 'Gone and never called me mother,' Boysie murmured. Then, aloud and strangled, 'Oh no,' remembering that he had put Rosy's address with his private papers in the slim-line Samsonite briefcase. If they had touched that.

'Ah,' said Griffin, cryptic.

'What do you bloody mean—ah?' They *had* tried to force the briefcase, he could tell by the feel and weight. They had tried to open it with the flash mechanism set. Slowly Boysie unlocked the case, his face drooping in agony as the little pile of ashes was revealed.

'Reminds me of the old days.' Griffin over his shoulder. 'The crematorium. Beautiful way to finish up, in one of them loverley urns on the mantel. Always with your family.'

Boysie wasn't listening. How the hell could he get hold of Mu-lan now? The club? What was the name of that blasted club?

'Goin' ter tell me what went wrong or not?' Griffin was at it again.

'For Gawd's sake, shut your flaming cake-hole, you macabre old devil!' Boysie well away. 'Yes. All right. In a minute I'll tell you the whole thing.' The club? *Sexy?*

No, it was not The Sexy even though Warbler had talked about a girl called Sexy. Who was she? Sexy ... Sexy ... Sexy Hexy—that was it. But the club? *Ritz?* Yes. But Ritz something. *Ritz Arsenal?* No. *Cardinal?* No, something *al*, though. *Cannibal? Kursal?* Ritz Kursal. Boysie looked happy again. He tiptoed to the telephone and began to search for Ritz Kursal in the directory. Jotted the number down, dialled with care. No reply. Not surprising as it was only two in the afternoon. Boysie snarled an oath and turned to see Griffin waiting with an impatient look, foot-tapping.

'Ha-ah,' said Boysie with a plastic grin, gritting his teeth. 'And where are you staying, Mr. Griffin?'

'Here, Mr. Oakes. Where else?' Expansive. 'Thought I'd do meself proud this time. On expenses.' A smooth chuckle. Then, 'You goin' to tell me now, are yer? What went wrong like?' Ever so sly. You devil sly.

'Yes,' said Boysie grimly, his mind tampering with the possibility of London HQ ringing through or Warbler turning up: the already planned night-game with Mu-lan spoilt for a second time. 'Yes. I'll tell you. But I think we'll talk in your room, Mr. Griffin. Over a little luncheon perhaps.'

'On expenses,' said Griffin, expressionless.

'Of course. On expenses,' said Boysie, leading Griffin to the door.

'You seem, Mr. Oakes, to have landed yerself—if you don't mind me sayin' so—on what could be termed the 'orns of a dilemma.' Pronouncing the word 'die-leema.'

Boysie nodded, biting his lower lip. For the first time since re-entering the West, he began squaring up to the problems—the cable to Mostyn had merely been re-action. Now he regretted having sent it. Griffin talked on.

'And what do yer intend to do about it, sir? That's the

real question, ain't it?'

Boysie continued to bite his lip and nod in frantic agreement. They sat in Griffin's suite (520), down the hall from Boysie's room, over the remains of what was meant to be a light lunch. Smoked salmon, cold ham and salad, with some fruit, cream, coffee, and a couple of bottles of the Piesporter Goldtröpfchen he had enjoyed so much during dinner with Warbler—Geerusalem, only three days ago. When the meal arrived it turned out to be a banquet over which Boysie poured out the bulk of his troubles to Griffin.

'Yer own bloomin' side lands yer in schtuck. Then the other bloomin' side puts yer right in the sh—in the mire.'

'And I have to be on board Kamikazi Airlines Flight whatever it is in the morning,' replied Boysie. 'Wish to God I'd never sent that bleedin' cable. Better to just walk in on them. Mission completed and all that.'

'You gonna do that? Goin' back to London?'

'Seems the only sensible thing.'

'Sensible. Christ!' said Griffin.

'Why not? What's wrong with getting back to London?'

'If you can't tell me, Mr. Oakes...' Griffin trailed off. 'No that's not really fair is it, sir? Often a bloke on the outside sees things clearer than the bloke on the inside.'

'So what's wrong with returning to London?'

Griffin put on a senior-master look. 'Strikes me there are several contingencies 'ere.' Pompous. 'First there is nothin' viably wrong in your returnin' to London.'

'*Viably* wrong,' repeated Boysie, his face a chart of bewilderment, gazing at the preposterous Griffin.

'Yerse,' said Griffin, posh and all la-di-da. 'Yerse. Nothin' *viably* wrong with it. But as I see things, yer might 'ave some difficulty gettin' to London. See?'

'No.' Boysie placid.

'Do I 'ave to spell it out to yer, Mr. Oakes?' He took a long look at Boysie. 'Yerse. I do reely, don't I? Yer own side set yer up. Right?'

'Right.'

'Then it is just possible, not probable I grant yer, but possible, that they may try it on before yer get 'ome like. While yer still on foreign soil.'

'You mean it would not be so easy in England? Not so easy to get me?'

'It's easy anywhere, Mr. Oakes,' said Griffin gloomily. 'You should know that yerself. No, I felt it might be more to their taste to—well, puttin' it in a nutshell, to dump yer over 'ere.'

'Possible.'

'Yerse. An' it would also seem that yer mate Khavichev's gone and put the boot in an' all. 'E's given yer money and that, 'helped yer escape to the West. But 'e's also made an investment of yer. Right?'

Boysie did not reply.

'Right,' replied Griffin for him. 'Old Khavichev must still 'ave people over 'ere loyal to 'im. They goin' to be watchin' you, Mr. Oakes, you know. If you don't get on that plane tomorrow—the right plane—then they're not goin' to like it.'

'Suppose not.' Boysie feeling the first twitches of the dark, doleful cramp taking hold.

''Ound you, Mr. Oakes. 'Ound you till yer dyin' day. If you'll pardon the expression.'

'I can get the Department to take action from London.'

'If they believes yer. As well they might. They just might,' said Griffin jauntily. 'Then there's always the —er—the—Gorilka faction.'

'Gorilka faction?' Boysie's mind twisting into back spirals.

'May be out gunnin' for yer. May not.' Griffin with a

hint of finality.

'You're a proper little Job's bloody comforter.'

'I do my best, Mr. Oakes, my best.' He paused as though ready to slide a knife through Boysie's ribs. 'You'll not 'ave forgotten the Chinese gentlemen either, will you, sir?'

'The—the Chinese?'

'We don't really know where they stand, do we? Except that they've got yer Mr. Warren. Could know all about you as well. The Chinese. Damn——'

'I know,' said Boysie wearily, 'damn clever, these Chinese.'

Griffin chuckled. 'My little joke, Mr. Oakes. No offence. Strikes me you're in a certain amount of 'ot water from which we will 'ave to try and extricate yer.'

'We? Extricate?'

'I took the liberty o' usin' a sorta royal "we" like. I means *I* shall 'ave to extricate yer. Got any ideas?'

'Friend Griffin.' Boysie looked at the death man, somewhat moved. Griffin was loyal enough to stand by and really assist. 'You'd help me?'

'I'd try, Mr. Oakes. I mean, it wouldn't be right for yer to pay me fare and expenses over 'ere for nothin', would it? So while we're workin' together yer might as well 'ave a full service and pay me fee.'

'Your *fee*?' Bellow.

'Me extricatin' fee.'

'I might have known. Don't you ever do anything for love?'

'Very rarely, sir. I find the times I 'ave done it for people out of—er—respect, or love as you might say, they've let me down somethin' shockin'. Always try to keep things on a business level, sir. You remember that and you don't go far wrong. Now, sir, any ideas?'

'As a matter of fact I have.' Boysie superior; his brain doing some cut-rate overtime. He drew out the American passport, tickets, and itinerary provided by Khavichev. Consulting the Itinerary, Boysie grinned. 'I'm due to leave Tempelhof on Pan American Flight 869 at eleven tomorrow.' (Nasty stomach drop at the thought of flying. Raising fantasies of disaster.) 'Flight 869 takes me to Frankfurt. If you can get an independent booking on that flight and then two tickets on the first aircraft leaving Frankfurt for London after'—he examined the itinerary again—'after mid-day, we can slip at Frankfurt and be back in London before teatime.'

Griffin thought about it. 'Yerse. Not bad. Though they'll probably be watchin' in Frankfurt.'

'We'll be in transit. They can't do much there. Might even take the risk and cable Mostyn to meet me.'

Once again Griffin wrapped himself in a cocoon of cogitation. 'Could work. Might try it. In the meantime you'll just 'ave to 'ole up 'ere.'

'Oh no.' Boysie adamant. 'I've got a date tonight and I'm not going to miss out on this one.'

'Money.' Griffin equally adamant.

'Do what?'

'Me money. Me fare and expenses. If you're goin' to get away with this one, Mr. Oakes, I'm not 'aving you roamin' around Berlin playin' alley cats with some bird. Rather 'ave nothin' to do with it. Me, I'm for 'ome.'

Boysie groaned, seeing, his night's dally with Mu-lan going for the proverbial Burton. The previous strain was hitting him; suddenly he felt very tired. 'Look, Mr. Griffin, I need company.'

'Yer got me, ain't yer?'

'True, but this lady—well, I wouldn't climb over her to get to you.'

'Charmin'.'

'I've been through bloody murder. And I need relaxation. Sleep and then something to set me up.'

'Make yer forget, yer mean?'

'Maybe. I've had it. Had enough. When a man's had enough there're one of two things he can do. Get pissed or get a woman. Me. I prefer the latter, and I've had this one arranged since Saturday. It's all laid on.'

'Laid on. Appropriate,' mouthed Griffin. 'Who is she, this bird?'

'None of your business.'

'It's me business if I'm supposed to be 'elpin' yer.'

Boysie let out a deep breath and a groan of resignation. 'She works in a club.'

''Ostess?'

'Not quite.'

'Don't understand yer, Mr. Oakes. Reely don't understand yer. Yer can get the cream in London. What yer want ter get mixed up with some club girl for?'

'She's a good girl. A nice girl.'

'And yer gotta letch for 'er?'

'We hit it off.' Then lamely, 'She's Chinese.'

'Gawd's truth, yer do pick 'em. In yer state yer go and pick up a Chinese bird. 'Aven't yer got enough troubles?'

'I'm going to see Mu-lan tonight.'

'If I'm goin' ter 'elp yer, then yer not movin' out of this 'otel.'

Boysie's brain slid into some quick cunning turns. 'All right, I'll try to get her round here.'

'Long as I can keep an eye on things. Watch her like.'

Boysie thought again. 'Okay. If I can get her round here, you can watch. From a distance you can watch. Outside the door from a distance. If anything goes wrong, you can be my bodyguard. Get me out of it.'

'As long as the price is right I'll foller yer to the ends of the earth,' said Griffin as though he meant it.

'No need for the ends of the earth. For crying out loud, Mr. Griffin. Look, just keep an eye on me. Make sure I don't land up in some Russian or Chinese cooler. See me through.'

'Don't worry, Mr. Oakes. I'll be right behind you.'

'Well, get cracking. Me, I'm for kip. Got a long night ahead of me.'

Griffin nodded.

Boysie turned and spoke again. 'Oh, and you'd better nip into my room, take the phone off the hook. You can bring my best suit and what the Scriptures call a complete change of raiment as well.'

'Bloody valet now,' commented Griffin, making for the door.

Boysie stretched back on Griffin's bed and lit a cigarette. One long pull on the weed and he became conscious of his aching muscles. Fatigue, mental and physical, broke over him like a series of rolling Pacific breakers. He just had time to reach out and stub the smouldering cigarette into the bedside ashtray before floating into the highly coloured dreams of unsettled sleep.

Mostyn's reaction to Boysie's cable was akin to the symptons produced by an attack from a nest of hornets. He grabbed at the interior telephone—the green one with a direct line to the Chief's office. A brief conversation, with the Second-in-Command's spirits descending into a quagmire. Without doubt the Chief had lunched well and not wisely. When, on invitation, Mostyn reached his superior's office, he discovered a warm glow surrounding the Chief. The Chivas Regal bottle was at the ready.

'C'min, James. Seat. Take a pew, you old ram. A pew what's to do?'

The Chief rarely called Mostyn by his Christian name. When he did either it was the forerunner of disaster or the old boy was sloshed. Mostyn diagnosed the latter.

'Trouble, Chief. Big trouble. I think you should look at this.' He slid the cable across the table, almost upsetting the bottle on the way.

'Watch me pixilatin' Chiv-arse Regal. Fortnums. Three-and-a-half quid a blasted bottle y'have to pay for the damn stuff now.' The Chief gently turned the cable form to face him, moved his head to one side, and closed an eye to get decent focus. *'Client?'* he mumbled, reading with the undue care of one highly alcoholised. *'Your way? Rotten resign? Help immediate? Red and yellow lines? Donkey from forearm? Stop stop stop help? Old-corn?* Dunno a feller called Oldco——' Realisation pulled him into a near sober condition. 'Your boy, Mostyn.' He was shouting. 'Your bloody, half-baked, lecherous, loud-mouthed, bungling, beatnik, cretinous boy. The Oakes boy. Boy Boysie.'

'Quite,' said Mostyn, granite risen from his soul and produced hard from the vocal chords.

'Damned idiot's out.'

'Yes.' A chip of quartz this time.

'Whash it all mean? Bloody elusive cable. Chap off his crumblin' chump? Gone Doolali Tap?'

Mostyn looked down his nose, an action that normally made people uncomfortable (his other trick was staring at a victim's shoes, most off-putting). 'It's a perfectly normal sub-text cable.' Sharp, speaking like one who knows he holds a royal flush in hearts. 'It means, Chief, that something has gone horribly wrong. Iris is dead—we knew that this morning. Thing is——'

'Thing ish——' started the Chief, still under the weather. 'Thing ish we knew Oakes was in the bag s'mornin'.'

'True.' Patient. 'Now he's obviously out of the bag. Done a deal by going double—or at least pretending to. A deal for Redland against the Chinese, and he's out of his depth.' The truth was like a right hook from Mohammed Ali. 'Oh my God! Boysie among the Chinese. Something terribly wrong there. Boysie fighting the Red Guard and the PLA on his own. Rabbit abducted. Something very weird.'

'Get 'im,' said the Chief.

'Kill him?'

'No, you bloody fool. Try to do it subt-subtl—— Tried to do it cunnin' and failed. Get 'im back here. If the feller's had the *nous* to get away, deserves 'nother chance. Go down to Ops and raise Warbler. Oakes back in London, fast.'

Mostyn left the room without replying. He returned fifteen minutes later, face grave as a tomb. A glass bearing traces of Alka-Seltzer stood on the Chief's table. The Chivas Regal had disappeared, and the Chief looked a shade more presentable.

'Well?' from the Chief.

Mostyn's visage immobile, trouble crouching behind each word. 'Warbler has not been seen since Friday, and there's no reply from Oakes's suite at the Bristol Kempinski.'

'Who else've we got in Berlin?' Delivered with a hint of despotism.

Mostyn read the danger signs. 'Warbler's stringer. Man called Gazpacho. Poses as an American sergeant. Been missing since Friday as well. Only the radio man left, and he's no blasted good.'

'Snookered behind the yellow,' remarked the Chief with an air of resigned turmoil. 'Keep tryin' to raise 'em. We'll have to wait. See what happens next. Someone'll have to move, that's certain. One side'll break cover. May even have to go to MI6. Give it twenty-four hours and see.'

The Chief turned and leaned on the windowsill, watching the gloom gather outside. Across the road a young man was having a Jew's friendly with an obstinate traffic warden. The pigeons were doing their stuff on the building opposite; they were probably doing it on the

Special Security building as well. The Chief reflected that everything was heading their way disastrously. Nasty things dropping in the Department's direction. Descending from a great height. The Chief used a word rarely heard off the bridges of Her Majesty's warships.

Gorilka was coming at him, close, so close that the ghastly wrinkles of burnt skin showed up like deep fissures on cracked flagstones. He held a P38 the size of a bazooka. Gorilka's mouth split open, a smile like a jagged, wide surgical incision. The giant P38 burped flame. Boysie felt the thud as the bullet hit hard on his shoulder. There was a death-wish longing for an accurate shot that would put him out of his misery. The one-way ticket to oblivion. Another bang on the same shoulder. Then a voice.

'Come on, Mr. Oakes, sir. Wakey wakey, 'ands orf the joystick. Lovely evenin', moon scorchin' yer eyeballs out. Come on, you lucky lad. Upsey-daisy.'

Boysie emerged from the semi-insensibility of nightmare land, sweat rolling from brow to navel. He raked his fingers, spread wide, through his hair. Soaking with perspiration. His mouth felt like a dungeon, possibly the lower regions of the Bastille circa 1789.

'What the——? Christ!' Looking at the Navitimer. It was nine o'clock.

Griffin stood over him, smirking.

'Nine?' said Boysie sleepily, still concentrating on the watch, which was giving him double-vision trouble. '*Nine!* You haven't let me sleep the whole bloody night?'

'Nine in the evenin', Mr. Oakes. Sleepin' like a babe yer were. Snorin' yer 'ead orf.' Griffin gave his creepy smile. 'I "feex" everythin'.' A pseudo-Mexican accent tinged with Griffin's native cockney.

The phoniness incensed Boysie. 'You "feex"!' Nitric

acid flexing through the words. 'Such as?'

'Tickets. We go on the scheduled flight. The Pan Am. There is a connecting BEA to London from Frankfurt. BE 603. Leaves 12.05, waits for through bookings if there is any delay. Waits up to half an hour. 'Ow about that for organisation? Got yer cannon too.' He threw the P38 on to the bed. It hit the coverlet with a bump and rolled with a spectacular crash to the floor.

'For Christ's sake, go easy.' Nervous—about sixty decibels too high. 'Damn thing's loaded.' Boysie leaned off the bed and picked the weapon from the floor as though handling nitro-glycerine.

'Brought yer suit and change of raimon.'

'Raiment.'

'Raiment,' repeated Griffin.

Boysie gazed at him quizzically. 'Don't think I'll need the suit really if I'm going to lure me little lustrous Chinese lady into Room 504.' Thought wave switching. 'You took the phone off the hook?'

'Personally, as I said.' All very haughty.

'Good. Think I'll ring the club from here.' Boysie slid his legs off the bed and rummaged in his pockets for the telephone number. The paper was crumpled. He had to iron it out on his thigh before dragging a chair to the telephone. This time he got results. The signal buzzed a couple of times, then a voice throaty at the other end.

'Gut evening. Ritz Kursal.'

'Good evening.'

'You are English? Or American perhaps?' Obviously hoping for a GI to fleece.

'English,' Boysie curt. 'Can I speak to Miss Puberty, please?'

Boysie waited. In the background he could hear the beat group. At this distance through the telephone they sounded like a distorted psychedelic LSD record. Scraping as the phone was picked up. Fast, regular breathing, followed by the voice.

'Boysie? You a'right? You safe? It is you, Boysie?'

'Mu-lan?' Dead sentimental.

'Oh, thank God. Ver' much thank God. You a'right?'

'I'm fine.' Soft, mellow, talking as though caressing the erogenous zones: lower lip, throat, waist, ear, inside of elbow. Boysie could not allow himself to think any further.

'I glad, Boysie. I been ver' troubled last two, three days.'

'It's all right now.'

'So worried. In your palm I saw—I saw—most terrible.'

'You saw something else as well?' Boysie throaty.

A long pause. He could almost see the beautiful Chinese girl running her pink tongue lightly across the magnetic lips, moist cosmetic, invitation to more than a dance.

'Yes.' Whisper, a combination of larynx, luxurious shudder, and the still sliding tongue. 'Yes, Boysie. Truth what I tol' you. I not bad girl, but I see in hand.' Hesitation, fire in the telephone mouthpiece. 'I see you and—and myself. You come down to club?'

Boysie's brow crinkled. 'No, Mu-lan. Not the club. I couldn't.' Deeper ridges in the brow, realising he meant it. 'I couldn't watch. Couldn't watch you—your——'

'My performance?'

'Yep.' Quiet. 'The way I feel I couldn't watch you.'

Intake of breath from Mu-lan Tchen. 'That is good. Nicest thing said ever to me.' Silence again before she continued, 'Can we? Can we'—constriction—'can we meet? To——?'

'Be together?'

'I will be good for you, I promise. Strange. Short meeting, but I never feel this with other man.' Hardly audible. 'Never. Never.' Fading into emotional inaudibility.

'Yes.' Straight. 'Me too.'

'I finish midnight. Ha'-past midnight perhaps. You pick me up at club? Truly I have many delights'.

'No.' Rivet firm. 'You come here to me.'

'Your hotel?' Uncertainty behind the query.

'You don't mind, Mu-lan? Please.'

'No. No. It's just—oh, ver' silly. Hotels embarrass me. You in big hotel?'

'Bristol Kempinski.'

'Oh.'

'Darling, don't worry. It's so big no one will notice. Just walk in as though you own the place. Looking like you do, as fabulous as you do, nobody's going to ask questions. Straight up to Room 504. Fifth floor.'

The big decision, the cross-roads, left, right, or straight on, being fought out in the Ritz Kursal phone booth. Unbearable pause with a sliding tributary of sweat moving slow motion from Boysie's hairline down his right cheek.

'I do anything for you, Boysie. I—I——' Forcing words unfamiliar to her. At last they came out, calm and clear. 'I need you.'

'You'll come?'

'I come. After midnight.'

'Soon. Make it soon.'

'As soon as I get away from club.' Realisation filtering. 'Boysie, you called me "darling."'

'It's natural.'

'You good for me. I promise I be your woman. Your woman only.'

A tickle of hesitation itched into the back of Boysie's sex-fuddled mind. Lumbered. A clinger. He waited a moment, shrugged his shoulders, mentally breathing. 'That's show business. Relationships are show business. So it's Chinese this time, and beautiful.' A picture of Elizabeth paused vividly, but momentarily, in his thoughts before commitment. 'After midnight then.'

'Good. I be there, Boysie.'

'See you, darling.'

'Must go. Now must go.' Again the restraint. 'After midnight, Boysie—Boysie darling.' The phone clicked off with the eternal finality of death. Slowly Boysie replaced the receiver, hand hard on the instrument, leaning forward, head down.

'Yer don't 'arf land yerself in it, chum, don'tcher?' Griffin sat back in the armchair, superior eyes fixed on the back of Boysie's neck. 'Always get copped, don'tcher? Birds. Always land yer in the tom. Yer just arsk for it, Mr. Oakes.'

'*Fermez* your flipping *gâteau trou*.'

For the first time Griffin detected a note of true violence in Boysie's voice. 'That's me boy,' he said with a certain amount of pleasure.

They ordered coffee, which eventually arrived with all the Germanic trimmings, and sat around talking spasmodically—Griffin doing most of the word-making. Prattling on, reminiscing about his favourite subjects: the old days as an undertaker and the more palmy times after taking over the construction work of death.

At eleven-thirty Boysie got up. 'Going back to my room now then, Mr. Griffin. Get tidied up for my guest.'

'Mind if I get a breath o' fresh air 'fore I start me vigil?' Griffin was all smiles.

'I'm paying you big dough to have you close.' Boysie put out by Griffin's reluctance to stay with the job.

'Lock yer door and don't let anyone in. 'Cept the bir— young lady, of course. Back in twenty minutes. Just want a breather. Walk around the block and 'ave a look at the sights.'

Boysie gave a symbolic shrug.' Make sure it's only twenty minutes.'

'Faithfully, I gives yer me word.' Griffin raised two fingers in a V to his forelock. 'Cubs' honour.' He approached the door. 'Eh, they don't 'arf go in for this ban-the-bomb stuff 'ere, don't they?'

'Ban the bomb?' Boysie turned, sharply puzzled.

'Yeah, sign's a bit twisted up but must 'ave cost a packet, revolvin' on topper that big building.'

'What are you talking about?' Impatient.

'That bloody great ban-the-bomb sign twirling on topper that place near the bombed-out church down the bottom of the Kurfürsten-whatname. Thing they always use in them spy pichers.'

'Ban the Bomb.' Razor sarcasm. 'That's the blooming Mercedes-Benz building. The Merc symbol is the whirly-gig. Ban the bomb.' Contemptuous.

Boysie followed Griffin's instructions and locked the door of 504 on return, checked that the telephone was off the hook, looked under the bed and in the wardrobe, then tested the window catches. Shave, shower, and liberal application of Brut (sales slogan—*After Shave, After Shower, After Everything*). 'Before everything,' he murmured, between humming snatches of 'Mack the Knife.' 'Be prepared,' he said loudly, looking into the mirror—the mental process set off by Griffin's previous Cub salute. Grey silk pyjamas with red piping by Budd, slippers on and a shuffle through to the bedroom, picking up the short black quilted smoking jacket. As he started to swing it on, Boysie caught a glimpse of himself in the wardrobe mirror; quick thought that the grey streaks had become more prominent on the sides of his hair. Boysie grinned, slid his arms into the jacket sleeves, then took the risk of using the phone to order a couple of Moët '59 magnums. After leaving the telephone off the hook again, he carefully inspected the murderous-looking P38, making sure it was loaded with safety catch on, and slipped the weapon within easy reach under the bed. He stretched out full length and checked the time. Ten minutes past midnight. At twenty past the champagne arrived, and at two minutes after the half hour (he was lying with eyes cemented to the Navitimer) came a low tapping on the door. Boysie moved like a leopard, slowed as he reached the door, pausing to compose himself.

'Who is it?' Lips close to the keyhole.

'Me. Mu-lan. Boysie?' The unmistakable accent.

She looked even more desirable than his memory recalled. The shining pitch of hair, light striking off the olive complexion of her oval face, figure unbelievable under the tight green and gold cheongsham. At the club Boysie had only briefly noticed her eyes. Under the pencil-slim arches of eyebrow the almond pupils seemed deeper than he remembered. Now they held him with utter adoration, deep, boring through his own eyes, making contact with the brain neutrons. The signals came through at maximum strength, flashing messages old as time to all nerve centres and organs. Mu-lan moved quietly into the room and shut the door behind her.

'Oh, Boysie, it is so good, so good to see you 'gain.'

It was all she said before her arms twined like luscious baby boa constrictors round his neck. Her mouth closed on Boysie's in the kiss of eternal life with variations, bodies so close they seemed to be dissolving into each other. The kiss lasted a full two minutes, then a break, but still holding close, smooth skin of cheek upon cheek, Mu-lan's heavy breathing in Boysie's ear, bellies and things moving, writhing, trying to intermingle. At last they broke away. Boysie held her shoulders, stepping away and looking at her, gulping the form, face, and eyes in massive brainfuls. The eyes, the almond eyes, plunging into his soul. (Was it Rupert Brooke? He was not talking about eyes, but what was the line? 'Granchester?' The village schoolroom smelling of chalk and flora collected on nature rambles. A twelve-year-old Boysie standing up and reciting the previous night's homework.

Brooke's 'Granchester.' A line somewhere? The line? Mu-lan's eyes above the mouth slightly parted in a gasp of sensuality. But the eyes. Brooke? Coming. Coming. Not about eyes. Not even almond eyes. Green. Water. Yes. *Beside the river make for you*—that's it—*A tunnel of green gloom, and sleep/Deeply above; and green and deep/The stream mysteriously glides beneath,/Green as a dream and deep as death.* Change it, and there were Mu-lan's eyes. *Almond as a dream and deep as death.* Sorry, Rupie baby, but they were Mu-lan's eyes you were writing about, not just if there was still honey for tea, and the church clock standing at two-fifty.)

'Oh, Boysie. It is so good to be with you. So, so good.' She broke his train of consciousness—which was heading on to a branch line anyway.

'You don't know how good it is to see *you*, little Chinese Mu-lan Tchen.' As he said it, Boysie mentally noted that he must relock the door.

'I be your woman? Yes?'

'My woman.' Affirmative.

'What the English boys call them? Like me? Birds. I be your bird, Boysie.'

Boysie smiled, unforced; for a change he was not putting on the big act, the massive seductive sophist. 'Okay. My Chinese bird. My Chinese pigeon.'

'*Baak gup.*'

'Back up?'

Tinkle of stereo laughter. '*Baak gup.* Chinese for pigeon.'

'Okay, Mu-lan. *Baak gup.* Drink?'

'Must we, my so good Boysie?'

'Champagne.'

'Oh well.' Mu-lan's bell of joy again.

They finished one magnum of the Moët, talking, verbally making love. There was joy, sentimentality, nostalgia, fear for the future, and the divine feeling of being 'a little lower than the angels.' Boysie had no qualms about Elizabeth. Now she seemed cold, unreal, far away and never been when you put her against this throbbing live girl. Mu-lan finished the dregs in her last glass of champagne and stretched a hand towards Boysie's thigh. The fingers stroked like a warm beach breeze, zephyrised. 'You ge' into bed, Boysie. I clean up, then come to you. Show what kin' o' woman I be to you.'

Boysie reached out for her, but Mu-lan had moved away with a fast swerve from the bed. The laugh again. 'I show you what Chinese woman can do for man.'

In spite of himself, Boysie was burning hot, trembling. Was this it? How many had he had? Fourscore and ten? Christ, double that; treble it and think of the number you first thought of. If he sat for a day making a list he would never get them all down. Boysie took off the jacket and hoisted himself between the sheets. Some he could remember, would never forget. The first—you always remember the first. Sixteen years old, a haystack, pain and tears. Iris he would not forget, nor Chicory Triplehouse. Others he would rather not even think about. Water running from behind the bathroom door. The water stopped. Silence. The long wait and then the door opening.

She had unpinned her hair so that it hung, a black waterfall, down to the velvet shoulders. Boysie could hear his heart and feel the quiver run from ears to thighs. Mu-lan's figure was even more perfect than he had imagined when he last saw her at the club. She walked slowly towards the bed, upright and without the overlay of conscious sex which was part of her strip trade onstage.

'Am I right for you?' Husky. The tone did not deny the truth that she really did need him. 'They tell me men like their girls partly dressed.' She wore only a milk-white brassière and tight plain briefs, nylon and transparent.

'Quickly.' All Boysie could force from his throat.

She climbed into the bed her left hand deftly pressing the table-lamp switch. Darkness and two bodies close. The brassière off, briefs slowly pulled down, while Mulan's fingers, moving with the delicate touch of apple blossom drawn over flesh, undid buttons and tugged gently at the pyjama cord. 'Let me, Boysie. Lie still. I give you all a man could want.'

Fingers slid between twin pairs of thighs, lips and tongues spun and twisted, stroked and hardened. Boysie felt as though a tightly wound spring, low between his legs, had been released. Now they were the same person. Two into one. One being vibrating, hard, panting, murmuring, the creak of the bed, the whispered words, and the moaning shudder.

Three times it happened, and Boysie, the experienced, the know-all-about-it Boysie, the sexual expert, became conscious of the terrifying truth that until this moment he had known nothing at all. After the third time they just lay whispering, wrapped, arms and legs twisted in a fantastic human sculpture. And so into the tranquil, satisfied, dreamless sleep, cushioned by exhausted joy.

The shriek slashed through Boysie's dark unconsciousness. Horror, sudden, like a cut-throat razor slicing across the carotid artery. Again and again. Boysie came out of the drifting pleasure of sleep with a lightning flash to full consciousness. Mechanically he turned towards Mulan. The beautiful almond eyes were wise with fear, looking beyond him with mouth half open to emit the next scream. Everything happened quickly. Boysie swivelled in the bed, his hand moving down for the P38. As he turned he caught an impression of a figure; a hand, fingers together, thumb extended, bearing down on Mu-lan's mouth to stifle the oncoming scream. From somewhere else another hand grasped Boysie's wrist. He was off balance but still managed to pull down with force, then up quickly, throwing his wrist away from the leverage and the clamped fingers. The action worked. The grip was released and a short body fell heavily against the bed. Boysie sprang on to the floor—a crouched position, flexed to take off against the attacker. His eyes did a fast circle of the room. The answer came back negative. To fight back meant complete defeat.

There were four of them, all small, with Eastern faces, almost certainly Chinese. One held Mu-lan, struggling, against her pillow. Boysie's man was making a quick recovery from the bed; another leaned against the door, arms folded. The fourth was about five paces from the bed to Boysie's right; he held a heavy automatic with its dangerous circular eye centrally positioned on Boysie's forehead.

Boysie's original assailant was back on his feet. He also had a gun out. Nausea rose unpleasantly from Boysie's esophagus; the old shakes setting in. The familiar trouble. Christ. He clenched his teeth, mind fumbling for the next move. But the brain would not function on an aggressive line. Typically, Boysie looked from one automatic pistol to the other. Identical. Probably the Chinese version of the Russian Tokarev 51. Bloody hell, what does it matter? What to do? Thoughts were side-tracking, branching off into inconsequentialities.

The Chinese whom Boysie had thrown spoke. 'Mr. Oakes, your friend Mr. Warren wishes to see you. You are to come with us.' Voice and face both dead as stiffs on marble slabs.

Boysie did not reply. He looked from one man to the other in turn. All wore grey suits and similar raincoats. Each had the same expression. Callousness combined with deadly efficiency.

The leader turned his head slightly towards the operator holding Mu-lan's head on to the pillow. '*La.*' Almost an aside, nodding towards the struggling figure. Mu-lan's captor made an almost imperceptible chop with his right hand, landing behind the girl's left ear. Mu-lan gave a minute grunt and went limp.

Boysie straightened and began to move.

'No, Mr. Oakes. Stop.'

Boysie stopped. 'If you've——'

'Killed her? No. Unconscious for ...?' He looked questioningly towards the man who had struck Mu-lan. '*To mo?*'

'One hour, comrade,' his partner answered in English.

'One hour,' repeated the leader, irritated at being shown up.

Boysie looked at each of the men in turn. Impossible to tell them apart. Saffron quadruplets.

'Now you get dressed.' Movement of the automatic pistol.

Boysie, mind fluctuating again, thought the guy spoke English with frightening accuracy. Get dressed? What to do? Obedience. The only answer. Then wait for his chance. Concentration now back on its normal narrow-gauge track; the Chinese were either going to kill or abduct him. Whichever, it entailed getting him out of the hotel. Slipping them in the process? Maybe. Chance anyway.

As he walked to the bathroom (picking up clothes on the way) with one of the intruders close behind, Boysie felt a surge of rage against Griffin. What the hell was he up to? Keeping an eye on him. Bodyguard. Boysie guard. That was the job. Well-paid job. Griffin was on to the Nelson touch. ('The Admiral clapped his telescope to his blind eye and said, "I see no something signal."' Or words like that.)

Boysie took his time dressing.

'No need to shave,' the Chinese said when Boysie picked up his razor.

'Don't worry, I'm not going to slice myself. Harry Caraway or whatever you call it.'

'Hara-kiri is Japanese suicide custom. We Chinese.' This one was not as perfect with the Anglo-Saxon as his chief.

Boysie altered to the pompous frequency as he started to lather his face. 'The British soldier is taught to shave daily in the field. I presume we are in the field—a bog rather than a meadow, I admit.'

The stocky Chinese was not following Boysie's ham humour but took no action as the shaving progressed. He looked on indifferently while Boysie donned clean underwear, light grey shirt, favourite Oleg Cassini tie, and the dark green worsted. To set the effect there were his most provocative cuff-links—the ones with two pairs of feet, one set pointing upwards wide apart, and the others close together, centred downwards.

Mu-lan still lay unconscious, breathing deeply, when they returned to the bedroom. The four men's faces were unchanged. No fraction of humour. Only the deadly mask quality. There was something minutely different about the room that took a minute to figure. The small writing table had been pulled centrally into the space between bed and window, with a stand chair placed in front. The table was set for one—a deep soup plate and spoon. There was extra baggage also, unnoticed before: a bulky leather briefcase.

The commander of the party spoke. 'Mr. Oakes, we have a long journey. You have not had breakfast?'

'No.'

'Then you need some sustenance.' Turning to the man still leaning against the door, 'Pong.'

The lounger straightened up.

'Remiss of me, Mr. Oakes.' The party boss sounded

polite though the eyes remained enigmatic. 'Very remiss of me. I have not introduced my colleagues. 'This'— hand towards the doorman—'is Mr. Pong.'

And I thought I had troubles with my initials, thought Boysie.

The leader continued, indicating the interloping bathroom guard. 'Mr. P'ao Shou. The other gentleman is Mr. Ch'ing Suan. I am Li Chi.'

'Hi.' Boysie holding back latent fear, raising his right hand in a fast circle of greeting. 'And Mr. Warren wants to see me?'

'Among others. General Kuan Hsi Shi, our director, wishes to talk to you also.'

'Director?'

'Yes.'

'Of the Jen Chia? Your espionage network?'

'Perceptive, Mr. Oakes. The Jen Chia.' Nod.

'In Albania?' Boysie trying to make it ice-box cucumber cool.

'A small distance away from Albania. A few thousand miles. But in this age of extraordinary travel, what is that?'

'Yeah.' Boysie looked glumly at the armoury still hanging around in people's hands. Breakfast, they said. If he could get someone else into the room. Even a waiter. He grinned like a toothpaste commercial. 'You're right, I haven't eaten breakfast. Will you join me? I'll ring down.' Half a pace towards the telephone. Mr. P'ao Shou's automatic swung in the classic back-hand pistol-whip movement, fast but without force, metal burning cold against Boysie's cheek, the muzzle nicely positioned to take the whole of his left ear away, and probably a large portion of the occipitalis and auricularis superior muscles with it. It snapped across Boysie's mind to try a couple of disarming moves. Instead he played at being a waxwork. Safer. Li Chi looked at him. Waxworks were on Boysie's mind; he was sure that the expressionless face of Li Chi was done in the Chamber of Horrors at Madame Tussaud's. Or was it in that place on Times Square, New York?

'No need for the room service for breakfast, Mr. Oakes. We have brought excellent delicacy which will see you through the day. Very sustaining.' He motioned to Pong, who clicked the briefcase open and drew out a Thermos flask, which he shook vigorously.

Li Chi spoke again. 'Maybe you think this strange for breakfast but I promise it is unique. Give great strength to your journey ahead.' Pong was pouring a steaming grey-brown soup into the tin bowl.

'What the hell's this?' Aghast was the only word for Boysie's inflection.

'Most invigorating. Special mushroom soup.'

'Mushroom? Toadstool most likely. Not for me, Mr. Li Chi. No. If you're going to kill me, do it quick. With a bullet. You've got enough hardware.'

'Kill you?' Li Chi wonderingly. 'Who wishes to kill you?'

'Okay, the pistols would be a bit noisy.'

'Always silencers,' interpolated P'ao Shou.

'Fool.' Li Chi showed emotion for the first time. Anger. 'Where you do your training, Shou? At Western spy movies? No such things as silencers. Do not underrate, Mr. Oakes. He knows such things.'

'Well, I'm not sitting here gulping down poison soup.'

Li Chi sighed. 'If we really wanted to kill you there are other silent methods.' Boysie's eye caught a movement from Comrade Ch'ing Suan. From his raincoat Ch'ing Suan took a heavy Walther LP-53 air pistol and a wooden cocking grip. With the grip he pulled down on the tightly sprung barrel. He returned the cocking grip to his pocket. The hand came out again, this time holding a clear plastic cylindrical phial between thumb and forefinger. He raised it to the level of his nose, eyes tracking in on Boysie. Through the plastic Boysie saw a blue-feathered air-gun dart, point down, resting on a circle of foam rubber.

'A little old hat, but a curare-tipped dart from an air pistol is still very quiet. Induces peacefulness. Eternal.'

'Old hat but it works,' agreed Boysie. Nothing could disguise the tonal quiver. 'Old hat? Your English is exceptional, Mr. Li Pee——'

'Chi.'

'Okay. Chi. For a Chinese your English is pretty collopial.'

'Colloquial you mean, Mr. Oakes.' The Chinese smiled. 'Naturally it is good. Harrow and Trinity, old boy. Trinity, Cambridge, of course.'

'Of course.' Sickly perplexity.

Silence. Ch'ing Suan still held the nine-and-a-half inches of barrel that was still broken ready for loading. Li Chi and P'ao Shou gripped their automatics with a dangerous diffidence, while Pong stood gently rubbing his hands together, palm to palm, then crossed palm to back, nasty movements predicting that Pong, if called upon, could do most unattractive things to the human body.

'Please drink your soup, Mr. Oakes.' Gentle pressure on Boysie's right arm from Li Chi, pushing towards the table.

'If we wanted to kill you we could do it without any fuss, here and now. I want you to be fit for the journey, old chap. The soup is a real gourmet's dish, made from specially cultured Mexican mushrooms. There's a good fellow. Drink it while it's hot, eh?'

'Hobson's choice.' Boysie sat down like a man with inflamed haemorrhoids, took a shallow spoonful of the liquid, and sipped. It was exceptionally tasty, but Boysie was determined to remain awkward. 'It could do with a shade more seasoning,' he said.

Li Chi turned to Pong. 'Salt and pepper for Mr. Oakes.' Pong's briefcase came into play. 'Black or white pepper?' enquired Li Chi.

'Black, I think.' Boysie playing at being Robert Carrier casing a restaurant.

Pong placed a wooden pepper mill and salt cellar on the table and Boysie camped it up—a sprinkle of salt, a grind of pepper, a sip, an additional soupçon of pepper. Another sip. A nod of pleasure. Visage serious.

Five minutes and Boysie had spooned up the last mouthful.

'Good.' Licking lips. 'Excellent. Magnifico.'

The Chinese all showed signs of preoccupation with their watches.

'We must go now. Quickly I'm afraid.' Li Chi.

There was a harsh pop from behind Boysie. Heart leap, but it was only Ch'ing Suan closing the air pistol and unloading, firing empty at the floor. Boysie had the feeling of 'what the hell.' He would play along. Might lead to something. The crocus foursome did not seem to be life-takers—as far as he was concerned anyway.

In the car park Boysie caught sight of his Jensen as they edged him carefully towards the black Merc 200 SE. It was a fine day, a slight chill, but sun and no sign of clouds. Pong took the wheel with P'ao Shou beside him. Boysie sat comfortably in the back between Li Chi and Ch'ing Suan. Feeling of mild elation and acute awareness that Li Chi was constantly glancing at his watch. The car started and they rolled out, heading on to the Kurfürstendamm.

'Going by air, I suppose?' Boysie unperturbed. Unconsciously he registered surprise at the lack of fear. Then sun became brighter and hotter. Li Chi looked at his watch once more. 'To be fair, Mr. Oakes, I think I should give you a small warning.'

'Oh?' No sense of worry.

'Nothing to be afraid of. Nothing at all, but your mushroom soup was made from a particular Mexican mushroom which contains undeniably mystic qualities. I tell you this so that you will not get frightened if you happen to experience a few odd sensations.'

Definite interest on Boysie's part—no anxiety. 'Oh? What kind of sensations?'

'Nothing much. You have heard the word psychedelic?'

This time an upsurge of panic. 'Hallucinations? Dope which brings on hallucinations? I knew that bloody soup was spiked. You've been feeding me—what's it called? LSD? Lysergic acid. That damn drug. You could kill me.' Shrieked.

'Calm yourself. No one is going to kill you. And we have not given you LSD. There is a relationship, but nothing to worry about. In fact, some years ago a Dr. Hoffman ate thirty-two of these very same mushrooms. He was perfectly all right.'

Boysie had a mental picture of some greybeard scoffing a huge platter of red, white, and blue fungi. The late Walt Disney kind of mushrooms.

'You will be unharmed,' continued Li Chi. 'We only used thirty in your soup. The ancient Aztecs ate them all the time even though they do contain a drug—teonanacatl. It may make you lose a sense of time and place, that's all.'

Boysie could hardly hear the last word. He glanced out of the car window, at a white and blue sign pointing them towards Tempelhof airfield, yet something was wrong. The buildings. He was in Berlin but this was not Berlin. The glare of sun pierced like a flame thrower. Light rebounded from stucco walls. White, flat roofs. Now a church. Not German. Boysie had never been to Mexico but this was recognisably a Mex-Spanish appearance, the white and red shades, cloisters, tall oblong campanile. There were sombreros? Ponchos? Bright skirts along the pavements. Germans? Stupid? Perhaps some carnival? A parade? An office block changed dimensions. Desperately Boysie screwed up his eyes and shook his head. Berlin. Berlin. He was in Berlin. Yet the office block rose decorated in fantastic whirls, patterns, murals. Between the buildings he glimpsed mountains, aridity. Boysie turned towards Li Chi. The man was not the Li Chi who had been seated there a few moments before. This man's features were visibly altering, nose straight, face broadening, skin pigmentation darkening, and the smooth Chinese hair changing into a long, coarse mane. The whole body transmogrified. Li Chi looked at Boysie. This was not a Chinese. A Mexican Indian. An Aztec. Something long gone. A high priest. The whole interior of the murk twisted, focus zooming in and out, warping. For Boysie it was as though he were watching some fantastic movie by a tricksy director. The remaining Chinese were also transmogrified, facially, bodily— even clothes. All were Mexican Indians. Even the car was not a car. They still moved smoothly enough but with a slight wavering motion. Then it was a car again. The Indian who had been Pong switched on the radio. Klemperer was whipping hell out of the Berlin Philharmonic, and the Berlin Philharmonic was bashing the blazes out of Wagner—'The Ride of the Valkyrie.'

Boysie's auditory system was all to blazes. 'Always liked old Herb Alpert and the Tijuana Brass,' he said, tapping away with his right foot and meaning it.

A grunt from the Mex who had been Li Chi. The car was not a car again. This time he got it. A canoe. They were riding fast over broad smooth waters in a canoe. Plains and hills on either side, and clumps of buildings in the distance, Persil clean. A bunch of *charros*—those incredible Mexican horsemen—galloped past, waving, the horses' hooves billowing up clouds of red dust. Land again, and the Indians 'helped him from the canoe. Colours. The mind. Mind. Colours in brilliant distinction and distortion. Smiling faces suddenly pocked with deep blue circles. A wide stretch of black turning to green, then black again. Silver. Big and silver. Wings. Grotesque. A great winged silver creature ahead. The ground kept tilting. The bird's beak flashing in the sun. Focus. No focus. Enormous bird. What? Some immense harpy eagle sprayed silver. Harpy eagles were Mexican birds. Could be. But this size? Nearer. Wasn't there an Aztec god? Ridiculous. Read it somewhere. The Plumed Serpent, God of Learning. Really close now, nothing but pulsating stacks of feathers so bright that Boysie could not open his eyes fully. Everything shone. Blistered with silver. They were walking up into the bird, right up some orifice, a dark well which changed to red. Crimson. Only the outlines of the four Mexican Indians, and he could smell the red, a light perfume getting stronger and stronger. Actually smell colours.

The bird was in a fury of noise. Unbearable roaring. Red changing to violet. Violet to black. Suddenly white. White and black, curving-thrusting-whirling past him. A tiny spot of purple growing larger and larger, striped with white. Forming a barrier around him so that he was being drawn into the colours, each with its own smell and noise. Electronic noise. 'Musique Concrète' reversed on a tape. Far away, then so loud that he had to clamp his hands over his ears. Red once more. Crimson. Gallons of blood into which he was being pulled. Terror. Hysteria within. He was not a person any more. Not an individual but a colour. Red. Blue. Gold. Gold. More gold. There was not any more gold. Red flecks in the gold. The red flecks were himself. He was a series of red flecks spreading into a Cineramic pattern, pieces of his body and mind dragged magnetically into this screen of colour. The screen altered. The colour now elliptical. Sounds changed. Colour fading. A purr. A hum. His hand on his knee in focus. Heartbeat strong. The purr louder. People. Normality and a sense of relief. He was sitting in the Jensen, only someone else was driving. A voice. Shouting.

'He's coming round, it's okay.'

Another voice from in front. 'Good timing. I'm going in now.'

Christ, thought Boysie, looking at the instrument panel, they've cut me bloody steering wheel in half. Eyes not yet in focus. Li Chi sat beside him. Was it still the Merc and not the Jensen? No. A low range of mountains below. The four Chinese were there with him, seated in a pattern of five as on a playing card, and it was a light aircraft not a car. Losing height, the mountains (high hills really) dipping away to the right. Below and in front, a scatter of ragged fields. A runway, short and cleaving through dirty yellow grass. Pong shifted his left foot, aligning the plane on the centre of the runway, nose angled and the motor throttle back. Lower and lower over the fields, a grey tracklike road to the left, no traffic. Nearly touching the grass. In front to the right, a long sprawl of buildings. Boysie, normally terrified by any kind of flying, particularly on take-off or landing, merely experienced extreme thankfulness at being alive. The runway threshold coming up.

'You feel okay now?' from Li Chi.

'Mushroom soup.' Boysie made the words sound vomit-ridden.

'You experienced the Mexican phenomena? Everything Mexican? Then the colour symptoms?' Li Chi speaking loudly, asking with grave interest.

Boysie closed his eyes and shook his head as though trying to dislodge a wasp from his ear. 'I was a colour. Lots of colours. That stuff's bleeding dangerous. Turn you mad.'

Pong was a good pilot. Only a slight judder as they touched down and started their ride across the narrow piece of concrete.

'Where are we?' asked Boysie.

'Does it matter?' Li Chi putting on the inscrutable style. 'Time and space have had no meaning for you in the last hours. Like an anaesthetic. Amazing, that teonanacatl, eh?'

'Where are we?' Boysie repeating the question, hard. The dazed state passing quickly.

'China.' Li Chi blandly.

'You're joking. *China!*' Shouted. 'How long have I been——'

'In the psychedelic state? For many hours. Three long aircraft rides.'

'Where in China?' Still disbelief.

'It doesn't really matter, but not far from Peking.'

'Peking? I don't sweating well believe it.'

'As you prefer.' Li Chi indifferent.

They were slowing to a halt, taxiing over the grass. Boysie began to take in the surroundings. The low hills, trees, unfamiliar architecture of the buildings—even those obviously prefabricated. All had an alien atmosphere. Bumping over the grass towards the sleek black car. It had a hint of the large version of the Peugeot 404, certainly the body work was inspired by Farina, but the whole thing was bigger, heavier, four doors, roomy. Boysie's memory index pinpointed—it was a Chinese-built Red Flag. The aircraft stopped. Edging off. Two more Chinese climbed out of the car—blue denim uniforms, cheap peaked caps. Boysie was helped from the aircraft, and as soon as his feet touched the grass the quiet politeness of Li Chi and his associates vanished. The pair from the car, one either side of him, gripped in effective come-along armlocks. Four arms twisted expertly and painfully hard up behind his back.

'Now you meet General Kuan Hsi Shi, Oakes.' Li Chi aggressive. 'A pleasant surprise. Into the car.' He added a few words to the guards, and Boysie found himself, still held tightly, in the rear of the automobile. The ride was fast—the interior of the car tinny and utilitarian—ending at the entrance to a three-story building surmounted by a typically ornate hexagonal roof, emblazoned with Chinese characters in blood-red. Boysie got the big hustle again. A long corridor, short flight of steps, and a door from behind which came the sound of non-harmonic music echoed in stereo.

Li Chi opened the door. He spoke in English. 'The prisoner Oakes, Comrade General.'

'Enter.' The voice was familiar, and Boysie was jostled through the door into a spacious office. The trappings were a blend of East and West: one wall completely decorated with weapons juxtaposed with two large crudely painted pictures. Boysie's quick glance picked out a 38 Special, a Colt 45, and a Japanese 8-mm. Nambu. The music came from stereo speakers set at right angles on opposite sides of the long wall facing the door. In the centre of the room a big ornate oblong desk, minutely tidy, complete with coloured telephones, intercom, and a small television.

The man at the desk had his back to the door, sitting in a swivel chair swung round to face the rear wall and a five-by-seven-foot green board on which were pinned photographs. LBJ, Harold Wilson, Mr. Kosygin, and Bobby Kennedy were recognisable. So, to Boysie's amazement, was a clear copy of Mostyn's face, Warren's, and his own. The man at the desk raised his right arm. The hand held an air pistol. Thunk, and a small red dart smacked into the board, placed accurately between the eyes on Boysie's photograph.

'Nice to see you again,' said General Kuan Hsi Shi,

swinging round after the manner of tycoons on television. For a moment Boysie did not recognise him. The drooping moustache had gone, revealing a partly Oriental face, not fully Chinese.

'Sit down,' said the General, smiling. 'I look different? *Ja*, Herr Oakes?'

General Kuan Hsi Shi was Boysie's Berlin contact. The erratic, amusing Warbler.

A movement behind Boysie to the left. A hand touching his shoulder. A voice whispering, 'Now I can get even about that foot, buddy.'

'You remember our friend Gazpacho?' General Warbler Kuan Hsi Shi looked past Boysie at the American sergeant. 'He is my chief aide: American born, but we know him as Shi T'ung K'u. And that, Oakes, L, Boysie, Brian Ian, Number 267953, Major of the British Department of Special Security—that can be translated in one English word—Tormentor.'

VI. CAT

Helter skelter, hang sorrow,
care'll kill a cat, up-tails all,
and a louse for the hangman.
                              Jonson,
              Every Man in His Humour

'I DEMAND to see the British Consul.' It was the only thing
Boysie could think of, and it sounded flat and preposterous against this bizarre situation—his Department
contact, as German as sauerkraut, turning out to be a
Chinese Intelligence officer. A general. And then this son-
of-a-bitch American, Gazpacho, the Tormentor. The
People's Liberation Army, Red Guards, hallucinatory
drugs, a rubble of confusion. The whole party, started
from the Chief's office in Whitehall, had turned into the
biggest con game since the gullible tourist had been sold
the Tower of London. Boysie dizzily faced the flood of
facts. He was the patsy, the universal fall guy of all
time.

'It must be all strange for you, Boysie. Difficult to
comprehend. But, as the Christian Bible says, "In the
fullness of time all things shall be accomplished."'
Warbler wore the same blue denim uniform as the two
soldiers who had frog-marched Boysie into the office. Of
course the quality of the denim was better and the cut
almost as good as anything from Savile Row. He leaned
forward to switch off the stereo set. 'I prefer Shosta-
kovitch myself'—smiling—'but that is considered deca-

dent.' Hand thumping the table at the final syllable. 'You wish to see your Consul. There is an Embassy and an Ambassador in Peking. Not far from here, but quite honestly we would rather keep this in the family. Our little family.'

'How come you're a German *and* a Chinese, General?' Boysie weak and beginning to lower himself into a chair before Warbler's desk. Gazpacho's fingers closed about his neck, pulling upwards. 'Stay on your feet, bud.'

'Oh, it's all right, K'u. Let him sit.' A pause augmented with a grin powerful enough to turn Frankenstein green with envy. 'For the meantime he can sit.'

Boysie sat, a heap of dejection. He looked around. Grief, those pictures were atrocious. Children's drawings in garish colours with overt, simple revolutionary messages. Below one of them hung a scroll of Chinese characters looking like preliminary architect's drawings for some new housing estate.

'What's that mean?' All track of the predicament and seriousness of his circumstances seeping from Boysie.

'Quotation from the great leader. From Chairman Mao. Translation: *This army has an indomitable spirit and is determined to vanquish all enemies and never to yield.*'

'Thought you'd had troubles over Mao's doctrines.'

'Chairman Mao's battle and thought will always continue. If it came to it, we would continue underground. You asked how I can be German and Chinese. In fact I am Chinese. Officially. I am a believer——'

'Good number. The Monkees. Top of the hit parade earlier in the year,' muttered Boysie.

'—a believer that China will, as Chairman Mao has always maintained, eventually master the world.' Warbler bit lightly on his right-hand index finger. 'You ask how I can be Chinese when I am so obviously German.'

'It's not so obvious now. I can see you're a mongrel.'

'Mongrel is good. And right.'

'The answer is easy. German father and Chinese mother. Mixed marriage.'

Warbler sighed. 'Unfortunately no marriage. A convenient arrangement, that is all.' He allowed himself another smile. 'Funny, it all happened in Paris. They were both students——'

Gazpacho interjected, 'Shouldn't we be getting on with the biz?'

Warbler placed his hands together in an attitude of prayer. 'Yes. There is not much time and many questions.'

'Your snatcher said Warren wanted to talk with me?' Time was a factor Boysie should play on.

'Oh dear.' Warbler saddened. 'They are such liars, those men. Warren is here. I doubt if he is in a fit condition to talk with you. But I suppose they were telling the truth. In a warped way. I am certain he would like to talk with you. You will see him. But there are matters which must be cleared up.'

'You're not kidding. There are things I want to know as well. That firing-range farce. Was that your fix?'

Warbler nodded. 'We had to play you along.'

'And the dummy ammunition? The dummies in East Berlin so that I couldn't carry out the operation even if I wanted to?'

Warbler silent, choosing the correct sentence. 'Yes, it was us. But that still does not rule out the fact that you were being sent on a suicide mission anyway.' He waved his hand, dismissing that portion of the events. 'What we really want to know is your connection with the Warren business. What you talked about with Khavichev. Why you were allowed to leave the East at all after facing such grave charges. Also, how much you know. If you know as much as Warren.'

'Look.' Boysie thrashing around with his fingers and

153

hands. 'Okay. I was sent in to do a job. Subversive activities between Great Britain and the USSR. We wanted Warren out, they wanted Iris in.'

'Iris MacIntosh?' Warbler.

'Yeah. Iris MacIntosh. We couldn't afford to let her go. It was the only way. Sure they arrested me. But there was no evidence. I wasn't caught in the act. They couldn't make it stick. The Ambassador intervened. They let me out, then your hoodlums jumped me, souped me up with Aztec purple hearts, and I ended up here. I *want* to see the Ambassador.' Why should he tell them about his talks with Khavichev? High-powered suppositories to the lot of them.

'You cannot see the Ambassador, I must make that plain. And you expect me to believe you knew nothing of the information Warren was taking out of Moscow?'

'How could I?'

'Through Khavichev. The information concerned us.'

'You mean the Jen——'

'The Jen Chia. Chinese Intelligence. You know that much.'

'I'm trained.'

Warbler shrugged. The two guards nudged in on the chair. Gazpacho moved round the desk to stand behind Warbler, who stared with a freezing scepticism at Boysie. 'Why then were you booked to fly to Albania? To Tiranë?'

'I was routed back to London. Via Frankfurt.'

'I want to know how much of Warren's information you have and what went on between yourself and Khavichev.' As an aside he added, 'You know Khavichev has been arrested and returned to Moscow?'

Boysie did not speak, lowering his head. Damned if he was going to tell them.

'It is very strange,' continued Warbler. 'The truth we need.' Five seconds by the sweep hand of the Navitimer.

'One way or another. You see, all sources of this information must be cut off. We must have the truth.'

Boysie clenched his fists tightly, forcing his brain on to simple things like trees and meadows, soft summer rain to lay the dust of terror welling up inside him.

'I wish to see the British Ambassador.' For the third time. 'And while we're at it, where am I? What is this place?'

Warbler spoke without hesitation. 'You're quite near Peking. It is a camp. Our main interrogation centre, so please do not try to escape. The guards are good, and at night we have watch dogs of great efficiency. Actually they are watch cats, six of them. The cat family. Pumas. We ship them in from South America and train them to kill people. Our own men they will not touch, but—well, they cannot resist prisoners. Very vicious, the puma.'

A buzz from the intercom. A winking red light. Warbler pressed the Speak button. A short conversation in Chinese. Then Warbler spoke to Gazpacho. 'Get Oakes changed. Start the process. Information quickly. Within twenty-four hours. *He* is on the way here now.'

'*He* is coming here?' Gazpacho accented the *he* as though it was God.

'Within two hours. Get Oakes changed and—the truth. We must have the truth.'

Boysie had no chance to think. The musclemen took over, bodily lifting him from the room. The ceiling swayed and swivelled, walls angled, glimpses of floors as they half dragged, half carried him down endless passages. The atmosphere was of a hospital; tiles, scrupulous cleanliness. Boysie's head clouted a door as Gazpacho led the party into a small room.

'Strip and put these on.' Gazpacho's face tight with hatred. The guards dropped Boysie. Throbbing bruises on shoulders and back. Gazpacho was pointing to a light-yellow, thin denim outfit, slacks and a jacket that buttoned to the neck. Sandals and a straw coolie hat lay nearby. Boysie rolled over slowly. 'What the hell's this meant to be?'

'Prison uniform, boy. You're in the cooler so you wears the clothes.' Gazpacho's smile edged across his face like a tombstone engraver's chisel. 'Help's our pets as well. The pumas.' He pronounced it 'poomaws.' 'The prison gear gives off a scent. Makes 'em real hungry. Now move.'

'Horlicks.' Boysie quivering with the rage of indignity. 'If you want me in that stinking fifth-rate Carnaby Street stuff, you'll have to get me into it yourself.' Which was precisely what Gazpacho and his brace of yellow gorillas did. Boysie completely helpless. These boys were pros. Struggling and kicking made no difference. They knew all the holds and counterholds. Within minutes Boysie lay on the floor in shame, clothed in the ill-fitting chill yellow garb.

'Now get up.' Gazpacho administered a light kick with his right heel.

Boysie painfully rolled over and got to his feet.

'Sandals,' snapped Gazpacho.

Boysie shuffled into the sandals as someone jammed the coolie hat on to his head, the loose chin strap hanging forward. Boysie moved his head back and the hat slid behind his neck, the strap loose against his throat. In spite of everything he opened his mouth. 'I feel a bloody twit in this, and there's nothing I can tell you. Told old Warble-face everything.'

'We shall see.'

The guards put on the forearm locks and held him to lead him out of the room. A few paces and they were out of the building and walking over a strip of grass towards a small square brick building. Boysie tried to get his bearings. He could see the track of road to his right, on the wrong side of a high barbed-wire fence. The light was beginning to fail and a low mist rose from the grourd. He glanced back. Over Gazpacho's shoulder, about a hundred yards away along the wire fence, was the main gate—a crude structure of rough poles and spiked wire, low huts on either side, and at least one armed sentry on view.

'Back to the drugs I suppose,' said Boysie to Gazpacho as an excuse for looking back.

'Drugs?'

'Well, you want to check out if I'm lying or not. Thought that was the latest kick. Even the Russians used mescaline in Hungary for extracting the old unvarnished.'

'Shut up and look to your front.'

Boysie was quite pleased that he had remembered that bit of useless information about the mescaline, gleaned from a Department file and stored by accident in his grasshopper mind.

'There are more exact methods,' Gazpacho said. A few steps later he added, 'Still got a long way to go on the drug techniques. Never be certain a client's telling the truth. Maybe he just imagines he is. Pain threshold's still the best.'

Sickness, always Boysie's reaction to anxiety and fear. Next to, and in line with, flying and spiders, his greatest terror fell into the physical-torture category. Tremors, the recognizable desire for a private or public convenience, and the soft impression that stomach and legs were made of frog spawn.

The hut was bare except for a powerful pair of lamps and a chair that looked suspiciously like the hot seat Boysie detested at his dentist's. The last time he had come across a chair like this was in similar circumstances—a cellar in the south of France. A man called Sheriek. That was during the disastrous Operation Coronet. A million years and two million blunders ago. A stampede of terror as Boysie realised he was about to get the works. He pushed back with all his weight. One of the guards lost footing for a second, but Gazpacho stepped in. It took only about thirty seconds before Boysie was strapped into the chair: metal clamps on wrists, ankles, thighs, and throat.

Gazpacho stood before him. 'The questions are simple, fella. I wanna see ya get top marks. Alpha plus. One hundred per cent in this examination. So let's go. Do you know about Warren's information? What passed between you and Khavichev? Why were you going to Tiranë? Answer.'

'I told you all I know.' Despite the terror, Boysie held on. Grim determination was the cliché underlying the sweat now oozing from him.

'I'll count to three, buddy, and you'd better talk. One ... two ... three ...'

Boysie remained silent. The back of Gazpacho's hand caught his right cheek, then the palm on the left. Again and again. Boysie thought his cheekbones were cracking. There was a definite trickle of blood from his face. Gazpacho wore two rings on the right hand; they glistened as he rubbed the hard skin.

'Talk.'

A precise halo of stars spun inside Boysie's head. He still held on. 'Nothing.' Barely able to get the word out. Gazpacho's hand swung again and again. Five seconds pause. Then again. Again. Again. The hard swing. Partial knockout.

Boysie came to with water dripping from his face. A couple of satellites joined the stars. Foolishly Boysie found himself trying to identify them. Warbler now stood with Gazpacho. Boysie could just make out what was being said.

'We'll make it one every hour.'

'You're the boss.' Gazpacho. 'In my experience I really think this guy's gonna be tough to break. Or he's telling

158

the truth.'

'Start with the third upper molar. The right one.' Warbler clipped out the words like a callous NCO on parade.

'Okay.'

Before Boysie had a hint of what was to happen, two pairs of hands, palms like steel, closed in on his head and jaw. So weak was he from Gazpacho's workout that the two Chinese guards prised his mouth open with the ease of experienced music-hall strong men ripping telephone directories in half. It was impossible to close his mouth. Boysie felt a metal clamp, encased in firm rubber, pulled down tight on the inside of his lower gums; then a similar appliance on the upper. Grunting noises from the back of his throat as it filled with saliva. A choking sensation, and Warbler's voice loud against his ear.

'Stop those noises. If you are willing to talk, signify by opening your eyes. In the meantime, close them tight. If you open them under false pretences things will be worse.'

A touch of metal on Boysie's lips. With shrieking terror he knew the truth and what the metal object was—a pair of dental pliers. Certainly. Their milled jaws were closing hard over one of the big upper teeth at the rear of his mouth. They were going to pull a tooth without anaesthetic. Slow, unbearable. Eyes jammed closed. Try to operate psychologically. Try, Boysie. Try. For Elizabeth. For pride. Stand it. Pretend there is sticking plaster over the eyes. The pliers moved and the first stab of pain shot through his head like an arrow. The pain grew, a balloon of expanding revulsion. He could hear the pain screaming, increasing as the tooth was slowly twisted. God, would they ever stop! The nerve ends seemed to reach right up through the scalp as though part of the brain were slowly being torn away. Excruciating agony. Searing. Burning. Stabbing and stabbing.

Boysie braced and strained against the metal bands binding him to the chair. Christ, they were doing it slowly! Twisting the tooth to and fro. Loosening it, playing with this one tiny piece of dentine, jiggling at the sensitive nerves so that the anguish smothered his whole body. Never in his whole life had he felt such positive sensations. Through the blinding convulsions Warbler's voice came trickling out of a mist that endlessly crucified exposed nerves in spasmodic nightmare rashes.

'Talk, Oakes. Talk.'

The over-all ecstatic raw flogging of Boysie's entire nervous system continued. Don't open the eyes. No. Stop. For Jesus' sake, stop! Pain. Pain. PAIN. So he could see it and hear the soundless screech. Rolling, systematic, electronic screams of pain. Then a last crisis, shooting like white hot needles from gums to brain, then traversing the body. Blackness. Dark grey. Grey. Light grey. Terrible throbbing and raw bruises filling his mouth, now freed from the clamp. Miles away through the grey well Gazpacho's voice. 'Threshold's pretty high.'

Boysie heard his own voice, weak signals, blurred by the singing in his ears and bloody saliva washing round his exploding mouth and gums. 'Don't know a bleeding thing. Why are you doing this to ...?' Dark grey again, then back to light. Warbler's voice.

'Take him to join his friend. In one hour we will try the upper third left molar. I noticed it was in need of attention anyway.'

Distantly Boysie felt the shackles being unclamped. Dreamingly, even distantly, he sensed the bruising. Semi-consciousness. The idea that they were carrying him from the room. Then fresh air and light. Night had not yet come. The sound of an engine. Warbler's voice.

'He's early. Just coming in to land. Carry on with Oakes. I must be there to meet him.'

Full, though ruined, consciousness returned. They were carrying him back towards the main gate. Past the gate. He had thought the agony over, even if only temporarily, but now reaction grew to full flower; the definite hard sore points where they had clamped wrists, ankles, thighs, and neck burned, Worse. The inside of his mouth—as though claws had torn and ripped ribbons of skin and flesh from the gums, roof, and sides of his cheeks, all exploding in fire reaching up into his head.

They had let his feet down and pulled him, holding him up, trying to make him walk. Boysie could not even grit his teeth for the pain inside the mouth. They were coming up to a large building. Concentrating hard, almost in hysteria, Boysie tried to retain a sense of direction. The main gate was about fifty yards away directly behind. Music—a blare of music coming from the building, which looked like an aircraft hangar, the double doors partly open. A long block of brilliant light cut from the space between the doors. It was like going into a refrigerator. Inside Boysie felt the bitter cold, like plunging into a vat of ice cubes. The clash of music, martial and strongly Chinese, thumped against his ears, pile-driving, making his head grow and expand until he thought it would shatter into fragments.

Boysie was beginning to succumb to weakness, with the ragged mouth, bruised body, and now the cold and cranium-splitting music amplified from at least six speakers. The building was a converted hangar, stone floor sharp with reflections from a dozen or so tower lights, almost a film studio. The great lamps all mounted at different heights and angles in the same direction, yet even the terrific heat generated by them had no effect on Boysie's freezing temperature.

Amid the litter of what appeared to be scrap metal, aircraft parts, and work benches, Boysie's eyes beamed in on a sight of fantastic horror. To the left stood a circular cage: steel bars, set at one-inch intervals round a circumference of about eight feet, the whole contraption rising in a curve, like a parrot's cage, to a height of around ten or eleven feet. Inside the cage was a man, feet on the floor but arms raised and hands cuffed to a chain hanging from the top centre. He was thinner than when Boysie had last seen him passing through one of the passages of Department Headquarters. Now, dressed like Boysie, Rabbit Warren looked at the point of death. Body sagging and head drooping. The face painted with parchment pallor, dried patches of blood on clothing and face. An arm pulled Boysie roughly to the right. Ten feet or so away from Warren's cage stood an identical enclosure, its steel door open and dangling handcuffs spread wide to receive a new victim.

The hard-boiled yellows in blue were not gentle. Boysie's ear struck a bar as they pushed him into the open cage. A dismal attempt to stop his arms from being raised and locked into the handcuffs proved fruitless. The door clanged shut with an echo. A sound effect from some documentary movie on life in jail. For the first five minutes Boysie thought the strain from wrists to shoulders would drag his arms from their joints. Slowly, numbness set in. Gazpacho and the guards left, the sound of their boots clicking over the stone floor, then ending abruptly, like ghosts, as they went out on to the grass.

Boysie could see nothing. The glare from the huge lights blocked out all view, heat on the eyeballs devouring the retinas. The music blared on, all part of the psychological torture. The sense of time vanished; then, suddenly, the music stopped. The silence was unnerving, yet, in spite of utter discomfort, Boysie found it an immediate stimulant to his senses. More alert. Less conscious of pain. From the right Warren's heavy breathing wheezed like a death rattle. Then came a hoarse whisper.

'Who are you?'

'Oakes. L. Special Security.'

Warren's words were faint; it was obviously difficult for him to speak at all. 'Told me the Russians had got you. You're a fake. Bloody fake.'

'Russians let me go. These boys have just given me a session. The teeth. Want to know how much I'm concerned in your business.'

'Makes no difference now. No chance here. Done for. Makes no difference. Madrigal. Madrigal's the man. The source. The stirrer. Madrigal. Strikes. Mad ...' The voice trailed off into a wheeze. A second later the music blared out again.

'Boysie started to droop, handcuffs playing hell with his arms. Oddly, he thought, the usual profound fear had gone. Weakness? The aftermath of torture? The impossible circumstances? Had they banished anxiety? Swept out the inbred cowardice. Time slipped away in a montage of silly mixed thoughts.

The music cut out as though someone had snipped the tape recording with cutter's shears. He was alert once more. Footsteps. Boysie's natural inclination was to feign unconsciousness. 'Lie doggo,' as the Chief would say. He let all weight go on to his arms. Traces of searing pain from wrists down to feet, knees bent, the body swinging. The footsteps came nearer.

Warbler was the first to speak. 'Warren is on the left, Oakes right. We have had two days on Warren. K'u's taken him to the limit. Nothing, Madrigal, nothing at all.'

The following voice was new, containing elements which once heard could not be forgotten. 'Wh-wh-what about Oa-Oakes?'

He sounded young, a cultured, smooth English accent. Nothing sinister; if anything, there was a studied charm coupled with a definitive, even attractive, stutter. It crossed Boysie's mind that if he were young and good-looking he would be a wow with the birds.

Gazpacho answered the man called Madrigal. 'Gave him a pretty high work-out and the tooth technique. He's a deceptive bastard. Took more than I thought. Nothing there though.'

'L-looks in a bad way. B-both of them. B-b-bad,' said Madrigal.

'Don't fancy the chances with either.' Gazpacho, respect peeping through. 'Not in the available time.'

'Is it really so short, Madrigal, sir?' Warbler's undertone was of complete veneration.

Madrigal's reply was not entirely audible. It sounded like, 'I must leave for Hong Kong tonight.' Boysie certainly got the words 'I must leave' and 'Hong Kong.' The rest was indistinct. 'This sh-shop has t-t-to be clo-s-sed up by dawn.'

'As soon as that, sir?'

'As s-s-soon as that. Im-per-ative.'

Boysie, still dangling in simulated insensibility, with muscles racked, locked in on Madrigal's voice. He had to remember that voice.

Gazpacho rapidly took over. 'Orders then, sir. I can get cleared in a couple of hours. What about these two?'

Endless silence. Then Madrigal's voice.

'K-kill th-em.' As though talking of greenfly on his prize roses. 'I mu-ust go. Ju-just get everything t-tied up. There's st-still a great d-deal to do and we must n-not fail. Remember wh-what has been said by the wo-workers of China.' For the next sentence his stammer disappeared, so did the charm. 'The cunning fox cannot escape the hunter's eyes; the sinister gang cannot deceive people armed with Mao Tse-tung's thought.'

'He was the greatest subversive of them all, Madrigal.' Adoration in Warbler's tone. 'Come, sir, we will see you off. Fu and Lee Fook can look after these two, can't they?'

'Sure.' Gazpacho was very near Boysie's cage; you could hear his breathing close. 'Oakes here is out. He won't be able to move far.' Footsteps crossing to the Rabbit enclosure. 'I'm not sure, but I guess Warren has nearly had it. Fu and Lee Fook can drag 'em over to the sand pit, finish 'em there, and dig 'em in. Okay?'

'That is best.' Either Warbler or Madrigal was grating the toe of a shoe irritatingly on the floor. It set Boysie's damaged mouth singing with anguish.

Gazpacho snapped out brief orders in Chinese and got a reply from one of the two guards.

'Okay, we can go. Nothing to worry about.'

'G-good.'

The hesitant voice of Madrigal was followed by the sound of retreating feet. Then the noise of the guards, Fu and Lee Fook, walking across the hangar. Boysie remained in the unconscious position. Who was to be the first? They were heading for Warren. The echo of locks being drawn, the click of a key, the handcuffs coming off. Then the horrible collapsing bumping of Warren's unconscious body tumbling to the ground. Muttered words in Chinese, then the dragging sound as they heaved Warren to the door. No noise. Chatter in Chinese, sounding as though one of the men was telling the other he could manage by himself. The dragging noise once more, receding out of the door, and one pair of footsteps approaching Boysie's cage.

Be ready. This is where it's going to count, and he would be fighting blind through the brilliance of the floodlights. Boysie allowed his eyelids to open a fraction. The Chinese was at the cage door, luckily silhouetted against one of the floods. Small but broad-shouldered. He had to unsling his sub-machine gun, if that was what it was, place it on the ground, to deal with the cage door.

Door open. Strong hands gripping Boysie's wrist as the key was inserted into the left handcuff. Boysie let the hand droop, then, as the cuff unlocked, allowed his hand to flop down swinging. Little yellow bonce must have thought it was a cinch.

The key clicked in the second handcuff. Boysie, acting on sense of direction, let his whole body fall forwards towards the Chinese. Not slack this time but with force, willing strength and springing from his heels. The guard was taken off balance. Boysie summoned every ounce of weight and pushed forward. The Chinese toppled backwards. There was no noise. He did not even cry out.

Boysie's hands shot up in the direction of his opponent's throat. The man was stunned, but the pain suffered at the hands of these inhuman humourless bastards had triggered rage in the hidden black spots of Boysie's unusually anti-violent mind. Automatic training was all that was necessary. His thumbs slid up the semi-conscious man's neck, expertly seeking the vital pressure points—the neck arteries, which carry blood to the brain. It was a trick used as far back as Roman times. Death in a matter of three seconds, and not a sound.

Boysie stood up, easing his aching limbs and lightly trying out his tongue against the raw patches of his mouth; the gaping hole where the third upper molar had been felt like the crater of Vesuvius. He took a deep breath and realised it was no good standing about like a spare what'sit at a wedding. Bending down, he scrabbled on the floor for the late lamented guard's gun. He picked it up and hurried to the light for a quick check. Easy. A French MAT 49. Bet that's been through Vietnam, thought Boysie. Compact, simple to handle, with a telescopic stock. Loaded with one magazine. Set on safe. One magazine—about twenty rounds of ammunition. Careful. Boysie set the weapon to single shot and started to edge from the hangar. The main gate, he knew, lay somewhere to the right along the barbed-wire fence. He moved quietly in the darkness, a group of lights round the gates acting as a guide. Better not try straight over the wire—it could be electrified or at least wired to an alarm system. He pulled the coolie hat forward from the back of his neck on to his head. Somehow even the straw gave a feeling of protection. There was a lot of activity coming from the main group of buildings on the far side of the gate. As he drew near, with joy, Boysie saw the gates were open. Two heavy trucks were drawing out, and no sign of a guard under the amber fluorescent lights which glowed round the exit area. By this time he had reached the back of one of the huts flanking the gates; another truck was rattling through. Should he risk running for it? There were lights in the hut on the far side. Lights meant guards and guns. Should really have tried to strip the strangled Chinese and squeeze into his uniform. Time. Soon they would find out. From far off, across the fields, beyond the runway, a muffled rapid burst of machine-gun fire. Boysie closed his eyes. That would be from the sand pit. Rabbit gone.

Chance it. A quick dash. He clicked the gun to automatic. If it meant a run and exchange of fire, it would be safer to do it fast with a rapid rate. His right foot moved forward, ready, when another engine note approached from the direction of the main complex. A car with lights dipped. A Red Flag. Probably the one that had brought him from the aircraft. Instead of going straight through, the car stopped short of the huts. Crouching low, Boysie watched. Only one occupant, the driver, climbed out and headed towards the lighted hut, leaving the engine still running. Opportunity golden as the Midas touch. The driver, in civilian clothes, moved without hurry, mounting the wooden steps and entering the hut. Boysie ran softly to the car and heaved the door open, ready to slide over into the driving seat.

The door was easy, and he already had one foot inside the car when the snarl came from directly behind. He wheeled round, gun to the hip. The puma was about twenty yards away, beginning its run for the spring, teeth bared, coming at speed. One of the watch cats Warbler had warned about. Seconds seemed to be reduced by seven-eighths. The cat was big and heavy, about eight feet long. Boysie's finger did not make the trigger before the animal sprang. Violently Boysie twisted to the right. The puma tried to alter course in mid-air, failed, and landed heavily on the car's passenger seat. Immediately turned with an angry, frustrated, violent growl, to leap out and spring again.

It was so close Boysie could smell the beast, now out of the car and a few feet from him. The smell of childhood circuses. This time the trigger finger was ready, though still not fast enough for the vicious cat. The animal reared up, jaws open and claws extended, reddish-brown mane turned luminously yellow by the lights. Boysie pressed the trigger in two bursts of five, felt the kick, smelt the burning charge, and saw the puma's abdomen rip open. The cat was pushed backwards, though its forepaws still dropped in Boysie's direction. He side-stepped an inch too late. The dying puma's left paw fell, scratching down his shoulder and arm, the thin yellow material rending, claws ploughing three deep furrows nearly to the elbow. To begin with Boysie felt no pain. The puma fell, a thud of finality, rolling over and kicking once at his feet.

A shout from the hut. Boysie's one thought was the car. Propelled by fear and purpose he dived for the door, scrabbling into the driving seat, conscious of figures appearing on the porch of the hut. Pedals. Feet searching in the dark, hands feeling for brake and the gear lever, hoping to hell it operated in the normal H pattern. Foot down on clutch, the other on accelerator. In gear, then out of clutch, gunning the engine. The Red Flag hopped and bounced forward, into second, crack and bump. They were shooting. Crash of glass as the rear window smashed. The car slewed, hit in the back by a quick burst of fire. Then he was through the gate, foot hard on the accelerator, holding the car in a wild skidding turn, tyres squealing, agonised. Into third and top gears, foot hard down, other toes searching for the dip switch to give him full beam. He was travelling, estimating sixty-five ... seventy ... seventy-five. Glance into the mirror, nothing coming up behind. At last the foot on the dip switch. The lights spread ahead, giving full visibility just in time to correct for an unexpected sharp bend. Bump brake, change down, accelerate. The back swung but he was round in a wild turn.

Boysie settled at the wheel. Must try to relax. Pain began to emerge. Not simply the wound from the puma, but the whole body ache and the dragon-fire mouth. Weakness. He must have lost a lot of blood. Constantly. Christ, he was driving on the left, wrong side of the road. Another bend coming up. Boysie edged over to the right and took the turn around sixty. Lights ahead. Some kind of village. Then, as he drew nearer, more lights. Another vehicle. But on the wrong side, heading straight for him. The oncoming car winked its lights hysterically. Collision course. Boysie began to pump the brakes and wrench the wheel over. It was a large lorry refusing to give way. In the dazzle he caught sight of a massive wheel bearing down on the rear of the car. Jumble, glass and metal giving way, rending, buffeting. Boysie could not hold her. The car spun, slowed, hit the shoulder, and bolted through some kind of hedge. Spasm in his arm as the machine rolled over. A swipe to the head, then silence except for the lorry's engine, still grinding, going away from him. The driver did not want trouble.

Boysie had no idea how long he had been lying in the

wrecked car. All senses were shrouded in a weak, throbbing ache. Here and there a rapier stab of hurt. There was blood around. Finally he hauled himself up, reaching for the door handle above him. Topsy-turvy land. The lock worked, and he had enough strength to push up and climb out, sliding down on to damp grass. Cold drenched him, bloody freezing, he thought, hanging on to the remains of the car. Dizzy. The clump of lights was quite near, to the right. A village. What was the use? He knew it was impossible even to exist. A strange land. They would be out looking for him. The tattered yellow prison costume. Mostyn, or Khavichev, or Madrigal, Warbler, Gazpacho, the Department had won. If he had the guts he would search the car for the gun and blow his head off. Somewhere near Peking. Injured. No money. The saga of Boysie Oakes had ended. Drunkenly he staggered away from the savage scrap heap until he reached the road, slowly weaving towards the lights. You never knew, the people there might be friendly; might give him warmth, food even, before they handed him in and the authorities plastered lead across his chest and dug the remains into the sand pit next to old Rabbit.

The village had a familiar look. A mirage? Perhaps death had already overtaken him. Familiar. Lights glinted through partly drawn curtains. Laughter, and a piano, from the first building. Boysie collided with the brick work. Fun was happening inside, you could hear it. He felt his way along the wall. A door. Knock? No need to be polite. Boysie turned the handle and stumbled into warmth thick with cigarette smoke and the smell of beer. Blurred familiar faces. White men, leather-skinned, cloth caps, glass mugs, a bar, and a red-faced man in shirt sleeves, wide red braces. Silence as all heads turned towards him. The man behind the bar opened his mouth.

'What the 'ell we got 'ere then?'

Accent? Accent? Indian? No, Welsh. Wales Welsh.

'What the 'ell we got 'ere then? Bloody Fu Man Chu?'

The black curtain partly rang down as Boysie felt his knees buckle. Sprawled on the floor, he was still alive and could hear. Voices dovetailed. 'Brandy, bach. Evan bach, get the brandy.'

'For God's sake, someone fetch Jones the police.'

'Come on, boys, on to the couch with him.'

A glass touching sore lips. The liquor stung.

Boysie heard his own voice as from the bottom of a well. 'Where am I? Where? Peking?'

'Come on now, boyo. Don' you worry.' the man said a word which was unmistakably Welsh but unpronounceable. 'You know,' he continued, 'near Borth. On the Aberystwyth Road. Lie back, bach. They'll be getting an ambulance. You'll be all right, boyo. Just rest.'

The hum of conversation got softer and softer until it disappeared altogether. Floating, then no feeling but the drift over dark seas.

VII. OWL

The clamorous owl, that nightly hoots
*   and wonders*
At our quaint spirits.

Shakespeare,
A Midsummer Night's Dream

'DAMNED idiot's turned up in Bath?' the Chief thundered behind his desk at Mostyn.

'Borth, Chief.'

'Borth? Oakes in Borth? Where the hell's that? Bulgaria?'

'Wales.'

'Wales. Might 'ave known it. Send him on a blisterin' mission to Berlin and he turns up in Wales with a posse of chip-eaters and Methodist ministers all singing "Sospan Fach" or the "Hallelujah Chorus."'

As soon as Mostyn had heard the news of Boysie's reappearance, he dashed as though pursued by a hurricane to the Chief's office, entering unannounced, an unprecedented act, which caught the old devil, feet on desk, thumbing through the current issue of a colourful girlie magazine. The Chief's spate about Wales stopped abruptly as he noticed Mostyn's interest in the sexy periodical.

'Her-humph,' he croaked, slipping the magazine into the desk drawer. 'Always go through the lot, Mostyn. Faces y'know, faces. Never sure whose picture might turn up in one of these. Borth in Wales, eh? Where? And what was he up to? Breaking all Ten Commandments with some Gwyneth or Megan? St. Patrick should never have driven all those snakes out of the place to begin with.'

'St. Patrick did that in Ireland, Chief, and it's a bit more complicated, I'm afraid.' Mostyn briefly went over the story of Boysie's arrival at the pub. The Chinese clothes. The injuries. 'They've got him in Machynlleth Hospital.'

'Machynlleth? Bloody wog-sounding name. Get 'im out, Mostyn. No time for standin' on ceremony. Out. And out of the service.'

'Chief, it's tricky. Police took him in and he rambled on about working for us——'

'Deny it. Wrestler's rectums, man, it's all in the book, isn't it? Fella's alone in the field. No help from us. There's an end to it.'

'They've called in the Special Branch.' Mostyn fought to sound calm.

The Chief blew like a burst boiler. 'Finished, Mostyn. That damn man was never any good. Advised against him in the first place, didn't I?'

'No, you bloody did not.' Mostyn's fangs bared. A showdown imminent. 'It was all your idea and you know it. And I'm not carrying the can for anybody. Not even you, Chief.'

The Chief gave his famous beetle-browed frown, but Mostyn went on. 'He is delirious and saying he was in a Chinese Interrogation Centre and that they fed him hallucinatory drugs.'

'Well, there's a get-out for you. Oakes off his chump.'

'Chief'—Mostyn in his patient voice—'let's not fool ourselves. You know as well as I do that the SB've known about Boysie's affiliation with us for a long time. They must even know what his job was. Practically everyone else seems to. MI5 and 6 now operate on entirely new

173

systems, and we're right behind the times. We pretend, Chief. Live in the past. Good God, we even use amateurs and our professionals all put on big acts. Cover doesn't mean a thing any more, even the top men hide behind attitudes, class consciousness, or the brand of cigarettes they smoke. It's a farce. We're out of date, and if something really big comes up, we either make a complete cock-up of it or scrape through by the non-existent skin of our teeth. The boys wander around Europe, fooling nobody, and as for the pay system, we squander money on people like Boysie or poor old Jimmy De Nob who used to be with M Section while the lads down the road in the Limited Destruction category are reduced to fiddling expenses. It's ludicrous.'

The Chief reached for the drinks cupboard, face a delicate purple. He removed the usual Chivas Regal bottle, thought twice about it, then returned the whisky to the cupboard. In a low voice he said, 'Get him back to London. Debrief him. Enforce the Official Secrets Act for life and wave him bye-bye. I'll try and put a word in at the Home Office. Been on the brink of amalgamating us for years. Excuses now. Do me best to keep the show goin'. Just get crackin', eh?'

Mostyn nodded and left, in a hurry to get to his telephone.

The pulling of strings was one of Mostyn's specialities. The following day Boysie was brought back to London and seclusion in a select clinic near Montague Square.

A Roedean-bred nurse looked down her nose when Mostyn arrived and openly grimaced when he asked for Boysie's room number.

'I'm afraid you have to get permission to see him,' she drawled. 'There are *policemen* there.' Nostrils twitching as though the cops were contaminating her as well as the clinic.

'No need to worry about them, old darling.' Mostyn

vocally caressing a silk nightdress. He flashed his Security Card.

'Oh,' said the nurse, betraying the fact that she read spy novels and never missed screen skulduggery. 'Very good, sir. Second floor. Room 200. I'll have to ring and let them know you're on your way up.'

'You do that, darling. I love being on my way up.'

The girl blushed as Mostyn headed for the lift.

There were two Special Branch men on duty. Mostyn did not know the one outside the door. Inside the room—white, with all the accoutrements of private clinics—Superintendent Glaisher sat by the bed. Boysie was dozing, and Glaisher toyed with *The Times* crossword.

'Wotcher Glaish.' Mostyn making light of the affair. Glaisher was not as bad as some of them (departmental jealousy can be a terrible thing). 'What news on the Rialto?'

'Eh?' The bald, ox-shouldered policeman eased himself out of the chair. 'The Rialto? Which one? Coventry Street? Pepys Road? Or St. James's Road?'

'Glaish, you amaze me.' Mostyn had forgotten the Super was a movie addict. 'Not cinemas. Shakespeare, you a *Times* crossword man and kosher with it.'

'Kosher?' Perturbed. 'How——?'

'The Special Branch hasn't got all the secrets. Glaishenheimer, isn't it? Before you did the deed with the deed poll?'

Glaisher shrugged. 'A man should live. If only to satisfy his curiosity. What Rialto?'

'Quotation, laddy. Billy the Kid from Stratford. Shylock, one of the mighty clan. *Merchant of Venice*—and don't say "it shouldn't happen to a Doge." It's an old gag.'

Glaisher shrugged again, hands spread wide. 'So I don't know my Shakespeare.'

'Yet you do *The Times* crossword.'

'Never finish it. Two clues I got today only.' He studied the paper. 'How about an anagram on something connected with espionage, Colonel Mostyn?'

'Pys,' said Mostyn, straight-faced. 'How's the boy doing?' He nodded towards Boysie.

'He sleeps well. Considering his job.'

'Shame on you. I've read the first report. What's your verdict?'

'Everyone here thinks he's a nut-case. Talks about being abducted to China, torture for no reason. He's been in a punch-up—nasty scratches, tooth missing, severe bruising. One of the doctors thinks he's been experimenting with junk. We're doing a routine check of the area. Regional Crime Squad's helping.'

'Can I talk to him?'

'Alone? Little secrets?'

'Of course.'

'Of course. An exception. For you I'll do it.'

Glaisher left, and Mostyn bent his lips to Boysie's ear. 'Boysie boy.' The mating call of a dove. 'It's Uncle. Nuncey Mostyn.'

Boysie opened his eyes. He had been awake all the time. 'Wondered when you'd get here.'

'Thought I'd wait until you felt a little brighter. They'll be letting you out in a few days. Had a nasty time. By the way, one of our men brought your car back from Berlin. It's in the usual place. New keys.' He quietly placed the small bunch of keys on the bedside table, then repeated, 'Yes. Had a nasty time.'

'Thanks to you.'

'Care to talk about it?'

'You're not going to believe it. Haven't told all to the jacks naturally, but you're not going to believe it.'

'Try me, old son. Try me.'

Boysie leaned back on the pillows. 'To begin at the

176

beginning. There was darkness, then a man called James George Mostyn——'

'Cut it. This is an official debriefing.' Mostyn had his briefcase open and a cassette tape recorder ready to run.

Boysie talked.

An hour later Mostyn left the clinic in a troubled haze. Dummy ammunition. Warbler. Gazpacho. Khavichev. Tickets to Albania. Mexican mushrooms. China. Warren. Torture. Pumas. Wales. A man called Madrigal on his way to Hong Kong. 'Gone right round,' he said to the Chief later, after they had listened to the tape recording. 'Put him to sleep. Only humane thing to do.'

'Under the present circumstances we'll have to put him out to grass, I'm afraid.' The Chief had been sober for two days, a record. Reputations hung by threads, and most of the bluster had gone. 'By the way,' he added, 'they found Warbler and Gazpacho. The real ones.'

'Yes?'

'On a bombed-out site near the Spandau Citadel. Severe cases of laryngitis.'

'Laryngitis?'

The Chief passed an index finger across his throat. 'Fatal infection caused by a service utility knife.' He placed both hands, palms flat, on the desk, head bent. 'The Special Branch is doing an all-out check, Old Mostyn. Home and Foreign Offices in a tizz. Boysie's story's mad, but the barometer's fallin' fast. Some aspects puzzlin'. Think we should do somethin' to show willin'.' The Chief looked a beaten man. 'This Madrigal. Check the files and cuttings. Oakes says he's gone to Hong Kong and that Warren said he was the man—the Source, he said—used the word "Strikes." How're we fixed in Hong Kong?'

'Only that alcoholic journalist with a flair for guess work.'

'Then someone'd better go out. You wouldn't care——'

'*No.*'

'Didn't think you would. Can you provide?'

'We're a bit thin on the ground. Could get that amateur bloke, what's his name?—Evol—J Branch use him. Or there's the Glare girl.'

'Don't really think so. What about your gun-dog Martin?'

Martin had risen from being a leg-man to the dubious position of Operations Controller to Mostyn. He had been highly involved with Boysie in the Coronet and Amber Nine business. A bit thick, Martin was at least zealous.

Mostyn's face crept into a smile. The thought of Martin in Hong Kong looking for someone called Madrigal appealed to his sense of humour. Within three hours Martin, brimming with trepidation, was on his way to Hong Kong, and Mostyn had six operatives combing all possible areas for a man with a stammer called Madrigal. At six-thirty that evening, Special Security's Cipher Department received a cable from Lisbon. After decoding, it read:

GOT OUT WITH REQUIRED INFORMATION WILL BE HELD UP FOR ONE WEEK BUT TIME LAG NO WORRY WAIT ME RABBIT

'That settles it.' The Chief was at the Chivas Regal bottle again.

'I recall Martin?' asked Mostyn.

'Leave it for a while. The coding's right so it looks as though Oakes has either bungled or been conned. If Rabbit is really out, we might be in the clear. Just get rid of Oakes, that's all I ask. For the sake of NATO, the

Common Market, Her Majesty's Inspector of Taxes, and the Chelsea Pensioners—get rid of him. Pension him off. Please.' The Chief's final word was a plea from the heart.

Boysie was discharged from the clinic on the following Wednesday. Neither the Special Branch nor the Department had offered him any further information regarding his recent experience. They took him back to the flat off Chesham Place in a police car. Elizabeth had visited the clinic regularly and tonight she was coming back to the flat. The scars were healing, and life began to look more bearable. He had been in the flat for only a few minutes when the telephone rang.

It was Mostyn, hearty and surprisingly pleasant. 'Home again, home again, jiggedy-jig, old son.'

'Yep. Great feeling, sir. You want me to come into the office today?'

'No-oo.' Mostyn undecided. 'Tell you what. Why not have a spot of lunch together? The old choppers up to a curry yet?'

'I should think so.' Boysie apprehensive about the friendly attitude. Too artificial for Mostyn.

'Where?'

'Let's make it Veeraswamy's. Say, one o'clock?'

'Fine.'

'Good. See you there.'

'Okay.'

'Oh, and Boysie?' Mostyn with a studied afterthought.

'Yes?'

'You'll be coming down by car, won't you?'

'Suppose so.' Warily. 'Why?'

'Then I needn't bother, Oaksey. I'll dice with death back to the treadmill with you. Be good, and don't forget to lock up, will you?'

Boysie left the flat just after twelve-thirty—casual grey suit and a raincoat—clouds had been threatening all morning. His mind was made up. He needed some kind of 'out' from the Danger Man game. A job in Central Files, Records, anything. Mean a cut in salary, of course, but he would have a go. The worst Mostyn could do was refuse. Couldn't really fire him. No one in the Department was fired. Or were they? Have to ask.

Mostyn was early, sitting at one of the circular tables in the foyer, sipping a pink gin, served by an elegant Indian lady. Small talk—a straight gin for Boysie—then into that extraordinary world of London's most famous Indian restaurant, reeking with memories of the old days of British rule, spiced air, the discreet eroticism of the sitar and sarod as background music, and those ambiguous symbols VR everywhere—which could well mean Veeraswamy's or Victoria Regina. No one ever asked. They both chose the same food—Chicken Vindaloo with Persian pulao rice, chapatis, lychees, and coffee. The chat over the meal was as minute as a pinhead. Halfway through the lychees (which had a cooling effect on Boysie's cavity, enflamed again by the Vindaloo), Boysie tried to turn the words into something more substantial.

'Er—any news about Madrigal?'

'Hey-nonny-no. What were the nurses like at that clinic, laddy?'

'There was a blonde night sister who always——' Boysie started. 'I asked you——'

'And I said hey-nonny-no.' Mostyn's face like a piece of the Mount Rushmore Memorial.

Coffee followed, and Boysie remembered his thoughts about people getting chucked out of the Department and his plan to be moved.

'Often wondered, sir, anyone ever get fired from the Department?'

Mostyn paused before answering. 'Fired?'

'Yes.' Nervous titter. 'You know, fired. Get the sack.

Out on the neck, the book, the old tin-tack.'

'Dismissed?'

'Yes.' Uncomfortable.

'Glad you asked that, old son. Normally one is pensioned off, sent to prison—for a breach in the regulations of the Official Secrets Act, of course—or DD.'

'DD,' repeated Boysie, bewildered.

'Feet first. Discharged Dead. In your case we're making an exception.'

'In my case?'

'In your case we're simply letting you go. I believe that's the polite term in the City.'

'But I wasn't going to ask about me. I just wanted a change—Records, Files...' He slowed down as Mostyn began shaking his head in a positive manner. 'Anything...' A weak nervous grin as he came to a stop.

'You're under the Official Secrets Act for life, Boysie old son, but it's the handshake, I'm afraid.'

Stunned. 'The handshake? You mean after all I've done? The risks? The bloody golden handshake and that's all?'

'Not golden, Boysie. Copper maybe, but definitely not golden.' Mostyn tossed a sealed envelope across the table. 'Five hundred quid in new notes.'

'Five ...?' Disbelief mingled with anger. 'You dirty, scheming, cheating, blood-sucking, snide bastard!'

'Orders, chum.' Unruffled. 'Sorry. It's been a bore. Admit I've been a bastard to you at times, but we've got on. Basically. Directly from the top. God's orders.'

Boysie picked up the envelope. Mostyn's hand whipped out, grasping his wrist. 'First of all the keys, please. Keys to the car and flat.'

'But my gear?'

'*Our* gear. You ought to have read the small print when we signed you on.' He began to quote from memory: '*At any time the Department can dismiss the*

above-named Brian Ian Oakes without notice or dis-
closure of reason. Accommodation provided by the De-
partment, complete with all contents at time of dismissal,
shall become the property of the Department together
with the motor vehicle provided for the use of the above-
named—need I go on?'

Stymied, snookered, checkmate. 'You mean I'm just
left with what I stand up in?' A deflated Boysie. In-
credulous.

'Naked we came into the world and all that sort of
thing. And the five hundred of course. In the circs we've
been very generous. Contractually no obligation to pay
you a red cent, let alone a pile of green, blue, or brown
backs.' Even the supercilious Mostyn felt a tweak of
worry. Boysie's clear ice-blue eyes were fixed on him to the
point of incredible hatred. Those eyes were the first thing
Mostyn had ever noticed about the man—long years ago
when the big, handsome tank sergeant gunned down two
Nazi agents in Paris, saving the Colonel's life. (How was
he to know the whole thing had been accidental? A
safety catch in the 'off' position, a stumble, and two
incredible shots that had shaken Boysie for years after-
wards.) The chips of ice were held so steadily on Mostyn
that British Special Security's Second-in-Command had
to look away. 'The keys, please, Boysie.'

Boysie stood up. Mostyn was suddenly conscious of the
man's height. With a double clang the two sets of keys
hit the table; the ones to the flat rebounded and ended
up on Mostyn's plate. Boysie snatched up the envelope
and tore it open. People were beginning to stare, and
two of the waiters hovered at the ready. Carefully Boysie
counted out the money. Loudly. Everyone in the vicinity
was interested. 'Four-sixty ,,, four-seventy ... eighty ...
ninety ... five hundred. Only just right. And I'm worth
five hundred pounds to you. Finished. A closed book.
Okay, so I'm floccipaucinihilipilificatious——'

'What?' Mostyn aghast, yet near laughter at the strange abuse.

'You heard. Look it up for yourself. I sat up all night once learning how to pronounce the bloody thing because it sounded like a high-class bit of obscenity. It means that you've rendered me worthless, so watch yourself, big daddy.' Boysie grabbed his coat and slammed out, almost upsetting an appetising Bhuna Gosht about to be served to a swinging young lady sporting a red fox Mary Quant coat.

In the street, Veeraswamy's magnificently regal doorman grinned with his traditional salute. 'Taxi, sir?'

'Please.' Boysie was dried up with shock. The taxi arrived, and he automatically asked for the Savoy. Halfway up the Strand the future financial outlook reared ugly. 'Make it the Strand Palace, will you? Got some business there first,' he shouted through the cabbie's partition.

The girl at Reception knew her stuff. Yes, they did have a single with bath, how long would he want it for? Uncertainly Boysie said a few days. She booked him in for a week and asked about luggage.

'Got to go back to the station and pick it up,' Boysie lied. The girl looked suspicious and withdrew the card by which Boysie could obtain his key from the hall porter. 'We can hold the room until six, Mr. Oakes. If you collect your baggage you will be able to move in.'

Boysie knew the score. 'Sure. Back within an hour.' He headed for the nearest telephone booth, took out notebook and pen, and dialled his bank. The manager was out but the chief clerk had Boysie's file to hand. Shattered, Boysie left the booth. For years he had lived off a magnificent salary with almost unlimited expenses. Always in credit, he spent freely, never bothering about the day when rain might fall. Now it was a hailstorm. His credit account showed only two hundred pounds.

Seven hundred and the clothes he stood up in, no job, and few prospects. He left the hotel and slouched back up the Strand, trying to work out priorities. Clothes. At least he had to have clothes. He dug into the five hundred pounds and picked up a reasonable suitcase at the first available shop before making his way to Cecil Gee's in the Charing Cross Road.

It had been years since Boysie had bought off the peg. He ended up with a formal suit, two pairs of slacks, a sports jacket, six ties, five shirts, three sets of cuff-links and assorted underwear. On the way back to the Strand Palace he lashed out on a couple of sets of pyjamas and one pair of shoes. His total of seven hundred had now dwindled to just over five.

In the hotel room Boysie rang down for a bottle of scotch, soda, and half a Courvoisier. A jumbo scotch, the radio percolating an assortment of pop, a cigarette between lips, Boysie stretched out on the bed and began to aim his addled mind in the general direction of ways and means.

Mostyn arrived back at Headquarters to find the sexy receptionist—known in private as Snake Hips—looking like death. Eyes rimmed red from tears. 'Colonel'—on the verge of breaking down—'the Chief. Straight away.'

'Mostyn's stomach pulsed a prediction of some gigantic disaster. 'What's up, love?'

'Oh, Colonel Mostyn...' The wretched doxy disintegrated, tears and sobs.

Mostyn ran to the lift. The Chief had cracked and taken the coward's way out, he thought. Instead he found the old sailor happy, awash with whisky, and grinning. 'Fix it, Mostyn?'

'Boysie?'

'Oakes, yes.' A small tipple to top up the glass.

'It's done.' Mostyn unemotional.

'Special Branch've got someone doing a temporary surveillance on him. Just until it blows over.'

'Till what blows over?' Mostyn's speech hesitant.

The Chief reached into his desk drawer, pulled out a cheque, and pushed it over to his Second-in-Command. 'Treasury's authorised payment to you. There's a letter of resignation for your signature, of course.'

Mostyn glanced at the cheque. Fifty thousand pounds. His skin glowed red. 'What do you mean, letter of resignation? Why do they want *my* head? I've just done this to Oakes for a pittance. Now it's me. Why?'

'Oh, not just you, little Mostyn. Far from it. We're finished. Washed up, disbanded, cut off in our prime. As from midnight, the Department of British Special Security ceases to exist. Our work's been taken over by the major branches. Disaster, old chap, has struck.'

'Doesn't seem to worry you too much.'

'No,' said the Chief, all jaunty. 'They're makin' me a peer. House of Lords. Services rendered an' all that cock.'

'Fireproof.'

'Asbestos, Mostyn. Asbestos. And no real responsibility. There's joy for you. If you'd sign the letter, please.'

Mostyn looked at the few typewritten lines. The bulk of his adult life had been given to the Department. Twice he had been severely injured. Several times there had been minor things like a broken leg or wrist. Now it was over. No argument. Mostyn scrawled his signature above the capital letters JAMES GEORGE MOSTYN.

'Good times, Mostyn, good times. Over now. Not sorry. Suggest you get your personal effects out of the office and move off like a doped racehorse. George's Mafia'll be movin' in soon enough.'

'Anyone being retained?'

'Only half a dozen. Can't tell you who now you've resigned. They're forming a special unit to deal with

Communist agitation in industry—manipulation of walk-outs, strikes, that sort of business. Things're bad in that direction, I gather.'

'I know. We have been working on it, remember?'

'Course. Course. We'll meet again, old Mostyn. Dinner soon, eh?'

'I expect so.' Mostyn charity cold.

'Is one thing, think you ought to know about.' The Chief solemn suddenly.

'What?' Mostyn past caring.

'There've been developments in Wales. Until the day after Oakes turned up, there was an unused film set well off the main road, about five miles from the pub.'

'A film set?' Urgency.

'Meso-Grabstone-Maul Productions've been doin' a blasted stupid spy film. Set in China. Representation of a prison camp.'

'Then Boysie——'

'Wait. They finished the film weeks ago but didn't bother to dismantle until now. Hidden away very well. Little airstrip and everything. Local police did a search. That cable, Mostyn, the one from Rabbit. Fake. They found Rabbit this mornin'. On the old film-set site. Buried in a heap of sand and shot to pieces.'

'It really happened then?'

'Looks like it. Special Branch'll be on to Oakes again, no doubt. Nothin' to do with us any more, though. Thank God.'

'Christ,' murmured Mostyn, shaking his head, 'only happen to Boysie. Nobody else would be fool enough to think he was in China when he was really in Wales.'

The Chief drummed his fingers on the desk, then perked up. 'Last drink then, Mostyn.' You could not tell if the Chief really felt happy or simply covered despair with layers of alcohol.

'No thanks.' Mostyn stood up and offered his hand in

186

farewell. 'Good-bye, Chief.'

'Come on, you bloody lubber. Old times' sake. Drink.'

'No thank you.' Biting at the words, Mostyn turned to leave the room, then whirled round. 'I've been wanting to say this for years. As the Chief of a security department you would make a bloody good front man for a public lavatory. You're a drunk, a stupid old buffoon, and a damn great pain in the arse.'

The Chief rose unsteadily. 'And I have something to say to you, Mostyn. As my Second-in-Command, you have proved yourself to be a sly, intriguing, bastard son-of-a-deckhand's syphilitic sister.'

'Thank you, Chief, and good-bye.' Mostyn walked to the desk and put out his hand. 'You greasy bugger.'

They shook hands.

'Thank you, Mostyn, and good-bye,' said the Chief. 'You unmitigated whore's godfather.'

Mostyn turned slowly and left the room, his shoulders drooping slightly.

The Chief, alone among his pictures of life past, poured himself another drink.

Around five o'clock Boysie, who had consumed a third of the whisky, made up his mind. Griffin, what had happened to Griffin? Perhaps he could help if the yellow men had not got him. Boysie dialled the number. It rang six or seven times before the receiver clicked up at the other end. Nobody spoke. Sound of breathing.

Boysie broke the silence. 'Mr. Griffin?'

'Mr. Griffin's residence. Who's calling, please?' The voice had sepia qualities.

'A friend. Who's speaking?'

'Mr. Griffin's manservant.'

Lord rot us, 'Griffin's man.' Bertie Worster and Jeeves already.

'Tell him it's Mr. Oakes.'

'Mr. Oakes. Very good sir.'

During the short wait Boysie's mind sifted Griffin's situation. A residence. Not a common old garden home but a residence. Before, it was either Griffin himself or some girl who answered the phone. Perhaps partial retirement had brought about a change in Griffin's status. There had been signs during the last months.

'Mr. Oakes?' Griffin's unmistakable voice.

'Griffin.' The bark of a Doberman. It should really have been a snarl.

'Thank 'eaven yer 'arbour light.'

Boysie did a dumb act. Irritated. 'Harbour light?'

''Arbour light—all right. Been worried to—well, yer know——'

'*You've* been worried? What about me? And what happened to you?'

'They clobbered me. Clobbered me proper. 'Onest, I played it straight. Was taking sight o' yer door long before the Chinese bint—sorry, Mr. Oakes—before the young lady arrived. Didn't sleep nor nothin'. Just go' a bleedin' great thump crost the back o' me neck. Came to in 'orspital. Yankee Military 'orspital. The goods.'

'I want to see you.'

'Yeah? Yeah, yer right. We should meet. Look, yer never been out my place before. Come an' 'ave a bite. Bi' o' nosh.'

'How do I get to you?'

'Don't yer worry. I'll send Rubin wiv the car. Where are yer? 'Ome?'

'No. Strand Palace Hotel. Room 200.'

'Be there in 'arf an hour. Okay?'

'All right.'

''Ave ter take pot luck. As yer find us like.'

Boysie did not answer.

'See yer then.'

'See you.'

Twenty minutes later the telephone rang, the hall porter saying that Mr. Oakes's car was waiting. By the porter's desk stood a six-foot Jamaican with shoulders to match, stylishly got up in grey livery with a discreet 'G' embroidered in gold on his cap. This was a bit much, even for Griffin, but the Jamaican turned out to be the chauffeur. The car was a black Phantom V with all the gear.

'Mr. Griffin says you can help yourself to a drink,' said Rubin curtly as he opened the door. Boysie settled comfortably in the rear, found the cocktail cabinet, and helped himself to a small brandy.

They slid off in the direction of Harrow, but within minutes Boysie lost track. Eventually gates and a drive, sweep of lawn to the left, and broad stone steps leading up to the front door. The house was large, exquisitely Georgian, smelling of money. Griffin came out on to the steps to greet him.

'Nice to see yer, Mr. Oakes. Come in, come in.' And to Rubin, 'Yer can get the nosh ready now.'

'Very good, sir.'

''Ave ter get rid of 'im. Too posh. Never relaxes. Bu' I 'ate apartheid. Like 'avin' spades round, so I give 'im the job.'

The hall was magnificent, like something out of *Homes and Gardens* but without the pictures being touched up. Griffin led the way into a large room decorated and furnished with the same distinguished touch. One wall was entirely bare but for a quietly lighted 'Mona Lisa.'

'Wonderful copy,' said Boysie, going close to the picture.

'Copy?' Griffin with a cunning grin. 'You think they've got the real one in Paris?'

Looking around, Boysie saw a number of *objets d'art* that seemed extraordinarily familiar.

'Sit down, Mr. Oakes. A drink?'

'No. No thanks. Enough already. I've lost my flippin' job.'

'So I 'eard.'

'You heard?'

'Well, Mr. Oakes. You know 'ow it is in our sort o' business.'

'No, I don't know how it is.'

Griffin looked embarrassed. 'All right, cock. I'll be fair wiv yer——' They were interrupted by the door opening and a slim teen-age blonde sneaking into the room.

'Ooh, sorry Griff. Didn't know——'

'Not now, 'Ortense. I'll be wiv yer later. Business meetin'. Rubin'll bring yer somethin' upstairs. Won't be late. Promise.'

'All right, dahling, I understand.' She paused, looking lecherously at Boysie. 'Who's your friend?' The voice was definitely top drawer and the whole aspect dazzling.

'Buzz orf, 'Ortense. See yer later.'

The girl pouted towards Boysie and withdrew.

'Birds,' said Griffin, throwing up his hands, 'death o' me they'll be.'

'You're old enough to be her father.'

'So? She's old enough to be fathered. She's real as well. An 'On. Real class there. 'Er old woman's a lady in 'er own right, then she marries a lord, 'Ortense's dad, divorces 'im, and goes and marries another lord.' Griffin smugly. 'Fella by the name of Mamian or somethin'.'

'Don't know how you do it,' said Boysie, exasperated.

'Well, she's gotta go and all. Been 'ere six months. 'Ave 'er if yer like. Little present. Be glad to give 'er away. Exhaustin' me she is.'

'You were just going to be fair with me.'

There was an embarrassed pause. 'Yeah, well, like anyone, I gotta earn me livin'. Point is that Colonel

Mostyn's used me a few times as well.'

Boysie was on his feet, fists clenched. 'You mean you were getting paid twice over?'

'Steady on, Mr. Oakes, please. No, not twice over. But I knew the score. I mean, you was screwin' Mostyn, weren't yer, so I didn't think there was no 'arm. Take larst year, for instance. That job in Switzerland. The Member of Parliament. Mostyn wanted me to do it, but, as yer well know, I had a stinkin' cold. Even so, when you arsked I came over to do it, didn't I?'

'Can't win, can I?'

'Highly unlikely.' Griffin grave.

A tap at the door. Rubin, attired in black trousers and white high-collared jacket sporting brass buttons. 'Dinner is served for you, sir.' To Griffin, with a bow from the waist. 'And for your friend.' No bow for Boysie.

Crossing the hall, Boysie stopped to admire an exquisite console table. 'This real as well?'

'Beautiful piece.' Griffin all sly smiles. 'Genuine Burgh, mid-eighteenth century. Mate o' mine picked it up in Christie's. Auctioneer wasn't 'arf mad.'

The dining room looked like a regimental officers' mess. A long, polished Jacobean table with matching chairs, military prints decorating walls of muted pond-green silk, silver glinting in the light thrown from half-a-dozen magnificent candelabra. Two place settings were laid, one at each end of the table. Boysie seemed a mile apart from Griffin. All conversation had to be projected across the glass gleam of opulence.

'Want to talk business really,' began Boysie.

Rubin hovered over a side table.

Griffin held up his right hand. 'After we've eaten, if yer don't mind, Mr. Oakes. Never mix business with pleasure. After we've eaten.'

Conversation was difficult at long range, the food

excellent—soufflé de homard, duckling rouennais, cassoulet princesse, and a Château La Tour at which Boysie had to do a double-take. An imposso Château La Tour. 1847. It just could not be.

'You surprise me, Mr. Griffin. I didn't expect...' Boysie shouted during the duckling.

'You thought it would be a semi with G-Plan furniture, china ducks migratin' across the walls, and a frozen-food dinner.' Griffin unperturbed.

Boysie lowered his eyes.

Griffin continued. 'Done very well for meself in me own way. Tried to develop taste. No real income-tax problems in my line. I like a good life. Like yer, Mr. Oakes.'

After the cassoulet princesse, Griffin suggested coffee and liqueurs in the 'drarin' room.'

When Rubin had left them alone with the percolator and bottle, Griffin leaned back in his armchair. 'Yer out of a job. Flat broke. And yer wants 'elp.'

'In a nutshell, Mr. Griffin.'

Pause.

'Well, Mr. Oakes. I 'ave a rule. I never lends money and I never borrows it. But there are other ways. What yer got in the kitty?'

'About five hundred quid.'

'Keep yer in fags for a couple o' weeks. Yer gotta find a job, that's for sure. May be able to 'elp with that anon. In the meantime we gotta tide yer over. You've played fair wiv me, so I'll play fair wiv yer. I mean, I can't see yer goin' back to life in a bed-sitter nor nothin' like that.'

'Unthinkable.' Boysie doing his Noel Coward.

'Yeah. You a gamblin' man?' Snap question.

'Not really. The horses you mean?'

'Blimey, no. Never touch the gee-gees, Mr. Oakes. Yer don't stand an earthly. Only gamble when yer certain to win. And when you've won—vamoose. Out quick.'

'Yes, I've heard professional gamblers have to be disciplined. Haven't really got the temperament myself.'

'Oh well, we can build that in, so to speak. As it were. You played the wheel? Roulette?'

'Two or three times. Total disaster.'

'Yeah, well I can fix it so it's not disaster.'

'How and where?' asked Boysie, dejectedly lighting a cigarette.

Griffin gave him a thin smile. Enigmatic. The right hand moved towards the bell push set into the wall nearby.

Rubin appeared like the Genie of the Lamp. 'Sir?'

'Get me the time of trains to Manchester tomorra. Quick.'

Rubin disappeared. Boysie even expected a puff of smoke.

'I don't lend money,' Griffin continued, 'but I feels I owes yer somethin'. I'm goin' to finance a little gamblin' session. Make yer a grand anyway. Sometime tomorra yer'll be travellin' ter Manchester. Gamblin's no good 'ere in London. Difficult ter rig. I pay's yer expenses—train, 'otel—Grand 'otel's about the best place.'

'I've got to go to Manchester?' Disgust.

'So? Loverley place, Manchester.'

'Venice with drains.'

'Chum, it may not be too 'ot. But it's a loverley place. Cultural as well. All them new buildings. Old and new mergin' into a comprehensive 'ole. The Town 'all. Free Trade 'all. The 'Alle Orchestra. The seductive baton of Sir John Barber's-brolly, City Art Gallery, Woolworth's. Blimey, Mr. Oakes, it's Britain's second city. And the night life. Really swings.'

'Like a metronome do,' said Boysie with superior insolence.

Rubin did his Slave-of-the-Lamp piece again, handing

193

Griffin a sheet of paper. The strange, paradoxical murderer studied it for a moment. Rubin had gone. Silently.

'You'll be travellin' up on the four o'clock train from Euston tomorra afternoon. Arrive Manchester Piccadilly Station at six-forty-four. Tickets and reservations'll be at yer 'otel in the mornin'. Book in at the Grand, then 'ang around until just before eleven. At eleven o'clock you 'ave to arrive at the Night Owl Club. Good, 'igh class gamin' joint orf Market Street. Find it easy enough. When yer go into the gamblin' room you'll see a chemin table. On the right there're three roulette tables. Yer goes ter the middle one, buyin' one 'undred quid's worth o' chips on the way. The croupier will be a tall fellow with blond 'air. Looks a bit of a poof but don't be fooled. Watch the wheel. After you've been there for a few minutes the zero will come up. Then the red nineteen——'

'But how——?'

'The blond croupier owes me a favour and knows I'll do for 'im if 'e don't play. And the middle table's the bugged one.'

'Bugged?'

'Yeah. Bent. Gassed. Electromagnus in the bulb behind the backtrack. Good man—well trained—just turns the switch for a moment at the right second, ball 'as a steel core and stops a second, then falls into the right slot. You want ter get a Scarne's *Guide Ter Gamblin'*, mate, it's all there.'

'Manchester, here I come.'

'I'll 'ave it all set. Any change of plan, Mr. Oakes, and I'll let yer know. Tickets, expenses, and that at yer 'otel in the mornin'. Nice ter 'ave seen yer again. Glad to be of some 'elp. Yer don't know it, but you'll be doin' me a favour and all.'

Boysie did not sleep well. In the past few days he had

become a changed man, alternating between fits of jangling fear and moments of calm, almost calculated diffidence, about the future. Now, cornered and suffering the final indignity of having to go to Griffin for help—financial help—some of the old neuroses were filling the vacant spaces of his subconscious. Those vacuums from which he had cleaned out the more fearsome moments of the last week. He should have not had to go to Griffin. There *was* money. Something? Where? What? Eventually sleep overcame him.

He woke with a start. He automatically noted the time: 8.32. Khavichev. That was it—Khavichev and the account in Switzerland. The numbered account. There *was* money.

Lighting a cigarette, Boysie tried to reach back into the room in East Berlin, to the conversation. Remember. Remember. Nothing. Try again. Visual. Be visual first. Khavichev was on the bed, sitting waiting for something. They had made the deal, Boysie had accepted. He had just come in from the bathroom. Christ, Khavichev had said a draft for twenty thousand pounds was already on its way. But what bank and what number? 'The details will be posted to your London address.' He could hear Khavichev saying it. Details to the flat. Hell. No. For heaven's sake. The mail waiting for him at the flat. He had not even opened one letter. There had been about half a dozen. Had them in his hand when Mostyn phoned. The raincoat. He had shoved them all into his raincoat pocket, intending to read them if he had to wait anywhere.

Boysie was out of bed and over to the wardrobe. Rummage. A forgotten handkerchief in the first pocket together with some dregs of tobacco and a pair of old theatre tickets. Then, in the other pocket the letters. A couple of bills. Airmail from the States (that would be Chicory's latest, she never missed a month). Airmail from

Switzerland. It was there, postmarked Zurich. Boysie ripped open the envelope. Khavichev had kept his side of the bargain. Two hundred and forty-five thousand Swiss francs. Twenty thousand quid. He had enough money in hard cash to buy an air ticket to Zurich now. By to-morrow he could be rolling in it. In England, Boysie always carried his real passport wherever he went—taking it from the safe and slipping it into his jacket pocket had been a reaction, as mechanical as breathing, before leaving the flat for that final, undignified lunch with Mostyn.

Happily, he ordered coffee, shaved, dressed, and went down to Reception. Through their Travel Bureau in the foyer he would probably be able to fix his flight there and then. The hall was crowded, and Boysie paused, automatically, at the Messages and Mail counter. 'Mr. Oakes, Room 200? Yes, there was a small package. He ripped it open. Money, about two hundred pounds, a rail reservation for the four o'clock Euston to Man-chester, and a cable confirming room reservation in the name Oakes. Boysie began to get greedy. Why not? Take Griffin's offer and make an extra thousand on the side. Finally he stopped in front of the Travel Bureau, grinned, and asked if there were any direct flights from Manchester to Zurich. The answer was affirmative, and at this time of the year there should be no difficulty in getting a walk-on booking. Boysie nodded.

At three-forty-five he walked on to Platform Four at Euston and found his reserved seat in Carriage G, Compartment A. The whole compartment was reserved, yet only one of the seats was already occupied—by, it seemed to Boysie, a long pair of fatally gorgeous legs.

She looked young enough to be still a schoolgirl; only the wide grey cat's eyes, peeping from beneath a fringe of hair the colour of ripe corn, betrayed that age had little to do with innocence or experience.

Boysie's gaze got as far as her mouth before his famous self-introductory smile froze. She was using the same pout as last night.

'Hey, you're 'Ortense. An Honourable.' Unconsciously echoing Griffin.

'You're Boysie. Nice Boysie, Griff said.'

Boysie's seat was opposite the Hon's. He sat, limp, a suspicious mind now treading the questionable alleys of why Griffin had so obviously placed this bird on his shoulders. 'And what else did *Griff* say?' He stressed Griffin's unfamiliar diminutive.

The girl's voice was tipped with sugar. No offensive uppercrust drawl. This was not Chelsea game, or Kensington kindling. 'Griff said that I should stick with you, keep you out of trouble, and be a good girl.'

'In other words, Honourable Hortense, he's given you your cards and passed you on to me.'

'Mmmm.' She hummed a happy affirmative. 'And please don't call me Hortense, or Honourable either. Griff used to be terribly—you know—proper.'

Griffin ought to be put away, thought Boysie. What right did he——? Oh well. His eyes were captivated by the long legs, the firm form and confidence of youth. 'What,' he asked, leaning forward, 'what were you to do if I already had someone in tow?'

'Griff said you wouldn't because your regular works during the day. Anyway, he checked to make sure she'd not arranged time off.'

'Thinks of everything, doesn't he?' mused Boysie. He had asked Liz, but she had been furious with him about the previous evening—having arrived at the flat to find the lock changed and 'that plain girl' (Elizabeth's words) in charge. Boysie was certain she did not believe his story, but it would have to wait until he had got the loot from Switzerland. That was more important than anything else.

The corn-coloured girl laughed.

'And if I don't call you Hortense, what *do* I call you? Horty?'

'Ooooh, don't,' squealed the Hon. 'That is my name, Hortense. Hortense Barnstaple.' She paused, disgust in a wrinkled nose. 'The Honourable Hortense Barnstaple. Isn't it ghastly? Friends call me Honey. Honey Mambo.'

'Yes. That's better. Honey. A——'

'Don't say it.'

'What?'

'A taste of Honey. They all say it. The older men, that is.'

'I'm not an older man, darling.' Boysie all camp. 'Let's make two things quite clear from the outset. One, I'm a middle-aged swinger——'

'A raver.' She giggled. 'And, Boysie, you aren't even middle-aged. Don't look it anyway.'

'Thanks. Second point, this is a one-night stand. I'm flying on to Zurich tomorrow. So it's a one-night stand.'

'We'll see, shall we,' said Honey confidently, wriggling her bottom. 'We'll see.'

Long before they reached Manchester, Boysie and Honey were, at least if not intimate, firm friends. Boysie had her life story off her as fast as wheat puffed from a gun barrel. The usual kind of downfall came pouring merrily from her lips. Her own father she had never known, her stepfather hard and strict, counterbalanced by a prosaic mother. Cheltenham reared in the background like a stage prop in her life. Her family rifted, then the drift from convention, followed by a succession of older men. Behind the pretty face and innocent pout lay an amoral animal whose cravings were almost satisfied at the age of twenty-one. Boysie suddenly felt he understood her predicament. Father-figure replacing father-figure. This was really scrambled. One young girl in search of a family. He began to sense shame in himself. A puzzling sensation for one who had rarely thought twice about leaping into bed with any young thing that offered.

The feeling returned when they arrived at the Grand to find Griffin had again played the jester and booked them into the bridal suite. Ought to be helping this girl, not shacking up with her, Boysie began to think. Ought to get her back to her family. Then she came out of the bathroom, minute frilly pants and bra, miles of leg and sunbeams of smile, served up for the asking. He sighed. Was he getting too old for the high life?

The Night Owl was easy to find. It was just as Griffin had described—including the queer-looking croupier and the zero coming up followed by a red nineteen. Boysie adhered to instructions. In less than an hour he walked out of the club twelve hundred pounds to the good but with three double Courvoisiers inside him. Boysie was not a hard-drinking man. He liked his brandy, but somehow the body never had a great tolerance for alcohol. One, even two doubles kept him happy. Three constituted a danger limit tending to distort action and common sense. The old smell of success was back in Boysie's mind.

'Back to the hotel?' asked Honey in tones meaning only one thing.

'No. Don't think so. Feel in a winning mood.' Boysie listing to port.

'Make up thee mind, lad, where's t' be?' The taxi driver with that blunt, familiar rudeness which some Northerners pass off for straight talking.

That did it. 'I've made up my mind, thank you, driver.' Boysie getting truculent. 'Which is the very best gaming club in town?'

'Well, if it's joost brass you want to chook around, tha's coom out o' a pretty fast place 'ere. Only oone better, that's The 'Ong Kong. New opened a moonth or so ago. Big brass there.'

'Sounds like a bloody Chinese restaurant,' slurred Boysie.

'Aye, we've gotta Chink eatin' place called 'Ong Kong an' all,' replied the driver. 'Bu' there's this gamin' 'ell as well. All doon up with fancy women dressed oop as geishas and pagodas and that, shouldn't woonder.' Getting his geography mixed.

'Then take us to it, driver. To The Hong Kong.'

'If tha wants to lose tha brass.'

'Oh, Boysie, and I . . .' Honey snuggling.

Boysie's perverted sense of values acted up again. She would be safer with him at The Hong Kong tables than in a velvety double room at the Grand Hotel.

'The Hong Kong,' he said firmly.

The cab pulled away from the curb and Honey slipped a hand into Boysie's. 'Thought you wanted some time alone with me, darling,' she said. 'After all——'

'Nicer place than you'd imagine,' he was talking loudly, eyes fixed out of the cab window and heart racing. He had to keep it down. This was not going to be like any of the other quick knock-offs in his life. He was determined. And when Boysie got determined he usually went wrong.

The Hong Kong was silk smooth, well lubricated and full of what they call in Las Vegas 'high-rollers'—men and women untroubled at dropping the odd thousand or two in a night. To add atmosphere, The Hong Kong was littered with Chinese: cigarette girls, hostesses, croupiers, and a décor which suggested that customers had left the glitter of the largest city in the north of England and been swept on some jet magic carpet into the big, exciting life of the Orient. It was a large, clever, and psychologically sound confidence trick. Like the big casino-hotels on the Vegas Strip, The Hong Kong was geared to gambling on a twenty-four-hour scale, with clientele sucked into a situation where time had nothing to do with the stark realism of life outside. It was a place where one became totally involved.

At the door there were the usual formalities, a membership card with an unknown sponsor appearing from nowhere. Inside, the foyer and an ornate flight of steps leading up to the Kowloon Room, dining, dancing, and a nightly cabaret. But the tables beckoned first, and Boysie, now playing the role of the last of the big spenders, cashed in for five hundred pounds' worth of chips. He stopped at the first roulette table, grinning at Honey, who looked dubious.

'Get the old system going here, baby, and we'll really make it.'

'Careful, Boysie, please.' Griffin had given her instructions to look after Boysie, and she was worried.

A cocktail waitress was at their elbow. Gin and tonic for the lady; a large brandy, Courvoisier, for himself.

When he had been at the table for less than thirty minutes, half of his Night Owl winnings had gone. He got up solemnly, took Honey's arm, and made for the foyer.

A young, dinner-jacketed man barred their way. 'Maybe you don't want to gamble any more, but the show's just starting in the Kowloon Room. Some great acts to-night.' Persuasive. Boysie looked at Honey. She did not want to go. Boysie, definitely well under by now, still managed to keep control of his intentions. Must tire her out. Not that he didn't fancy her. It would be—no. A definite no.

'Come on, Honey. Let's see the show.' Before she could remonstrate he had her elbow clamped in his right hand and forced her towards the stairs.

The Kowloon Room was a large circular pad with imitation windows brilliantly lit like a stage set, looking out on to views of Hong Kong bay, the island itself hanging in a blaze of lights and colour like a peak draped with sparkling necklaces, to the right. Someone had put a lot of money, thought, and knowledge into the place.

Out of character, on a dais, a Latin-American quintet rattled out a rhumba. Their table was towards the rear of the room but with a good view of the dance floor—the size of a small road roundabout. The prices were enormous. One glance at the menu and they had your trousers down. As unsteady as he was, Boysie's main thought was to get Honey as sloshed as possible. Quickly he ordered a toxic, king-sized Appendicitis De Luxe for each of them. If Honey played, it should do the trick—Grand Marnier, lime juice, gin, and egg whites, on top of the gin she had already consumed. He could slip his under the table. Do anything he liked. Concentration. He must recoup by getting to Zurich as soon as possible. He did not even know the air times. There might not even be a direct flight tomorrow.

A roll on the drums did not seem to make much difference to the lively chatter around the tables. Through the haze Boysie could see that the habitués of the Kowloon Room were not all slink and high-rollers—more a mixture of those who had lost heavily downstairs and were ready to call it quits, ending the evening with a giggle; middle-class couples being daring for the night; at one or two tables heavy-faced men a bit out of their depth.

The persuasive gent from the foyer stood in the middle of the dance floor at a microphone, taking over as *compère*. A bit of heckling from some chinless wonders in the front row as he announced the first act—a coloured girl with a voice that tried hard to be Shirley Bassey's but missed by a good octave. One of the chinless set, very drunk, made loud comments and was shushed violently by people at nearby tables. Honey held Boysie's hand tightly during the sentimental numbers and, to Boysie's delight, swigged long at her Appendicitis De Luxe. The coloured singer ended on 'you can have him.'

'Now, folks. You've had one bit of sex appeal.' The *compère* was back at the mike. 'But here's something quite out of the ordinary.' Boysie's stomach twitched. A brace of stagehands were pushing an ornate chaise longue on to the floor. A pile of clothes at one end. The high-buttoned boots in place. 'You've all seen strippers. At least I hope you have. But here's one with a real difference.' The build-up was not as good as Merry Fern's back in Berlin. 'Not a stripper but a dresser. From China, the Kowloon Room proudly presents a young lady just back from a sensational tour of Europe. Miss Rosy Puberty.'

Boysie hunched into his seat and tried to look inconspicuous. Rosy appeared, spot-lighted, from the far corner of the room, to tremendous applause. The act was almost identical with that he had seen at the Ritz Kursal, only, for the sake of British hypocritical decency, his ravishing Mu-lan walked on, not naked but wearing *le minimum*—a tiny white G-string. The rest followed, the audience excitedly rapt as usual. In the glare of lights she could not possibly have seen Boysie. Even so his face must have betrayed him. Honey leaned over the table, her voice now definitely showing the first signs of inebriation.

'Sexy, darling. You embarrassed? Come back to the hotel and I'll show you better than that.'

Rosy's performance had produced its desired effect, completely ignoring Shakespeare's semi-truism, spoken by the porter in the Scottish play, that drink 'provokes the desire but takes away the performance.'

During the clamour of applause Boysie took the

opportunity of ordering another Appendicitis for Honey. It had been a shock to come suddenly upon Mu-lan again. Thoughts raced. Should he sneak out and make contact? Or get her address from the management? No. Keep clear—the still voice inside.

The *compère* again. 'That's all the sex we have to offer you, I'm afraid. But tonight we are more than proud to present a man respected throughout the world for his strange and baffling talents. We are lucky enough to have him here under a four-month contract. When you've seen him once, you will want to come back again and again. Ladies and gentlemen, the greatest mind-reader living. Born in China of British parents, this young man has taken over twenty years to develop his extraordinary powers—ten of these years were spent in a Buddhist monastery. I ask you to concentrate on the fantastic Professor Madrigal.'

The hair rose on the back of Boysie's neck like the quills of a porcupine at bay. He felt sick, eyes riveted to the artists' entrance. Professor Madrigal. Hong Kong. He had heard Madrigal say that he had to be in Hong Kong. Could it have been at The Hong Kong? Boysie had not seen the face, but by God he would never forget that voice. 'K-kill th-em.' Breathlessness. Heartbeat in his ears. Blood to the head.

Voices were deceptive. Boysie really did not know what to expect. In his inner consciousness, Madrigal's face and form had appeared to him in a hundred guises, ranging from a warped Gorilka-like figure to an inscrutible Charlie Chan. The centipedes, which had been moving rapidly along both his small and large intestines, came to a rapid halt as Professor Madrigal walked into view. This could not possibly be the ogre of his nightmares, that shadowy figure lurking and stuttering in the horrific hangar. For a second there was an association of ideas working hard in Boysie's mind and bringing with them an almost psychosomatic reaction—the smell of the hangar, glare of light, the pain and fear.

This Madrigal was young, slim, and immaculate in a smoke-grey DJ with black silk lapels. His face was so English that tradition, the outmoded order of British squirearchy, Olnui pancake race, and the Changing of the Guard seemed to be almost foreign by comparison. The man who stood in the centre of the Kowloon Room's floor, modestly accepting the scattered applause, could have barely reached his late twenties or early thirties. His face, slim and in direct proportion with his body, was, at first sight, too good-looking: a high forehead, eyes steady and certain, a light hazel, swiftly moving around the room, summing up his audience, mentally weighing individuals and parties, sorting the sheep from the goats, separating the difficult and sceptical from those who would go along with him for the sake of pure entertainment. His hair, showing the preliminary signs of thinning from the forehead, was groomed straight back, the natural waves brushed and cut down to avoid any hint of showiness; flat ears, long Romanesque nose, friendly mouth, and strong jaw line.

Madrigal's hands held no stage props, no pseudo-mind-reader equipment in evidence. The impression was of an entertainer approaching his audience with direct confidence. He emanated friendliness and a relaxed approach. A casual glance by any intelligent observer would mark him as a professional—in the street he could be taken for a doctor, lawyer, even a young tycoon. Certainly he had the static of power almost visibly around him.

Boysie sighed out his worry. Madrigal? Coincidence. But as soon as the man opened his mouth, the centipedes were rapidly on the move again, joined immediately by any army of red ants progressing in columns of four through Boysie's stomach, while a small plague of locusts ate their way along his spinal chord. In front of his public, Madrigal's distinctive stammer was reduced to an attractive, hinted impediment, but the voice remained unmistakable. The tall, pleasant young man with the easy relaxed smile demanding audience attention in the Kowloon Room was without doubt the Madrigal who had, out of hand, ordered the summary death of Rabbit Warren and Boysie Oakes. The man whom General Kuan Hsi Shi (Warbler, as Boysie knew him), Shi T'ung K'u (the Tormentor, Gazpacho), and all the parchment-yellow boys at the camp on Bloody Island or Peking or Wales or wherever it was held in ridiculous deference as a mastermind.

Boysie, while keeping his attention on Madrigal, tried to pretend that he was invisible, sinking lower into the chair, mind split between the horror of finding this man, by accident, and the racing thoughts of how he could rid himself of Honey Mambo without hurting a conscience which wrestled within him. The confusion dissolved as Madrigal started his performance. Hatred bubbled like a witch's cauldron. For the first time, Boysie wanted to kill in cold blood. Thoughts of the inhuman, senseless, and calculated torture, the arrogance, and the evident fact that Madrigal overlorded some dreadful operation, Chinese-backed and aimed at the Western world, brought death into total perspective. Boysie wanted Madrigal's blood. Paradoxically, he signalled to a waiter, indicating that Honey should have another drink—unconsciously getting her out of the way for a grand kill. The destruction of Madrigal.

Madrigal himself, oozing charm as a fatal bullet wound seeps out blood, was in the midst of his preliminary spiel.

'M-my name is Madrigal—an English name going back to the time when witchcraft was ri-ife in this country and anyone with the kinds of talents I have acquired would be highly suspect. As I-I've said. My name is Madrigal.

Madrigal the mind-reader. I want to demonstrate to you some of the amazing things that are possible with just a little practice—twenty years' practice, concentration, and self-denial in my case—and your cooperation.'

The chinless drunk made a loud comment. 'You wanna learn to shtand up shtraight for a shtart.'

Madrigal glanced at him in contempt and carried on. 'Now, I see a lady sitting at this table on my right.' He walked to the table—two men and two girls; a dark nervous girl giggled as the charm was aimed straight at her. 'I wonder if you'll help me by coming on a journey in the mind?'

She nodded.

'I-I w-w-want you to imagine you are going to visit the house of a friend. You w-walk along the road and come to this p-person's h-house. Will you do that? Imagine you are actually doing it.'

The girl nodded shyly.

'You open the gate and walk up the path. Are you d-doing that?'

The girl nodded again.

'You are just about to ring the d-doorbell when you notice the n-number of the house. It's in large n-numbers. Large figures. The n-number of your friend's house. You've followed me so far, yes?'

Once more she nodded.

'Now.' Madrigal completely oblivious to everyone but the girl. 'I want you just to think of this n-number. The n-number you see on your-your friend's h-house.' He had taken a card from his pocket, a pen from the inside of his jacket. 'All right, fix it in your m-mind. See it big. The n-number of this friend's h-house. Go on, k-keep thinking of it.'

The girl gave a minute nod.

Madrigal's eyes locked with hers. His pen moved down to the card, boldly writing something. The tension eased.

'Now. Please, I ask you not to change your mind, otherwise b-both of us will be in t-trouble. I have committed myself. I have wr-written a n-number on this card. The n-number I believe is identical with that of your friend's h-house. The n-number you have been thinking of. Would you tell the l-ladies and gentlemen what that n-number is?'

Hesitation. Then the girl said clearly, 'Seventy-nine.'

Madrigal tossed the card on to the table. 'Read what I have wr-written, please.'

The girl looked stunned for a moment and then laughed nervously. 'You are right. Number seventy-nine.'

It was a smash opening. Madrigal smiled knowingly, about to turn away. The drunk, only two tables to the left, started to act up again. 'Noshing in that. Shimple. Noshing clever about that.'

'I'll come to you in a minute. I promise you.' Madrigal turned back to the girl's table. 'While I'm over here, I wonder if you'd try something else. I'd like to show you an experiment in hypnotism. Is there a package of cigarettes on the table?' A pack of Players was at her boy friend's elbow. 'I wonder, for the sake of entertaining everybody, if you would remove the silver paper from that pack of cigarettes and strip off the backing?'

The girl followed instructions.

'Now just roll the silver paper into a tight ball, as tight as possible, now place it on your palm. Okay? Concentrate on me. Concentrate. The silver paper is getting hot. Warm. Hot. Hotter. Hotter. It will become so hot that you cannot bear to hold it.'

The girl yelped with pain and threw the silver paper to one side. Laughter, even from the girl. Applause, which finally dwindled. The drunk started turning very nasty. Loudly he shouted out, 'You're a bloody fraud. Wouldn't dare to do anything with me.'

Boysie could see the fury building in Madrigal's face.

The mind-reader crossed to the centre and stood directly in front of the stupid sloshed one.

'You look fine to me.' The imbiber undoubtedly an ex-officer in some smart regiment—the battalion know-all, hated by many and disliked by most. 'Frightened,' he goaded Madrigal. 'That's what you look like. Frightened.'

Madrigal's guard dropped for a second. 'Madrigal fears no man.' He spat out. 'Have you got some cigarettes?' A slight pause before adding, 'sir.'

'Course.'

'Then I'll try the same experiment I tried with the young lady just now. Take out the silver paper, strip off the lining of thin paper, and roll the silver paper into a small ball. Now, don't just place it in your palm like the young lady did, grip it tightly in your fist.'

The drunk fumbled a little before getting it right.

'It's going to be hot,' said Madrigal quietly. 'Hot. Hot. Hotter.'

The drunk was uncooperative. 'Feelsh perfectly normal to me,' he said. 'Fact if anything'sh getting colder.'

'Right.' Madrigal with a terrific snap. 'That silver paper is going to burn through your hand. You're going to feel a lot of pain.'

It took a matter of seconds. The drunk emitted a shriek of anguish and dropped the paper, nursing his hand. Madrigal smiled and turned his back, walked quietly away.

Even from where he sat, Boysie could see the large blister, raw red, on the man's palm. There was no more trouble with the drunk. Madrigal carried on with his act, giving an amazing display of completely unpredictable items. He named addresses and telephone numbers known only to individuals in the audience, spelt out the serials of five-pound notes in a man's wallet, did the impossible. It was a performance of extraordinary ability. Fascinating and fantastic. The mind-reader ended up by selecting a young woman at random and asking her to think of any great, well-known public figure and to concentrate on this man or woman. He sat, now in the centre of the floor, holding a sketching board and charcoal in front of him. The woman concentrated, Madrigal sketched, occasionally looking up at her, and finally asked the name of the person of whom she had been thinking. It was the Prime Minister. Madrigal turned the board to face the audience. There was a perfect charcoal sketch of the PM.

The mind-reader left the floor to tremendous applause. The clapping continued, and he slowly, almost sheepishly, returned. When silence came, Madrigal spoke —again the soft persuasive, even gentle voice.

'You seem to have liked my w-work. S-so to end I will do one very small item. An-an illustration of how the mind can control the m-mind. A short demonstration in hypnosis. As th-this is only going to be a brief demonstration I wonder if you will allow me to choose my vi-victim—I mean, of course, my subject. I assure you that nobody is going to be made to look st-stupid.' He was edging towards a table where one or two of the heavier, rough-hewn men sat. Madrigal fixed his eyes on one of the party, singling him out. 'You, sir,' he said. 'I promise there will be no embarrassment. Would you help me?'

The man, broad-shouldered, with a face that would not have been out of place in a boxing ring, was uncertain. His friends began to heckle him, but eventually he nodded acceptance.

'Good. If you'll step this way.' Madrigal led his subject on to the floor and seated him facing to the left. 'Can I ask you, sir, have you ever been hypnotised before?'

'Nay, lad.' A broad Manchester accent matching the man's build.

Madrigal smiled. 'I get the impression that you don't altogether believe in hypnosis.'

'Never really thought abou' it. Don't 'old mooch with this sort o' thing.' Uneasy.

'I'm sorry about that, sir.' Madrigal genuinely apologetic. 'Perhaps we had better choose another subject.'

'Nay. You 'ave a go. See what thee can do.'

'All right.'

Madrigal seemed to change. Or was it Boysie's imagination? This was still part of a demonstration, but Madrigal gave the impression of projecting his whole being towards the hard man facing him in the chair. It was as though the performance did not really matter. The man in the chair mattered.

'I shall need a little cooperation from you,' Madrigal said, authority mingled with the calm quality of his voice, an authority which cut through any pleasantries. 'Just relax with your hands on your knees. That's it. Now pick some point in front of you and look at it. Don't take your eyes off it. Keep looking at that point. Relax. Relax. I want you to relax your whole body. Everything. Keep looking at the point. Now relax as you have never relaxed before. Imagine you are so completely unwinding that your body is almost melting in relaxation. Start at the toes. Relax the toes. Keep your eyes fixed on that one point. Now let all the muscles go as you relax. Relax the whole of your feet. Now the ankles and calves. The knees and thighs. They're disappearing. Keep your eyes fixed on that one point.' The room was silent but for Madrigal's voice, cool and directed solely at his subject.

Boysie glanced across at Honey. She had almost finished the last Appendicitis and was definitely wavering, nearly reacting to Madrigal's soft, continuous flow of talk, which went on without a pause.

'You are feeling tired. Very tired. Eyes still open but

keep looking at the same spot. Now go on relaxing. Relax your stomach muscles. You have no stomach. Now the chest. You're feeling very tired. You can hardly keep your eyes open. Your eyelids feel like lead weights. Relax the shoulders. Arms. Hands. Fingers. Feel the cloth of your trousers under your fingertips. Your fingertips are going into nothing. So tired. Important. Relax your neck. Like jelly. Your neck's like jelly. Now the face. Chin. Cheeks. Even your hair. Keep your eyes on that one spot. Relax. Your eyelids are drooping. There are lead weights hanging from them. Pulling them down. You are falling asleep. You just cannot keep your eyes open. In a moment I am going to count to five. When I reach the figure five, next time I say five, your eyes will close and you will be in a deep hypnotic sleep. You will be able to hear everything I say and do everything I tell you to do. You will be under my control and nobody else will have this power over you.'

Boysie's hair bristled. It may have enthralled everybody else in the room, but for Boysie it was an act of power which meant something more than just ordinary entertainment or a showy demonstration of hypnosis.

'In one minute you will sleep as you've never slept before. You will be able to answer me but do nothing without me.' Madrigal paused, his face like rock, eyes fixed on the bulky man in the chair. Boysie's mind was clear. For the time being his alcohol intake made no difference. He was enmeshed in something of extreme importance. Intuitively he knew.

Madrigal was still speaking. '... one ... two ... three ... four ... five.' The subject's eyes snapped shut like a Venus flytrap. The whole body rigid, still. The face a mask. No movement but for the regular breathing. Everyone in the room still concentrated. Madrigal turned to the audience. 'You see, ladies and gentlemen, the subject, a normal man like any of yourselves, is in a deep hypnotic trance. If anyone has doubts about this, I ask you here and now to come forward. Anybody.' He underlined the word. 'Just come forward, and I'll do exactly the same for you.' Nobody moved.

Madrigal's eyes darted around the room. 'All right. Very quickly I will demonstrate how our friend here is under complete hypnotic control. I have nothing in my hand, as you can see.' He showed his right hand to be empty on both sides. Placing his thumb and forefinger together, he addressed the tranced man. 'If you can hear me, raise your right hand.'

The subject's right hand moved upwards and then dropped back on to his knee.

'Just a simple test of reaction. I am going to prick you very lightly on your right hand with a pin. Just a tiny pricking sensation. I am holding the pin now.' He again showed the audience that his hand held nothing, then brought down the thumb and forefinger in a swift jab, as though stabbing the man's hand.

The subject winced and jumped with pain.

'That'—Madrigal to the audience again—'shows how far auto-suggestion can go under hypnosis. Now, something else.' To the subject, 'Do you ever go fishing?'

'Yes.' Grunted, as though through layers of cotton wool.

'All right. You are sitting by the river bank and you are going to fish. You have all the equipment with you. Bait your hook and then cast the line.'

In perfect mime the subject went through the routine of baiting and casting. Tension eased a little, and the audience began to laugh.

'You see, it's easy to make somebody think he is elsewhere. We'll try just one more.' Then, to the subject, 'Okay, that's enough fishing for today. You've earned a drink. There's a pint of beer, your favourite beer, in front of you now. Go ahead.'

The big fellow went ahead. You could almost taste the stuff and see the mug as the beer went down, the man's throat making perfect swallowing motions. The audience was in hysterics. Boysie noticed that the band was quietly easing itself back on to the dais. The subject put down his imaginary pint and drew the back of his right hand over his mouth.

More laughter from the audience, then Madrigal was addressing them again. 'These are just small simple things. I am now going to wake the patient—if we can call him that. But before we do, I will show you one of the most amazing things about hypnosis. The phenomena of post-hypnotic suggestion. Watch and listen very carefully.'

He addressed the subject again. 'In a few moments I am going to wake you. I will count from five to one. When I next reach the number one you will be wide awake. You will remember nothing except that you have had a short sleep. You will feel happy and contented. You'll wake up smiling. We will speak briefly, after which I'll take out my handkerchief and blow my nose. As I do this the band will start to play a waltz. You will immediately imagine that you have a partner and waltz back to your table. Do you understand?'

'Yes.' Again the muffled affirmative.

Then once again Madrigal addressed the audience. 'You will see how post-hypnotic suggestion works. I must remind you that we do not want to embarrass the gentleman, and in order to plant the idea firmly in his mind I am again going to repeat my instructions by whispering them in his ear. Excuse me one moment.'

Madrigal bent over the man, speaking softly, lips close to the ear. Was Boysie imagining it, or was there more concentration this time? More stress? Madrigal straightened up. 'Right'—he snapped at the subject—

'you will now waken. Five ... four ... three ... two ... one.'

The subject's eyes snapped open. A grin slowly spread across his large face as he got to his feet and stretched. 'By Gow, that were joost like goin' ta sleep. Is that wha' thee calls 'ipnosis?'

Titters among the classier sections of the audience. Madrigal slowly took out his handkerchief and blew his nose. The band started up a waltz, and the man, now looking larger and, in a way, more ridiculous, stretched out his arms, took hold of the thin air which was his invisible partner, and went through a series of light, perfect waltz steps back to his cronies. Laughter all round, including guffaws from the waltzing man.

Madrigal stepped forward to take his bow, and Boysie hurriedly summoned the waiter for the bill. All was not right. Dismissed or not, he had to get hold of Mostyn. But quick.

Honey was quite incapable. In the taxi she lolled against him, murmuring endearments and hanging on. Boysie prayed she would drop into a state of insensibility. It took both himself and the cab driver to get her out of the taxi when they arrived at the hotel. She managed to get across the foyer and into the lift without undue trouble, insisting constantly that she was all right. Once in their room it was all over. Boysie sighed with relief. Honey Mambo was actually flat out, fully dressed, on the bed and snoring.

Mostyn. No good ringing HQ. He slipped his address book from his pocket and checked on the number, Mostyn's private number, and picked up the phone. It took at least five minutes to get through.

'Mostyn.' Sleepy and discontented, the voice came tumbling sharply into Boysie's ear.

'What the hell're you ringing me up at this time of night for—this time of the morning. It's bloody two

215

o'clock. Anyway we don't belong any more.'

'I know. I'm sorry, Colonel, but it's important.'

'The answer is no. I can't lend you a penny.'

'I don't want to borrow money. I've found Madrigal. Something's up. Very funny. He's working in an incredible mind-reading act in Manchester, at a place called The Hong Kong. That's what he must have meant. He hasn't gone to Hong Kong at all. He's here.'

'Madrigal?' Mostyn still not completely awake, 'who the hell's—oh yes, I remember.'

'You know, at the Interrogation Centre——'

'Then tell it to the Special Branch, Boysie boy. I'm not your boss any more.'

'No, but you do run the perishing thing.'

'Perishing. It's perished. And do I hell run it. Thought bad news travelled fast. You don't know what's happened?'

'What?' Boysie in mid-Pacific.

'Special Security's been disbanded. Not only you out of a job, Boysie. The Chief's gone to the Lords, and I'm here on my own. Bloody pensioned off, so go somewhere else with your blasted Madrigals and fiddle-dee-dees. Good night.'

Final. No comeback. Just the phone clunking into place far away in London.

Boysie stood, receiver in hand, astonished, mind doing odd twists and rolls. The Department closed. Everybody out. The whistle had blown.

Honey snored on peacefully. For a second Boysie felt virtuous. A year, six months ago, even a month ago, he would have been undressing the girl and popping in beside her. Tomorrow, the day would have been ridden away on a sexual carousal. Now, this kind of thing was not for him. The Department had closed. Good-bye to the old life. The king is dead. Long live the king. Zurich and the twenty thousand pounds beckoned. He was tired, exhausted, but money always called.

Jiggling the receiver rests, he got through to the operator. Was Manchester Airport open at this time of night? It was, they had a twenty-four-hour service. Get him Manchester Airport then. It took less than a minute before a revoltingly wide-awake voice was on the line. Zurich? Next flight? Swiss Air had one going out at 03.20. It gave him an hour and a bit. They would put him on to Swiss Air. Another couple of minutes. Yes, there were vacancies, but he would have to hurry. Regulations. By rights you had to be checked in at least thirty minutes before the scheduled time of take-off, but there was a half-hour delay on this flight. (Wasn't there on all of them?) If it was a definite booking they would hold the seat for him until ten past three.

Boysie moved. Excuses to the night staff. His suitcase. A taxi quickly. A scribbled note to Honey:

Dear little Honey,
   Sorry about all this but have to get to Zurich. Leave your address here and I will be in touch as soon as possible. Money enclosed so you're not left on the rocks. I have no right, but why not try to make it up and go home to your father and mother. Thanks for everything.

Love,
Boysie

A fast taxi ride and an even faster check-in. Yet he still had time for another large brandy—the old stomach playing up, reacting to the thought of flying.

Take-off, as always, was pure hell: sweating, and the all-too-familiar vivid picture of the aircraft engulfed in flame. But soon they were heading steadily on course. Boysie loosened his seat belt (he never actually undid the wretched thing) and tilted the seat back. Fatigue took over. The next thing he knew was the hostess shaking his shoulder. She had tightened his belt before landing and they were taxiing in. It was six in the morning, chilly, and customs formalities waited. He was in Zurich.

Boysie found a hotel for one night and deposited his hastily packed suitcase. He made the bank before they were even open. Inside, everyone was polite and eager to assist, among the marble, chrome, and glass. The manager spoke English and tried to persuade him to keep some money on deposit. Boysie was tempted but won through, leaving with a package heavy with Swiss francs. He spent the rest of the day nipping from bank to bank, changing francs into sterling, dropping a couple of thousand on the deal. Never mind, now there were funds for the asking.

The following morning, in terror, he boarded a BEA Trident and headed for London, money stashed all over the place, even cellotaped to his chest and back— uncomfortable, as it made him crackle at every move.

Luckily the boys at Heathrow were busy when they finally landed. By mid-afternoon Boysie was back at the Strand Palace, determined not to push his luck. The cash had to last. Now to find a flat and start some new and less terrifying line of business.

VIII. DOLPHIN

Since once I sat upon a promontory,
And heard a mermaid on a dolphin's back,
Uttering such a dulcet and harmonious breath,
That the rude sea grew civil at her song.
　　Shakespeare, *A Midsummer Night's Dream*

TIME, the cliché runs, is a great healer. With some it heals quicker than most. Boysie Oakes had a happy knack of being able to push unpleasant things into the background. He opened with a new bank by popping a thousand pounds of his Russian-provided cash into a deposit account. The rest he kept in envelopes, moving them every twenty-four hours from safe-deposit box to safe-deposit box, on mainline railway and underground stations. Within a few months, he reckoned, he could get a fair old balance showing at the bank. Next, a year's lease on a splendidly appointed flat in Glendale House, among the lush lawns, fountains, and general amenities of socially opulent Dolphin Square.

Two weeks went by. Over eight million pints of milk were drunk in the London area, while one thousand three hundred children were born and a similar number of people died, all in London, two at the hands of murderers who were apprehended and charged within a matter of hours. A Cabinet Minister resigned. The Prime Minister visited Washington for two days of talks with the President of the United States, and the Minister of Labour made a Party political broadcast in which he stated that the rise in strikes, both wildcat and those supported by the Trade Unions, was, to say the least, alarming. Indeed, in two weeks there were four major strikes, a couple of them in the North of England.

In the meantime, Boysie searched his mind for plans which would give him a certain salary with the minimum amount of work. As usual, he merely put off the evil day, made it up with Elizabeth, and spent his now completely free time seeing the latest shows, eating well, and sleeping, with Elizabeth of course, even better. Elizabeth, with her sense of duty and public spirit, continued to work at the Board of Trade. The first fortnight went by.

The crunch came on a Monday bright with late spring and the good omens of summer. It also came through the same person who had started Boysie on his undercover and neuroticised career as Liquidator to the now defunct Department of Special Security—James George Mostyn.

Mostyn had become a bitter man. It was not an unnatural reaction. For years he had enjoyed power. Power and the sense of active service were the things which kept Mostyn on the ball. Financially he never had to worry. The golden-handshake cash was welcome, but the Mostyns were an old established family. Somewhere, way back, there had been a title. And it was public knowledge that a Lady Fitzroy Mostyn had been mistress to Henry II long before the king took up with 'the fair Rosalind.'

But Mostyn was restless, unsettled. The only world he knew was that of Security and Intelligence. He needed to work. In desperation the former Second-in-Command of Special Security applied for two jobs as security officer in industrial firms, but it was no good. The people at the top just looked blank when he outlined measures which he would obviously have to take if he obtained the post. On both applications he was turned down.

The ultimate idea came to Mostyn in a sudden explosion of inspiration while sitting over a gin and tonic in the Cheshire Cheese. There would have to be partners of course. He could not do it on his own. No, not necessarily partners. Better to have underlings. His own security service, a private and confidential organisation with Colonel Mostyn at the head. Industry, people with private problems; they would flock to him. So many were frightened to go straight to the authorities. Back to the old game with a difference. Not tied down by the flying mare of red tape. Not all that much anyway. Partners? Why partners? Far better to have underlings. The power puppeteer complex showed in a sardonic smile creasing Mostyn's lips. Underlings. Yes.

It was precisely at this moment that thought and coincidence ran headlong into each other. Mostyn took a sip of his drink and nearly choked as a voice, all too well known, came shyly from behind his left shoulder.

'Hello, Colonel. Mind if I join you? Care for a spot of the old mothers?' asked Boysie Oakes. The Cheshire Cheese was not one of his usual haunts, but loose ends bring individuals into the most unlikely meeting places.

'Oh, Christ.' Mostyn sighed. 'Thought I'd seen the last of you.'

'Bad pennies and all that.' Boysie grinned and made for the bar without waiting for Mostyn's acceptance.

Mostyn's eyes followed the broad shoulders, watching as the big buffoon pushed his way through the mill of tourists and journalists crushing for the liquid lift to carry them through the afternoon. Mostyn bit his lip. Underlings? He had held Boysie to ransom for a long time. Could he do it again? The docile killer had not done a fandango when the Department axed him, but a spot of bluff might help. At least he knew Boysie—his ways, limitations, armour chinks. It could be a starter. Smooth. Do it as cool and syrupy as he knew.

'*Prophesy not unto us right things, speak unto us smooth things, prophesy deceits,*' he murmured. No one like old Isaiah for saying the right thing.

Mostyn had mild doubts watching Boysie return to the table. The lad did not look broken. The sudden chop from the Department should have caused grievous bodily, mental, and financial harm. Mostyn, still confident that he was never wrong about human nature, would have staked his reputation on Boysie's going downhill fast. But his former menial looked clean, well cut, smart, and suavely turned out. Impossible though it might seem, Mostyn had to admit that he may have misjudged. Boysie gave all the signs of having landed on his feet the right way up. These signs were even stronger once conversation began. Boysie brimmed with pleasure, confidence streaming from every attitude, even the way he sat opposite his former boss was disturbing—no aggression, simply the posture of fused one-upmanship and careful diffidence.

'Cigarette, sir?'

Boysie was too casual. It made Mostyn uneasy. He waved his hand in a gesture of utter contempt for the habit. Silence, then Mostyn's naturally curious instincts got the better of him. 'Bit snappy on the phone the other night,' he began. Gently, don't let yourself get flustered and pushed into a corner. 'Sorry about that, Boysie old chum, but it was late and—well, you know. All been a bit of a blow. Didn't really want to know. You get in touch with Special Branch about that chap? What's his name? Madrigal?'

'No.' Boysie complacent. 'They haven't been near me, so I left it. Their headache now.'

'Not very public-spirited.'

'Sorry, sir, but I lost touch with public-spiritedness working for you.'

'Yes.' Mostyn pensive, trying to work it out. 'Doing

222

well?' he asked.

'Not doing at all—'cept in the most vulgar sense. Like what's-his-name in that Galsworthy book, waiting for something to turn up.'

'Dickens.' Mostyn's smile broadening, the tiger knowing he now had the upper hand.

'What?'

'Dickens, not Galsworthy. Micawber, character in *David Copperfield*—Dickens. Waiting for something to turn up, eh? You look prosperous enough to get along without anything turning up.'

'I had something put by for the old cold front. The rain scores.' Foxy.

'Didn't show on your bank account, laddie.' The old Mostyn, opinionated and full of self-assurance.

'You don't think I kept everything in my bank account, do you?' Boysie equally self-assured. 'The mattress, sir. Under the mattress? I'm a country boy, remember?'

Mostyn refused to be deflated. 'So you're now eating out your savings.' Sneer. 'A bed-sitter, and keeping up some sort of image for the sake of the dickie birds.' He touched Boysie's lapel lightly. 'Or should I say duckie birds?'

Boysie took a long drag at his cigarette, looked at it, then at Mostyn. With distaste he stubbed out the fag end and gave a supercilious one-sided leer. 'There is only one duckie bird, and I have an apartment in Dolphin Square.'

'My, my. The affluent society. A world of indifference, privacy, and solitude. Stuffed mattresses indeed. Who is your taxidermist?'

'I don't have a car.'

Mostyn, despite the somewhat shaking facts, remained his imperturbably true self. 'I failed miserably, didn't I, Boysie?' A fading sigh. 'Using a customed word like taxidermist and your mind immediately turns to public transport. A taxidermist is an animal stuffer. Birds a speciality.'

'So I am a taxidermist.' Shrugging. They sipped their drinks before Boysie spoke again. 'And how are you making out, sir? Enjoying retirement?'

'No, I'm not.' Firmly. It slipped out before Mostyn could stop himself. He paused for a moment before plunging. 'Better the devil you know.' He knew Boysie and how to handle him. Casually putting his glass on the table, he settled back in the chair, eyes fixed on Boysie's face. 'You've got nothing in view? No offers? Company directorships or things like that?' Sarcastic and snide.

'Like old times, hearing you talk like that.' Boysie found himself unruffled. 'Why? You've got something in mind?'

'Matter of fact I have.' Mostyn leaning across the table, speaking low as if speaking love. 'Could be a bundle in it. It's an idea. You want to talk about it?'

'Depends.'

'No, it doesn't depend—except on the fact that you and I are security-trained. Let's go somewhere a little more discreet.'

'Such as my flat where you can drink my booze?'

'Precisely.' The thin, satisfied smile, as Mostyn rose, flicked a hand down the cuff of his right arm, removing imaginary dust, and reached for his umbrella.

The Dolphin Square flat was not as flashy as Boysie's old apartment off Chesham Place, but it reflected a more austere taste. Mostyn, while waiting for Boysie to pour the drinks, perused the bookshelves. Instead of the latest blood, thunder, guts, and rapid sex that had crammed Boysie's former library, he noted that Steinbeck, Hemingway, and Fitzgerald were to the fore. Even Saul Bellow was in there.

'Literary aspirations, eh?' Mostyn running the ferrule

of his umbrella along the books.

'Don't damage the spines, Colonel. Your own vertebrae could get snarled up.' Boysie passed over a drink and sat down. 'Sit and tell all.'

Mostyn settled himself with slight discomfort. 'Security, old Boysie. I've had a long time at the game now. Now I'm restless. Been my life and I've got to get back. You're out of a job. I trained you——'

'To kill.'

'All right, to kill. But you spent enough time in my office to know how security works. I mean, you could bug or tap. You know enough about networks, cells, set-ups, cut-outs.'

'Your clichés are showing, Colonel. You've been reading too many straight suspense books.'

'Okay, son.' Mostyn the hard man again—finger up like the 'Kitchener-Wants-*You*' poster. 'The words are public property. But how many people know the real stuff? Very few.'

'You want to get back into security. Why not apply? The M Sections are still operational.'

Mostyn laughed. A throaty cynicism. 'And the Political, not to mention the Diplomatic Agency. See that play on television the other night? Fellow said every diplomat is a legalised spy. The thing is that security doesn't necessarily concern spies. Outdated Oaksie. Mata Hari went out with Mata Hari. Good Christ, Buddha, Krishna, and Vishnu, you know ninety per cent of the Eastern defectors are wanted for criminal acts in their own countries.'

'What are you getting at?'

'The individual. The individual who needs security protection. The small industrial organisation whose own security officers know sweet FA—except how to run spot checks on how many people are knocking off company property. I'm thinking of a private security organisation.'

'A hepped-up detective agency?'

'Could put it like that, yes. A private detective agency dealing solely with security. No sleazy divorce cases and what the daily woman saw. A specialised firm. Very smart. Very pricey. But an organisation that gets results.'

'You'd want offices. A staff. Money.'

'Begin in a small way. I've got money. I'd put up the capital. Even give you a job to begin with.'

'Office boy?'

'PA to me. Twenty-five a week do you?'

'You're joking.' Boysie gulped at his drink, a ginger ale disguised as brandy. 'It's a great idea, Colonel. I'm with you. But I'm only with you on one condition.'

'And that is?'

'A share. I put in a share of the cash. Where were you thinking of offices?'

'I haven't been thinking. Tinkering with the idea in the back of my mind. But if I'm going ahead, why not here?'

'This flat isn't big enough to swing a tart's bar.'

'No, you idiot. Dolphin Square. Plenty of room, plenty of flats going. You've got one. I could get one, and we could rent a double to operate from. The kind of clients we are after would feel at home. What else do we need? Equipment—a secretary, private line, our own switchboard. Could be arranged quickly.'

'How much?'

'Start on a capital of, say, sixty thousand pounds.'

'Just the two of us?'

'If you like.' Mostyn could see from Boysie's face that the figure could not be split down the middle. 'You put up half? Fifty-fifty?'

Boysie hesitated. 'Sorry. No. You'd have the lion's share. I can manage ten thousnd.' Even that was pushing it.

'Mmmm.' Mostyn disquieted. He did not think Boysie

226

could find even that much.

'Okay.' Boysie quickly. 'What if we get swamped? How about some muscle?'

'Muscle?' Mostyn blank-eyed.

'Come off it. You know exactly what I mean. A third party. Our third party.'

'*Our* third party?'

'Charlie.'

'Charlie?'

'Charles Griffin.'

'Griffin? But——'

'I had dinner with Griffin the other night, Colonel.'

Mostyn's face flushed, the expression of a man who has been given a swipe and back-hander from a Lesbian wrestler. 'I see.'

Boysie was going full out. 'Officially, Charlie retired, but I think he'd appreciate a share in something like this.'

The silence was ear-splitting. Boysie's mind raced over the possibilities. Mostyn was right. They could make a bundle. Mostyn weighed the problem carefully. They would need at least three men in operation if things moved fast. Forty thousand was nothing to him. Sixty thousand was nothing to him. But it would help to have the odd twenty thousand thrown in by a couple of others. Griffin he could trust even more than Boysie. Boysie always made him nervous. Boysie and Griffin together would hold only a third of the shares.

Boysie waited.

At last Mostyn nodded. 'If he'll play he's in. Ten thousand from each of you and forty from me.'

Boysie gestured towards the telephone. 'You know his number as well as I do.'

Mostyn wearily heaved himself out of the chair. The phone call was a classic piece of confidence-building double-talk. Griffin was a businessman. By the time the telephone was replaced, the hook was baited. 'We're supposed to go straight round. I think you're right. Like me, he's bored stiff.'

As they got to Mostyn's car Boysie asked, 'You've been out there before? You know the way?'

'Many times.' Mostyn turned from the car door and smiled. It was one of the most sympathetic smiles Boysie had ever seen from Mostyn. The ex-Second-in-Command added quietly, 'Shakes you a bit, doesn't it?'

Griffin was enthusiastic. The plans were outlined. Ten thousand compared to the potential returns was nothing.

'It'll be a real pleasure workin' wiv yer both. What we gonna call the outfit?' He already had a cheque book open.

'Security Unlimited.' Boysie without inspiration.

Mostyn disregarded him, like a man pretending he did not have halitosis. 'What about Mostyn Secuior. Nice ring about that.'

'Look, mate'—Griffin's pen poised over the cheque book—'even though we got the smaller shares, if yer name's gonna be there, then our names gonna be there as well.'

'What about initials?' Boysie brighter.

'You may have something there.' Mostyn happier. 'MGB Limited.'

'Sounds like a bloody film company.' Griffin.

'Okay.' Boysie. 'First two letters then. BOMOGR.'

Stanislave Bomogr. I suppose. The Latvian Bomogrs, of course.' Mostyn at his oiliest.

'Got it.' Griffin with evil intent, 'only way it fits. GRIMOBO. GRiffin, MOstyn, and BOysie. I'll sign on that. GRIMOBO Ltd.'

Mostyn looked furious. 'MOGRIMBO,' he snapped.

Griffin closed his cheque book. 'GRIMOBO or nothin'.'

'MOGRIMBO,' repeated Mostyn.

'BOGRIMO,' said Boysie.

Twenty seconds' pause. Mostyn capitulated. It was too good a thing to louse up now. 'All right. So be it. GRIMOBO Enterprises. I'll settle for that.'

Smiles all round. Boysie's cheque book joined Griffin's on the table. Pens moved.

It took a week. When Mostyn started something he really put on full power. Lawyers. Registration at Old Street. Lease of premises. The quiet installation of a switchboard and safe. Dubious equipment, ranging from hand guns (Mostyn's contacts provided Firearms Certificates without a blink) to 'spike mikes', swizzlestick antennae, recording gear, microphones, and all the paraphernalia of intrusion. One of Mostyn's ex-secretaries, Virginia Cockfosters—a lady of uncommon virtue and bloodhound visage—was persuaded to leave her present post with a textile firm to become GRIMOBO's first secretary, while another ex-Department telephonist, a shapely little darling with a no-nonsense personality and the unprepossessing name of Kate Kooker, took over the switchboard.

They were ready to go. Mostyn, Boysie, and Griffin met together in the now converted double flat in Dolphin Square. Glasses were charged—lethally. Smiles wreathed all faces. What lay behind the smiles was a different matter. Not one of the trio would admit that they were not in it for the fun, kicks, or danger. In relative terms they were all there for one reason, Hard cash at anyone's expense.

'To GRIMOBO!' Mostyn raised his glass, and the thought flickered through his mind, I'm going to screw the arses of those two.

'GRIMOBO,' said Boysie, thinking, I'm going to screw the arse off Mostyn at least.

'GRIMOBO,' added Griffin. Under his breath he

muttered, 'Screw them.'

The next morning saw an advertisement in the personal column of a select newspaper:

GRIMOBO ENTERPRISES Small private confidential security organisation will undertake any lawful security work; industrial, political, private. Write Box B.432, The Times, E.C.4.

PART THREE

MADRIGAL

If you like it ... Macabre?

IX. CORGI

The Royal Corgi to unleash
And waddle swift to death across the heath.
Ernest Newman, *Peenemünde*

'AND this is Cockfosters.' Mostyn introduced his new secretary to Boysie and Griffin on the first official operational morning. Boysie, with a leery eye on the telephonist, Miss Kooker, bit his tongue. Griffin did not contain himself.

'Thought it was Dolphin Square,' he gurgled.

Miss Cockfosters nodded, unamused, while Mostyn looked livid and shuffled his feet.

'What we do then, guv'ner?' Griffin as perky as ever.

'Wait for public response.' Mostyn haughtily. 'Miss Cockfosters and myself are going to plan a tasteful publicity campaign.' The pair headed for the chairman's office.

'And the best of British, South American, and Peruvian luck to him. There's a Les if ever I——'

'Oooh. Mr. Oakes.' Miss Kooker coy.

'What's up, Kookie? You'll have to get used to worse than that. Specially if you're going to be working for him.' Boysie jerked his head in the direction of Mostyn's door. 'Right bastard he can be.'

Nothing happened on the first day. On the second they had fifteen letters, all from companies advertising their wares, which ran from office equipment to prophylactics. At mid-day Boysie, fed up with sitting around, took a walk up to a magic novelties shop in the Tottenham Court Road, and returned with a set of cards, which he placed at vantage points in the main office. The cards bore slogans like, 'Please Do Not Play with Your Yo-Yo during Office hours,' 'Look Alive Remember You Can Be Replaced by a Machine,' and near Mostyn's door, 'Be Reasonable . . . Do It My Way.'

On the third morning Mostyn removed the cards, and at 10.30 the telephone rang. There had also been a heavy mail, which neither Boysie nor Griffin had been allowed to see. The telephone rang again at 10.45. Mostyn made two outgoing calls, and Miss Cockfosters strode out into the main office. Mostyn wanted both Boysie and Griffin.

The Colonel looked pleased. 'We're in business, chaps. Things're beginning to pick up. I'm off in half an hour.' Looking briskly at his watch. 'Member of Parliament's wife being blackmailed. Sounds like our old friends.'

'Who?' asked Boysie dryly.

'Redland, of course.'

'No. Who's the bird?'

'The lady will remain anonymous for the time being. If I need to call you into the case, you will be briefed then. We work on the same principle as the Department. The "need-to-know" principle.'

'What's on for us then?' Griffin fed up to his second and third molars.

Mostyn smiled. Oh Gawd, thought Boysie. He knew that smile. 'For you Charles,' said Mostyn pompously, looking at Griffin, 'we've got a nice one. Tidy select boutique in Hall Green say they're getting their window-display ideas pinched by the opposition down the road.'

'An' where the 'ell's 'All Green?'

'Birmingham,' said Boysie with satisfaction. His grin faded as he saw Mostyn's eyes.

'Boysie boy, we've got a call from the Ministry of Pensions and National Insurance.'

'Yes.' Boysie knew what was coming.

'Oh, you've guessed.' Mostyn with pleasant greasiness conveying mock disappointment.

'Collecting off bleeders who owe loot to the Min of Pen and Nat Ins.'

'In a word.' Eyebrows raised looking like a lamb with a hyena wanting to get out. 'Sharp lad.'

Mostyn tossed a big manila envelope across the table to Griffin. A larger one followed for Boysie. 'Instructions. Good hunting, chaps.'

'GRIMOBO for ever,' grunted Boysie, disgruntled as he left.

Boysie stood one week of debt-collecting—days of searching for non-existent addresses and trudging after invisible men and women never home, gone abroad, visiting relatives, or passed away. It was a Thursday lunchtime when he returned to the office, sank into a chair, tenderly eased his shoes off, and exclaimed, 'Oh, my aching feet!'

Griffin, back from Hall Green after 'a righ' old rave up wiv some of them brummy dollies,' looked up from the table where he was engaged in a game of patience.

''Ard time of it then?' said Griffin. 'Wanna use Dr. Scholl's foot spray? Does wonders.'

'Money down the drain.'

'Does my feet a power of good.'

'No, this place. It isn't going to survive on jobs like these—collecting debts and fiddling about with petty little provincial boutiques.'

Griffin sniffed. 'Think yer wrong, Mr. Oakes. Gather we've gotta really big one on our 'ands. Yer was goin' ter be recalled this afternoon anyway. Conference three o'clock.'

'Oh? What's it all about, Kookie?' To the little telephonist.

Miss Kooker acted deaf and dumb.

'Sworn to secrecy,' said Griffin knowingly.

'Glad to hear she can swear at all.' Boysie picked up a copy of *The Times*.

The paragraph jumped out at him from the front page, at the bottom of column three. DEATH OF GENERAL KHAVICHEV. Boysie's stomach pulsed. A second of anguish. It was only a short piece:

General B. P. Khavichev who was the Russian officer in charge of Military Intelligence on the Eastern front during World War II died of a heart attack in Moscow yesterday, according to a Tass Agency Report.

Boysie felt tears welling up for no reason. He swallowed hard, hearing the broken Russian speaking to him from the past. '...*a short time of horror. A moment of fear. After that, rest, sleep. It is of little consequence. It has to happen one day.*' Boysie let the paper drop from his fingers. For a moment there was a terrible dread, then lightness. Khavichev was right. Out loud he said, 'Yes. It's of little consequence. It has to happen one day.'

'What?' From Griffin.

Boysie took a deep breath. 'Oh, nothing. Sorry.' A faraway voice. He was remembering—Khavichev's farewell, Berlin, Mu-lan, the four Chinese, Warbler, Gazpacho, Madrigal. Christ, he hated Madrigal.

'Oh, you're back, are you?' Mostyn stood in the doorway. 'You'd both better come in now. Something really big at last. Our first live one.' Inside the office, seated, Mostyn burst his plastic explosive bomb. 'At three o'clock this afternoon we have a VIP visiting us with what he regards as a pretty desperate security problem.'

'Not the PM wanting our help with the strikes?' Boysie flippant.

Mostyn did not smile. 'Not the Prime Minister, no.' Cold. 'But it is the strikes—or at least *a* strike, which could be connected to others.'

'Yeah, there 'as been a glut on the market.' From Griffin.

'In the North it's been going out of control completely. I don't have to tell you that. At least I hope I don't. Ten major walk-outs in two weeks, and now they've threatened rail and motor industries as well. There's been usual wild sniping, attacks on the trade unions, talk of corruption and Communist agitation.' Mostyn paused. Boysie and Griffin nodded in unison before their Director continued. 'Our client believes he has definite proof of outside interference. Politically bent union leaders, all that sort of balls.'

'Who's the mystery man then? The client?' asked Boysie lightly.

Mostyn seemed to inflate with pomp. 'None other than Lord Mamian.'

Boysie and Griffin looked at each other. Dismay. Boysie noting Griffin's face was ashen; Griffin seeing Boysie's face chalk white.

'What the devil's the matter? Never heard of him?'

'Not quite sure.' Boysie slow. On the defensive.

Griffin quickly interceded, ''Asn't gotta stepdaughter called 'Ortense, 'as 'e?'

Dark thunderclouds seemed to appear visibly over Mostyn's head as he flipped through the dossier in front of him, reading random excerpts. 'Born 1907 ... educated Bradford Grammar School ... scholarship to St. Edmund Hall, Oxford ... became member of Labour Party 1930 ... strong connections with trade-union movement ... took over as chairman of IWC Board 1934 ... 1939 entered Green Howards ... distinguished war service, finishing up as a colonel, full colonel, MC. DSO ... three Companies ... largest Mamian Electronics ... created first Lord Mamian of Stockport 1947 ... married ... Lady Elizabeth Barnstaple ... in 1940. Her second, yes, she has one daughter, Hortense. What have you been up to?' His piggy eyes darting between the two men. '*Boysie?*' The accusing finger.

Boysie was flustered. 'Nothing—er—nothing at all, Mostyn, sir. Clear conscience. Driven snow.'

'Er—let's put i' that we do know the 'On 'Ortense. Socially, as you might say.' Griffin had a greyish pallor now.

'Intimately?' Mostyn's question like a blast furnace.

'Definitely not.' Boysie ramrod straight.

Mostyn pondered, then accepted. 'Okay. This looks like the goods. A real break. If either of you have loused it up by playing mums and dads with Lord Mamian's daughter, I'll——' No need to say more.

'Only hope she doesn't show up here with Daddy,' murmured Boysie as he and Griffin left the office.

'Unlikely. Rift in the family loot I gathers. 'Asn't talked to daddy for years.' Griffin smug but with a niggle of worry pricking under the skin.

'I've got news for you,' said Boysie, his face like the mask of tragedy. 'I sent her packing. Told her to get back to her father and mother.'

'Oh Christ. Then we do 'ave to keep our bloomin' digits crossed.'

'Fingers, legs, toes, anything to hand.'

Boysie and Griffin lunched meagrely at a nearby pub. Brown ale and sandwiches. Boysie could not help thinking that this was a far cry from the palmy days at the Pizzala, Carlton Tower, Rib Room, or Claridge's.

There was a relaxation of tension when His Lordship arrived, on the dot of 2.59 p.m., accompanied only by a dewy-browed personal, and obviously very private, assistant. Both Boysie and Griffin smelt a fully fledged lawyer and accountant in him. There were brief introductions, the assistant taking a back seat. Mamian filled the room with a curt presence. He was a tall man, worn well for his age, not running to fat and still retaining a military bearing, waxed moustache, facial veins showed mildly blue against a high colour denoting the possibility of high blood pressure. He was also a man who cared little for the social niceties, one who had never bothered to drop his northern manner or to try to overlay his born-and-bred accent with a pseudo-film of BBC newsreader English. When they were all seated he snapped his fingers at Membersby (the assistant), who, with the fawning manner of a Uriah Heep, handed him a heavy folder.

'Ah've 'ad you checked out, Mostyn,' Lord Mamian began. 'You won't 'ave t' mind that. Good career, and ah'll tell thee now, ah'm puttin' complete faith in you and your organisation. Goin' righ' out on a limb comin' to you at all. But ah've no other choice. Truust a man so truust 'oo 'e truusts.' He indicated both Griffin and Boysie. 'That's one o' me mottoes. Truust a man so truust 'oo 'e truusts——'

Mostyn interrupted. 'Mr. Oakes and Mr. Griffin are my fellow directors. Both know a great deal about security matters. Quiet as a grave you might say.' He looked hard at the pair.

'Good. Then to business. I daren't go to MI5, Special branch, or whoever roons these bloody things nowadays. Got too much at stake.' He took a deep breath and bent his head, looking at the carpet. For a moment there was hesitation, then he jumped. 'Now we coom to confidential stoof. You all know m' largest company is Mamian Electronics—big plant near Bolton. First ah'm goin' to' break th' official Secrets Act and tell thee what we're doin' there. Test your knowledge first.' He looked at Mostyn, Boysie, and Griffin in turn. ''Ave you ever 'eard of CORGI? If so, wha' is it?'

Mostyn was in quickly. 'CORGI is Britain's first really large intercontinental ballistic missile project. The programme's been escalated over six years. It is Ultimate

Classified, mainly because the taxpayers would go bald as coots if they knew public money was going on such a weapon. CORGI is designed to have an orbital range, propelled by liquid fuel, and with a warhead estimated to be in excess of twenty megatons. The deal is arranged through the NATO force, though strategically it's designed to give Britain a correctly evaluated striking power should we have to go it alone. I mean, in the event of a split between ourselves and the United States and—or NATO.'

'Thee knows thee stuff, lad. Anything else?'

'CORGI is scheduled into service in Britain next year. Fully operational with the NATO strike forces by 1968. In order to protect the operation, from a security angle, its building is completely decentralised. Small and large firms provide components. Security-screened company directors of major organisations, Defence Staff, and final Assembly Plant Chiefs are the only people who know about it—except senior Military and Civil Security officers. Mr. Oakes here already knows because he had sight of the original directives when we worked together with Special Security. Enough for you, sir?'

'Aye. You're either a bloody clever enemy or the real thing. Ah'll plump for thee bein' real.' He clapped his hands together, as if punctuating his sentence with a full stop. 'The CORGI operation is in danger of a major holdup. Even a step down. Ah know of two firms up North makin' tiny bits and pieces tha' 'ave almost gone out of business because of labour disputes. Mamian Electronics 'ave a big piece o' th' pie, Colonel Mostyn. A very large segment as y' might say. We're makin' the Internal Computerised Command Guidance System. If we drop be'ind on production the 'ole programme is thrown out of gear. And we *are* bein' thrown out, gentlemen. Labour problems.'

Somewhere outside the windows there was a sudden

chatter of birds. Boysie was getting nasty reactions. Beads of perspiration and a rising pulse rate. It was like the former times when something of desperate import turned up at Special Security. The tense concentration and looks of concern.

Lord Mamian continued 'Ah've been a trade-union man since I were a little lad, bu' ah've never known anything like this. In two weeks we've been faced with three walkouts—over stupid things, little problems tha' ah can normally fix wi' a bit of man-to-man chat. Ah get on wi' th' lads, don't I, Membersby?' Sharply to the weasel assistant.

'Oh yes, my lord. One of the lads all right.'

'Seem to 'ave lost tooch some-ow. Thought I knew me men. Main trouble's one union—Amalgamated Union of Humpers and Grinders. Very important to us over the question of assembly. Most essential. An' now they're threatenin' the axe. Total strike over a stupid wage claim. Ah've gone with them all the way. Twice ah've gone with them. Bu' they raise th' odds every time I accept their offers. It's unnatural.'

Everyone else in the room was silent. Mamian's very presence precluded interruption at that point.

He continued. 'There's no doubt tha' ah've go' serious agitation on me 'ands. Outside interference. That's something ah know's been suspected by the authorities in smaller cases. Bu' if I take ma problem to National Authorities they're goin' to' cut me out. We'll be classified as Insecure an' zip goes a million. Two, three million. Ah'll 'ave nigh on a thousand lads out o' work, and ah'll personally go bust.'

'Tricky,' said Mostyn, trying to cover his feelings about big businessmen scared of running foul of Government Security. These were men he despised.

'Aye.' Mamian nodded. 'Tricky till yesterday when ah got the tip-off. We know who the agitator is. Thank Gow soom men've got consciences. Most men follow their leaders like sheep. One man didn't. Lad I were a' school wi'. 'Olds a senior position in th' union. No names——'

'No pack drill,' from Boysie, who was withered by a death-ray look from Lord Mamian.

'Aye. No pack drill. Any road, 'e came t' me last night, frightened, scared ou' of 'is wits 'e were. Strong union member as ah've said, bu' 'e was scared. Seems the local union executive leader—one o' my lads—'as been doin' the stirrin'. Could 'ave knocked me down——'

'Wiv a fevver.' Griffin's turn to get the eye treatment.

'Wi' a fevver,' repeated Mamian. 'This bloke spilt the beans. Ordered the union members to agitate. Put as much pressure on as possible. Even put forward the theory tha' they're involved in a project for mass destruction and tha' it's wrong. Ah know this man, Mostyn. 'E's always been far to' th' left but never anything like this. Overnight the man's turned into a Communist agitator. If ah chop 'im the 'ole lot'll be out in flash. If ah keep 'im on ah'm done for.'

'Can you put the finger on him for us?' Mostyn iceberg cold and twice as dangerous.

Lord Mamian placed a heavy dossier in front of GRIMOBO's Director. Mostyn opened it. Typewritten sheets. Details of a career. Even a page giving a complete rundown on the man's physical attributes. A photograph filled the centre of the page. Boysie had a side view, but he could see it plainly. A shudder. Something in the back of his mind. The face, even at this angle, was of a man he recognised. Someone he had seen somewhere. Where?

'Excuse me, Colonel Could I see that photograph?'

Mostyn looked up, annoyed. 'Why?'

'I think I may have something. Have to look and think though.'

Without grace, Mostyn withdrew the sheet and passed it to Boysie. The face was definitely familiar. He glanced at the name at the top of the form. Albert Elia Sowerton. That had no meaning. But the face. He sensed everyone in the room looking at him. Waiting. Mostyn's foot tapping irritably. Then Boysie cut through the barrier. Albert Elia Sowerton was the man at The Hong Kong. The man Madrigal had hypnotised. His brow creased, mind fighting for the real connection. He turned to Lord Mamian.

'Er—— Your Grace—I mean, Your Lordship—oh heck. I might have something here. I wonder if I could talk to Colonel Mostyn privately?'

'Don't see why. What's ya name again?'

'Oakes, sir.'

'Well, Oakes. Ah've been frank wi' all you lot. Don't see why you shouldn't be frank wi' me. In fron' o' me.'

Boysie struggled for words. 'This is slightly different. Sir, I'd rather make sure with the Colonel. Might be making a fool of myself.'

'Wouldn't be the first time, laddie,' jabbed Mostyn.

Mamian was quick at sizing up situations. 'Membersby, we'll wait in th' outer office.' To Griffin, 'You stayin'?'

Griffin raised his eyebrows questioningly at Boysie.

'Better raise some tea or something for Lord Mamian and his—his——'

'Assistant,' slimed Membersby.

Reluctantly, Mamian, Membersby, and Griffin left. Mostyn's fist hammered the desk as the door closed. 'What the devil are you playing at, Boysie? What's this about this twit's photograph?'

Boysie talked. He talked for some twenty minutes, giving a complete description of what had occurred after Mostyn had paid him off from the Department. In particular, he went through Madrigal's moves at The Hong Kong. 'The thing that bugs me is that Madrigal whispered into this fellow Sowerton's ear while he was under hypnosis. I felt there was something wrong then. Look, Mostyn, I know Madrigal. He is dangerous and highly implicated with the Jen Chia. Rabbit Warren had something to tell us about it. Khavichev knew there was some sort of plot.'

Mostyn looked serious. Could be. Chap had it in a novel once. Damn good yarn. Got a fellow to assassinate under hypnosis. Hang it all, the Chinese use it. Ever read Dr. Sargant's *Battle for the Mind*? Hypnosis is a medical technique now. Medical and security technique.' He sat for a moment, a waxwork among the politicians at Madame Tussaud's. Then, 'Get Lord Mamian back in here. I'll tell him we're dealing with it, and we'll be in touch. Five or six days should see us through.'

Boysie opened the door. Mamian and Co. were obviously impatient. 'Would you care to step in here a moment, gentlemen?' Boysie madly formal.

As Griffin passed into the room he muttered out of the corner of his mouth, 'Yer'd better ge' ou' there, Mr. Oakes. Someone to see yer.'

Mostyn looked up. 'Boysie. We'll need extra help. Remember Martin?'

Boysie remembered Martin all right. Martin, Mostyn's blue-eyed boy, the watch dog with a built-in warning twinge in his right kneecap, which seemed to operate whenever trouble loomed. Mostyn still talked. 'I gather he's what the theatrical profession call "resting" at the moment. Miss Kooker has his number. Get him over here. Like a dose of——'

'Thoughts?'

'Faster. Jet up 'is——'

Boysie nodded and went into the outer office. Honey Mambo stood by one of the windows. Hot flush. She turned towards him.

'Hello, Boysie.' Devastating.

'Hi—er—hi.' Boysie with raised hand, embarrassed

and eyes aswivel. 'I'm—I'm sorry about——'

'Running out on me?'

'Uh-huh.'

'Don't be, darling.'

She was coming near. The whiff of Imprévu. Constriction in Boysie's breathing. He sensed Kate Kooker watching with the fascination of a snake about to strike.

'I just wanted to thank you, Boysie. Best thing you could have done. I'd been making a mess of things. Please ring me some time.' A small black-gloved hand held out a card.

Boysie took it gingerly. He could feel the ancient vibrations passing between them.

'Just, thank you, Boysie darling.' A pair of arms reached up around his neck, pulling him towards her. Lips meeting. Tender. Violent. A wide mouth, small tongue darting with the speed of a sewing-machine needle.

The kiss ended as rapidly as it had begun, and Honey Mambo walked, slowly and with the steady carriage of seduction, towards the door.

'Crikey,' said Miss Kooker, 'they warned me about you.'

Boysie stood with his hand to his mouth, desperate for satisfaction. It seemed endless. Then he took out his handkerchief, wiping it across red-smeared lips, and turned to the telephonist.

The Director says you have the number of a man called Martin. Get him on the line. Run him to earth. Make sure he's here an hour ago.'

'Yes, Mr. Oakes. Certainly, Mr. Oakes.'

Lord Mamian and his lackey left, looking moderately happy, half an hour later. Within the hour Martin arrived. He spent five minutes along with Mostyn—financial arrangements, Griffin and Boysie decided. Then they were all back in there. Mostyn went through the details from the beginning. Repeating everything Lord Mamian had told them, filling in what Boysie had added, and completing the picture with a rough sketch of what he read into the situation.

'I want this place, The Hong Kong, checked out from top to bottom. I want to know who Madrigal has used as hypnotic subjects over the last few weeks, where people live, a recording of this mind-reading act of his, the works.' His attention turned to Griffin and Martin. 'Obviously Boysie can't case the place. If Madrigal spots him the balloon rises. It's up to you two lads. I'll issue the equipment, and I want you in Manchester tonight. Drive up. Take the Bentley. And remember, we've got to have results fast. Two or three days. Three at the most.' Martin and Griffin left within the hour.

For the following three days suspense invaded the Dolphin Square headquarters. On the evening of the third day Boysie was waiting for Elizabeth in his flat when the phone rang.

'It's on, Boysie'—Mostyn sounding jubilant—'the duet's back and it's definitely on. Over here now.'

'But I——'

'Now.'

Martin and Griffin were sitting in Mostyn's office when Boysie arrived. Mostyn looked repulsively complacent. 'Come in, old Boysie. The best chair for operative Oakes, gentlemen. Cigar?'

Boysie refused. 'What is all this?'

Boysie had known Mostyn long enough to read the signs.

'Couple of first-class men here, old Boysie boy. You've hit on it. No doubt at all. Briefly, The Hong Kong circularised a vast number of northern factories, public utilities, and even unions themselves when it opened a few months ago. Trade-union members get special cards and special rates. It'a gift.' He wrinkled his nose, as though reacting to a bad smell. 'People of that class cannot resist mixing with their betters at a lower figure. The joint has a regular run of trade-union people going through it every week. Martin, carry on.'

Martin looked surprised. 'Well, sir, what I told you. I saw Madrigal work twice. On both occasions he used men whom we later identified as highly placed members of trade-union organisations. Also, through surreptitious means, we back-checked on the kind of person Madrigal uses for such experiments.' Martin was being Gothicly arch. 'Actually they all conform. Nine out of ten are connected with industry, the railways, docks, public offices——'

'All right, you've made your point.' Mostyn waiting to get on with it. 'How was the knee by the way?'

'Like a jolly old Mexican jumping bean, sir. No doubt there's something up.'

'Griffin.' Mostyn looked at Charlie.

'Yeah?' Griffin had been far away.

'Your side. Tell little Boysie your side.'

'Ah. Yers. Well. First, Madrigal himself is seein' a lot o' this bird you was knockin' orf in Berlin. The Chinese bird.'

'Mu-lan?' Boysie swamped by sudden depression.

'Yeah. Also, The 'Ong Kong itself is owned by a couple o' fellas 'oo keep in the background.' He paused to pick up a brace of photographs from Mostyn's desk. 'Not well enough in the background to stop the old Minox though. Minox is a spy's best friend, eh?'

Boysie took the photographs. The depression turned to hatred and a violence he had rarely felt before.

'Recognise them?' From Mostyn.

'Warbler and Gazpacho. Chinese names of General Kuan Hsi Shi and Shi T'ung K'u, the Tormentor. When do we go?'

246

Mostyn looked at Boysie. In the past there were moments when he had been uncertain of the bungling, sometimes idiotic man. The chips of blue ice that were Boysie's eyes now flamed with white heat. Even clowns can be terrifying, he thought, before speaking. 'By rights we should hand over all this stuff to the Political and Military Intelligence Department. There's no doubt in my mind that Madrigal's involved in a psychological operation geared to disrupt industry and the normal running of the country. Don't really know enough about it, but I should imagine it's got something to do with post-hypnotic suggestion. Both men whom Martin saw being used as subjects went to Madrigal's apartment on the afternoon or early evening following their being publicly hypnotised——'

'Go' a nice place, Madrigal,' Griffin interrupted. 'Sixth-floor apartment in an old building in Ducie Street.'

'When do we go?' said Boysie.

It was amazing to Mostyn to see the grin of pleasure on Boysie's face. 'I'm not sure.' Long silence. 'Hang it, okay. Let's show them what the old SS can really do. Finish off what Rabbit Warren started. Just three of us, I'm afraid. Martin will have to mind the store.'

'Oh, thank you very much, sir.' Martin seemed happy about that, even though he was rubbing his right kneecap like a professional masseur.

'In the meantime'—Mostyn scratching his nose with the right index finger—'there's one extracurricular experience for you, Boysie.'

Boysie knew trouble was coming. He had got over the hump of anxiety. He was ready. Now the butterflies returned, accompanied by moths, battering at the wall of his stomach. 'What?' he said suspiciously.

Mostyn, top dog as always, split his mouth into the grimace of evil. 'You're going to be hypnotised. Hypnotised, old lad.'

X. FOX

But the little red fox murmured,
'O do not pluck at his rein,
He is riding to the townland
That is the world's bane.'
          Yeats, 'The Happy Townland'

It was nearly ten o'clock the following morning when a taxi dropped Boysie and Mostyn at the intersection of Queen Anne and Wimpole Streets.

'This way.' Mostyn pointed up Wimpole Street with his umbrella. Today was City gent day for him, bowler, pin stripe, and neatly furled brolly. Boysie had slung on some grey tweed Jaeger gear, not a wise move, for now he felt out of place, sauntering with the strutting Mostyn past the parked Rolls-Royces and Bentleys. He had got over the initial anger of realising he was to be sucker bait for Madrigal. Hypnosis frightened him. Having someone else completely control your actions, maybe even your thoughts, brought a creepy sensation.

'Can't really explain it all to you myself,' Mostyn had said. 'Don't know enough about hypnosis. But this chap Fox is the best man in the country.'

They crossed New Cavendish Street, and Mostyn again pointed with his umbrella. The houses looked all the same—brass plaques, doctors, dentists, specialists in every organ of the human body. London's wealthy hypochondriac belt. An elderly lady, dressed by Harrods, was

248

being helped down the steps of one house and into a waiting taxi. The world was full of overpriced garments, old people warding off the inevitable, a few debs sadly hearing the worst, and all paying for the best.

Together, Mostyn and Boysie mounted the steps. The brass plaque bore three names: Rainbow, Heston, and Bright. Mostyn pressed the bell push with a neatly leather-covered forefinger and pushed open the door. A starched lady was already on her way to meet them, clip-clopping high-heeled across the marble floor of a hall austere but for the bust of some eminent medic plaster-still on a bookcase heavy with leather and unpronounceable titles embossed in gold.

'Mostyn,' said Mostyn.

'Oh yes.' The lady, one would not dare call her a receptionist, spoke in the hushed tones usually reserved for funeral parlours. 'This way, please. He won't keep you waiting for long.'

'Walk the barrack way,' whispered Boysie. Mostyn shot him a look edged with a volley of arrows that would have made Agincourt look like a dart-club outing.

The room was large, the fireplace undoubtedly Adam, and the magazines surprisingly new. Last week's *Punch* cheek by jowl with the latest *Life*. Boysie noticed his hands were trembling again. The old, old shakes, linked with a palsied tremor in the lower part of the abdomen. Mostyn buried himself in the *Financial Times*. Boysie lit a cigarette, paced the floor between deep leather chairs, and hoped. The ten minutes felt like an hour. Then the crisp lady returned.

'This way, please.'

They crossed the marble hall and were led up a staircase, wide and ornate, seething with the ghosts of Victorian mammas, papas, and scuttling tweenies; through the door at the top of the landing and into another world, another waiting room comfortably contemporary with a large reproduction of Picasso's 'Guernica' slap in the middle of one wall.

'That ought to make any unstable patient feel at home,' said Boysie brightly.

The door opened and a small, chubby-faced, neat man trotted in.

'Colonel Mostyn. Nice to see you again.' He extended a hand to Boysie's Director, manners impeccable. Charm and a genuine aura of professional expertise surrounded the man. He turned to Boysie. 'And this is Mr. Oakes?'

'Mr. Oakes,' introduced Mostyn. 'Mr. Fox. An old and valued friend of mine.'

Boysie put out his hand. The grip was firm, friendly. Fox, thought Boysie, was an apt name. The small man had soft red hair groomed precisely back from the forehead. Fox? Yet there was no cunning in the eyes, only a deep perception.

'Fox?' queried Boysie, aloud this time.

'That's right.' A voice you could trust, but Boysie was not in the trusting vein.

'Your name wasn't on the door downstairs,' he said.

'Boysie.' Mostyn quiet, at his most persuasive. 'Trust, boy, trust. Mr. Fox and I have worked together many times. I want you to put yourself entirely in his hands. Do exactly what he says. He knows what it is all about.'

Fox led them in to his consulting room—muted green walls, a desk, chairs, padded couch, and the inevitable bookshelves. Fox seated himself behind the desk, pen in hand. Boysie and Mostyn faced him. Fox pressed an intercom button on the desk and spoke softly into the mike. 'I don't want to be disturbed. No interruptions under any circumstances.'

The recognisable voice of the receptionist came back with an affirmative. Fox looked from Boysie to Mostyn and back again.

'It's all most interesting,' he opened. 'I've listened to

this fellow Madrigal's performance—all the tape you sent over. At first I thought we might save some trouble and get him under the Hypnotism Act. You know, you're not allowed to give public demonstrations of hypnotism without a licence from the local authorities? Unfortunately he is in the clear. Not only has our friend Madrigal got a licence, but also he is really a professor. Four years' standing only, and it's the University of Tiranë. But he's a trained psychiatrist as well. No fool this one. Knows his stuff.'

'Could he be doing what I suggested to you?' Mostyn upright with hands clasped round the top of his umbrella.

Fox doodled on the paper in front of him. 'The old Svengali business,' he said at last. 'To be honest with you, it's not out of the question. Depends whom he is dealing with. His technique is quick, and very good, but he can only put people into what we call a stage of light hypnosis in that short space of time. It's not the ideal setting for the post-hypnotic suggestion he's obviously using.'

Mostyn grunted.

'The fact remains,' Fox continued, 'we don't know if he's resorting to drugs. Fingering his subjects and having something like sodium amytal slipped into their drinks. Also, a lot is dependent on what he whispers to them. The actual wording.' He stopped momentarily to complete a doodle with a flourish. 'Thing is, we know they go to his place, and that can mean he is in a position to put them into a much deeper stage. Make them far more susceptible.'

Boysie remembered something he had read. 'But isn't it true you can't make a person do something against his natural instincts under hypnosis?'

'To a point. But who knows what a man's natural instincts are? There was a classic case of the woman

Bompard in the late nineteenth century. She was accused of murdering her lover and pleaded she was under hypnosis at the time of the murder. All right. Under normal circumstances that woman would never have the moral intent or ability to murder. But deep down she could have easily wanted to murder her lover. Under hypnosis the act would be possible. Give her Dutch courage, so to speak.'

'In other words,' said Mostyn, 'if Madrigal chooses blokes who are inclined to left-wing agitation, he stands a good chance of pushing them over the edge.'

'Not just a good chance. The odds seem most favourable.' Fox smiled. Boysie warmed to this quiet young man. He knew what he was talking about without making it into a production number.

Fox was speaking again. 'The problem, as I see it, is that we have to put a barrier between Mr. Oakes and Madrigal.' He stopped short, hand to his mouth. 'Mr. Oakes does know of his mission?'

Mostyn nodded.

'I've got to get a ringside seat so that Madrigal will go for me. I'm the lucky lad he hypnotises. The one that gets sweet nothings whispered into his ear.' Boysie with a bitter twang.

'Yes.' Fox far away. 'And you've only got to *seem* to be hypnotised. My job is to prevent our friend Madrigal from actually putting you out.' He stood up. Right, Mr. Oakes—I believe they call you Boysie. Can I take that liberty?'

'Be my guest.'

'Good. We've got a lot of work to do.' He turned to Mostyn. 'I think you can go away and come back for the patient tonight. About seven? I shall probably need a final session with him tomorrow morning, and you can travel to—where is it? Manchester?—in the afternoon.'

Mostyn left them alone, and Fox began to pull the

slatted shades to cover the windows. 'Just make yourself comfortable,' he said over his shoulder. 'Take off your coat, loosen your tie, off with your shoes if you like, then lie down on the couch. Head on the pillow.'

Boysie obeyed like a trembling monkey. The room was dim now, and he could glimpse only the vague shadow of Fox standing at the foot of the couch. A click and a tiny spot of light appeared, suspended about five feet above the end of the couch.

'Okay?'

Fox's voice close. The doctor was sitting beside him, to the right. Darkness except for the pin-prick of light.

'Think we'll have a little music to guide us on our way.'

A piano started up from nowhere. Stereophonic. No, not a piano. A harpsichord. Bach's *Goldberg Variations*. Boysie used to have the recording at the Chesham Place flat. Helmut Walcha's version. Must get a new copy.

'You know the piece?' Fox asked.

'Yes.'

'Bach wrote it for a friend who couldn't sleep. Now you're going to sleep. A special kind of sleep. Look at that spot of light and relax. Keep both eyes fixed on the light and feel your body relaxing. Especially your legs and the muscles behind your neck.'

Boysie began to feel sleepy. His eyes stung. Bach mixed with Fox's quiet voice.

'Good. Good. That's very good. I think you're feeling too tired to keep your eyes open. Better close your eyes.'

Gently Fox nudged Boysie into a shallow hypnotic depth. Boysie was conscious of everything said to him, yet unable to activate his body without Fox's word.

The first session went on for an hour. Fox brought Boysie out of the hypnotic state, and they had coffee and biscuits together.

'I'm pushing it a bit,' admitted Fox, 'but our time is

limited. It's got to be a quick one. Still, you're reacting well.'

Back to the couch. Much deeper this time, with Fox constantly talking about Madrigal and himself. 'You'll find I am the only person who can place you into any hypnotic level. Dr. Fox is the only person who can hypnotise you. Remember that. Dr. Fox is the only person who can hypnotise you, tell me that.'

Obedient again, Boysie murmured that Dr. Fox was the only person who could hypnotise him. They continued, then broke again for tea. Boysie had lost track of time.

On to the couch once more. Now it was different. Fox would put Boysie under very quickly and bring him out again fast, implanting ideas, suggestions. Tomorrow night someone else would be trying to hypnotise him, but he would not have any success. Boysie would react correctly, but this man, he had to visualise the man— Madrigal appeared huge and aggressive—would not have the power to bring any hypnotic talent to bear. Boysie would remember this just as he would remember anything Madrigal said. He would obey only Dr. Fox. Dr. Fox was his sole control. Tonight he would sleep peacefully and be prepared for the next day.

Boysie did sleep well, his first dreamless sleep in months. On the following morning Mostyn and Griffin picked up Boysie at his flat. They drove, in the Bentley, to Wimpole Street, and the final session began.

The idea implanted on the previous day was hammered home into Boysie's subconscious. By the time he left it was quite clear what he had to do. There was implicit faith in Dr. Fox.

Just after noon Mostyn got behind the wheel of the Bentley; Boysie was beside him, Griffin in the back. They pulled away from the curb and headed for Swiss

Cottage, then north to Apex Corner, turning to the left towards Aylesbury and then picking up the motorway. They were on their way to Manchester and Madrigal.

Leicester and Derby went by. At last they made Stockport. Mostyn was adamant. Boysie was the set-up. They must not arrive together, so Boysie, with overnight bag and a wad of expense-account fivers tucked into his wallet, reluctantly left the Bentley to train it into Manchester. As Boysie slammed the car door, Mostyn leaned over, lowering the window.

'By the way, old boy,' said Mostyn, 'just to make certain, I've booked you a table for the show. Right up front. Name of Oldcorn.' He grimaced wickedly. 'Don't forget to tip the head waiter. Oh, and give us a call as soon as the operation's completed. Griffin and I will be at the Grand.'

Boysie ground his teeth and marched away. That was another thing that rankled. They were staying at the Grand. He had been booked in at the Palace. Boysie, as usual, never trusting Mostyn, did not like the idea of being split from his partners. As it turned out, the move was for the best. The Palace was good and comfortable. Boysie rested, went over the procedure in his mind, bathed, shaved, and changed into a dark suit.

For verisimilitude he arrived at The Hong Kong an hour and a half before the floor show was scheduled. Half an hour at the tables, he thought, then an hour for dinner. Play old Charlie's system again. This time in pounds instead of hundreds. Unexpectedly, luck was with him. Thirty minutes netted ten pounds, and Boysie left for the Kowloon Room with a sense of supremacy.

He ordered Perrier water with his meal. He could watch the bottle being opened. Fox said this was safe enough but he must drink nothing else. The possibility of hypnotic drugs was too great.

The coloured singer had been replaced by another

girl, white this time, trying to be Petula Clark and missing by two octaves. The same young man, the build-up for Mu-lan. Boysie squirmed in his chair. His table was dead centre of the floor and she spotted him almost immediately—on her first complete turn as she showed off that lovely body to the silent, appreciative audience. For a second their eyes met, and Mu-lan faltered. Throughout the whole business of dressing, her eyes returned to him again and again as though trying to speak—even as she took her call to the usual tumultuous applause.

A waiter was at Boysie's elbow with a glass. 'A Grand Marnier with compliments of the management, sir.'

'Oh, thank you.' Hoping he sounded real. Could be the signal. He might already have been spotted. The lights dimmed for Madrigal's announcement. With a quick move, Boysie drew the glass towards him, looked up in the direction of the *compère*, and tipped half the contents between his legs on to the floor. The lights came up for Madrigal's entrance. Boysie's eyes never left him once and, as good as he was, Madrigal could not resist at least two lengthy glances in Boysie's direction. In spite of the surveillance, Boysie managed to get rid of the remaining liquor under the table.

Madrigal had hardly changed his act, which still had a shattering impact on the audience. Boysie tried to keep his mind on what was to come, following Fox's directions.

Madrigal finished his thought-sketching effect and left the floor. There seemed to be a long pause before he returned. It was on. The mentalist had begun his hypnosis build-up. Hooked, he headed straight for Boysie.

The technique was exactly the same as before, only this time Madrigal seemed to be pushing the words, trying to get Boysie into a deep stage very quickly.

Boysie's mind fought Madrigal's relentless voice. '... relax the whole of your feet. Now the ankles and calves. The knees and thighs...' Fox's voice buried deep inside him repeating, 'Take no notice of what Madrigal says to you. Do as he tells you, but retain control of your body at all times. Keep control of your mind. Only I, Fox, can hypnotise you. Madrigal cannot control you.'

He was winning. Retaining his senses. Madrigal could not touch him or reach into his mind. The voice went on. 'In one minute you will sleep as you have never slept before. You will be able to answer me but do nothing without me...' Like hell I will, thought Boysie.

Now Madrigal was counting. '... three ... four ... five.' Boysie acted, closing his eyes with a sharp snap, keeping his body rigid and face a mask. From now on it was child's play. He raised his hand when told to, did the wince and jump of pain at the simulated pin-pricking, pretended to fish and knock back a pint of beer.

Now it was really coming. Madrigal talked to the audience about post-hypnotic suggestion. He gave the instructions. Now. Now. Madrigal was saying it. '... in order to plant the idea firmly in his mind I am again going to repeat my instructions by whispering them in his ear. Excuse me one moment.'

Boysie felt Madrigal's soft lips close to his ear. Then the voice, a whisper loud as a peal of bells. 'You'll do exactly what I have told you to do.' The mind-reader was very distinct, speaking slowly and stressing every word. 'You will also do one other thing. Tomorrow afternoon you will cancel all your appointments. You will dispense with all other loyalties and come to my apartment.' Twice Madrigal repeated the address in Ducie Street. 'You will come at exactly three-thirty tomorrow afternoon. We will greet each other like old friends. I will offer to tell your fortune. When the word *death* is said ... when the word *death* is said, you will return to the hypnotic state you are now in. When I wake you in a moment, you will do as I say. You will forget about coming to my apartment tomorrow until you wake in the morning. Only then will you remember. If you understand, raise your right hand slightly.'

Boysie lifted his hand half an inch. It would be shielded from the audience by Madrigal's body. Half-past three tomorrow. Fortune-telling. Death. His mind was so active with Madrigal's final words that he almost missed his cue for coming out of the trance. Again Boysie was a second or so behind Madrigal's nose-blowing signal and the band striking up before he waltzed back to the table, feeling, as he observed to Mostyn later, 'a right twit.'

It was over. Tomorrow afternoon Madrigal would get what was coming to him. Boysie could hardly wait to dash back to the hotel and call Mostyn. Careful though. Calm. Don't give cause for suspicion. The whole joint was probably loaded with Madrigal's boys. Boysie stayed at the table, smoking a cigarette, wondering if Mu-lan would try to get in touch. Common sense told him it was too dangerous to make any move in that direction. The cigarette finished, Boysie called for the bill, paid, and casually sauntered out—three quid to the good.

In the street he asked the doorman to get him a cab. The taxi drew up and the doorman opened the rear door, asking where he wanted to go.

'Put me off at the CIS building, please.' Boysie dropped half a crown into the doorman's hand, pleased at the subterfuge. As the cab drew away he leaned forward to the driver. 'Make that the Palace Hotel,' he said, 'will you?' Unaware of the snazzy little red TR4A on the taxi's tail.

Back in his room at the Palace, Boysie rang down for coffee and put a call through to Colonel Coots (even

Mostyn was using a pseudonym) at the Grand Hotel. The coffee arrived as he waited. The hotel had a fast room service and a slow telephone operator. Finally Mostyn's voice was on the line.

'Coots. Who is that?'

'Brian, sir. Sorry to trouble you but I'm afraid I've got to cancel all my appointments tomorrow afternoon. Got a date at three-thirty.'

'You all right?'

'Fine. Went like a dream. All in order, see you as arranged, sir.'

'Good boy.' Mostyn sounded happy as he put down the telephone.

Boysie lit a cigarette and poured a cup of coffee. Four lumps of sugar, then a knock at the door. Boysie felt unguarded. He was unarmed and the message had gone back. He stood close to the door for a second, cigarette still between his fingers.

Knocking again, soft but more urgent.

'Who is it?' hissed Boysie.

'Me. Mu-lan. Quickly. Le' me in'

Boysie slipped the bolt and swung the door back. Her sweet smell, the scent of her body close as she brushed past. Boysie closed the door, and Mu-lan turned, her back to the woodwork, her left hand on the door knob.

Boysie had taken a step back into the room, now he moved towards her, arms reaching forward. 'Thank heaven. Mu-lan. Little pigeon.'

'No, Boysie. Stop.' She was poured into a gold and red cheongsham. Her right hand shot up her skirt, a flash of thigh above stockings, black-bowed suspenders, and a matching garter holster nestling on the inside of her right leg. Boysie stopped, looking, puzzled, into the muzzle of a .22 gold-plated Bernardelli automatic.

'Christ. What's that? A cigarette lighter?' said Boysie, unsure.

'No, Boysie, please stay away. I mean it. Ver' sorry but should not be here. If anyone come I shoot you.'

'Shoot me? But I thought—— Mu-lan.'

'Listen.' Tears in her eyes.

Boysie was still fuddled. Why the tears? 'What is it, Mu-lan? Put that thing down.'

'Boysie, please listen.' Hysteria behind the usual placid exterior.

'Okay.' Boysie quiet and relaxed. 'What is it?' The girl was really crying now; mascara trickled with salt tears down her cheeks.

'All life,' she sobbed out, 'all life I been taught hate people like you. Hate you. From ver' first teaching I hate. Then you love me in Berlin. I deserve die, Boysie. Me I deserve die. If they catch me I die.'

'Hate me?' Boysie confused. 'You mean you're——?'

'I member of Jen Chia. Six, seven year now. But never have experience like loving you. That only reason I come. We not allowed privilege of love, Boysie. You un'erstand?'

'Yes.' Boysie quietly. Sober and waiting for his chance.

Out it came in a rush. 'Madrigal. Tonight he hypnotised you. Ver' clever at hypnotise. Tomorrow you remember you have appointment with him at flat Ducie Street. Ha'pas'-three in afternoon. They think you know of Jen Chia plans for slowing British economy. Making big trouble on strikes. General Kuan Hsi Shi and bad one, the American they call Shi T'ung K'u, are here. They meet Madrigal two o'clock tomorrow for final conference. You go see Madrigal ha-pas'-three. He hypnotise you again and send you to docks. He follow you. The General and Shi T'ung K'u wait. Take you on ship. China. Really take you China this time. Get much big information. Make much trouble. I come, Boysie, warn you.'

The gun was still steady in her hand though the body

trembled and tears had now built into soggy pools, washing her make-up into little island patches. She took a deep breath. 'We not allowed cry either. I traitor now. Chairman Mao once say, "We must be ruthless to our enemies, we must overpower and annihilate them." I not ruthless because I love you. But China will overpower and annihilate.'

Mu-lan's left hand moved on the door knob. Boysie did not try to stop her. The door closed. Her shoes made no sound on the carpeted corridor outside.

Boysie rested his hand on the telephone, then changed his mind. He had an early date with Mostyn and Griffin. Time enough to tell them then.

XI. PYTHON

I had an aunt in Yucatán
Who bought a Python from a man
And kept it for a pet.
She died, because she never knew
These simple little rules and few;
The Snake is living yet.

Belloc, 'The Python'

'THREE in one, eh? Madrigal, the unpronounceable
Warbler, and the equally obscure Gazpacho. The pick-
ings, plus information on Chinese Intelligence operation
in Britain.' Mostyn paced his room at the Grand Hotel.
It was like a war dance.

' 'Ypnotic spanner in the works.' Griffin looked up
from the racing page of the *Daily Express*. ' 'Orse runnin'
at Cheltenham today called Trilby. Reckon that's an
omen?'

They had gathered for a working breakfast in
Mostyn's suite—the table still littered with debris of
bacon, eggs, coffee, toast and marmalade. Boysie had
recounted the events of the previous evening, and the
whole trio now realised that the pattern of the events
had now changed drastically. Instead of just settling the
score with Madrigal they had the whole works.

Mostyn's war dance ended in a pose not unlike
Rodin's 'The Thinker'—but with clothes. He was
slumped in the chair, left arm dangling over his knee,
right elbow crooked with the fist bunched below the lips.

Boysie was finishing his coffee, the eternal cigarette in his mouth. He felt apprehensive over Mostyn's reactions— the first flush of victory now followed by this period of intensely concentrated thought. Mostyn preferred to play things by the book. He knew the book, lived with it. Look at the way he had reeled off those details about CORGI. Boysie knew exactly what was going on in his Director's mind. Mostyn shook his head. 'It's not on,' he said, almost a whisper.

Griffin put down the *Express*. 'Wha' ain't on then?'

'The whole thing,' said Mostyn, 'it's too bloody big.' His manner was still indecisive in spite of the words.

'For Pete's sake,' said Boysie.

'Use your noodle.' Mostyn still undecided. 'We've got three of their leaders for the asking. But this is on a national level. Christ, man, we can lay most of the recent British labour disputes smack on the Chinese doormat.'

'All the better then.' Griffin returned to Peter O'Sullivan, found he had exhausted that page, so flicked back to William Hickey. 'See that Princess 'as been at it again,' he commented.

'This is a job for Special Branch or MI5.' Mostyn doing it by the book again.

Love us, thought Boysie, the man's a bloody sadistic computer. 'The book, the book, the book,' he said aloud. 'Look, I want Madrigal. I want him like I've never wanted anyone before.'

'Personal vengeance,' said Mostyn, twelve denier. 'Speaking strictly, we're private citizens. It's a job for the professional Intelligence and Security boys.'

'You're not a pro any more then,' snapped Boysie.

That hurt. He saw Mostyn wince. You could hear the spools clicking in that computerised brain. The Director's hands dropped to his sides in defeat. 'Yes, I'm still a professional,' he said, biting at the words. 'A fact profes- sional——'

'Cu' orf in yer prime.' Griffin put down the paper.

Mostyn ignored him. 'We can always follow Warbler and Gazpacho. If they panic, make an arrest and hand 'em over to the Jacks.' He looked long at Boysie, then, 'And you want Madrigal on toast. All right, you've done it before and he's like a bloody animal anyway. Keep your date with him. Griffin'll show you how to go about the rest.' He got up and went into the bedroom.

'Yer reely wanna do 'im, Mr. Oakes?' Griffin steady.

Boysie nodded.

'Come over 'ere then.' Griffin had a pencil and paper on the table. He pushed back the plates of congealing egg yolk, brushed away some of the crumbs, and started to draw. Mostyn returned with a bulky leather briefcase, tinkered with his key chain, and placed a pair of Muden Transceivers—the Japanese walkie-talkies, about the size of a twenty-five box of cigarettes—on the table.

'You'll need those,' he said.

Griffin nodded over his shaky drawing. 'Wha' about the wire-cutters as well?' he asked.

Mostyn inclined his head towards the briefcase. 'You can take them in that. The other gear's in there too. I'll issue before we go.'

Griffin tapped his drawing with the pencil. 'Now, Mr. Oakes,' he began, 'last night, when yer was all tartin' it up at The 'Ong Kong, I took the liberty of casin' friend Madrigal's gaff, 'is sixth-floor apar'ment. Very nasty, a lift droppin' down six stories. We've always 'ad clean accidents before, and this should be as clean as a whistle.'

'Except the police are bound to treat it as murder. Or at least the vicious act of teenage hooliganism.' Mostyn peeping out from behind a corner of the *Guardian*.

'Shockin' these teenagers and wha' they gets up to,' said Griffin. 'Madrigal lives on the sixth floor. Nice place 'e's go' an' all. Bit weird, but nice. You know. Number 64, 'bout for'y feet from the lift and the stairs. Madrigal always uses the lift. I checked that larst night. Most of 'em do. Use the lift, I mean. Terrible, 'cause it's such an old affair. They services it regular but it ain't what yer might call reliable. An' it ain't goin' to be reliable this afternoon when Madrigal gets in.'

'No?' said Boysie without emotion.

'Definitely not. Now look 'ere, I've drawn it for yer. The lift's powered by a bleedin' great drivin' mo'or wha' works the cable drum. There's a control cable goes from the mo'or t' the lift.'

'Yes.' Boysie intent.

'Take no notice o' that. 'Cause that only controls the mo'or with the controls in the lift, the buttons like. The cable drum, now that's a different matter.' Boysie could see there were three lines descending down from the circle representing the cable drum.

Griffin talked on. 'There's three cables runnin' from this 'ere drum to the lift. Them's the cables wha' takes the strain. Cu' them, and——'

'Capow.' Boysie grinning.

'No, Mr. O, rather a caplunk-boing-boing-boing. See, there's this safety cable which operates the emergency brakes. No cable, no brakes.'

'Oh.'

'Don' go an' get depressed though. Thank 'eaven it's not a modern lift, they're right bastards, all sorts of brakes an' things. This baby's only go' the one safety cable. An' i' can operate quite normal without i'. So 'ere's wha' I suggest. You go' an appointment wiv' old Madders at 'arf-past-free. Right?'

'Right.'

'I comes wiv yer, carryin' the briefcase wiv a pair o' wire-cutters. Bloody great big ones we go' an' all. Up we goes. You gets orf at the sixth floor and goes t' see 'is nibs 'oo reckons he's goin' t' 'ypnotise yer ag'in. I keeps goin'—righ' up t' the top. Tenth floor. When I gets out of the lift at the tenth, I turns left an' there's this little fligh' o' metal steps, 'bout a dozen steps wiv a metal door. Control-room door, bleedin' great notice. DANGER UNAUTHORISED PERSONS KEEP OUT. There's a lock what's child's play t' pick. Up there larst nigh' I was for 'arf an hour. Anyway. I cuts the cable—the safety cable—leaves the door open, and spends the rest o' the afternoon riskin' life and limb goin' up an' down in the lift without a safety cable on i'. See?'

Boysie nodded.

'Easy from then on, ain' i'? Eventually yer'll come out o' Madrigal's place t' go to the docks—least 'e'll think yer goin' t' the docks. Ah'll be in the lift when it gets to the sixth floor. We opens and closes the door. I go down again, for the sake o' the right noise, and yer goes beltin' up the apples t' the tenth and the control room. When I gets t' the bottom, I opens and closes the lift door ag'in for——'

'Verisimilitude,' muttered Mostyn.

'Wha' 'e said. An' then I comes up t' the fifth floor. I walks up t' the sixth and positions meself near Madrigal's flat. As soon as 'is door 'andle turns I starts walkin' t' the stairs. I goes on down till I 'ears 'im shut the lift gate. We both go' our walkie-talkies switched on, an' I yells "right." You 'ears it up in the control room and acts accordin'ly.'

'Accordingly to what?'

'Accordin'ly t' the fact tha' there's a bloody great fireman's axe on the wall o' that there control room, and I reckon about three great mighty whacks wiv tha' across the cables on the drum'll do the trick. Whumpff ... whumpff ... whumpff ... squeach ... AAaaaaaagh. Crump. Bye-bye, Madrigal.'

Boysie nodded. He was not even smiling.

They went over the plan another couple of times and tested the walkie-talkies, much to Mostyn's annoyance.

'Well, we go' tha' taped then, boss.' Griffin rubbed his hands.

Mostyn slowly lowered his *Guardian*. 'Thank heaven for little churls. What time did you say Warbler and Gazpacho were due at Madrigal's place?' he asked Boysie.

'Mu-lan said about two.'

'We'd better go on watch about then ...'

' 'E's go' all the right lingo, 'asn't 'e?' Grinning Griffin. 'That's all them police programmes on the tele. "On watch." Did yer 'ear that? 'E'll be talkin' about keepin' obo next.'

'Cut it.' Mostyn sharp. 'There's a lot to do before we go over to Madrigal's. It'll be a light luncheon, I'm afraid. Also, I don't like it, but we'd better be safe.' His hand was in the briefcase. He removed three revolvers—Colt Pythons—and passed one each to Griffin and Boysie, keeping one for himself. 'Loaded,' he said, putting an oblong box of Winchester Western 357 ammunition on the floor. 'And take six extra rounds each. These are only to be used in emergency. Got it?'

Silently the team which made up GRIMOBO loaded their Pythons.

Warbler and Gazpacho stayed only a short time at Madrigal's apartment. It was just after two-fifteen when they emerged from the building. Like a pair of Siamese twins. Across the road, Boysie sat in the driving seat of a Hertz (take it or leave it where you like) rented Vauxhall Premier. The Bentley would have been too conspicuous. Mostyn sat, surrounded by thoughts, in the front passenger seat, drumming his fingers on the dashboard.

It irritated Boysie. 'Charge of the Light Brigade?' he queried sarcastically.

Griffin was in the back, curled up with a German thriller, *Jerry Cotton G-Man*.

Both Mostyn and Boysie turned and stared at Griffin's choice of literature. Griffin looked up and then glanced at the cover of the book. 'Carn't le' me language course go t' pot now, can I?'

A simultaneous shrug from Mostyn and Boysie. Cigarette smoke was fugging up the car. Mostyn began to wind down his window. His eyes focused on the doorway as the Siamese twins came out.

'Action stations.' Low. 'Here they are.'

Boysie already had the engine running. Three pairs of eyes watched Warbler and Gazpacho walking up the pavement. A blue Austin Cambridge taxi was coming towards them. Warbler's hand shot out in a *Sieg Heil* fashion. Beautifully executed. The taxi appeared to stop out of respect for the salute. I suppose there are German taxi drivers in Britain, thought Boysie. The two men climbed into the taxi, which shot past the Vauxhall, gathering speed. Boysie selected 'Drive.' Brake off. The car surged forward and performed an effortless one-point turn. The taxi screamed its way through the street, past Victoria Station and along Deansgate.

Boysie attached an imaginary bell to the front of his car, ringing it now and again. It did not seem to give them any priority when it came to jumping red lights. They were nearing the bottom of Deansgate when the taxi turned right.

'Where the hell're they going?' Boysie shouted at Mostyn.

'How the hell should I know? You said the Docks. Ever tried looking at a map? You can't expect me to do it all.'

'Quite right.' Griffin from the rear.

'I don't notice you pulling any muscles.' Mostyn angry. He consulted the street plan. 'They've turned into Liverpool Road. It's the right direction for the Docks.'

Right. Left. Then another right turn, bringing them

into Regent Road. The two cars roared on.

Mostyn tapped Boysie on the shoulder. 'Touch your forelock, old man, we're passing a police station. There, on your left.' Boysie switched off the imaginary bell.

Chauffeur-driven Griffin, in the back, sighed and turned the page. They were gaining on the taxi and both cars turned into Trafford Road at about the same time.

'Dock entrance on the right. Pull over opposite the gates. We'll watch from there,' shouted Mostyn, winding down the window that had only been half open.

The taxi turned into the main entrance and stopped under an archway bearing the legend MANCHESTER DOCKS.

'We at the Docks then?' asked Griffin, looking up from his book.

Warbler and Gazpacho got out of the taxi and paid off the driver. Gazpacho seemed to be helping Warbler. A security officer sauntered over. Gazpacho spoke, shrill, loud, and with a pronounced slur. 'Oo 'eck, I do 'ope we make it. We're stewards on the MV *Gardnia*. We're sho' bloomin' late and Fanny Haddock here isn't too well. She can't take her drink.' Warbler draped an arm round Gazpacho's shoulder and belched realistically.

'Go on. Clear orf t' yer ship, you bloody pair of pooves.'

'Thanks, luvvy,' said Gazpacho with a wilting right hand. 'Keep your back to the wall.'

The guard returned to his office, muttering, 'Gawd 'elp the Merchant Navy.' Gazpacho and Fanny walked to the end of the Dock Office and turned right.

'Time to go,' said Mostyn. 'Wonder if they take Diners Club cards here?'

'Eh?' from Boysie.

'You'll see. Drive into the entrance.'

Boysie swung the car through the archway. Once more the security guard shuffled over. Mostyn flashed a Diners Club card under the guard's eyes, saying, 'Special

Branch. Two men just came in. Half cut. Which way did they go?'

'Who? Oh, that pair o' screamers. MV *Gardnia*. Number 9 Dock. Turn right at the end of this building and you're there.'

'Thanks.'

The guard raised his hand to stop a straddle carrier that was about to cross their path. He saluted and waved them on. Mostyn turned to Boysie. 'Don't know what I used to do without Diners Club.'

'A lot more, probably.' Caustic.

They left the car by the grain elevator at the head of Number 9 Dock. Griffin stayed with it, their last line of defence.

'Brush up your German in the meantime.' Mostyn sly.

It fell on stony ground. 'Raver dust up some Chinks.' Griffin unhappy.

Mostyn and Boysie, the MOBO section of the outfit, set off in search of the Siamese Screamers, over ground crisscrossed with railway lines. A whistle sounded from behind. A DH 18, a Sentinel shunting locomotive, bearing down. Leap to the side, then a run across the lines and along the side of Shed Number 10.

'No good sticking together. You go right. I'll go left.' Mostyn snappy. Boysie wished he had never given him that Strategy game for Christmas.

'Okay, Monty.'

The security guard was not as stupid as he looked. He knew a top priority pass when he saw one. He also knew Mostyn, by face and reputation. 'Special Branch, huh!' His fingers trembled as he dialled the number. Ringing tone. A voice.

'Manchester City Police.'

'CID, please. Inspector Bannister. Hello. Willie Daw—

William Dawson, Manchester Dock Security, sir. Something strange. Special Security posing as Special Branch. Can you get over? ... Ten minutes? ... Good.... Thank you, sir.'

Telephone lines hummed.

'Hello, Regional Crime Squad? Bannister, Manchester CID. Call from the Docks. Special Security posing as MI6. Think it's up your street.... At the Docks in twenty minutes? ... Right.'

'Regional Crime Squad here, sir. Chief Inspector Shot. I understand you're the Northern Co-ordinator for the Department of Special Security.... What? ... Disbanded.... Well, with respect, sir, they can't have been, they're at the Manchester Docks now.... Yes, sir.... Yes.... You'll bring a squad of Military Police? ... Very good, sir.... Thank you.... Beg your pardon? ... Yes, I'll alert the Railways Police as well.... Certainly, sir.'

Boysie glanced at his Navitimer: 2.35. The Docks were quiet, except for the odd lighterman wandering lonely in Coventry or concern. The tea break was in session. The sky clear blue and the air spring-chilled, a thin mist hugging the ground giving the atmosphere an extraterrestrial feel. Great cranes loomed out of the earth. Dead. Waiting for the current to recharge their metal muscles. Giant piles of wood lay waiting in the immense Timber Dispersal Area to the right. The huge owl-hoot of ships, a lapping of water, the scream of seagulls—every sight and sound amplified in the still air. Death. For a place usually bustling with activity it was uncannily quiet. Somewhere, a million miles away, a train rattled over an obscure viaduct. At that moment Boysie knew he was alone.

Mostyn strutted impudently, enjoying himself. He heard the distant train as well. A similar reaction. Enjoyment turned to fear and a complete comprehension of the situation. He ran back across the lines, squeezed between two railway flat-top cars, and joined Boysie. 'Sweet FA over there.' Assurance slipping.

'Didn't think there would be, did you?' Boysie was on thin ice.

At the same moment they spotted Warbler trying to climb into a mechanical grab. Why? They looked around. Only one ship tied up on this pier. Boysie squinted. The name? MV *Garden*?? MV *Gardnia*, flying a Panamanian flag.

There was no gangway on the ship and the ropes had been cast off. Realisation.

'Mostyn. Warbler—he's trying to get to that ship. Three guesses who's operating the crane.' Boysie started to run. 'You take Warbler. I'll get Gazpacho.'

Mostyn ran, uncertain for a moment about taking the orders of an underling. Fifteen seconds and he scrambled over the side of the grab.

Boysie was at the foot of the ladder leading to the crane's cab. He started to climb. Instantly the fear of heights became an engulfing problem. Vivid recollections of the tower at Ruhleben. Up. The air clear, the wind vicious—eating at his bones, numbing his fingers. Mustn't slip. Must hold on. Get the bastard. Good incentive to climb. Get the rotten filthy bastard.

He reached the first stage and paused to regain breath. Vibrations. The crane was moving, the grab being hoisted. Boysie glanced down at the ship, turbulence foamed from the propellers. Christ, Warbler and Gazpacho knew, they were trying to make a break for it. The *Gardnia*'s smart white motor cutter still lay alongside the dock—for himself and Madrigal, Boysie presumed. Without thinking further, Boysie raced up the next two flights. Now he was at cabin level. Gazpacho inside, desperately operating the controls. Boysie slid the door open.

Mostyn thought of Liberation Day. Paris 1944. There

had been two men then. Now there was only one at the metal monster. Twenty-three years since he had made a fist intended to smash a man's face to pulp. The bottom of the grab was coated with variegated shades of mire, remnants of cargo handling through the years. A foul smell, iron and shit, as he slid into the basin and Warbler's foot caught him in the guts. Mostyn doubled up. But before Warbler could get both feet back on the metal he lost his balance on the grab's curved base. Mostyn leaped in and swung the full force of his buffalo-hide shoe at Warbler's temple. The aim was wrong. Mostyn's sole and heel only grazed the top of the General's head. Still, it hurt. The scream echoed round the iron chamber pot.

Mostyn threw himself on top of Warbler, hands groping for the scrawny neck. Must remember. In-fighting is like riding a bicycle or swimming. You never forget. Warbler's knee came up in the direction of Mostyn's crotch. GRIMOBO's Director had visions of Mostyn the Impotent. No performance tonight due to circumstances beyond our control. He rolled to one side, and the knee whipped through empty air. Leap. Knee in Warbler's stomach now. Hard. Hard. Harder. Trying to push his guts out. Must get leverage. The little man below him was making grunting, retching noises. Mostyn reached up. A chain dangled from the grab's side. Metal links greasy in his fingers. Mostyn grasped the chain and pulled. The bottom of the grab began to open. Warbler slipped and started to scream, then recovered with half of his leg dangling through the gap. Mostyn let go of the chain and the heavy sides of the grab sprang closed again, crushing into Warbler's leg.

Pinned between the iron jaws, Warbler lashed out— helpless, hysterical, blind mad with fear and pain. He clawed hopelessly at the slimey sides of the grab, then at the visible part of his crushed leg. Without warning the grab tipped sideways. Mostyn's arms shot upwards; he was sliding out of the metal bowl. Another lurch, and he reached out to snatch and cling to the big hook that secured the grab to the chains and pulleys of the crane. Below, there was an audible crack and shriek as Warbler's leg broke. Then only a soft whimpering.

Mostyn crooked one arm round the hook and made himself as comfortable as possible. Warbler's leg caused a permanent gap in the bottom of the grab; through it Mostyn could see a continually changing angle of water, railway lines, ant-like people, and toy boats. Unpleasant. What the hell was Boysie up to? He looked towards the crane's control cab.

Boysie had got the first punch—a straight kidney with the edge of his hand. Winded, Gazpacho fell across the controls. They reacted immediately, and Boysie saw the grab rise. Gaspacho spun round to face Boysie, the air thick with perspiration and heavy oil. Panting. Moving. Circling. No words. Kill or be killed.

Gazpacho's foot came up with a straight kick. Boysie spun the driver's revolving seat, and the boot meant for his groin, ripped the leather covering away. The cab began to revolve, a mild sensation of centrifugal force acting on both men. Boysie made a lunge at Gazpacho's left wrist in a vain attempt to pull down and unbalance the man; but he underestimated Gazpacho's strength. The treacherous American flexed his arm like a bull-whip. Boysie was thrown back against the cabin wall— the partition that separated them from the drive mechanism. The connecting door burst open, making the motor's monotonous drone louder. Boysie saw the grab still rising and tilting. Must get to those controls. The two men circled the driver's chair like a couple of hungry animals after the same morsel of food.

The revolving motion of the cabin was an added disadvantage. Strains of the 'Carousel Waltz' filled

Boysie's ears. Musical bloody chairs. Boysie was now circling towards the controls. He could see the names. *Luffing Lever*. What the hell is that? Boysie snatched at it. The grab began to swing dangerously towards the cab. Gazpacho was behind him now. Hands at the base of his neck. A sleeper hold. *Speed Control*. The words blurred as Boysie pushed the lever to *On Full*.

The grab swung violently. Gazpacho's hold was stronger. Get him off. Boysie forced back, hard and fast, with his elbows into the sides of Gazpacho's stomach. The hands on his neck relaxed, and Boysie, in a last attempt to take over the crane, heaved on the control marked *Hoist Lever*. The swing of the grab became more acute, and the whole structure of the crane began to shudder. Terror. Prophetic pictures of news headlines about CRANE DISASTER AT MANCHESTER DOCKS.

Boysie whirled round, wrenching Gazpacho with him. the man clung on. Boysie felt his back hit the rear of the cab; he brought his knee up between their close chests and kicked out. Gazpacho slid away from him, then spun and bumped, sickeningly, gut first, into the *Hoist Lever*. Boysie looked up to see the grab on a downward swing heading directly for the cabin, Gazpacho sprawled over the control panel. Boysie made a dash for the sliding doorway and slid down the first ladder as the metal grab, with Warbler's leg jutting beneath, battered into the cabin through the window, sending Gazpacho into the machinery room. There was the crunching noise of shattering glass and twisting metal, and the grab swung away once more. Boysie climbed the short ladder, back into the cabin, and dashed for the controls. He pushed the *Hoist Lever* into the *On Down* position.

The grab, still swinging, dropped, reached its apogee, then slowly returned to embed itself into the main metal trellis of superstructure. Boysie saw the jaws of the grab open as the metal basin hit. There was no scream, just the tiny broken body of Warbler dropping, dropping, dropping to the concrete and bouncing off into the water. Mostyn, shaken but triumphant, clung to the big iron hook. Unexpected the crane shuddered again and the motor stopped. Somebody must have pulled the switch on them.

Boysie wiped his forehead with his right sleeve. There was no sign of Gazpacho. No trace until he got to the motor room. Nausea, vomit, and horror, which made Boysie run for the metal steps. Gazpacho had been thrown back, by the grab's impact, into the motor room. Nobody had pulled the main switch. Gazpacho had been drawn into the giant driving cog wheels. The crane had stopped through a, now pulped, bodily malfunction.

Far below, Mostyn, still shaking, was gingerly easing himself from the hook on to the superstructure and second stage of the crane. Boysie joined him. Neither spoke. They were too busy staring at the main gate.

Way below them three black Wolseleys, two Black Marias, and three olive-drab Land Rovers were parked in convoy near the Renta-Hernia Vauxhall. There was no sign of Griffin; he had quietly allowed himself to slide to the floor of the Vauxhall and continued reading in peace. But police, uniformed and plain-clothed, bumped shoulders with troops around the Docks. They seemed to be searching without any idea of their quarry. An ant hill without order.

'How did that lot get into the act?' asked Boysie.

'Who are they anyway?' asked Mostyn.

They looked at each other, back to the swarm of police and military, and then at each other again, shrugged and started to climb down. A whistle sounded, long and shrill, as they reached the first stage.

'I have a feeling,' said Mostyn, 'that we should look lively. Tea break's over and here come the workers.'

The pair descended, to mingle with the shuffle of men

who were now filling the Dock area. As they passed into the crowd Boysie heard the cry of an outraged docker. ''Kme. Who's buggered me crane?'

'It was I,' muttered Boysie under his breath, quickening his walk.

As they threaded through the confusion, Mostyn turned to Boysie. 'You don't possibly think all those policemen and soldiers could be looking for us, do you, old darling?'

'Damn clever these Chinese,' replied Boysie.

They climbed into the car, and Griffin, braver now his partners had returned, slid up again. 'There ain't 'arf been some runnin' round 'ere while yer bin gone,' he offered.

Mostyn took the wheel this time, giving a kind of regal wave as the Vauxhall swept under the archway into Trafford Road. 'Be in good time for Madrigal,' he said.

'Gloves on, and I think we'd better wipe down the weaponry. Don't wanna leave no dabs around.' Griffin put down his book and rummaged busily in the briefcase.

'Want to wipe myself down first,' Boysie was dusting off traces of the fight.

'Griffin, old lad'—Mostyn completely his former self—'I do wish you'd stop using that terrible criminal slang. Very unprofessional. Calling dabs dabs. If you mean fingerprints, then say fingerprints. Dabs is a sloppy word. They don't encourage its use at the Yard.'

Griffin made some improbable suggestions as to what the Yard could do. Boysie had pulled the sun visor down and was neatly combing his hair in the vanity mirror. Griffin sniffed the air and looked towards Mostyn.

'You don't 'arf need a change of clothes. Don't 'arf pong.' he observed.

Mostyn did not take his eyes off the road. 'I am quite aware that I stink to high heaven. So would you if you'd been rolling around with a Chinese agent in a metal bowl half full of manure.'

'Kinky wiv it,' said Griffin, polishing his Python with a Persiled handkerchief.

Boysie did the same, keeping his handkerchief round the revolver's butt. A pair of soft suede gloves landed in his lap, thrown from the briefcase by Griffin.

'Is all this really necessary?' Looking at Mostyn.

'You'll get a better grip with suede,' was Mostyn's only answer.

They pulled up a good two hundred yards short of Madrigal's apartment building. It was well after three o'clock.

'Yer'd betta go first,' said Griffin. 'It's safer we don't go in together. I'll foller yer in a minute. Just wait for me at the lift.'

'You got everything?' asked Mostyn.

'I think so.' Boysie checked—Python revolver, gloves transceiver. He got out of the car. 'You bring the briefcase, won't you?' to Griffin in the back.

'I got tha' all right. No problem.'

'Good luck, Boysie boy. You wanted to get him. So get him.' Mostyn scruffy in the front of the car.

It was cold in the hall of the building. The lift had been left at one of the upper stages. Boysie slipped his right hand into a glove, pressed the *Descent* button, and lit a cigarette. The lift had hardly arrived before Griffin, jaunty and businesslike, arrived with the briefcase.

'Yer won't forget anythin', will yer, Mr. O?'

'Everyone thinks I'm a right nit,' said Boysie, Understandably edgy.

'No offence meant, but yer performance up there, up in Madrigal's place, it counts a lot.'

'Do you think I don't know? I'll give the performance of a lifetime. At the first mention of *death* I'll go as rigid as a——'

'Yer. That's wha' I means really. Do i' proper.' He paused for a thought. 'You'll be all right wiv 'im. Go' no doubt about tha'. It's when yer gets into tha' control room. No second thoughts or anythin'. We can rejig i' now if yer wants. I can do the whole thing.'

'I'll get Madrigal. One way or another.' A silence between them. Then Griffin opened the lift gate.

'Yer've reely growed up, ain't yer, Mr. Oakes? Joined the big league.'

'As far as people like Madrigal are concerned, yes.'

'Good boy.'

The lift slowly whirred upwards. As they neared the sixth floor Griffin spoke again. 'Don't forget now. Apartment 64. Stairs are on yer left, and when yer gets up t' the tenth, the control room steps are on the righ' of the lift. And, Mr. Oakes...?'

'Yes?'

'Don't forget t' switch yer transceiver on.'

'I won't forget anything,' said Boysie, grinding his half-smoked cigarette into the lift's floor.

'Naughty,' remonstrated Griffin, reaching forward with a gloved hand and scraping the fag end from the floor. 'This'll be a Crime Squad job, surprisin' wha' they might find out, even from a bit o' cast away snout.'

They nodded to each other as Boysie hauled back the gate and stepped out on to the sixth floor. As he walked up the corridor he could hear the lift going on up to the tenth floor with Griffin. It would only be a matter of minutes now until the safety cable would be useless, clipped apart by the big wire shears in Griffin's briefcase.

Madrigal opened the door, beaming. He was older than one would have imagined. Close up the crow's-feet lines around the eyes gave him away.

'M-my dear Mr. Oldcorn. You've come for your session. I'm so glad you could make it.'

The small hallway was deceptive. Madrigal led Boysie through the main room, large, high, and dim. The curtains were drawn, the only light coming from an angle-poised lamp, which showed a partly completed game of patience on the green baize table. Through the gloom Boysie could make out two doors, One to the kitchen and bathroom area, he thought, the other to a bedroom.

'We-we'd b-better get started straight away I think,' stammered Madrigal, picking up the patience cards.

'All right by me.' Boysie doing his best to imitate bewilderment. After all, he was not under hypnosis and had not the glimmer of an idea what it was all about or why he was there. Madrigal was at his elbow, placing a chair to one side of the table.

'You si-sit here.'

Boysie sat uncomfortable. The green baize reminded him of the tables he had been called upon to erect for village whist drives as a child. The Colt Python felt heavy in the waitsband of his trousers. Madrigal appeared at the other side of the table, sitting opposite, a pack of oblong blue-backed cards between his slim hands.

'I think we'll st-start by giving you a Tarot reading. The Major Arcana. You are familiar?'

'Not really.' Boysie had no compass bearings on this situation.

'W-w-well, there's nothing difficult.' He threw some of the cards, face upwards, on to the table, bizarre, coloured drawings, each card with a Roman numeral at the top and the title at the bottom. Boysie glimpsed *Le Diable*— a devil, wings and horns, standing above a naked man and woman leashed by their necks; *Temperance*—a chubby lady with blue hair and wings pouring something from a blue pitcher into a red one; and *L'Hermite* —an elderly gent carrying lamp and staff, looking as though he'd walked straight out of a Royal Shakespeare

Company production. Madrigal gathered the cards and handed them to Boysie.

'W-will you shuffle, p-please, then pass the cards back to me.'

The cards were large, even for Boysie's great fists. He shuffled awkwardly.

Madrigal went on speaking. 'While y-you're sh-sh-shuffling I would like you to ask the cards a question. Out loud if you like.'

'Okay. What does the future hold?' Boysie asked looking at the cards.

'Again.'

'What does the future hold?' A right load of old nonsense this was.

'Now hand the c-cards back to me.'

Madrigal cut and laid the top four cards, face upwards in a diamond pattern on the table. 'L-let's see what you've drawn.' Madrigal scrutinised the cards. 'Ye-yes. This is good. At the top you have *L'Empereur*, there is power here. Ne-ne-next *L'Amoureux*, the lovers.' Cupid straddled the sun, aiming towards a trio below. 'G-good. Trials can be surmounted. Then *Le Bateleur*, the magician or ju-ju-juggler. Again power. You are a man with mu-much power. Or about to find power. *La Papesse*, the female p-p-pope. The high priestess. Serenity, wisdom, and knowledge.'

Boysie looked up at Madrigal. The man was visibly shaking. Fear crossed the table between them like an electric current. The stammer got worse.

'Th-this is v-v-very g-good, Mr. O-Oldcorn. Very good. P-power, wi-wisdom. Th-the surmounting of trials. B-but the test c-c-comes with the final card and we will find this by a-adding together the numbers of these c-c-cards. You-you do it and t-t-tell me wh-what you've got.'

Boysie began to tot up. *L'Empereur* was four.

L'Amoureux six, and *Le Bateleur* one, bringing it to eleven. Two for *La Papesse*. Thirteen in all.

'Unlucky for some,' he said brightly.

'The number please.'

'Thirteen, of course.'

The tension seemed to go from Madrigal. From the light of the angle-poise Boysie could see that his adversary's face was more relaxed. The hint of a smile.

'C-c-card number thirteen.' Madrigal thumbed through the pack, placed it face upwards, centred between the other cards. Boysie looked down. The card crudely showed a skeleton, sizing a field of human heads, feet, and hands.

'The joker.' Boysie flippant.

'I'm-m af-f-fraid not, Mr. Oldcorn. This card brings good fortune to an end. Number thirteen is Death.'

Boysie took his cue promptly. At the word *death* he allowed his eyes to stare blindly ahead, His body in a paradoxical state of rigidity. Madrigal got up, waved a hand in front of Boysie's eyes, then returned to his seat. He began to speak slowly and softly with hardly a trace of stutter.

'You are already asleep. In a few moments I am going to count from one to five. When you next hear the number five your eyes will close and you will be deeply asleep. Deep. Deep. Deep. One ... two ... three ... four ... five.' Boysie closed his eyes. He had nothing to fear any more. Dr. Fox was his only hypnotic control. Fox had taught him about fear.

'We haven't much time,' said Madrigal. The same, soft voice. 'I'm going to give you something. Hold out your right hand.' Boysie did as he was told and felt a small oblong piece of cardboard on the palm of his hand. 'That is a ticket,' Madrigal continued. 'It will admit you to Manchester Docks. Go through the main gate and show it. Then ask where the MV *Gardnia* is tied up. They will direct you. Someone will meet you on the way. You are going on a long sea journey. It will be pleasant.'

Good luck, thought Boysie.

'I may even join you myself. You will go now. You are able to walk, talk, and act normally. Plenty of taxis pass this building. You know what to do? Answer.'

'Yes,' said Boysie, doing an imitation of a space-age robot.

'You have a ticket pocket in that jacket?'

'Yes.'

'Put the ticket in that pocket until it is required at the Docks. You have money?'

'Yes.'

'I will count five to one. The next time you hear me say one you will open your eyes and leave. You will carry out my instructions. Five ... four ... three ... two ... one.'

Boysie opened his eyes, stood up, and walked towards the door. In the passage, he did not look back. Madrigal had closed the outer door by the time Boysie was halfway to the lift. He inceased his pace, pulling on the gloves. Button. Press. The whir of the lift. Boysie looked back towards Madrigal's apartment. Nobody. The lift came up and stopped. Griffin stood there, grinning. Boysie nodded and opened the outer gate. Griffin slid the inner gate, then closed it. Boysie followed suit with the outer gate and turned away to run, tiptoes, up the stairs. Seventh floor, eighth, God, he ached from the fight. Ninth. Tenth. Now the small staircase and metal door with its warning. The door was unlocked, the fireman's axe clamped to the wall. In front of him, Boysie saw the big drum with four ridges on which the cables rode. One ridge was empty. No cable. Griffin had done his stuff. Griffin. The cables started to move.

Boysie whipped the transceiver from his pocket, switched on, and extended the telescopic aerial before reaching out for the fireman's axe. Underestimating, as usual, Boysie pulled too hard and the axe fell with a clatter, nearly taking his right foot off. He placed the transceiver on a ledge below where the axe had hung and bent down for the wooden handle. The axe was beautifully balanced. Boysie made like a headsman. Traitors, he said quietly to the cables. The cables stopped moving. Griffin had made it to the fifth floor. He could hear the gates. Silence. Then the cables moving again. Upwards? Madrigal?

Boysie held the blade of the axe above the centre cable. The mechanism stopped again. Gates. Open. Close. From the transceiver came Griffin's voice. 'Right.' Boysie raised the axe. Middle cable in one. The far side took two strokes, but his last all but embedded the axe into the drum. The cables snaked away through the slots in the floor. From below came a fading rumble. A bumping noise and then an echo. Undramatic. No screams, no cries, no hideous crashing of metal and wood. Boysie closed the telescopic aerial, switched off the transceiver, and slipped it into his pocket, then replaced the axe and left.

The building must have been empty or filled with deaf mutes and cripples. Nobody had rushed out of their flats, summoned by the noise. Boysie reached the fourth floor. There was only one person—Griffin.

' 'E weren' in i'.'

'Madrigal?'

'Well, we wasn' after King Kong, was we? Sorry, Mr. Oakes, bu' 'e tumbled us. Come ou' o' the flat and definitely opened the lift doors. I thought 'e was well in, bu' I saw the bloomin' thing goin' down. No' a soul in there.'

Boysie looked upwards.

'Wha' we do now then?' Griffin asked.

'There's only one thing to do.' Boysie started up the

stairs. Griffin watched him for a moment, mouth gaping, then ran beside him.

Madrigal opened the door to their knock, polite and courteous backing away into the main room, light now with the curtains pulled back.

'I expected you to return,' said Madrigal, herded by the twin Python revolvers.

'Why didn't you run for it then?', asked Boysie.

'The inevitable is inevitable, Mr. Oakes. The Tarot told us that this afternoon. Knowledge, wisdom, and serenity. The Death card could hardly cancel those. In a Tarot reading the Death card can mean many things. The abrupt ending of something—like losing your job. It can also mean death, not necessarily one's own death.'

'You mean you really go for all that stuff?'

'Of course.' Madrigal tremendously relaxed. 'It is my life.' He laughed. 'Was my life. You know everything of course. Very clever. Our section has had a fair run with your trade unions. But don't be mistaken. Our section is not the only one. Nor is our method the only method. It will go on and on until the glor——'

The Colt Python jerked twice against the glove, two explosions sounding like hand grenades in the confined space of the long room.

Boysie had never seen anyone shot at close range. On the television or at the pictures they simply doubled up, clutching their guts. Madrigal was lifted off his feet and flung across the room, spinning violently. When his back was towards them, the two men could see the great gaping exit wounds, as though someone had torn his flesh away. Madrigal hit the far wall with his shoulder, then bounced to the floor. The bedroom door was flung open, and Mu-lan ran out. She got three paces into the room, dishevelled, but beautiful as ever in her white underwear, hand to mouth. Her lungs filled to scream as she saw Madrigal.

The Python cracked again, and Mu-lan was pushed against the wall. She slid down in an untidy bundle of useless flesh, bone, and blood, leaving an ugly smear on the wallpaper.

Boysie's shoulders began to shake long before the gloved hand reached out and closed the door.

GRIMOBO WILL RETURN

A SELECTION OF FINE READING
AVAILABLE IN CORGI BOOKS

War

☐ 552 07943 X BATTLE   *C. S. Forester, Robert Carse etc.* 5/–
☐ 552 07936 7 THE DEVIL'S BRIGADE *George Walton and Robert Adleman* 5/–
☐ 552 08003 9 ESCAPE FROM GERMANY   *Aidan Crawley* 5/–
☐ 552 07871 9 COMRADES OF WAR   *Sven Hassel* 5/–
☐ 552 07959 6 THREE CAME HOME   *Agnes Keith* 5/–
☐ 552 07726 7 THE DIRTY DOZEN   *E. M. Nathanson* 7/6
☐ 552 07986 3 HIROSHIMA REEF   *Eric Lambert* 5/–
☐ 552 07910 3 THE GERMAN ARMY AND THE NAZI PARTY
                             (illustrated) *Robert J. O'Neill* 7/6

General

☐ 552 07704 6 THE VIRILITY DIET   *Dr. George Belham* 5/–
☐ 552 07566 3 SEXUAL LIFE IN ENGLAND   *Dr. Ivan Bloch* 9/6
☐ 552 08009 8 THE PLEASURES OF LOVE   *Barbara Bross* 9/6
☐ 552 07593 0 UNMARRIED LOVE   *Dr. Eustace Chesser* 5/–
☐ 552 07949 9 GROW UP—AND LIVE   *Dr. Eustace Chesser* 3/6
☐ 552 07950 2 SEXUAL BEHAVIOUR   *Dr. Eustace Chesser* 5/–
☐ 552 07951 0 YOU MUST HAVE LOVE   *Dr. Eustace Chesser* 3/6
☐ 552 07930 8 THE ISLAND RACE (fully illustrated in colour)
                             Winston S. Churchill 30/–
☐ 552 06000 3 BARBARELLA (illustrated)   *Jean Claude Forest* 30/–
☐ 552 07804 2 THE BIRTH CONTROLLERS   *Peter Fryer* 7/6
☐ 552 07400 4 MY LIFE AND LOVES   *Frank Harris* 12/6
☐ 552 07745 3 COWBOY KATE (illustrated)   *Sam Haskins* 21/–

Westerns

☐ 552 08006 3 TIMBAL GULCH TRAIL   *Max Brand* 3/6
☐ 552 07756 9 SUDDEN—TROUBLESHOOTER   *Frederick H. Christian* 3/6
☐ 552 07976 6 SUDDEN AT BAY   *Frederick H. Christian* 3/6
☐ 552 07991 X THE HOODED RIDERS, No. 22   *J. T. Edson* 3/6
☐ 552 08011 X THE BULL WHIP BREED, No. 23   *J. T. Edson* 3/6
☐ 552 08012 8 SAGEBRUSH SLEUTH, No. 24   *J. T. Edson* 3/6
☐ 552 07856 5 MAN OF THE FOREST   *Zane Grey* 3/6
☐ 552 07653 8 MACKENNA'S GOLD   *Will Henry* 3/6
☐ 552 07902 2 SHALAKO   *Louis L'Amour* 3/6
☐ 552 08007 1 CHANCY   *Louis L'Amour* 3/6

Crime

☐ 552 07872 7 THE KREMLIN LETTER   *Noel Behn* 5/–
☐ 552 07974 X PHOTO FINISH   *Jean Bruce* 3/6
☐ 552 07855 7 STRIP TEASE   *Jean Bruce* 3/6
☐ 552 07990 1 A CASE FOR THE BARON   *John Creasey* 3/6
☐ 552 08005 5 DOUBLE FOR DEATH   *John Creasey* 3/6
☐ 552 07912 X WIDOWS WEAR WEEDS   *A. A. Fair (Erle Stanley Gardner)* 3/6
☐ 552 07716 X AMBER NINE   *John Gardner* 3/6
☐ 552 08004 7 MADRIGAL   *John Gardner* 5/–
☐ 552 07905 7 HIDEAWAY   *John Gardner* 3/6
☐ 552 07988 X UNDERCOVER CAT PROWLS AGAIN   *The Gordons* 3/6

All these books are available at your bookshop or newsagent: or can be ordered direct from the publisher. Just tick the titles you want and fill in the form below.

CORGI BOOKS, Cash Sales Department, J. Barnicoat (Falmouth) Ltd., P.O. Box 11, Falmouth, Cornwall.

Please send cheque or postal order. No currency, and allow 6d. per book to cover the cost of postage and packing in U.K., 9d. per copy overseas.

NAME ....

ADDRESS ....

(OCT. 68) ....

THE GAMES

HUGH ATKINSON

THE BEST SELLING NOVEL THAT COULD SNUFF OUT THE OLYMPIC FLAME

"Packed with intrigue, excitement, sport, love – every emotion known to humanity."

Edinburgh Evening News & Despatch

🐾 CORGI BOOKS   552 07981 2   7s.6d.

SOON TO BE A MAJOR FILM